About

Melanie Milburne read seventeen in between s After completing a Mas decided to write a nov romance author was born. Melanie is an ambassador for the Australian Childhood Foundation and is a keen dog lover and trainer and enjoys long walks in the Tasmanian bush. In 2015 Melanie won the HOLT Medallion, a prestigous award honouring outstanding literary talent.

Anne Mather always wanted to write. For years she wrote only for her own pleasure, and it wasn't until her husband suggested that she ought to send one of her stories to a publisher that they put several publishers' names into a hat and pulled one out. The rest as they say in history. 150 books later, Anne is literally staggered by the result! Her email address is mystic-am@msn.com and she would be happy to hear from any of her readers.

Jennie Lucas' parents owned a bookstore and she grew up surrounded by books, dreaming about faraway lands. At twenty-two she met her future husband and after their marriage, she graduated from university with a degree in English. She started writing books a year later. Jennie won the Romance Writers of America's Golden Heart contest in 2005 and hasn't looked back since. Visit Jennie's website at: www.jennielucas.com

Summer of Love

Summer of Love: Summer Nights

MELANIE MILBURNE

ANNE MATHER

JENNIE LUCAS

MILLS & BOON

First Published in Great Britain 2021
By Mills & Boon, an imprint of HarperCollins*Publishers* Ltd
1 London Bridge Street, London, SE1 9GF
www.harpercollins.co.uk

HarperCollins*Publishers*
1st Floor, Watermarque Building,
Ringsend Road, Dublin 4, Ireland

SUMMER OF LOVE: SUMMER NIGHTS
© 2021 Harlequin Books S.A.

Their Most Forbidden Fling © 2013 Melanie Milburne
A Forbidden Temptation © 2016 Anne Mather
A Night of Living Dangerously © 2012 Jennie Lucas

ISBN: 978-0-263-30040-6

Printed and bound in Spain
by CPI, Barcelona

THEIR MOST
FORBIDDEN FLING

MELANIE MILBURNE

To Tony and Jacqui Patiniotis and their sons,
Lucien, Julius and Raphael, for their generous
support to the National Heart Foundation in
Hobart. This one is for you!

CHAPTER ONE

MOLLY SAW HIM first. He was coming out of a convenience store half a block from her newly rented bedsit. He had his head down against the sleeting rain, his forehead knotted in a frown of concentration. Her heart gave a dislocated stumble as he strode towards her. The memories came rushing back, tumbling over themselves like clothes spinning in a dryer. She didn't even realise she had spoken his name out loud until she heard the thready sound of her voice. 'Lucas?'

He stopped like a puppet suddenly pulled back on its strings. The jolt of recognition on his face was painful to watch. She saw the way his hazel eyes flinched; saw too the way his jaw worked in that immeasurable pause before he spoke her name. 'Molly…'

It had been ten years since she had heard his voice. A decade of living in London had softened his Australian outback drawl to a mellifluous baritone that for some reason sent an involuntary shiver over her skin. She looked at his face, drinking in his features one by one as if ticking off a checklist inside her head to make sure it really was him.

The landscape of his face—the brooding brow, the determined jaw and the aquiline nose—was achingly familiar and yet different. He was older around the eyes and mouth, and his dark brown hair, though thick and glossy, had a few streaks of silver in it around his temples. His skin wasn't quite as weathered and tanned as his father's or brothers' back on the farm at home, but it still had a deep olive tone.

He was still imposingly tall and whipcord lean and fit, as if strenuous exercise was far more important to him than rest and relaxation. She looked at his hazel eyes. The same shadows were there—long, dark shadows that anchored him to the past.

'I was wondering when I'd run into you,' Molly said to fill the bruised silence. 'I suppose Neil or Ian told you I was coming over to work at St Patrick's for three months?'

His expression became inscrutable and closed. 'They mentioned something about you following a boyfriend across,' he said.

Molly felt a blush steal over her cheeks. She still wasn't quite sure how to describe her relationship with Simon Westbury. For years they had been just friends, but ever since Simon had broken up with his long-term girlfriend Serena, they had drifted into an informal arrangement that was convenient but perhaps not as emotionally satisfying as Molly would have wished. 'Simon and I have been out a couple of times but nothing serious,' she said. 'He's doing a plastics registrar year over here. I thought it'd be good to have someone to travel with since it's my first time overseas.'

'Where are you staying?' Lucas asked.

'In that house over there,' Molly said, pointing to a seen-better-days Victorian mansion that was divided into small flats and bedsits. 'I wanted somewhere within walking distance of the hospital. Apparently lots of staff from abroad set up camp there.'

He acknowledged that with a slight nod.

Another silence chugged past.

Molly shifted her weight from foot to foot, the fingers of her right hand fiddling with the strap of her handbag where it was slung over her shoulder. 'Um… Mum said to say hello…'

His brows gave a micro-lift above his green and brown-flecked eyes but whether it was because of cynicism, doubt or wariness, she couldn't quite tell. 'Did she?' he asked.

Molly looked away for a moment, her gaze taking in the gloomy clouds that were suspended above the rooftops of the row of grey stone buildings. It was so different from the expansive skies and blindingly bright sunshine of the outback back home. 'I guess you heard my father's remarried…' She brought her gaze back up when he didn't respond. 'His new wife Crystal is pregnant. The baby's due in a couple of months.'

His eyes studied her for a beat or two. 'How do you feel about having a half-sibling?'

Molly pasted on a bright smile. 'I'm thrilled for them… It will be good to have someone to spoil. I love babies. I'll probably babysit now and then for them when I get back…'

He continued to look at her in that measured way of his. Could he see how deeply hurt she was that her father was trying to replace Matt? Could he see how guilty she felt about *feeling* hurt? Matt had been the golden child, the firstborn and heir. Molly had lived in his shadow for as long as she could remember—never feeling good enough, bright enough.

Loved enough.

With a new child to replace the one he had lost, her father would have no need of her now.

'You're a long way from home,' Lucas said.

Did he think she wasn't up to the task? Did he still see her as that gangly, freckle-faced kid who had followed him about like a devoted puppy? 'I'm sure I'll cope with it,' she said with the tiniest elevation of her chin. 'I'm not a little kid any longer. I'm all grown up now in case you hadn't noticed.'

His gaze moved over her in a thoroughly male appraisal that made Molly's spine suddenly feel hot and tingly. As his eyes re-engaged with hers the air tightened, as if a light but unmistakable current of electricity was pulsing through it. 'Indeed you are,' he said.

Molly glanced at his mouth. He had a beautiful mouth, one that implied sensuality in its every line and contour. The shadow of dark stubble surrounding it gave him an intensely male look that she found captivating. She wondered when that mouth had last smiled. She wondered when it had last kissed someone.

She wondered what it would feel like to be kissed by him.

Molly forced her gaze to reconnect with his. She needed to get her professional cap on and keep it on. They would be working together in the same unit. No one over here needed to know about the tragic tie that bound them so closely. 'Well, then,' she said, shuffling her feet again. 'I guess I'll see you at the hospital.'

'Yes.'

She gave him another tight, formal smile and made to move past but she had only gone a couple of paces when he said her name again. 'Molly?'

Molly slowly turned and looked at him. The lines about his mouth seemed to have deepened in the short time she had been talking to him. 'Yes?' she said.

'You might not have been informed as yet, but as of yesterday I'm the new head of ICU,' he said. 'Brian Yates had to suddenly resign due to ill health.'

She gripped the edges of her coat closer across her chest. *Lucas Banning was her boss?* It put an entirely new spin on things. This first foray of hers into working abroad could be seriously compromised if he decided he didn't want her working with him. And why would he want her here?

She was a living, breathing reminder of the worst mistake he had ever made.

'No,' Molly said. 'I hadn't been informed.'

'Is it going to be a problem?' he asked with a direct look she found a little intimidating.

'Why would it be a problem?' she asked.

'It's a busy and stretched-to-the-limit department,' he said. 'I don't want any personal issues between staff members to compromise patient outcomes.'

Molly felt affronted that he thought her so unprofessional as to bring their past into the workplace. She rarely spoke of Matt these days. Even though she had lived with her grief longer than she had lived without it, speaking of him brought it all back as if it had happened yesterday—the gut-wrenching pain, the aching sense of loss. *The guilt.* Most of her friends from medical school didn't even know she had once had an older brother. 'I do *not* bring personal issues to work,' she said.

His hazel eyes held hers for a beat or two of silence. 'Fine,' he said. 'I'll see you in the morning. Don't be late.'

Molly pursed her lips as he strode off down the street. She would make sure she was there before he was.

Lucas glanced pointedly at the clock on the wall as Molly Drummond rushed into the glassed-in office of ICU. 'Your shift started an hour ago,' he said as he slapped a patient's file on the desk.

'I'm so sorry,' she said breathlessly. 'I tried to call but I didn't have the correct code in my phone. I'm still with my Australian network so I couldn't call direct.'

'So what's your excuse?' he asked, taking in her pink face and the disarray of her light brown hair. 'Boyfriend keep you up late last night, or did he make you late by serving you breakfast in bed?'

Her face went bright red and her grey-blue eyes flashed with annoyance. 'Neither,' she said. 'I was on my way to work when I came across a cat that had been hit by a car. I couldn't just leave it there. It had a broken leg and was in pain. I had to take it to the nearest vet clinic. It took me ages to find one, and then I had to wait until the vet got there.'

Lucas knew he should apologise for jumping to conclusions but he wanted to keep a professional distance. Out of all the hospitals in London, or the whole of England for that matter, why did she have to come to his? He had put as much distance as he could between his past and the present. For the last ten years he had tried to put it behind him, not to forget—he could never, would *never* do that—but to move on with his life as best he could, making a difference where he could.

Saving lives, not destroying them.

Molly Drummond turning up in his world was not what he needed right now. He had only recently found out she was coming to work here, but he had assured himself that he wouldn't have to have too much to do with her directly. He had planned to become director at the end of next year when Brian Yates formally retired. But Brian being diagnosed with a terminal illness had meant he'd had to take over the reins a little ahead of schedule. Now he would have to interact with Molly on a daily basis, which would have been fine if she was just like any other young doctor who came and went in the department.

But Molly was not just any other doctor.

She wasn't that cute little freckle-faced kid any more either. She had grown into a beautiful young woman with the sort of understated looks that took you by surprise in unguarded moments. Like yesterday, when he'd run into her on the street.

Looking up and seeing her there had made his breath catch in his throat. He had been taken aback by the way her grey-blue eyes darkened or softened with her mood. How her creamy skin took on a rosy tinge when she felt cornered or embarrassed. How her high cheekbones gave her a haughty regal air, and yet her perfect nose with its tiny dusting of freckles had an innocent girl-next-door appeal that was totally beguiling. How her figure still had a coltish look about it with those long legs and slim arms.

He had not been able to stop himself imagining how it would feel to have those slim arms wrap around his body and to feel that soft, full mouth press against his. He had his share of sexual encounters, probably not as many as some of his peers, but he wasn't all that comfortable with letting people get too close.

And getting too close to Molly Drummond was something he wanted to avoid at all costs.

'I haven't got time to give you a grand tour,' Lucas said, forcing his wayward thoughts back where they belonged. 'But you'll find your way around soon enough. We have twenty beds, all of them full at the present time. Jacqui Hunter is the ward clerk. She'll fill you in on where the staff facilities are. Su Ling and Aleem Pashar are the registrars. They'll run through the patients with you.' He gave her a brisk nod before he left the office. 'Enjoy your stay.'

'Dr Drummond?'

Molly turned to see a middle-aged woman coming towards her. 'I'm sorry I wasn't here to greet you,' the woman said with a friendly smile. 'Things have been a bit topsy-turvy, I'm afraid.' She offered her hand. 'I'm Jacqui Hunter.'

'Pleased to meet you,' Molly said.

'This has been such a crazy couple of days,' Jacqui said. 'Did Dr Banning tell you about Brian Yates?' She didn't wait for Molly to respond. 'Such a terrible shame. He was planning to retire next year. Now he's been sent home to get his affairs in order.'

'I'm very sorry,' Molly said.

'He and Olivia just had their first grandchild too,' Jacqui said shaking her head. 'Life's not fair, is it?'

'No, it's not.'

Jacqui popped the patient's file, which Lucas had left on the desk, in the appropriate drawer. 'Now, then,' she said, turning to face Molly again. 'Let's get you familiarised with the place. You're from Australia, aren't you? Sydney, right?'

'Yes,' Molly said. 'But I grew up in the bush.'

'Like our Lucas, huh?'

'Yes, we actually grew up in the same country town in New South Wales.'

Jacqui's eyebrows shot up underneath her blunt fringe. 'Really? What a coincidence. So you know each other?'

Molly wondered if she should have mentioned anything about her connection with Lucas. 'Not really. It's been years since I've seen him,' she said. 'He moved to London when I was seventeen. It's not like we've stayed in touch or anything.'

'He's a bit of a dark horse is our Lucas,' Jacqui said, giving Molly a conspiratorial look. 'Keeps himself to himself, if you know what I mean.'

Molly wasn't sure if the ward clerk was expecting a response from her or not. 'Um…yes…'

'No one knows a whisper about his private life,' Jacqui said. 'He keeps work and play very separate.'

'Probably a good idea,' Molly said.

Jacqui grunted as she led the way to the staff change room. 'There's plenty of women around here who would give their eye teeth for a night out with him,' she said.

'It should be a crime to be so good looking, don't you think?'

'Um…'

'He's got kind, intelligent eyes,' Jacqui said. 'The patients love him—and so do the relatives. He takes his time with them. He treats them like he would his own family. That's rare these days, let me tell you. Everyone is so busy climbing up the career ladder. Lucas Banning was born to be a doctor. You can just tell.'

'Actually, I think he always planned on being a wheat and sheep farmer, like his father and grandfather before him,' Molly said.

Jacqui looked at her quizzically. 'Are we talking about the same person?' she asked.

'As I said, I don't know him all that well,' Molly quickly backtracked.

Jacqui indicated the female change room door on her right. 'Bathroom is through there and lockers here,' she said. 'The staff tea room is further down on the left.' She led the way back to the office. 'You're staying three months with us, aren't you?'

'Yes,' Molly said. 'I haven't been overseas before. The job came up and I took it before I could talk myself out of it.'

'Well, you're certainly at the right time of life to do it, aren't you?' Jacqui said. 'Get the travel bug out of the way before you settle down. God knows, you'll never be able to afford it once the kids come along. Take it from me. They bleed you dry.'

'How many children do you have?'

'Four boys,' Jacqui said, and with a little roll of her eyes added, 'Five if you count my husband.' She led the way back to the sterilising bay outside ICU. 'One of the registrars will go through the patients with you. I'd better get back to the desk.'

'Thanks for showing me around.'

Molly spent an hour with the registrars, going through each patient's history. Lucas joined them as they came to the last patient. Claire Mitchell was a young woman of twenty-two with a spinal-cord injury as well as a serious head injury after falling off a horse at an equestrian competition. She had been in an induced coma for the past month. Each time they tried to wean her off the sedatives her brain pressure skyrocketed. The scans showed a resolving intracerebral haematoma and persistent cerebral oedema.

Molly watched as Lucas went through the latest scans with the parents. He explained the images and answered their questions in a calm reassuring manner.

'I keep thinking she's going to die,' the mother said in a choked voice.

'She's come this far,' Lucas said. 'These new scans show positive signs of improvement. It's a bit of a waiting game, I'm afraid. Just keep talking to her.'

'We don't know how to thank you,' the father said. 'When I think of how bad she was just a week ago...'

'She's definitely turned a corner in the last few days,' Lucas said. 'Just try and stay positive. We'll call you as soon as there's any change.'

Molly met his gaze once the parents had returned to their daughter's bedside. 'Can I have a quick word, Dr Banning?' she asked. 'In private?'

His brows came together as if he found the notion

of meeting with her in private an interruption he could well do without. 'My office is last on the left down the corridor. I'll meet you there in ten minutes. I just have to write up some meds for David Hyland in bed four.'

Molly stood outside the office marked with Lucas's name. The door was ajar and she peered around it to see if he was there, but the office was empty so she gently pushed the door open and went inside.

It was furnished like any other underfunded hospital office: a tired-looking desk dominated the small space with a battered chair that had an L-shaped rip in the vinyl on the back. A dented and scratched metal filing cabinet was tucked between the window and a waist-high bookcase that was jammed with publications and textbooks. A humming computer was in the middle of the desk and papers and medical journals were strewn either side. Organised chaos was the term that came to Molly's mind. There was a digital photo frame on the filing cabinet near the tiny window that overlooked the bleak grey world outside. She pressed the button that set the images rolling. The splashes of the vivid outback colour of Bannington homestead took her breath away. The tall, scraggy gum trees, the cerulean blue skies, the endless paddocks, the prolific wildflowers after last season's rain, the colourful bird life on the dams and the waters of Carboola Creek, which ran through the property, took her home in a heartbeat. She could almost hear the *arck arck* sound of the crows and the warbling of the magpies.

Her parents had run the neighbouring property Drummond Downs up until their bitter divorce seven years ago. It had been in her family for six generations, gearing up for a seventh, but Matthew's death had changed everything.

Her father had not handled his grief at losing his only son. Her mother had not handled her husband's anger and emotional distancing. The homestead had gradually run into the red and then, after a couple of bad seasons, more and more parcels of land had had to be sold off to keep the bank happy. With less land to recycle and regenerate crops and stock, the property had been pushed to the limit. Crippling debts had brought her parents to the point of bankruptcy.

Offers of help from neighbours, including Lucas's parents, Bill and Jane Banning, had been rejected. Molly's father had been too proud to accept help, especially from the parents of the boy who had been responsible for the death of their only son. Drummond Downs had been sold to a foreign investor, and her parents had divorced within a year of leaving the homestead.

Molly sighed as she pressed the stop button, her hand falling back to her side. The sound of a footfall behind her made her turn around, and her heart gave a jerky little movement behind her ribcage as she met Lucas's hazel gaze. 'I was just...' she lifted a hand and then dropped it '...looking at your photos...'

He closed the door with a soft click but he didn't move towards the desk. It was hard to read his expression, but it seemed to Molly as if he was controlling every nuance of his features behind that blank, impersonal mask. 'Neil emails me photos from time to time,' he said.

'They're very good,' Molly said. 'Very professional.'

Something moved like a fleeting shadow through his eyes. 'He toyed with the idea of being a professional photographer,' he said. 'But as you know...things didn't work out.'

Molly chewed at the inside of her mouth as she thought about Neil working back at Bannington Homestead when he might have travelled the world, doing what he loved best. So many people had been damaged by the death of her brother. The stone of grief thrown into the pond of life had cast wide circles in the community of Carboola Creek. When Lucas had left Bannington to study medicine, his younger brother Neil had taken over his role on the property alongside their father. Any hopes or aspirations of a different life Neil might have envisaged for himself had had to be put aside. The oldest son and heir had not stepped up to the plate as expected. Various factions of the small-minded community had made it impossible for Lucas to stay and work the land as his father and grandfather had done before him.

'It wasn't your fault,' Molly said, not even realising how firmly she believed it until she had spoken it out loud. She had never blamed him but she had grown up surrounded by people who did. But her training as a doctor had made her realise that sometimes accidents just happened. No one was to blame. If Matt had been driving, as he had only minutes before they'd hit that kangaroo that had jumped out in front of them on the road, it would have been him that had been exiled.

Lucas hooked a brow upwards as he pushed away from the door. 'Wasn't it?'

Molly turned as he strode past her to go behind his

desk. She caught a faint whiff of his aftershave, an intricately layered mix of citrus and spice and something else she couldn't name—perhaps his own male scent. His broad shoulders were so tense she could see the bunching of his muscles beneath his shirt. 'It was an accident, Lucas,' she said. 'You know it was. That's what the coroner's verdict was. Anyway, Matt could easily have been driving instead of you. Would you have wanted him to be blamed for the rest of his life?'

His eyes met hers, his formal back-to-business look locking her out of the world of his pain. 'What did you want to speak to me about?' he asked.

Molly's shoulders went down on an exhaled breath. 'I sort of let slip to Jacqui Hunter that we knew each other from…back home…'

A muscle in his cheek moved in and out. 'I see.'

'I didn't say anything about the accident,' she said. 'I just said we grew up in the same country town.'

His expression was hard as stone, his eyes even harder. 'Why did you come here?' he asked. 'Why this hospital?'

Molly wasn't sure she could really answer that, even to herself. Why had she felt drawn to where he had worked for all these years? Why had she ignored the other longer-term job offers to come to St Patrick's and work alongside him for just three months? It had just seemed the right thing to do. Even her mother had agreed when Molly had told her. Her mother had said it was time they all moved on and put the past—and Matthew—finally to rest. 'I wanted to work overseas but most of the other posts were for a year or longer,' she said. 'I wasn't sure if I wanted to stay away from home quite that long. St Patrick's seemed like a good place to start. It's got a great reputation.'

He barricaded himself behind his desk, his hands on his lean hips in a keep-back-from-me posture. 'I've spent the last decade trying to put what happened behind me,' he said. 'This is my life now. I don't want to destroy what little peace I've been able to scratch together.'

'I'm not here to ruin your peace or your life or career or whatever,' Molly said. 'I just wanted some space from my family. Things have been difficult between my parents, especially since Crystal got pregnant. I'm tired of being the meat in the sandwich. I wanted some time out.'

'So you came right to the lion's den,' he said with an embittered look. 'Aren't your parents worried I might destroy your life too?'

Molly pressed her lips together for a moment. Her father had said those very words in each and every one of their heated exchanges when she'd broached the subject of coming to London. 'Do you want me to resign?' she asked.

His forehead wrinkled in a heavy frown and one of his hands reached up and scored a rough pathway through his hair before dropping back down by his side. 'No,' he said, sighing heavily. 'We're already short-staffed. It might take weeks to find a replacement.'

'I can work different shifts from you if—'

He gave her a dark look. 'That won't be necessary,' he said. 'People will start to ask questions if we make an issue out of it.'

'I'm not here to make trouble for you, Lucas.'

He held her gaze for an infinitesimal moment, but the screen had come back up on his face. 'I'll see you on the ward,' he said, and pulled out his chair and sat down. 'I have to call a patient's family.'

Molly walked to the door, but as she pulled it closed on her exit she saw that he was frowning heavily as he reached for the phone...

CHAPTER TWO

LUCAS WAS GOING through some blood results with Kate Harrison, one of the nurses, when Molly came into the ICU office the following day. Her perfume drifted towards him, wrapping around his senses, reminding him of summer, sweet peas and innocence. How she managed to look so gorgeous this early in the morning in ballet flats and plain black leggings and a long grey cardigan over a white top amazed him. She wasn't wearing any make-up to speak of and her shoulder-length hair was pulled back in a ponytail, giving her a fresh-faced, youthful look that was totally captivating.

'Good morning,' she said, her tentative smile encompassing Kate as well as him.

'Morning,' he said, turning back to the blood results. 'Kate, I want you to keep an eye on Mr Taylor's white-cell count and CRP. Let me know if there's any change.'

'I'll ring you with the results when they come in,' Kate said. She turned to Molly. 'Hi, I'm Kate Harrison. I heard on the grapevine you're from Dr Banning's neck of the woods.'

Molly's gaze flicked uncertainly to Lucas's. 'Um… yes…'

'I looked it up on an internet map,' Kate said. 'It's

a pretty small country town. Were you neighbours or something?'

'Sort of,' Molly said. 'Lucas's family ran the property next door but it was ten kilometres away.'

'I wish my neighbours were ten kilometres away,' Kate said with a grin, 'especially when they play their loud music and party all night. Nice to have you with us, Dr Drummond.'

'Please call me Molly.'

'We have a social club you might be interested in joining,' Kate said. 'A group of us hang out after hours. It's a good way to meet people from other departments. Nobody admits it out loud but it's sort of turned into a hospital dating service. We've had two marriages, one engagement and one and a half babies so far.'

'Dr Drummond already has a boyfriend,' Lucas said as he opened the file drawer.

'Actually, I would be interested,' Molly said, sending him a hard little look. 'Apart from Simon, I don't have any friends over here.'

'Great,' Kate said. 'I'll send you an invite by email. We're meeting for a movie next week.'

Lucas waited until Kate had left before he spoke. 'I'd be careful hanging out with Kate's social group. Not all the men who go have the right motives.'

She gave him a haughty look. 'I can take care of myself.'

'From what I've heard so far about your plastics guy, he doesn't seem your type.'

Her brows came up. 'And you're some sort of authority on who my type is, are you?'

He gave a loose shrug of his shoulders. 'Just an observation.'

'Then I suggest you keep your observations to yourself,' she said, her eyes flashing like sheet lightning. 'I'm perfectly capable of managing my own private life. At least I have one.'

'Just because I keep my private life out of the hospital corridors doesn't mean I don't have one,' Lucas clipped back.

Jacqui came into the office behind them. 'Whoa, is this pistols at three paces or what?' she said. 'What's going on?'

'Nothing,' they said in unison.

Jacqui's brows lifted speculatively. 'I thought you guys were old friends from back home?'

'Excuse me,' Molly said, and brushed past to leave.

'What's going on between you two?' Jacqui asked Lucas.

'Nothing,' he said with a glower.

'Could've fooled me,' Jacqui said. 'I saw the way she was glaring at you. It's not like you to be the big bad boss. What did you say to upset her?'

'Nothing.'

Jacqui folded her arms and gave him a look. 'That's two nothings from you, which in my book means there's something. I might be speaking out of turn, but you don't seem too happy to have her here.'

The last thing Lucas wanted was anyone digging into his past connection with Molly. It was a part of his life he wanted to keep separate. The turmoil of emotions he felt over Matt's death was something he dealt with in the privacy of his home. He didn't want it at work, where he needed a clear head. He didn't like his ghosts or his guilt hanging around.

'Dr Drummond is well qualified and will no doubt be a valuable asset to the team at St Patrick's,' he said. 'All new staff members take time to settle in. It's a big change moving from one hospital to another, let alone across the globe.'

'She's very beautiful in a girl-next-door sort of way, isn't she?'

He gave a noncommittal shrug as he leafed through a patient's notes. 'She's OK, I guess.'

Jacqui's mouth tilted in a knowing smile. 'She's the sort of girl most mothers wish their sons would bring home, don't you think?'

Lucas put the file back in the drawer and then pushed it shut. 'Not my mother,' he said, and walked out.

Lucas was walking home from the hospital a couple of days later when he saw Molly coming up the street, carrying a cardboard box with holes punched in it. He had managed to avoid her over the last day or two, other than during ward rounds where he had kept things tightly professional. But as she came closer he could see she looked flustered and upset.

'What's wrong?' he asked as she stopped right in front of him.

Her grey-blue eyes were shiny and moist with tears. 'I don't know what to do,' she said. 'My landlord has flatly refused to allow me to have Mittens in my flat. He's threatening to have me evicted if I don't get rid of him immediately.'

'Mittens?'

She indicated the box she was carrying. 'Mittens the cat,' she said, 'the one that got hit by a car on my first day? I had to take him otherwise the vet would've sent him to the cat shelter and he might've been put down if no one wanted him.'

'Didn't the owner come and claim him?' Lucas asked.

'It turns out he doesn't have an owner, or none we can track down,' she said. 'He hasn't got a collar or a microchip. He's only about seven months old.'

He angled his head, his gaze narrowing slightly. 'What were you planning to do with him?'

Her expression became beseeching. 'One of the nurses mentioned you lived in a big house all by yourself. She said you had a garden that would be perfect for a cat. She said you'd—'

Lucas held up his hands like stop signs. 'Oh, no,' he said. 'No way. I'm not having some flea-bitten cat sharpening its claws on my rugs or furniture.'

'It's only for a few days,' she said, appealing to him with those big wide eyes of hers. 'I'll find another flat, one that will allow me to have a cat. *Please?*'

Lucas could feel his resolve slipping. How was he supposed to resist her when she was so darned cute standing there like a little lost waif? 'I hate cats,' he said. 'They make me sneeze.'

'But this one is a non-allergenic cat,' she said. 'He was probably hideously expensive and now we have him for free. Well…not free exactly…' She momentarily tugged at her lower lip with her teeth. 'The vet's bill was astronomical.'

'I do *not* want a cat,' he said through tight lips.

'You're not getting a cat,' she said. 'You're *babysitting* one.'

Lucas rolled his eyes and took the box from her. His fingers brushed against hers and a lightning strike of electricity shot through his body. Her eyes flared as if she had felt it too, and two little spots of colour pooled high in her cheeks. She stood back from him and tucked a strand of hair back behind her ear, her gaze slipping from his. 'I don't know how to thank you,' she said.

'My place is just along here,' he said gruffly, and led the way.

Molly stepped into the huge foyer of the four-storey mansion Lucas owned. The house was tastefully decorated with an eclectic mix of modern, art deco and antique pieces. Room after room led off the foyer and a grand staircase to the floors above. There was even a ballroom, which overlooked the garden, and a conservatory. It was such a big house for one person. It would have housed three generations of a family with room to spare. 'You don't find it a little cramped?' she asked dryly as she turned and faced him.

The corner of his mouth twitched, which was about the closest he ever got to a smile. 'I like my space,' he said as he shrugged off his coat and hung it on the brass coat rack. 'I guess it comes from growing up in the outback.'

'Tell me about it,' Molly said with feeling. 'I'm starting to feel quite claustrophobic at that bedsit and I've barely been there a week. I don't know why Simon suggested it.'

'Does he live there with you?' he asked.

'No, he's renting a place in Bloomsbury,' she said. 'He offered me a room but I wanted to keep my independence.'

'Are you sleeping with him?'

Molly frowned to cover her embarrassment. She had only slept with Simon once and she had instantly regretted it. She couldn't help feeling he had only slept with her as a sort of payback to his ex Serena because he'd been so hurt by her leaving him. Molly had mistaken his friendliness as attraction, but now she wasn't sure how to get out of the relationship without causing him further hurt. 'I can't see how that is any of your business,' she said.

His eyes remained steady on hers, quietly assessing. 'You don't seem the casual sleep around type.'

She felt her cheeks heat up a little more. 'I'm not a virgin, if that's what you're suggesting. And there's nothing wrong with casual sex as long as it's safe.'

His gaze slowly tracked down to her mouth.

Something shifted in the air—an invisible current that connected her to him in a way Molly had never felt quite before. She felt her lips start to tingle as if he had bent his head and pressed his mouth to hers. She could almost feel the warm, firm dryness of his lips against her own. Her mind ran wild with the thought of his tongue slipping through the shield of her lips to find hers and call it into erotic play. Her insides flickered with hot little tongues of lust, sending arrows of awareness to the very heart of her. She ran the tip of her tongue out over the surface of her lips and watched as his hooded gaze followed its journey.

The mewling cry of Mittens from inside the box broke the spell.

Lucas frowned as if he had completely forgotten what he was carrying. 'Er...aren't we supposed to rub butter on its paws or something?' he asked.

'I think that's just an old wives' tale,' Molly said. 'I'm sure if we show him around first he'll soon work out his territory. I don't suppose you happen to have a pet door?'

He gave her a speaking look. 'No.'

'Oh, well, he'll soon let you know when he wants to go in or out. Maybe you could leave a window open.'

'No.'

Molly pursed her lips in thought. 'How about a kitty litter box? Then you wouldn't have to worry about him getting locked inside while you're at work.'

'Read my lips,' he said, eyeballing her over the top of the box. 'I am *not* keeping this cat. This is an interim thing until you find a pet-friendly place to stay.'

'Fine.' She opened the folded over lid of the box. Mittens immediately popped his head up and mewed at her. 'Isn't he cute?'

'Adorable.'

Molly glanced up at him but he wasn't looking at the cat. 'Um...I brought some food with me,' she said, and rummaged in her handbag for the sample packs the vet had given her.

Mittens wound himself around Lucas's ankles, purring like an engine as his little cast bumped along the floor.

'I think he likes you,' Molly said.

Lucas glowered at her. 'If he puts one paw out of place, it will be off to the cat shelter.'

She scooped the cat up into her arms, stroking his soft, velvety little head as she looked up into Lucas's stern features. 'I'll just feed him and give him his medication and get out of your hair,' she said.

'The kitchen is this way,' he said, and led the way.

Molly stood back to watch as Mittens tucked into the saucer of food she had placed on the floor. 'He's been wormed and vaccinated,' she said.

'Desexed?'

'That too,' she said. 'He might still be a bit tender down there.'

'My heart bleeds.'

Molly picked up her handbag and slung it across her shoulder. 'He'll need to use the bathroom once he's finished eating. Do you know you can actually train a cat to use a human toilet? I saw it on the internet.'

He didn't look in the least impressed. 'How fascinating.'

'Right, well, then,' she said, and made a move for the door. 'I'll leave you to it.'

'What are you doing for dinner?' Lucas suddenly asked.

Molly blinked. 'Pardon?'

His mouth twisted self-deprecatingly. 'Am I that out of practice?'

'What do you mean?'

'I haven't asked anyone to stay to dinner in a while,' he said. 'I like to keep myself to myself once I get home. But since you're here you might as well stay and share a meal with me. That is if you've got nothing better to do.'

'You're not worried what people will think about us socialising out of hours?' she asked.

'Who's going to know?' he said. 'My private life is private.'

Molly felt tempted to stay, more than tempted. She told herself it was to make sure Mittens was settled in, but if she was honest, it had far more to do with her craving a little more of Lucas's company. It wasn't just that he was from back home either. She felt drawn to his aloofness; his don't-come-too-close-I-might-bite aura was strangely attractive. His accidental touch earlier had awoken her senses. She could still feel the tingling of her skin where his fingers had brushed against hers.

'I haven't got anything planned,' she said. 'Simon's going to the theatre with his friend. There wasn't a spare ticket.' She saw his brows lift cynically and hastily added, 'I didn't want to see it anyway.'

Lucas moved across the room to open the French doors that led out to the garden. He turned on the outside light, which cast a glow over the neatly clipped hedges that made up the formal part of the garden. A fountain trickled in the middle of a pebbled area and a wrought-iron French provincial setting was against one wall where a row of espaliered ornamental trees was growing. Mittens bumped his way over and went out to explore his new domain. He stopped to play with a moth that had fluttered around the light Lucas had switched on.

'It's a lovely garden,' Molly said. 'Was it like that when you bought it?'

'It had been a bit neglected,' he said. 'I've done a bit of work on the house too.'

'You always were good with your hands,' she said, and then blushed. 'I mean, with doing things about the farm.'

His lips gave a vague sort of movement that could not on anyone's terms be described as a smile. 'Would you like a glass of wine?' he asked.

'Sure, why not?' Molly said. *Anything to make her relax and stop making a fool of herself,* she thought.

He placed a glass of white wine in front of her. 'I have red if you prefer.'

'No, white is fine,' she said. 'Red always gives me a headache.'

Lucas went about preparing the meal. Molly watched as he deftly chopped vegetables and meat for the stir-fry he was making. He worked as if on autopilot but she could see he was frowning slightly. Was he regretting asking her to stay for dinner? He wasn't exactly full of conversation. But, then, she was feeling a little tongue-tied herself.

'So why an intensivist?' he asked after a long silence. 'I thought you always wanted to be a teacher.'

'My teacher stage only lasted until I was ten,' Molly said. 'I've wanted to be lots of things since then. I decided on medicine in my final year at school. And I chose intensive care because I liked the idea of helping to save lives.'

'Yeah, well, it sure beats the hell out of destroying them.'

Molly met his gaze over the island bench. 'How long are you going to keep punishing yourself? It's not going to bring him back.'

His eyes hardened. 'You think I don't know that?'

Molly watched him slice some celery as if it was a mortal enemy. His jaw was pulsing with tension as he worked. She let out an uneven sigh and put her wine down. 'Maybe it wasn't such a good idea for me to stay and have dinner,' she said as she slid off the stool she had perched on. 'You don't seem in the mood for company. I'll see myself out.'

He caught her at the door. His long, strong fingers met around her wrist, sending sparks of awareness right up to her armpit and beyond. She looked into his eyes and felt her heart slip sideways. Pain was etched in those green and brown depths—pain and something else that made her blood kick-start in her veins like a shot of pure adrenalin. 'Don't go,' he said in a low, gruff tone.

Molly's gaze drifted to his mouth. She felt her insides shift, a little clench of longing that was slowly but surely moving through her body.

His body was closer than it had ever been. She felt the warmth of it, the bone-melting temptation of it. She sensed the stirring of his response to her. She couldn't feel it but she could see it in his eyes as they held hers. It sent an arrow of lust through her. She wanted to feel him against her, to feel his blood surging in response to her closeness. She took a half a step to close the gap between their bodies but he dropped her wrist as if it had suddenly caught fire.

'I'm sorry,' he said, raking that same hand through his thick hair, leaving crooked finger-width pathways in its wake.

'It's fine,' Molly said, aiming for light and airy but falling miserably short. 'No harm done.'

'I don't want you to get the wrong idea, Molly,' he

said, frowning heavily. 'Any...connection between us is inadvisable.'

'Because you don't mix work with play?'

His eyes were hard and intractable as they clashed with hers. 'Because I don't mix emotion with sex.'

'Who said anything about sex?' Molly asked.

His worldly look said it all.

'Right, well...I'm not very good at this, as you can probably tell,' she said, tucking a strand of hair back behind her ear. 'I try to be sophisticated and modern about it all but I guess deep down inside I'm just an old-fashioned girl who wants the fairy-tale.'

'You're no different from most women—and most men, for that matter,' he said. 'It's not wrong to want to be happy.'

'Are *you* happy, Lucas?' Molly asked, searching his tightly set features.

His eyes moved away from hers as he moved back to the kitchen. 'I need to put on the rice,' he said. 'You'd better keep an eye on your cat.'

Molly went outside to find Mittens. He wasn't too happy about being brought back inside, but she lured him back in with a thread she found hanging off her coat. She closed the door once he was inside and went back to where Lucas was washing the rice for the rice cooker. 'What can I do to help?' she said. 'Shall I set the table in the dining room?'

'I don't use the dining room,' he said. 'I usually eat in here.'

'Seems a shame to have such a lovely dining room and never use it,' Molly said. 'Don't you ever have friends over for dinner parties?'

He gave a shrug and pressed the start button on the cooker. 'Not my scene, I'm afraid.'

'Do you have a housekeeper?'

'A woman comes once a week to clean,' he said. 'I don't make much mess, or at least I try not to. I wouldn't have bothered getting anyone but Gina needed the work. Her husband left her to bring up a couple of kids on her own. She's reliable and trustworthy.'

Molly cradled her wine in her hands. 'Do you have a current girlfriend?'

He was silent for a moment. 'I'm between appointments, so to speak.'

She angled her head at him. 'What sort of women do you usually date?'

His eyes collided with hers. 'Why do you ask?'

Molly gave a little shrug. 'Just wondering.'

'I'm not a prize date, by any means,' he said after another long moment. 'I hate socialising. I hate parties. I don't drink more than one glass of alcohol.'

'Not every woman wants to party hard,' she pointed out.

He studied her unwaveringly for a moment. 'Not very many women just want to have sex and leave it at that.'

Molly felt a wave of heat rise up in her body. 'Is that all you want from a partner?' she asked. 'Just sex and nothing else?'

Had she imagined his eyes looking hungrily at her mouth for a microsecond? Desire clenched tight in her core as his gaze tethered hers in a sensually charged lock. 'It's a primal need like food and shelter,' he said. 'It's programmed into our genes.'

Molly was more aware of her primal needs than she

had ever been. Her body was screaming with them, and had been from the moment she had laid eyes on him on the street the other day. It still was a shock to her that she was reacting so intensely to him. She had never thought herself a particularly passionate person. But when she was around him she felt stirrings and longings that were so fervent they felt like they would override any other consideration.

'We're surely far more evolved and civilised than to respond solely to our basest needs?' she said.

His eyes grazed her mouth. 'Some of us, perhaps.'

The atmosphere tightened another notch.

'So how do you get your primal needs met?' Molly asked with a brazen daring she could hardly believe she possessed. 'Do you drag women back here by the hair and have your wicked way with them?'

This time his gaze went to her hair. She felt every strand of it lift away from her scalp like a Mexican wave. Hot tingles of longing raced along her backbone. She felt a stirring in her breasts; a subtle tightening that made her aware of the lace that supported them. Her heart picked up its pace, a tippity-tap-tap beat that reverberated in her feminine core.

His eyes came back to hers, holding them, searing them, penetrating them. 'I'm not going to have my wicked way with you, Molly,' he said.

'But you want to.' *Oh, dear God, had she really just said that?* Molly thought.

'I'd have to be comatose not to want you,' he said. 'But I'm not going to act on it. Not in this lifetime.'

Molly felt an acute sense of disappointment but tried to cover it by playing it light. 'Glad we got that out of the way,' she said, and picked up her wine. 'You're not really my type in any case.'

A short silence passed.

'Aren't you going to ask what my type *is*?' she asked. 'Oh, no, wait. I remember. You already have an opinion on that, don't you?'

'You want someone strong and dependable, loyal and faithful,' he said. 'Someone who'll stick by you no matter what. Someone who'll want kids and has good moral values in order to raise them.'

Molly raised her brows in mock surprise. 'Not such a bad guess. I didn't know you knew me so well.'

'You're like an open book, Molly.'

She dropped her gaze from his. He was seeing far too much as it was. 'I need to use the bathroom,' she said.

'The guest bathroom is just along from the library.'

As Molly came back from the bathroom she took a quick peek at the library. It was a reader's dream of a room with floor-to-ceiling bookshelves stacked with old editions of the classics with a good selection of modern titles. The scent of books and furniture polish gave the room a homely, comfortable feel. She ran her fingers along the leather-bound spines as if reacquainting herself with old friends.

She thought of Lucas in his big private home with only books for company. Did he miss his family? Did he miss the wide, open spaces of the outback? Did he ever long to go home and breathe in the scent of eucalyptus and that wonderful fresh smell of the dusty earth soaking up a shower of rain?

Molly turned from the bookshelves and her gaze

came upon a collection of photographs in traditional frames on the leather-topped antique desk. She picked up the first one—it was one of Lucas with his family at Christmas when he'd been a boy of about fifteen. His parents stood proudly either side of their boys. Lucas stood between his brothers, a hand on each young shoulder as if keeping them in place. All of them were smiling; their tanned young faces were so full of life and promise.

Within two years it would be a very different family that faced the camera. The local press had hounded the Bannings after the accident. And then the coroner's inquiry a few months later had brought the national press to their door. Sensation-hungry journalists had conducted tell-all interviews with the locals. Even though the coroner had finally concluded it had been an accident and Lucas was not in any way to blame for Matt's death, the press had painted a very different picture from the gossip and hearsay they had gleaned locally. They had portrayed Lucas as a wild boy from the bush who had taken his parents' farm vehicle without permission and taken his best friend for a joyride that had ended in his friend's death. Jane and Bill Banning had visibly aged overnight, Lucas even more so. He had gone from a fresh-faced teenager of seventeen to a man twice that age, who looked like the world had just landed on his shoulders.

Molly reached for the other photo on the desk. Her heart gave a tight spasm as she saw Matt's freckled face grinning widely as he sat astride his motocross bike, his blue eyes glinting with his usual mischief.

The last time she had seen her brother he hadn't

been smiling. He had been furious with her for going into his room and finding his stash of contraband cigarettes. She had told their parents and as a result he had been grounded.

For every one of the seventeen years since that terrible day Molly had wished she had never told their parents. If Matt hadn't been grounded he might not have slipped out with Lucas that night behind their parents' backs. Matt had hated being confined. He'd got claustrophobic and antsy when restrictions had been placed on him. It was one of the reasons he had been thrown from the vehicle. He hadn't been wearing a seat belt.

'I thought you might be in here,' Lucas said from the doorway.

Molly put the photo back down on the desk. 'I hadn't seen that picture before,' she said, and picked up another one of Ian and Neil with their current partners. 'Neil's been going out with Hannah Pritchard for quite a while now, hasn't he? Are they planning on getting married?'

'I think it's been discussed once or twice,' he said.

She put the photo down and looked at him. 'Would you go home for the wedding?'

His expression visibly tightened. 'Dinner's ready,' he said. 'We'll have to make it short. I have to go back to the hospital to check on a patient.'

Molly followed him back to the kitchen, where he had set up two places, one at each end of the long table. He seemed distracted as they ate. He barely spoke and he didn't touch his wine. She got the feeling he had only eaten because his body needed food. He seemed relieved when she pushed her plate away and said she was full.

'I'll walk you home on the way,' he said, and reached for his coat.

'You're not going to drive?'

His eyes shifted away from hers as he slipped his hospital lanyard over his neck. 'It's only a few blocks,' he said. 'I like the exercise.'

They walked in silence until they came to the front door of Molly's bedsit. 'I'll let you know as soon as I find another place to rent,' she said. 'I hope it won't be more than a few days.'

'Fine.'

'Thanks for dinner,' she said after a tight little silence. 'I'll have to return the favour some time.'

'You're not obliged to,' he said, and glanced impatiently at his watch. 'I'd better get going.'

'Bye.' Molly lifted her hand in a little wave but he had already turned his back and left.

CHAPTER THREE

LUCAS DIDN'T LEAVE the hospital until close to three a.m. and the streets were deserted as he trudged home. The chilly wind drove ice-pick holes through his chest in spite of his thick woollen coat and scarf. He shoved his hands deep into his pockets and wondered what it was like back home at Carboola Creek. He loathed February in London. It was so bleak and miserable. If the sun did manage to break through the thick wad of clouds it was usually weak and watery, and while the snow was beautiful when it first fell, it all too soon turned to slippery brown slush.

He thought longingly of Bannington Homestead. If he closed his eyes he could almost smell the rain-soaked red dust of the plains. It seemed a lifetime ago since he had felt the bright hot sun on his face.

He opened the door of his house and a piteous meow sounded. 'Damn you, Molly,' he muttered as the little cat came limping towards him with its big possum-like eyes shining in welcome. 'Don't get too comfortable,' he addressed it in a gruff tone. 'You're not staying long.'

The cat meowed again and ribboned itself around his ankles before moving way to play with the fringe of the Persian carpet. Lucas caught a faint whiff of Molly's perfume in the air as he moved through the house. It was strongest in the library, or maybe that was just his imagination. He breathed in deeply. The hint of jasmine and sweet peas teased his nostrils, reminding him of hot summer evenings sitting out on the veranda at the homestead.

He let out a long weary sigh and picked up the photograph of his family. His parents were in their sixties now. They were still working the land alongside Neil. Ian was the other side of town on another property. His parents had come over to London for visits a few times. He had loved having them here but it made it so much harder when they left. His mother always cried. Even his stoic father had a catch in his voice and moisture in his eyes. Lucas had come to dread the airport goodbyes. He hated seeing them so distraught. He had not encouraged them to return and always made some excuse about being too busy to entertain visitors.

Lucas wondered if they missed him even half as much as he missed them. But it was the price he had to pay. He put the photo back down and looked at Matt's photo. He saw echoes of his mate's face in the pretty features of Molly. That dusting of freckles, the same uptilted nose, the same light brown hair with its sun-bleached highlights.

Was that why he felt so drawn to her?

Not entirely.

She was all woman now, a beautiful young woman with the whole world at her feet. He saw the way the male staff and patients looked at her. It was the same way *he* looked at her. He had been so close to pulling her into his arms and kissing her. He had wanted to press his mouth to the soft bow of hers to see if it felt as soft and sweet as it looked.

But he could just imagine how her parents would react if he laid a finger on their precious daughter. He thought of what *his* parents would feel. They wouldn't say anything out loud, but he knew they would find it hard to accept Molly. It wasn't her fault, but any involvement with her would make moving on from the past that much more difficult for them and for him. Did he want her so badly because he knew he couldn't have her? Or was it just that she was everything he had always wanted for himself but didn't feel he deserved?

When Molly got to work the next morning Su Ling, one of the registrars, pulled her over and said in an undertone, 'Keep away from the boss. He's in a foul mood. We had a death overnight—David Hyland in Bed Four. He went into organ failure and Lucas was here until the wee hours with him and the family.'

Molly glanced at the empty bed and felt a sinking feeling assail her. David Hyland had only been forty-two with a wife and two young children. He'd developed complications after routine gall-bladder surgery and Molly had only spoken to his wife the day before about how hopeful they were that he would pull through.

Deaths in ICU were part of the job. Not everyone made it. It was a fact of life. Miracles happened occasionally but there was only so much medicine and critical care could do. She wondered if every death on the unit brought home to Lucas the death that haunted him most.

'Don't you have anything better to do than to stand there staring into space?' Lucas barked from behind her.

Molly swung around to face him. 'I was just—'

'There are two families waiting in the counselling rooms for updates on their loved ones,' he said in a clipped, businesslike tone. 'I would appreciate it if you got your mind on the job.'

'My mind is on the job,' she said. 'I was on my way to speak to the Mitchell family now. Do you have any further updates on Claire that I should make them aware of?'

His eyes looked bloodshot as if he hadn't slept the night before. 'Claire is stable,' he said. 'I can't give them anything other than that. We'll try and wean her off the sedation again tomorrow. We'll repeat the scans then as well.'

Molly watched as he strode away, barking out orders as he went. Megan, one of the nurses, caught her eye and raised her brows meaningfully as she walked past with a catheter bag. 'He obviously didn't get laid last night.'

Molly hoped her face wasn't looking as hot as if felt. 'Obviously not,' she said, and headed off to the counselling room.

Molly was waiting for a coffee at the kiosk later that day when Simon breezed in. 'Hello, gorgeous,' he said, throwing an arm around her shoulders and planting a smacking kiss on her mouth. 'How's tricks?'

Molly tried to wriggle out of his embrace. 'Stop it, Simon. People are watching.'

'Don't be such a cold fish,' he chided as he tried to land another kiss. 'Are you still angry with me for blowing you off last night? I told you the theatre was booked out.'

'I believe Dr Drummond told you to stop.'

Molly felt a shiver run down her spine at that strong, commanding voice. She turned to see Lucas eyeballing Simon the way a Doberman did a small, annoying terrier.

'Who's this?' Simon asked, with a pugnacious curl of his lip.

'This is my boss,' Molly said, blushing in spite of every attempt not to. 'Lucas Banning, head of ICU.'

Simon's lip curled even further. 'Aiming a bit higher, are we?' he said.

Molly wished the floor would open up and swallow her whole. She glanced at Lucas but his expression gave little away apart from a glint of derision in his eyes. She turned back to Simon. 'I'm not sure what you're implying but I would rather you—'

'You won't put out for me but I bet you'll put out for him if he promises to fast-track your career,' Simon said with his sneer still in place.

Molly was desperate to get away before any more people joined the audience. As it was, she could see one of the nurses dilly-dallying over the sweeteners as she shamelessly eavesdropped. 'I think you've got the wrong idea about our friendship, Simon,' she said. 'I'll call you later.'

'You do that,' he said, throwing Lucas a death stare before looking back at her. 'You have some explaining to do.'

Molly walked out of the kiosk without collecting her coffee. She had only gone three or four strides when

Lucas caught up with her. 'Are you out of your mind?' he asked. 'What are you *thinking*, dating that jerk?'

She kept walking with her head held high. 'It's none of your business who I date.'

'I beg to differ,' he said. 'He's distracting you from your work.'

Molly rolled her eyes. 'He's doing no such thing.'

'He's totally wrong for you,' he said. 'I can't believe you can't see it.'

She stopped and glared at him. 'My private life has absolutely nothing to do with you.'

His gaze held hers for a long tense moment and she saw a pulse beating at the edge of his mouth. 'You're right,' he said. 'Go and break your own heart. See if I care.'

Molly frowned as he strode ahead of her down the corridor. She could be mistaken but she could almost swear that was jealousy she had seen glittering in his eyes.

Lucas put some kitten biscuits in the saucer on the floor. Mittens crunched his way through a little pile before lifting his head and giving a soft purring meow of appreciation.

'You're welcome,' Lucas said. 'But don't think for a moment that I'm warming to you because I'm not.'

The doorbell sounded. For a moment he thought he had imagined it. But then it sounded again. He wasn't expecting visitors, he never had them. Even the most fervent religious proselytisers had given up on him.

He opened his front door to find Molly standing there with a shopping bag in one hand. She looked tiny, standing there in the cold. Her coat looked too big for her and her hat and scarf framed her heart-shaped face, giving her an elfin look that was unbelievably cute. 'I've brought more supplies for Mittens,' she said. 'I hope you don't mind me calling in without notice. I was worried you might be running out of food for him.'

'I picked up some more at the corner store on the way home,' he said.

She handed him the bag. 'I won't come in. I'm busy.'

'Going out with lover boy?' Lucas said as he took the bag.

Her eyes clashed with his. 'What's it to you?'

'Nothing,' he said, wishing it was true. 'I just wouldn't like to see you get hurt. He's a player. I heard a rumour he's got his eyes on Prof Hubert's daughter. As career fast tracks go, you can't get much better than that.'

She gave him a cold look and took a step backwards. 'I'd better get going. I'd hate to take advantage of your warm hospitality.'

'Aren't you going to say hello to your cat?' Lucas asked.

She raised her chin. 'I wasn't sure if I was welcome,' she said. 'The way you spoke to me today in ICU was deplorable.'

He leaned a hand on the doorjamb. 'You want me to apologise? Sorry, but I'm not that sort of boss. If you can't suck it up then you'd better find some other job where you can get your ego stroked all day.'

'You were out of line,' she said, shooting him a little glare. 'You know you were. You were taking out your frustration on your staff. That's not how to run a department like ICU.'

'Are you telling me how to do my job?' he asked.

She held his challenging look. 'I'm telling you I won't be bullied and harassed by you just because you had a bad day.'

'Did you happen to speak to David Hyland's wife and family?' Lucas asked. 'They were expecting him to make it. *I* was expecting him to make it. Do you know what it felt like to go out there and tell them he had died while we were trying to resus him?'

'I know what that feels like. I've had to—'

'His wife looked at me as if I had just stabbed her in the heart,' he said. 'The kids looked at me in bewilderment. Those are the faces that keep me awake at night. Not the bureaucrats who insist on reducing admission times whilst contributing nothing to the running of the hospital other than sipping double-shot caramel lattes and shuffling a bit of paperwork around their desks. Not the CEO who hasn't got a clue what it feels like to be up all night, worrying about a desperately ill patient. It's the families that come back to haunt me. They want me—*they expect me*—to make it all better, to fix things. But I can't always do that.'

'I'm sorry,' she said, nibbling at her lip, her eyes losing their defensive glare. 'A death is hard on everyone.'

Lucas blew out a breath and held open the door for her. 'I should warn you that I'm not good company right now.'

'Maybe I'm not looking for good company.'

He closed the door and turned and faced her. 'What are you looking for?'

She gave a little shrug of one of her slim shoulders. 'I'm not sure…just any company, I guess…'

Lucas kept a wide berth even though he wanted to reach for her and hold her close. He wanted to block out the hellish day he'd had with a bit of mindless sex. But sweet little Molly Drummond wasn't the right candidate. He had a feeling it wouldn't be mindless sex with her. Those soft little tender hands of hers would not just unravel him physically. They would reach inside him and unpick the lock on the vault of his soul. 'Would you like a drink or something?' he asked.

'I'm fine,' she said. 'I won't stay long. I just wanted to check on Mittens. Oh, you got him a litter tray.' She turned and smiled up at him disarmingly. It was like a ray of sunshine after a wet week. It seemed to light up the foyer, or maybe that was just his imagination.

'Yeah, well, he kept me awake half the night howling to be let out,' he said, keeping his voice gruff in case she had noticed his guard slipping momentarily. 'I don't mind tossing and turning over patients but I draw the line at stray cats.'

'Do you think he's settling in?'

'I don't think there's any doubt of that,' he said wryly. 'He's taken up residence on the end of my bed. I tried to shoo him off but he was back within minutes.'

She was still smiling at him. 'You big softie,' she said.

Lucas glowered at her. 'Have you found alternative accommodation yet?'

Her smile faded and her shoulders went down in a little slump of defeat. 'I've rung heaps of agencies but there's nothing close to the hospital, or at least none than I can afford. And no one wants to rent a place for just three months. I don't know what else to do. Simon offered to share his place with me but I'm not sure I want to do that.'

Lucas felt as if each and every one of his spare rooms had suddenly developed eyes and was staring at him pointedly. His thoughts zigzagged in his brain. It wasn't as if she would be in the way. He would probably never even run into her. It was a big house. Too big really, but he'd liked the thought of working on something in his spare time. He'd *needed* something to distract himself. He really should have sold it by now and bought some other rundown place to renovate. It seemed a shame that no one but him got to see how comfortable and convenient it was before he moved on. Molly had already hinted at his lack of hospitality. What would it hurt to have a houseguest for a week or two?

'You could always stay here until something becomes available.' He hadn't realised he had said it out loud until he saw the surprised look on her face.

'Here?' she said. 'With you?'

'In one of the spare rooms,' he said. 'I'd charge you rent and expenses. I'm not running a charity.'

'Are you sure?'

Lucas wasn't one bit sure. He still didn't know why he had uttered those words. But he had and he couldn't unsay them. Besides, he was already looking after her wretched cat. Better that she moved in and took charge of its feeding and toileting. It could sleep on her bed, not his. And he would willingly suffer the invasion of his private domain for a week or two rather than see her move in with Simon-up-himself Westbury.

'I'd expect you to do your share of the cooking while you're here,' he said. 'And I would prefer it if you entertained your men friends off site.'

'It's a very generous offer...' Her perfect white teeth nibbled at her lower lip. 'But what if people think we're actually living together as in *living* together...you know, as a couple?'

Lucas couldn't stop a vision of her lying naked in his bed taking over his mind. He wondered what it would be like, waking up beside her each morning. Seeing her sunny smile, feeling her arms around him, smelling the scent of her on his skin, his body sated from long, passionate hours of lovemaking. He pushed the thoughts aside like a row of books toppling off a mantelpiece. 'I don't waste time worrying what other people think,' he said. 'What I do outside the hospital is no one's business but my own.'

'What about our families?' she asked.

He gave her a grim look. 'Don't you mean *your* family?'

'I don't think my mother will have a problem with it,' she said, frowning a little. 'My father is another story.'

'Isn't it time you lived your own life?' he asked. 'You're twenty-seven years old. You shouldn't have to justify your actions to him or anyone.'

'I know,' she said. 'That's one of the reasons I came to London. I wanted to break free. I think my father still sees me as a little girl who needs protecting.'

'Yeah, well, given your choice in men so far, I'm inclined to agree with him,' Lucas said.

'I know Simon gave you the wrong impression,' she

said. 'He's not usually so…possessive. I think it was all show, to tell you the truth.'

'He's a prize jerk,' Lucas said. 'I thought you had much better taste than that.'

Her grey-blue eyes flashed. 'Perhaps I should have you assess every potential partner to see if they meet your exacting standards,' she said. 'Would that satisfy you?'

Lucas had a feeling he wasn't going to be satisfied by anything other than having her to himself, but he wasn't going to admit that to her. She wasn't his to have. He had to remember that. She was his best mate's little sister. Any chance of a future together had died along with Matt. 'Do you need a hand moving your things across?' he asked. 'I have an hour free now.'

His offer to help appeared to mollify her. 'That would be very helpful,' she said. 'Thank you.'

Molly put the last of her things in the spare room furthest away from Lucas's master suite. She still couldn't quite believe he had made her the offer of temporary accommodation, although she suspected it had more to do with discouraging her from moving in with Simon. It was very dog in the manger of him, given he'd made it clear he wasn't going to pursue her himself. Perhaps he wanted to prove to himself that he could keep his hands off her. Lucas's house was certainly big enough for them to avoid intimate contact. They didn't even have to share a bathroom. There were six to choose from as well as his en suite.

But even sharing a space as large as this had its complications. There was her attraction to him, for one thing. She couldn't seem to control it. Every time he looked at her she felt a stirring of longing deep inside. She *ached* to feel his mouth on hers. It was almost an obsession now. She didn't think she would rest until she had tasted him. And then there was his body: that strong, tall body that was so lean and fit and in its prime. She wanted to explore its carved muscles, smooth her hands over the satin-wrapped steel of his back and shoulders, hold him in her hand, feel the throb of his blood against her palm. Her body got moist thinking about it. Her nerves got twitchy and restless, the contraction-like pulse deep and relentless in her core.

She gave herself a mental shake. She was probably only fixated on him because he had said he wasn't interested in acting on his attraction to her. It was the contrariness of human nature—wanting something you knew you couldn't have.

Molly took Mittens with her downstairs and placed him on the floor near his kitten milk and biscuits. It was raining outside; the droplets of water were rolling like diamonds down the glass of the windows and French doors. It was hard not to think of home when the weather was so dismal. The cold seemed to seep right into her bones. The bedsit had felt like an icebox, but at least Lucas's house was warm, even if his manner towards her was not.

She heard his firm tread behind her as he came into the room. 'Are you all settled in?' he asked.

'Yes, thank you,' Molly said, turning to face him. 'It's a lovely room and so spacious. Much nicer than the bedsit, I can assure you.'

He gave her one of his brisk, businesslike nods. 'I'm

going out for a while,' he said. 'I have some paperwork to see to at the hospital.'

'You work too hard,' she said.

'I get paid to work hard.'

'Surely not this hard,' Molly said. 'You look like you didn't sleep at all last night. Why do you drive yourself so relentlessly? No, don't tell me. I already know.'

His mouth flattened grimly. 'I would prefer it if you kept your opinions to yourself. You might currently share my house but that's all you're going to share. I don't need you to take on the role of a caring partner. Do I make myself clear?'

'When was the last time you had a partner?' Molly asked.

It was a moment or two before he spoke. She wondered if he was trying to remember. 'I can assure you I'm no monk,' he said.

'Tell me the last time you had sex.'

His brows snapped together. 'What *is* this? Do you really think I'm going to give you a blow-by-blow account of my sex life?'

'You've felt at perfect liberty to comment on mine,' Molly pointed out.

'That's because you were conducting it in the hospital cafeteria.'

'That is not true!' she said.

'You'd better keep a lid on your public displays of affection if you want to keep your job,' he said.

Molly felt her back come up. 'Are you threatening me?'

His eyes warred with hers. 'Not personally, but I think I should inform you the current CEO is a stickler for professional behaviour at all times,' he said. 'Patients come to St Patrick's for health care, not to witness a cheesy soap-opera love scene in the middle of the corridor. If a patient complains to him it would be one look at the CCTV and you'd be fired on the spot.'

'And I bet you'd be the first to be glad to see me go,' she said with a resentful look.

'So far I've heard nothing but good reports about you from patients and staff alike,' he said. 'I would hate to see all that come undone by behaviour that would be considered puerile in a high school, let alone in a professional setting.'

Molly set her mouth tightly. 'I can assure you it won't happen again.'

'Make sure that it doesn't,' he said, and strode out.

When Molly came downstairs in the morning Lucas had already left for work. His housekeeper was in the kitchen, unloading the dishwasher. She smiled and straightened as Molly came in. 'I'm Gina,' she said. 'Dr Banning told me you and the little cat are staying for a few days.'

'Yes,' Molly said. 'I hope that's not going to make extra work for you?'

'Not at all,' Gina said. 'It will be good for Dr Banning to have some company in this big old house of his. You're from his home town in Australia, yes?'

'Is my accent that obvious?' Molly asked with a self-deprecating smile.

'Not your accent,' Gina said. 'Your looks.'

'My...looks?'

'The photo in the library,' Gina said. 'You're Matthew Drummond's sister, yes?'

Molly frowned. 'You know about Matt?'

Gina nodded solemnly. 'Dr Banning's mother told me when they visited a few years ago. Very sad. Such a tragic accident.'

'Yes…yes, it was.'

'It is good that you are still friends,' Gina said.

Friends? Molly thought. Is that what she and Lucas were? 'Um…yes,' she said. 'Our parents were neighbours for years and years. We sort of all grew up together, same school, same teachers even.'

'He is a very kind man,' Gina said. 'But he works too hard. I tell him he needs to find a nice girl, get married and have some kids. It would help him to have something other than work to occupy his mind, yes?'

'Um…he does seem very career driven,' Molly said.

'He uses work to forget,' Gina said. 'He saves lots of lives but he can never bring back the one he wanted to save the most.' She shook her head. 'Sad, very sad.'

Molly gave the housekeeper a pained smile. 'I have to get going,' she said. 'It was lovely meeting you.'

'I hope you're still here when I come next week, yes?' Gina said with a twinkle in her chocolate-brown eyes.

'Oh, no,' Molly said hurriedly. 'I hope to find another flat well before then.'

'Have you found another flat?' Jacqui asked in the staff tearoom a couple of days later.

Molly closed the newspaper rental guide with a dispirited sigh. 'I've looked at five so far but none of them allow pets,' she said. 'The ones I've looked at

CHAPTER FOUR

LUCAS WAS IN his office, writing up some notes, when he got a call from Alistair Brentwood in Accident and Emergency. He'd had hundreds of calls over the years from various doctors in A and E, but something about this one made the hairs on the back of his neck stand up as soon as Alistair gave him the rundown on the incoming patient.

It was like hearing his and Matt's accident replayed back to him. The names and ages had changed but it was so similar he felt like he had been swept up in a time warp. The horror of that night came back to him in hammer blows of dread. He felt them pound through his blood as he listened to his colleague's description.

'Lucas, we've got a male, twenty-one, with a serious head injury,' Alistair said. 'Blunt chest trauma and haemodynamically stable. I can see a bit of lung contusion on his chest CT, abdo is OK, but his brain scan looks like global contusions and oedema. His GCS was three at the scene but picked up to six in here. One pupil fixed and dilated, the other sluggish. Pretty serious closed head injury. You got a bed for him up there?'

'Thanks,' Lucas said, mentally gearing up to face the shattered family. He would have to deal with them on a daily basis, helping them come to terms with the severity of their loved one's injuries. 'We're right to take him. Have the neurosurgeons assessed him yet?'

'Yes, they'll put in an ICP monitor when he's settled in the unit. If he survives it's going to be a long haul,' Alistair said matter-of-factly. 'Name's Tim Merrick, he was the passenger. The driver got off very lightly—a Hamish Fisher. He's going to the ward for obs.'

Lucas felt a cold hand press hard against his sternum. *Two shattered families*, he thought. Lives that just hours ago had been normal would now never be normal again. He wondered if Hamish Fisher had any idea of what lay ahead for him—the guilt, the despair, and the what-ifs and if-onlys that would haunt his days and nights for the rest of his life. 'OK. I'll come down now if he's ready,' he said.

'Yeah, he's fine to go.'

'Dr Drummond, this is Tim Merrick, twenty-one-year-old male from a MVA,' Lucas said with his usual clinical calm as the patient was transferred to ICU. *Just another patient*, he kept saying inside his head, but it wasn't working as it normally did. This was somebody's son, someone's brother.

Someone's best friend.

A cold, sick feeling curdled his stomach. Bile rose in his throat. His chest felt as if it was being compressed by an industrial vice. He was having trouble breathing. He could feel sweat beading between his shoulder blades. His temples pounded.

Scenes from seventeen years ago kept flashing through his mind on rapid replay. Matt's parents looking ashen and gutted as they came in to where their son's broken and bloodied body lay on a hospital gurney. Molly standing there, holding her mother's hand, her grey-blue eyes wide with fear and dread, her little face as white as milk but for the nutmeg-like dusting of her freckles. Lucas's parents looking shocked. Their faces seeming to age in front of him as he falteringly tried to explain what had happened.

The doctors with their calm clinical voices and the police with their detached demeanours as they took down his statement and asked questions he could barely answer for the ropey knot of anguish that had risen in his throat.

Lucas blinked a couple of times and brought himself back to the moment. 'He's got a severe closed head injury, but not much else. Neurosurgery are coming up in twenty minutes to put in an ICP monitor. Can you set him up on the ventilator?'

'Sure,' Molly said.

'I'm going to start mannitol and steroids, and do the paperwork,' he said. 'Some relatives have just arrived. I'll go and talk with them. We're going to pull out every stop here to give him a chance of recovery.'

'I'll run the CO_2 slightly up and put in a central line, and get the ICP monitor set up ready to connect,' Molly said.

'Good,' Lucas said. 'He's got right pulmonary contusion, and I've just got the official CT report. He's also got a small pneumothorax on the right.'

'Good that was picked up,' Molly said. 'We could've blown that up overnight on the ventilator. I'll put in a right chest drain after I've set the ventilator.'

'Thanks.' He drew in a heavy breath that felt like it had a handful of thumbtacks attached. 'I'll talk to the relatives. He's got a severe head injury, but he could recover. He's only young. He's got to be given the maximum chance.'

Once Molly had put in Tim Merrick's chest drain she went back to the central office where Aleem Pashar was going through the patient notes that had come up from A and E.

'Not sure why the boss is insisting pulling out all the stops,' Aleem said. 'The CT scan's not looking good. Look.'

Molly took the report and read through it with a sinking heart. A positive outcome was very unlikely. What had Lucas been thinking? Surely he of all people knew the data on severe brain injuries? It wasn't fair to give the family unrealistic expectations. They needed to be gently prepared for the imminent loss of their loved one. It might be days, or weeks, sometimes even months, but someone as badly injured as Tim Merrick might not leave ICU alive, or if he did, he would be severely compromised.

'I sure wouldn't want to be the one who was driving,' Aleem said as he leaned back against the desk. 'Can you imagine living with that for the rest of your life?'

Molly frowned as she looked at the registrar. 'Pardon?'

'Tim Merrick's mate,' he said. 'He was the one driving. All he got was a fractured patella.'

Molly bit her lip. Was that why Lucas was doing everything he could to keep Tim alive? He was reliving his own nightmare through the driver. He would be feeling the anguish of the young man, having been through it himself. Keeping Tim Merrick on life support indefinitely was his way of giving the young driver time to come to terms with what had happened. But while she understood Lucas's motives, she wasn't sure she agreed with giving the family false hope. They could end up suffering more in the long run.

'No alcohol involved, which is one thing to be grateful for, I suppose,' Aleem said. 'Apparently he swerved to avoid a kid on a bike. Missed the kid but as good as wrote off his best mate. Can you imagine having that on your conscience? I'd never get behind the wheel again.'

Molly put down the CT report. 'I think I'll have a word with Tim's parents. Dr Banning should be finished with them now.' She turned at the door. 'Can you ring the orthopaedic ward and find out the driver's name? I think I'll visit him before I go home.'

'Will do,' Aleem said, and reached for the phone.

'Mr and Mrs Merrick?' Molly gently addressed the middle-aged couple who were still sitting huddled together in the counselling room.

There was no sign of Lucas, although Molly could pick up a faint trace of his light aftershave in the small room, suggesting he had not long ago left. A pile of used tissues was on the table beside the wife and she had another one screwed up in her hand. The husband was dry-eyed but his Adam's apple was going up and down like a piston.

'I'm Dr Drummond,' Molly said. 'I've been looking after your son in ICU. He's on the ventilator now and comfortable.'

'Can we see him?' the wife asked, absently tearing the tissue in her hand into shreds.

'Yes, of course,' Molly said. 'But first…I think I should warn you that ICU can be an upsetting place. There are lots of machines making all sorts of noises. You are free to come and go as you like but we have a strict hygiene policy to reduce the risk of infection. Did Dr Banning go through all this with you?'

The wife nodded. 'He said Tim's stable for the time being. He said we should talk to him as much as possible…that it might help bring him round.'

'It will certainly do no harm to sit with him and talk to him,' Molly said. 'Has Dr Banning been through Tim's scans with you?'

'He said it's too early to be certain what's going on,' the husband said. 'There's a lot of swelling and bleeding. He said he'd like to wait till that settles before giving a more definitive diagnosis.'

Molly could see the sense in what Lucas had told the Merricks but she wondered if he was just buying time. She had seen the scans. Bleeding and swelling notwithstanding, Tim was critically injured and nothing short of a miracle could turn things around.

She took the parents to their son's bedside and watched as they spoke to him and touched him. It was heart-wrenching to think that in a few days they might lose him for ever.

It was impossible not to think about her brother's death at times like this, how that night in A and E had been such a surreal nightmare. Her parents had done the same as the Merricks. They had touched and stroked Matt, talking to him even though they had already been told he had gone. Molly had seen Lucas on their way out of the hospital. He had been standing with his parents, his face so stricken it had been like looking at someone else entirely. Matt had lost his life, but in a way so too had Lucas. Nothing would ever be the same for him again.

'Dr Drummond?' Mrs Merrick's voice interrupted Molly's reverie. 'Can I talk to you for a minute?'

'Sure,' Molly said.

Mrs Merrick looked at her son again, tears rolling down her face. She brushed at them with her hand and turned back to Molly. 'Tim would hate to be left an invalid. He wouldn't cope with it. We talked about it only recently. A relative—his cousin—had a serious accident at work and was left a quadriplegic. He's totally dependent on carers for everything now.

'Tim said it would destroy him to be left like that. That he would rather die. He insisted on drawing up an end-of-life directive. We tried to talk him out of it. We thought only old or terminally ill people signed them but he was adamant. I suppose what I'm saying is…I want to know what we're dealing with here. I want to do the right thing by my son. I want to be…' She glanced at her husband and continued, '*We* want to be prepared for whatever is ahead.'

'I understand,' Molly said. 'We'll keep you well informed on Tim's progress. There are protocols to go through in regard to end-of-life directives. I'll speak to Dr Banning about it.'

'There's one other thing,' Mr Merrick said as he

came and stood by his wife. 'I want to be clear on this. We don't blame Hamish for what happened to Tim. This is an accident—a terrible, tragic accident. It could've been the other way round. We're devastated for Hamish as well as ourselves.'

Molly felt a lump come up in her throat. She could remember all too well the dreadful words her father had shouted at Lucas and his parents in A and E all those years ago. Everyone had known it had been the raw grief talking but it hadn't made it any easier to witness. If only her father had demonstrated even a fraction of the dignity and grace of the Merricks. 'I'm going to see Hamish now,' she said. 'I'll tell him you're thinking of him.'

Molly went to the orthopaedic ward where Hamish Fisher was spending the night prior to having his knee repaired the following morning. She found him lying in a four-bed ward with the curtains drawn around his bed. Curled up there with his back to the room, he looked a lot younger than twenty-one. Her heart ached for him. He looked so alone and broken. From this day forward his life would never be the same. She wondered if in seventeen years' time he would be just as locked away and lonely as Lucas.

'Hamish?' she said. 'I'm one of the ICU doctors, Molly Drummond.'

Hamish opened his reddened eyes. 'He's dead, isn't he?' he said in a bleak tone.

'No,' she said, taking the chair beside the bed. 'He's on a ventilator and at this point he's stable.'

The young man's chin shook as he fought to control

his emotion. 'But he's going to die, isn't he?' he said. 'I heard the ER doctors talking.'

'No one can say for sure at this stage,' Molly said.

He swallowed convulsively. 'I swerved to avoid a kid on a bike,' he said. 'It all happened so quickly. I saw this little kid coming out of nowhere and I hit the brakes but there must have been oil on the road. I lost control...'

Molly put her hand on his where it was gripping the sheet with white-knuckled force. 'Tim's parents don't blame you,' she said. 'They're with Tim now but I'm sure they'll come down to see you when they get the chance. Do you have anyone here with you? Your parents?'

He shook his head. 'I haven't got a dad. My mum is on her way. She's been on a cruise with friends. She'd saved up for years to go... She's flying home tonight.'

'It's important you have people around to support you,' Molly said. 'I can organise for the hospital chaplain to visit you. It helps to talk to someone at a time like this.'

'Talking isn't going to turn back the clock, is it?' Hamish said.

She gave his hand another squeeze. 'Just try and take it one day at a time.'

Molly didn't see Lucas again until later that night. He came in just before midnight, his face looking drawn and his eyes hollow, as if two fingers had pushed them right back into his head.

'Are you OK?' she asked, rising from the sofa where she had been flicking through a home renovating magazine without managing to remember a word of what she had read.

He scraped a hand through his hair. 'Yeah,' he said. 'Why wouldn't I be? It was just another day at the office.'

'It was hardly that,' Molly said.

He dismissed her with a look and turned to leave. 'I'm going to bed.'

'Lucas?'

His back looked concrete tight with tension in that infinitesimal moment before he turned to look at her. 'I've handled hundreds of critically ill trauma patients,' he said. 'This is just another case.'

She came over to where he was standing. 'It's not just another case,' she said. 'It's like you and Matt all over again.'

A stone mask covered his features. 'Leave it, Molly.'

'I think we should talk about it,' she said. 'I think my parents should've talked to you about it long ago. It was wrong to blame you the way they did. Tim's parents are obviously shattered by what's happened but at least they're not blaming Hamish.'

'That will come later,' he said grimly.

'I don't think so,' she said. 'I think they realise it could just have easily been Tim behind that wheel. It's devastating for them to face the prospect of losing their son but—'

'They are *not* going to lose their son,' Lucas said with implacable force.

Molly frowned at him. 'Lucas, you can't possibly think he's going to survive more than a few days or a week or two at the most.'

A thread of steel stitched his mouth into a flat, determined line. 'I've seen plenty of critically injured patients come off ventilators. He deserves every chance to make it. I'm not withdrawing support.'

'But what if that's not what Tim would've wanted?'

'We'll find out what he wants when he wakes up,' he said.

'What if he doesn't wake up?' Molly asked. 'You saw the scans. It's not looking good right now.'

'Early scans can be misleading,' he said. 'You know that. There's bleeding and swelling everywhere. It can take days or even weeks to get a clear idea of what's going on.'

'I don't think it's fair to give his family false hope,' she said. 'I think they're the sort of people who need to know what they're up against right from the get-go. They want to be prepared.'

His eyes were hard as they clashed with hers. 'I hate to pull rank here but I have a lot more clinical experience than you,' he said. 'His parents are still in shock. This is not the time to be dumping unnecessary and distressing information on them.'

'Tim Merrick signed an end-of-life directive,' Molly said. 'His mother told me. They all did it a couple of years ago after a relative was made a quadriplegic in a workplace accident.'

Lucas drew in a short breath and then slowly released it. 'So?'

'So his wishes should be acknowledged,' Molly said. 'He didn't want to be left languishing in some care facility for the rest of his life. Evidently he was quite adamant about it. He couldn't bear the thought of being dependent on others for everything.'

He moved to the other side of the room, his gait stiff and jerky as if his inner turmoil was manifested in his body. He rubbed the back of his neck. The sound of his hand moving over his skin was amplified in the silence.

'He would want the ventilator turned off, Lucas.'

'It's too early to decide that.'

'There might be a time when it's too late to decide,' Molly pointed out. 'What will you say to him then? "Sorry, we disregarded your directive because we thought you were going to wake up and be back to normal"?'

He cut his gaze to hers. 'I've seen patients with much worse injuries walk out of ICU,' he said.

Molly gave him an incredulous look. 'You think Tim Merrick is going to walk when he can't even *breathe* on his own? Come on, Lucas, surely you haven't abandoned the science you were trained to respect and rely on? He's not going to walk again. He's probably not going to do anything for himself again. And you're prolonging his and his family's agony by insisting on keeping him hooked up to that ventilator.'

'What about Hamish Fisher?' he asked, nailing her with a look.

Molly released a little breath. 'Lucas, it's not Hamish Fisher lying in that bed.'

'No,' he said. 'But he's the one who's going to spend the rest of his life wishing to hell it had been.'

Molly felt the anguish behind his statement. She saw the agony of it on his face. For all these years he would have given anything to trade places with her brother.

But that's not how fate had decided things would be. 'I know this is difficult for you,' she said. 'But you have to keep your clinical hat on. You can't let what happened to you all those years ago influence your decision in managing Tim Merrick's care.'

He looked at her for a long, tense moment. 'Just give him some time,' he said. 'Surely he deserves that?'

'Are we talking about Tim or Hamish?' Molly asked.

He walked to the other side of the room and looked out of the window at the blizzard-like conditions outside. Molly saw his shoulders rise and fall as he let out a long, jagged sigh. She wanted to go to him, to wrap her arms around him and hold him close. But just as she took the first step towards him he turned and looked at her.

'I had a patient a few months back,' he said, 'a young girl of nineteen who'd fallen from a balcony at a party. She fell five metres onto concrete. It was a miracle she survived the fall. She had multiple fractures, including a base-of-skull fracture. She was in a coma for a month. Just when she was showing signs of waking up she got meningitis. The scans looked as if things were going downhill. Every other doctor and specialist involved with her care was ready to give up. I refused to do so. In my view, she just needed more time. I was right. She was young and fit and her other injuries were healing well. After another week she started to improve. It was slow but sure. She's back at university now, doing a fine arts degree. She comes in now and again and brings cupcakes for us all.'

'I'm glad it worked out that way for you and for her,'

Molly said. 'But there are just as many cases where it doesn't.'

He held her look for a long moment. 'The day she walked out of hospital with her parents I went to my office and closed the door and cried like a baby.'

Molly could picture him doing it. He had depths to his character that could so easily go unnoticed in a brief encounter. He was dedicated and professional at all times and yet he was as human as the next person. It was perhaps his humanity that made him such a wonderful ICU doctor. He didn't want anyone to suffer as he had suffered. He worked tirelessly to give his patients the best possible chance of recovery.

His own personal tragedy had moulded him into the man he was today—strong, driven and determined. He was a leader, not a follower. He expected a lot from his staff but he didn't ask anything of them he wasn't prepared to do himself. She could not think of a more wonderful ally in the fight for a patient's life. But she wondered if it all took its toll on him personally. Was that why he was all work and no play? He simply had nothing left to given anyone outside work.

'It must have been an amazing moment to see her walk out of hospital,' she said.

'It was,' he said. 'I know doctors are meant to keep a clinical distance. You can't make sound judgements when your emotions are involved. But once the patient is in the clear, sometimes the relief is overwhelming. I've had staff go on stress leave after a patient leaves. It's those sorts of miracles that make our jobs so rewarding and yet so utterly demanding.'

'How do you deal with the stress?' she asked.

'I fix stuff.'

'Fix stuff?'

He wafted a hand at their surroundings. 'There's nothing quite like tearing down a wall or painting or replastering or refitting a kitchen or bathroom,' he said. 'I'm thinking of selling in the spring. I've just about run out of things to do.'

'But this is such a fabulous house,' Molly said.

He gave a shrug. 'It's just a roof and four walls.'

'It's much more than that, surely?' she said. 'You've put so much work into it. It seems a shame not to get the benefit of it for a while.'

'Don't worry,' he said as he hooked his jacket over one shoulder. 'I'll give you plenty of notice before I let the realtor bring potential buyers through.'

Molly bit her lip. 'I'm having trouble finding anywhere else to live so far.'

'There's no hurry. You can stay here as long as you need to.'

'But not for the whole three months.'

He held her look for a beat. 'I can't imagine that you'd want to. I'm not the most genial host.'

'I think it's best if I keep looking,' she said. 'I'm having a hard time convincing everyone we're not a couple.'

'And that embarrasses you?'

Molly found his green and brown gaze mesmerising. 'No, not at all,' she said. 'Does it embarrass you?'

His eyes moved over her face, as if he was committing her features to memory. The silence throbbed with a backbeat of electric tension. She felt it echoing in her blood and wondered if he could feel it too. His eyes dropped to her mouth, pausing there for an infinitesimal moment. 'In another life I would've kissed you the other night,' he said in a gravel-rough tone. 'I probably would've taken you to bed as well.'

Molly looked at his mouth. She could see the tiny vertical lines of his lower lip and the slight dryness that she knew would cling to her softer one like sandpaper does to silk. 'Why not in this life?' she asked softly.

He reached out and brushed her lower lip with the pad of his index finger. His touch was as light as a moth's wing but it set off a thousand bubbly, tingly sensations beneath her skin. 'I think you know why not,' he said, and stepped back from her.

Molly felt like the floor of her stomach had dropped right out of her as he turned and left the room. She put her hand to her mouth, touching where his finger had so briefly been…

CHAPTER FIVE

LUCAS LOOKED AT the bedside clock and groaned. Another hour had gone by and he still couldn't sleep. His body felt restless, too wired to relax enough to drift off. He wondered if Molly was faring any better. But of course that was his problem—thinking about Molly.

He couldn't *stop* thinking about her. About how soft her plump lower lip had felt against the soft press of his fingertip. How luminous her grey-blue eyes had been when she had looked at him. How husky and sexy her voice had sounded. How he had wanted to pull her into his arms and kiss her, to taste her, to feel her respond to him.

He groaned again and threw off the bedcovers. Having her under the same roof was a form of self-torture. What had he been thinking, inviting her to stay with him? The house had changed since she'd moved in. And it wasn't just her little cat, who right at this moment was curled up on the foot of his bed, purring like an engine.

Molly made his big empty house seem warm and inviting. It was subtle things, like the way she had brought a bunch of flowers home and put them on the kitchen table in a jam jar because he hadn't ever thought to buy a vase. It was the fragrance of her perfume that lingered in the rooms she had wandered into. It was seeing the little array of girly things in the guest bathroom she was using—the lotions and potions, the hairdryer and straightening iron. And it was the not-so-subtle things, like her sexy black wisp of lace knickers hanging to dry over the clotheshorse in the laundry.

It wasn't just the house that had changed since she'd moved in. *He* had changed. He no longer came home wanting to be alone. He came home and looked forward to seeing her, hearing her, being with her. It wasn't enough to see her at work. He wanted more. He wanted to talk to her and to have her talk to him. He wanted to see her smile, hear her laugh.

He wanted her.

But he couldn't have her without the past overshadowing everything. How long before her parents—either singularly or jointly—expressed their misgivings? Such antagonism would poison any alliance between them as a couple. But it wasn't just the family stuff that gave him pause. How could he make her happy when he had nothing to offer her? He was used to being alone. He didn't know how to live any other way. He would end up hurting her, just like he hurt everyone who dared to care about him.

Molly was out of his league, out of bounds, forbidden.

But he still wanted her.

Molly woke to the sound of mewing outside her door. She threw off the bedcovers and padded over to let Mittens in. 'So now you want to sleep in my room, do you, you traitorous feline?' she said.

The little cat blinked up at her guilelessly and mewed again.

'Don't just sit there looking at me like that,' Molly said. 'Are you coming in or not?'

Mittens wound his body around her ankles and then padded off towards the stairs, stopping every now and again to look back at her as if to tell her to follow him.

Molly shook her head in defeat and reached for a wrap. She followed the cat to the kitchen downstairs, where she poured some cat biscuits into the dish on the floor and watched as he munched and crunched his way through them. 'You'd better not make a habit of this,' she muttered. 'I can't see Lucas waiting on you whisker and paw for nocturnal top-ups.'

There was a sound behind her and Molly turned and saw Lucas standing there dressed in nothing but a pair of long black silk pyjama trousers that were loose around his lean hips. Her eyes drank in the sight of his broad muscular chest. The satin skin with its natural tan, the carved pectoral muscles, the tiny pebbles of his flat male nipples, the ripped line of his abdomen and the dark hair that trailed beyond the waistband of the trousers. 'Um...I was just feeding Mittens,' she said, waving a hand at the cat, who was now licking his paws and wiping them over his face in a grooming session.

'So I see,' Lucas said.

'I hope I didn't wake you, nattering away to him,' Molly said.

'I wasn't asleep.'

She looked at his drawn features—the bloodshot eyes, the deep grooves that ran each side of his mouth. *Don't stare at his mouth!* She brought her gaze back up to his eyes and felt a tremor of want roll through her. He was so arrantly sexy with his dark stubbly regrowth and his hair all tousled.

'Can I make you a hot drink or something?' she asked, and started bustling about the kitchen to stop herself from reaching for him. 'I bought some chocolate buttons the other day. They're my weakness. That's why I put them on the top shelf, so they're not in my face and tempting me all the time.' She reached up on tiptoe in the pantry but she couldn't quite reach the packet in her bare feet.

Lucas's arm reached past her and took the packet of chocolate buttons off the shelf. 'Here you go,' he said.

He was *incredibly* close in the tight space. Molly could smell his warm male smell. She could see the individual points of his raspy regrowth along his jaw. She could see the dark flare of his pupils as he held her gaze in a lock that had distinctly erotic undertones. Her fingers touched his as she went to take the packet from him but he didn't release it. She gave it a little tug but still he held firm. She nervously sent the tip of her tongue out over her lips and gave the packet another little tug.

She felt the faintest loosening of his hold, but just as she was about to claim victory, his fingers wrapped around hers. The electricity of his touch sent a shockwave through her senses.

He gently tugged her towards her him until she was flush against his pelvis, her stomach doing a complete flip turn when she encountered the ridge of his growing erection. She lowered her lashes as his mouth came down, down, down as if in slow motion.

As soon as Molly felt the imprint of his mouth on

hers, a rush of sensation spiralled through her. His kiss was light at first, experimental almost, a slow, measured discovery of the landscape of her lips. He gradually increased the pressure but he didn't deepen the kiss. But somehow it was all the more intimate for that.

He cupped her face in his hands, his lean, long fingers gentle on her cheeks. It was a tender gesture that made her insides melt. She felt the rasp of his unshaven jaw against her chin as he shifted position. It was a spine-tingling reminder of all the essential differences between them: smooth and rough, hard and soft, male and female.

He gently stroked his tongue along the seam of her mouth. It wasn't a command for entry but a tempting lure to make her come in search of him. She pushed the tip of her tongue forward, her whole body quivering when it came into contact with his—male against female. It made fireworks explode inside her body. It unleashed something needy and urgent inside her. She gave a little whimper as his tongue touched hers again, a stab and retreat that had an unmistakably sexual intent about it.

Molly pressed herself closer, her insides clenching with desire as she felt his erection so hot and hard against her belly. His tongue glided against hers, calling it into a circling, whirling dance that made her senses spin like a top.

Had she ever been kissed like this?

Not in this lifetime.

He increased the pressure of his mouth on hers, interspersed with gentle but sexy thrusts and glides of his tongue. His hands slid up into her hair, his fingers splaying out over her scalp where every hair shaft was shivering and quaking in delight.

He broke the kiss to pull at her lips with his mouth, teasing little tugs that made her belly flip and then flop. Then he caressed her lips with a slow, drugging sweep of his tongue before covering her mouth again in a kiss that had a hint of desperation to it.

Molly felt her bones turn to liquid as his mouth worked its mesmerising magic on hers. She had never felt so turned on by a kiss. Hot darts of need pierced her. Her breasts felt tight and sensitive where they were pressing against his chest. Her inner core was moist and aching with that hollow feeling of want that nothing but sex could assuage. She moved her lower body against him, loving the feel of him responding to her so powerfully.

He took a deep breath and pulled back, holding her with his hands on her upper arms. 'We need to stop,' he said, breathing raggedly. '*I* need to stop.'

'Right…of course…good idea. We definitely should stop,' Molly said, suddenly embarrassed at how passionately she had responded to him. Would he think her too easy? Too forward? That was ironic as she was quite possibly the most conservative lover on the planet. But somehow he had unlocked a part of her she hadn't known existed.

He dropped his hold and rubbed at his face with both of his hands. 'I knew this was going to happen. I'm sorry. It's my fault. I was the one who crossed the line. It won't happen again.'

'We kissed,' she said, trying to be all modern and laid back about it. 'What's the big deal?'

His expression tightened. 'This is not just about a kiss and you damn well know it.' He moved to the other side of the kitchen. 'I don't need this right now.'

'Maybe this is just what you need,' Molly said. 'You're too focussed on work. That's why you can't sleep. You haven't got an off button.'

'Don't tell me how to live my life.'

'You're not living your life, though, are you?' she said.

His brows snapped together. 'What's that supposed to mean?'

'You have no life,' Molly said. 'You work ninety-to a hundred-hour weeks. You bite people's heads off. You push people away. You can't even remember the last time you got close to someone.'

'I had sex three months ago.'

Molly arched her brow. 'On your own or with someone?'

He rolled his eyes. 'With a woman I met at a conference.'

'Did you see her more than once?'

'There was no point,' he said. 'The chemistry wasn't right.'

'So it was a one-night stand.'

'There's nothing wrong with a one-night stand as long as it's safe.'

'And you like to be safe, don't you, Lucas?' Molly said. 'Safe from feeling anything for anyone. Safe from having anyone feel anything for you.'

She could see the tension in him. It was in every line and contour of his face. It was in the set of his shoulders and the tight clench of his fists. She could even feel it in the air. It made the atmosphere crackle like scrunched-up baking paper. 'What are you trying to do, Molly?' he asked. 'Push me until I lose control?'

She stepped up to within an inch of his body. His nostrils flared like those of a wild stallion as her scent came to him. Her breasts almost touched his chest. He held himself rigid, every muscle on his face set in stone, his body a marble statue. 'This is what you're frightened of, isn't it, Lucas?' she said as she placed a hand on his chest where his heart was thumping. 'Wanting someone. *Needing* them.'

He covered her hand with his and pulled it off his chest, the strength and grip of his fingers making her wince. 'I want you out of here by the end of the week,' he said, dropping her hand as if it was poisonous.

'Why?' she asked. 'Because you don't like letting someone see how incredibly lonely you are when you haven't got work to distract you?'

His jaw looked like it had been set in concrete. 'If you're not careful I'll throw you out tonight.'

'I don't think you mean that,' Molly said.

'You want to put it to the test?' he asked.

She looked at the steely glint in his eyes and backed down. 'Not particularly.'

'Wise of you,' he said.

'I'm only doing it because of Mittens,' she said. 'If it wasn't for him, I would've left before this.'

'You shouldn't have come in the first place.'

'You invited me!'

'I meant to London,' he said. 'You should have known it would cause trouble. But that's probably why you came. You could destroy my reputation with a word to the right person and you damn well know it.'

Molly frowned as she looked at him. 'I didn't realise you had such an appalling opinion of me. Do you really think that's why I'm here?'

'I've paid for what happened to your brother,' he said. 'Every day of my life since I have paid for that error of judgement. I can't bring him back. I can't undo what's done. I just want to be left to get on with my life. Is that too much to ask?'

'But you're not getting on with your life,' Molly said. 'You're stuck. Just like I'm stuck. Matt haunts us both. We both feel guilty.'

'You have no need to feel guilty,' he said. 'You weren't driving the car that killed him.'

'Why did you go out that night?'

He closed his eyes as if trying to block out the memory. 'I didn't want to go,' he said. 'Matt was pretty wired. He was in one of those moods he got into from time to time. I didn't find out until later that he'd been grounded, otherwise I wouldn't have agreed to go. But he always wanted to push the boundaries. He wanted the adrenalin rush. That's why I insisted on getting back behind the wheel. I thought he was being reckless. I didn't mind going for a drive to hang out, but doing tailspins and doughnuts wasn't my thing. I didn't see the kangaroo until it was too late. If I'd had more experience or if we'd been in a later model car, I would probably have handled it better. I lost control on the gravel. I didn't even realise he hadn't done up his seat belt until I saw him hit the windscreen.'

'Matt wouldn't have gone out at all if it hadn't been for me,' Molly said.

'What do you mean?' he asked.

'I found his stash of cigarettes and told my parents,' she said. 'That's why they grounded him. He was upset with me about it. I've always blamed myself for what happened. I wish I'd kept my mouth shut.'

Lucas frowned. 'You were just a little kid,' he said. 'You did the right thing. Matt shouldn't have been smoking, especially as he had asthma. He stole those cigarettes from Hagley's store. I was furious with him about it. But he was always pulling pranks like that.'

Molly let her shoulders drop on a sigh. 'I can't help blaming myself. Not just about Matt, but about my parents. Once he was gone…I wasn't enough for them. I couldn't make them happy. I couldn't keep our family together no matter how hard I tried.'

He came over to her and placed a gentle hand on her shoulder. 'Your parents were having trouble well before Matt's death,' he said. 'He told me about it heaps of times. You might not have noticed, being so much younger. Young kids tend to see what they want to see. Matt was sure your parents were heading for a breakup. His death probably just postponed it for a few years.'

Molly looked up into his face. His eyes were kind, his touch so gentle it made her melt all over again. 'I've never really talked to anyone about this before,' she said. 'Everybody always clammed up as soon as I came into the room. It was like the mere mention of Matt's name would damage me in some way. I guess they thought they were protecting me, but in the long run it made it so much harder. I had no one to talk to about him, about how much I missed him, about how guilty I felt. It must have been like that for you too.'

His expression spasmed in pain as he dropped his hand from her shoulder. 'It was one of the worst things about the whole tragedy,' he said. 'I lost my best mate and then no one would ever talk to me about him. My parents did their best but they didn't want to upset me. My brothers didn't know how to handle it. It was as if Matt had never existed.'

'I don't think Matt would want us to keep punishing ourselves for what happened,' Molly said. 'He would want us to be happy—to get on with our lives. Can't you see that?'

'I'm not going to take advantage of you,' he said, his mouth flattening in resolve. 'You're a long way from home. You're way out of your depth. You're uncertain about your relationship with Simon whatever his name is. I'm not going to add to your confusion by conducting an affair with you that will only end in tears.'

'It doesn't have to end in tears,' she said. 'We could have a great relationship. We have a lot in common. We have the same values. We have the same background.'

He gave her a bleak look. 'How long do you think a relationship between us would last?' he asked. 'Your parents would be up in arms about it. It would devastate them. It would devastate my own parents. Do you think they haven't suffered enough? They've paid a high price for my mistake. I won't have them suffer anything else.'

'You're wrong, Lucas,' Molly said. 'It wouldn't devastate them. It might actually help them, and my parents too. Can't you see that? It would help them to realise life goes on. We could help them heal.'

'I can't do it,' he said. 'I *won't* do it. You're not thinking straight. You're caught up with the nostalgic notion of me being your brother's best friend. That's all it is, Molly. You're not attracted to me for any other reason.'

'This is not about Matt,' Molly said. 'This is about us.'

'There is no us without Matt,' he said. 'Can't you see that? He's a shadow that will always be over us. You will always see me as the person who was responsible for his death. I get that. I totally understand and accept it because it's true. But I don't want to spend the rest of my life being reminded of it. Every time I look at you I see Matt. Every time you look at me you see the man who tore your family apart. How long do you think a relationship with that sort of backstory will last?'

'There is such a thing as moving on,' Molly said. 'We can't change the past but we can move on from it.'

'I'm sorry, Molly,' he said. 'You're a sweet girl. You're exactly the sort of girl I used to think I would one day settle down with. But that was then, this is now. I don't want to complicate my life with emotional entanglements.'

'There will come a day when work won't be enough any more,' she said. 'What will you do then?'

He gave her a wry look. 'I'll get myself a cat.'

'Funny.'

'That's me,' he said. 'A laugh a minute.'

'You're never going to allow yourself to be happy, are you?' Molly said. 'This is the hair shirt you've chosen—to live the rest of your life without love and connection. But it's not going to bring Matt back. It's not going to do anything but make you and the people who love you miserable. I feel sorry for you. You're like a tiger in a paper cage. You're the only one who can free yourself but you're too stubborn to do it.'

'Why are you so interested in my happiness?' he asked. 'You're the last person who should be worrying about how I feel.'

'You're not a bad person, Lucas,' Molly said. 'You just had a bad thing happen to you. You need to forgive yourself for being human.'

He touched her on the cheek with a slow stroke of his finger. 'Sweet, caring little Molly,' he said. 'You've always had a soft little heart. Always rescuing lame ducks and hopeless cases and getting yourself hurt in the process.'

She looked into his hazel eyes as tears welled in her own. 'I don't know how to live any other way.'

He leaned down and pressed a soft kiss to the middle of her forehead as if she were ten years old. 'Go back to bed,' he said. 'I'll see you in the morning.'

Molly slipped out of the room but it was a long time before she heard him make his way upstairs.

CHAPTER SIX

LUCAS WAS RECALIBRATING Tim Merrick's respirator the following morning and talking Catriona, one of the more junior nurses, through it. 'The pressure has gone up, which indicates pulmonary oedema,' he said. 'This means the lungs are stiff, and the ventilator pressure has to be turned up to inflate the lungs and get enough oxygen on board to give the brain the best chance of recovery. If the oxygen level in the blood drops, the brain damage will worsen instead of improve.'

'Is he likely to recover?' Catriona asked with a concerned look.

'We're doing all we can to make sure he does,' he said. *Don't die. Don't die. Don't die.* It was like a chant he couldn't get out of his head.

He had visited young Hamish on the ward first thing this morning. It was like looking at himself seventeen years ago. Hamish had the same hollow look of anguish in his eyes, the same shocked, this-can't-be-happening expression on his face. It was gut-wrenching to witness. It brought back his own anguish and guilt in great swamping waves.

Lucas turned to the nurse again. 'Can you run some blood gases through the analyser? I've got inflation pressure up another notch and oxygen is on one hundred per cent. I'm going to administer some frusemide to increase urine output to try and dry out the lungs a bit.'

A few minutes later Catriona called the readings out to Lucas.

'Damn,' he said. 'He's getting respiratory acidosis and we still haven't got the O2 up.'

'The X-ray's here for his chest film, Lucas,' Molly said as she came over.

'Maybe that will show something reversible,' he said. 'If we can't get that oxygen level up then the chance of recovery is going to slip away. Hypoxia and cerebral oedema is a bad combination.'

They looked at the images on the screen. 'You still think he's going to make it?' she asked.

Lucas stripped off his gloves, tossed them in the bin and walked over to the lightbox. 'It's still too early to say with any certainty,' he said. 'It might be a couple of weeks or more before that swelling goes down.'

'He's got a decerebrate posture—the clawed hands,' Molly said. 'I can't imagine how his parents must be feeling, to see him like that.'

'Emma Wingfield looked as bad at this stage, if not worse,' he said. 'Young brains have a knack of beating the odds and recovering. By the time people are admitted here with a tube in every orifice even their relatives don't recognise them. A few months later they'll walk in here with a box of chocolates—you'd never have guessed it was them under all that technology.' *He just hoped Tim was going to another one of them.*

'He's got a big effusion on the right,' Molly said.

'Yeah,' he said, looking at it. 'That's definitely worth draining. Might significantly improve lung function.'

Su Ling came across. 'Dr Banning?' she said. 'We've got a response from Claire Mitchell.'

Lucas called to Aleem, who was coming in with blood reports. 'Can you get set up here for me to do a drain?' To Molly he said, 'Come with me. It'll take half an hour for him to set up. I could use you over here.'

'What's happened?' he asked, when they got to Claire's bed.

'She's opened her eyes and she's fighting the ventilator,' Su Ling said.

It was the best news Lucas had had all day, maybe all year. 'Talk to her, Molly, while I look at the pressure.'

'Claire, can you hear me? It's Dr Drummond,' Molly said gently. 'You've had an accident and you're in Intensive Care. You're going to be all right. We've got you on a machine to help you breathe.'

'Her intracranial pressure's through the roof,' Lucas said. 'It's good she's responding but we're going to have to sedate her to get the pressure down. We need a few more days to wean her off the supports.'

'I'll give ten IV diazepam and up the sedation for twenty-four hours,' Molly said.

'Good,' he said. 'Another twenty-four hours and we'll turn down the sedation, see if she's less agitated and the IC pressure doesn't go up so much. I'll go and have a word with her parents. Are they here?'

'They left just half an hour ago to grab a coffee,' Su Ling said. 'They won't be long.'

'Right,' he said. 'I'll do that drain first.'

'I can do the drain,' Molly said, swinging her gaze to his. 'You can't do everything all at once.'

She had a point but Lucas wasn't going to let her know it. 'Call me if you have any difficulties,' he said, and left to find Claire's parents.

'Dr Drummond,' Jacqui said as Molly came into the office after a break later that day. 'This is Emma Wingfield. She's a previous inmate of ours. Emma, this is Dr Drummond. She's from Australia, like Dr Banning.'

'Hello,' Molly said with a smile. 'I've been hearing wonderful things about you. Dr Banning told me you were one of his star patients.'

Emma blushed, making her look far younger than nineteen. 'I owe him my life. He's the most amazing man.' She held out a plastic container. 'I've made him brownies. They're his favourite. Is he here? I'd love a quick word with him.'

'I don't think he's back from a meeting with the CEO,' Jacqui said, glancing up at the clock. 'It's been a pretty crazy day around here. He was late leaving so the meeting will probably run overtime.'

'That's OK,' Emma said. 'I'll wait. That is if I'm not in the way?'

'Not at all,' Jacqui said. 'Why don't you take a seat in one of the counselling rooms and I'll get him to come to you as soon as he gets back?'

Emma tucked the brownie container under one arm and left with another shy smile.

Jacqui turned and looked at Molly. 'I didn't have the heart to tell her you were living with Lucas,' she said. 'Her first real crush. Don't you just ache for her?'

Molly felt a blush steal over her cheeks not unlike the one young Emma had just experienced. 'I told you I'm not involved with him. I'm just sharing his house temporarily.'

'Yeah, but I've got two eyes in my head,' Jacqui said. 'He can barely take his eyes off you and you blush every time he walks into the room. So what gives? What's the deal with you guys? Did you have a fling in the past or something?'

'No, of course not,' Molly said. 'I was just a kid when he left to come over here.'

Jacqui tapped her finger against her lips. 'But there's something between you, isn't there?'

Molly gave a little sigh. 'He and my older brother were best friends,' she said, hoping to fob her off.

'Ah, now I get it,' Jacqui said. 'Lucas thinks your brother wouldn't approve of him making a move on his kid sister. That's typical of him, ever the gentleman. So what does your brother do? Is he a doctor too?'

'Um…no.' She paused for a moment before continuing, 'He died a while back. A car accident.'

'I'm so sorry,' Jacqui said. 'How dreadful for you and your family. And for Lucas too, to lose a best mate.'

'Yes…yes, it was dreadful,' Molly said. 'But it was an accident. It wasn't anyone's fault. It was just one of those things.'

Jacqui looked past Molly's left shoulder. 'Ah, here he is now,' she said as Lucas came in. 'You have a visitor— Emma Wingfield. She's waiting in one of the counselling rooms. She's brought you brownies.'

'Right.' Lucas gave a brisk nod and walked back out again.

Jacqui rolled her eyes. 'One of us should probably tell him,' she said. 'You know what men are like. You have to hit them over the head with something before they see it.'

Molly chewed at her lip. 'I'll have a word with him later.'

Molly found him in his office, going through some journals at the end of the day. 'Can I have a quick word?' she asked from the door.

'Sure,' he said, placing the journal he'd been reading to one side. 'What's up?'

She rolled her lips together to moisten them. 'Um… it's about Emma.'

He frowned. 'Emma?'

'Emma Wingfield.'

'What about her?'

Molly shifted her weight from foot to foot, feeling a little out of her depth and uncertain. Maybe she should have got Jacqui to say something. Would he misread her motives for bringing Emma's infatuation to his attention? 'I may be speaking out of turn but I couldn't help noticing she's rather attached to you,' she said.

His eyes held hers steady. 'And your point is?'

She felt her cheeks fire up. 'She's very young. You should be careful you don't give her the wrong idea. She could get very hurt.'

'I was her doctor, for God's sake,' he said. 'Anyway, she's just a kid.'

'She's nineteen, almost twenty,' Molly said. 'That's old enough to have a relationship with a man who is technically no longer her doctor.'

'I'm not having a relationship with her,' he said. 'She comes in from time to time to say hi to all the staff who looked after her. I told you that the other day.'

'She only wanted to see you today,' Molly said. 'She barely said a word to anyone else. I think she fancies herself in love with you.'

'That's rubbish,' he said. 'Why would she be in love with me?'

'You're handsome and kind and you saved her life,' Molly said. 'That's just for starters. I'm sure there are a hundred reasons why she has a crush on you. Just about every single woman at St Patrick's fancies you like crazy so why should she be any different?'

His eyes measured hers for a pulsing moment. 'Why indeed?'

Molly knew her cheeks were bright red but carried on regardless. 'I think you need to let her down gently. She's young and vulnerable. She's been through a traumatic experience and is still finding her way.'

'Emma wants to do something for the unit,' he said. 'Some fundraising. That's why she wanted to meet with me as unit director. I said I'd help her do something. I'm not sure what. We're still at the brainstorming stage. Maybe you could offer some suggestions. I haven't got a clue about that sort of thing.'

'I'd be happy to help,' Molly said. 'I was involved in a dinner dance for our unit back home. It was a great success. Everyone talked about it for months afterwards.'

'I'll arrange a meeting between the two of you to get things rolling,' he said.

'I still think you should be careful in handling Emma,' Molly said. 'I'm sure her reasons for the fundraising are very noble, but you still have to keep in mind she could be actively seeking time alone with you.'

'Thanks for the tip-off,' he said. 'But I'm sure you're mistaken. Anyway, I think she already has a boyfriend.'

'Yes, well, that doesn't always signify,' Molly said.

His brow came up in an arc. 'Are you speaking from experience?'

'Not necessarily.'

'How is Simon what's-his-name?' he asked. 'I saw him chatting up one of the young midwives in the cafeteria this afternoon. He sure gets around, doesn't he?'

'He's a free agent,' Molly said. 'He can chat up whoever he likes.'

'So you're no longer an item?'

'We weren't really one in the first place,' she said, blowing out a breath. 'I was what you'd call a rebound fill-in for him. I was feeling a bit lonely at the time but now I wish I'd never let him cry on my shoulder. I can see why his ex left him. He's quite narcissistic and controlling.'

'And possessive.'

'That too.'

There was a little silence.

'I might be a bit late coming home this evening,' Molly said. 'I'm going to a movie night with Kate Harrison's group. I was…um, wondering if you'd like to come too.'

'Why would I want to do that?' he asked.

'It would be good for you,' she said, 'to take your mind off work for a change. Things have been pretty stressful what with Tim Merrick and all. I thought it'd be nice to get out and socialise a bit so—'

'I already have an engagement this evening.'

'Doing what?'

'Do you really want me to spell it out for you?' he asked with a sardonic quirk of his brow.

Molly blushed. 'Oh, right… Sorry, I didn't mean to embarrass you or anything…'

He picked up his journal again. 'Close the door on the way out, will you?'

CHAPTER SEVEN

MOLLY WAS DISTRACTED all the way through the movie. She couldn't stop thinking about what Lucas was up to and who he might be with tonight. Who was it? She didn't think it was anyone from the hospital. She felt agitated at the thought of him bringing someone back to his house.

What if his lady friend spent the night? She herself would no doubt encounter her in the morning. It would be beyond embarrassing. It would be heart-breaking to see him with someone else. She couldn't handle it. She didn't want to handle it. She hated the thought of some woman coming back just to sleep with him. Would they be interested in who he was as a person? Would they take the time to get to know him? To understand what had made him the quiet, reserved man he was?

Of course not.

He wouldn't allow them to. He had let no one into his private world of pain. He shouldered his guilt and anguish with dogged determination. He had no joy in his life, or at least none that she could see. He was isolated and deeply lonely but he wouldn't allow anyone to get close to him.

Molly didn't join the others for drinks after the

movie. She caught a cab back to Lucas's house and went inside with an ear out for the sound of voices, but it was as silent as a tomb. She checked the sitting room but it didn't look like anyone had even been in there. The cushions on the sofa were all still neatly arranged. The coffee table was neat with its glossy book of iconic photographs from around the world centred just so. There were no condensation rings from drinks or crumbs from nibbles.

Maybe he'd decided to stay at his date's place, or maybe he'd booked a hotel room, she thought in stomach-plummeting despair. She didn't want him to make love to someone who didn't know him, who didn't care for him…*who didn't love him.*

Molly was about to head upstairs after feeding and playing with Mittens when the front door opened and Lucas came in, bringing a waft of chilly air with him.

'How was your date?' she asked.

'I had to take a rain-check,' he said as he shrugged himself out of his jacket. 'I got a call from the hospital. Tim Merrick's temperature suddenly skyrocketed. He started leaking CSF from one ear.'

'Oh, no…' Molly frowned in concern. Leaking cerebrospinal fluid and a fever probably meant meningitis had occurred. The damage to his brain could increase if it wasn't quickly controlled.

'It's a setback,' he said. 'But I hope we've caught it in time.'

Molly watched as he rubbed a hand across the back of his neck. He grimaced as if his muscles were in knots. 'You look tired,' she said.

'Yeah, well, eighteen-hour days do that.'

'I could massage your neck for you if you like,' she offered.

'You'd break your fingers working on my golf balls of tension,' he said. 'I'll be fine. I just need a couple of hours' sleep.'

'I'd like to do it for you,' Molly said. 'It won't take long. I'm pretty good at it. I used to do my dad's neck and shoulders all the time.'

He looked at her for a long moment. 'You sure you want to get that close to me?' he asked.

'Will you bite if I do?' she asked with an arch look.

'Guess there's only one way to find out,' he said.

A few minutes later Molly had him sitting on one of the sofas in the sitting room. She stood behind him and started kneading his neck through his shirt. His muscles felt like concrete and his shirt wasn't helping matters as it kept bunching up. 'I think you'd better take your shirt off,' she said. 'I can't get into those muscles the way I want to.'

'It's been a while since a woman's asked me to strip for her,' he said as he unbuttoned his shirt.

'Ha ha,' Molly said. 'Now, stay put while I get some massage oil.'

When she came back with some perfumed oil he was sitting bare chested on the sofa. She drank in the sight of his broad tanned shoulders and the leanness of his corded muscles. She poured some oil into her hand and emulsified it before placing her hands on his shoulder.

'I'm sorry if my hands are cold,' she said. 'It won't take long to warm them up.'

'They're fine,' he said with a little groan. 'Perfect.'

'You're so tense.'

'You should feel it from my side.'

Molly smiled and kept massaging. She loved the feel of his warm male skin underneath her hands. After a while he started to relax. She worked on his neck muscles right up to his scalp, turning his head to the right and then to the left to loosen the tension.

'You missed your calling,' he said.

'When was the last time you had a massage?' she asked as she worked on his scalp with her fingertips.

'Can't remember.'

Molly kept stroking and gliding her hands over his shoulders. Over time the movements of her hands became less vigorous and more like caresses. She breathed in the musky scent of him as she worked her way down over his pectoral muscles. She heard him draw in a breath as her fingers skated over the top of his abdomen. It was daring and brazen of her but she couldn't leave it at that. She inched her way down, taking her time, stroking each horizontal ridge of toned male flesh.

The air became loaded with sensual intent as she found the cave of his belly button surrounded by its nest of coarse masculine hair.

He suddenly captured her hand and stilled it against the rock-hard wall of his stomach. 'Molly.' His voice was as rusty as an old hinge.

'Yes?'

He pushed her hand away and got to his feet, turning to face her across the sofa, his eyes dark and full of glittering desire. 'What the hell are you playing at?' he asked.

'I was massaging you.'

'The hell you were,' he said. 'Do you have any idea

how hard this is for me? Do you think I don't want you? Of course I do. I can't think of a time when I've wanted someone more.'

'Then why are you fighting it?'

He flicked his eyes upwards as he turned away. 'For God's sake, you know why.'

Molly came from behind the sofa to stand in front of him. 'No, I don't know why,' she said. 'We're both adults. There's no reason we can't have a relationship. This has nothing to do with anyone else but us.'

He dragged a hand over his face in a weary fashion. 'I can't promise you a future because of the past. The past *I'm* responsible for.'

'We can make the future *in spite* of the past,' Molly countered. 'Haven't we both suffered enough? Why should we spend the rest of our lives grieving over what we've lost instead of celebrating what we still have?'

'It will always be there between us,' he said. 'It won't go away. It will fester in the background until one day it will blow up in our faces. I can't risk that.'

'Life is full of risks,' she said. 'You can't protect yourself from every one of them. Loving and losing are part of what a rich human life entails.'

'I lost everything when Matt died,' he said heavily. 'I lost my best mate. I lost my family. My community. The future I'd envisaged for myself. It was all gone in the blink of an eye.'

'So you're going to punish yourself for the rest of your life because you don't feel you deserve to be happy?' Molly asked. 'But what about my happiness?'

He closed his eyes briefly. 'I can't make you happy.'

'You're not even prepared to give it a try, are you?' she asked. 'You've made up your mind. You're going to live a life of self-sacrifice. But it won't achieve anything. All it will do is make you end up lonely and isolated. Pretty much as you are now. You're jammed on replay. Lonely, lonely, lonely.'

He gave her an irritated look. 'I'm not lonely. I like being alone. I don't need people around me all the time.'

Molly rolled her eyes and turned away. 'Good luck with that.'

He snagged her arm and turned her back to face him. 'What's that supposed to mean?'

She gave him a direct look. 'Why did you ask me to stay here with you?'

'You needed a place to stay in a hurry,' he said. 'I couldn't see you tossed out on the street. I wasn't brought up that way.'

'I think you asked me to stay with you because deep down you're tired of being alone,' Molly said. 'You're sick of rattling around in this big old house with no one to talk to. The occasional dates and one-night stands aren't cutting it any more. You're yearning for something more meaningful.'

'You're wrong,' he said, snatching up his shirt and shoving his arms through the sleeves.

'Am I?'

'I don't need to be rescued, Molly,' he said, glowering at her. 'I'm not going to be another one of your lame-duck projects. Find someone else to rehabilitate.' He turned and strode out of the room, closing the door with a snap behind him.

* * *

Over the next few days Molly only saw Lucas at work. He barely seemed to spend any time at home at all. He left in the morning before she got up and he came back when she was already tucked up in bed. She didn't know when he ate or slept. She found herself listening out for him at all hours of the night, not really settling until she heard him come up the stairs and close his bedroom door. He drove himself relentlessly. She wondered how long he could keep doing it. The job was demanding at the best of times, but he had taken on extra shifts as if work was all he wanted to do.

Molly had the weekend off and spent it shopping and sightseeing. But on Sunday night she felt at a loose end. She hadn't seen Lucas all weekend, although she had noticed he had fed Mittens and cleaned his litter tray.

After watching a movie she wasn't really interested in, Molly took a long soak in the bath before preparing for bed. She spent a couple of hours trying to relax enough to go to sleep but she kept jolting awake when she thought she heard Lucas's key in the lock.

Finally, at three in the morning, she gave up and came back downstairs for a drink. On her way back up she noticed there was a light on in the library. It seemed she wasn't the only one having trouble sleeping. She padded to the door, which was ajar, and gently pushed it open. Lucas was sitting on the comfortable sofa in the middle of the room with his head resting against the back, his long legs stretched out in front of him, crossed at the ankles. His book was lying open on his lap and his eyes were closed, as if he had fallen asleep in mid-sentence.

He looked much younger in sleep. His features were less harshly drawn and the normally grim set of his mouth was relaxed. His hair was tousled as if his hands had been moving through it, and his shirt was crumpled and the first three buttons undone, showing a glimpse of his sternum.

She walked over to him but still he didn't stir. She watched his chest rise and fall on each slow and even breath. After a moment she carefully took the book from his lap and placed it on the nearby side table.

Still he slept.

Molly reached out with her hand and ever so gently brushed a lock of hair off his forehead. His eyelids flickered momentarily but didn't open. He made a small murmuring noise and let out another long exhalation.

She picked up the throw rug that was draped over the end of the sofa and gently spread it over him.

He didn't stir.

She touched his face with her fingertips. His stubble caught on her soft skin like silk on coarse-grade sandpaper. She sent her fingertip on an even more daring journey to trace over his top lip and then his bottom one. His lips were dry and warm and so very, very tempting…

She hesitated for a moment before she leaned down and pressed a soft-as-air kiss to his mouth. His much dryer lips clung to hers as she gently pulled back. But then he gave a little start and opened his eyes, his hands wrapping around hers like a snare captured a rabbit.

'I was just…making sure you were warm enough,' she said.

For a moment he said nothing. Did nothing. Just sat

there with his eyes meshed with hers, his warm strong hands holding hers captive.

The silence swelled with sensual promise.

'I didn't mean to wake you...' Molly said. 'You looked so...peaceful.'

He gave her hands a gentle little tug to bring her down beside him on the sofa. 'Why aren't you in bed?' he asked.

'I couldn't sleep.'

His eyes moved over her face as if he was memorising every tiny detail. He paused longest on her mouth. 'Isn't it the handsome prince who's supposed to kiss Sleeping Beauty to get her to wake up?' he asked.

Molly moistened her lips with a quick dart of the tip of her tongue. 'Yes, but I'm already awake so what would be the point?'

His eyes smouldered as they came back to hers. 'This thing between us...it's not going to go away, is it?'

'Not in this lifetime.'

A corner of his mouth lifted.

'Hey, you almost smiled,' she said, touching his lip with her finger.

He captured her finger with his mouth and sucked on it erotically while his gaze held hers. Molly felt her stomach drop. The sexy graze of his teeth and the rasp of his tongue made her shiver with delight. He tugged her closer, a gentle but determined tug that had a primal element to it. His eyes were dark with desire as he pressed her down against the cushioned sofa, his long lean body a delicious, tantalising weight on her.

His eyes made love with hers for endless seconds. 'I told myself I wasn't going to do this,' he said.

Molly looped her arms around his neck. 'I want you to do this,' she said. 'And I'm pretty sure you want to do this too.'

His mouth tilted wryly. 'I guess I can't really deny that right now, can I?'

She moved against the hard press of his erection. 'Not a chance.'

He brought his mouth down and covered hers in a hungry kiss. It was a kiss of longing and desperation, a kiss that spoke of deep yearnings that hadn't been satisfied for a long, long time. His tongue stroked the seam of her mouth to gain access, thrusting between her lips to meet her tongue in a sexy tangle. Molly clasped his head in her hands, her fingers threading through his hair as he worked his sensual magic on her mouth. Her breasts were tingling against the hard wall of his chest, her pelvis on fire where his erection probed her boldly.

One of his hands lifted her hips to bring her even harder against him. She gave a little gasp of pleasure as his other hand cupped her breast through her wrap. But it wasn't enough for him. He tugged open the wrap and went in search of her naked flesh. She shivered as he bent his head to suckle on her. Her nipple was sensitive and tightly budded but he seemed to know exactly what pressure to subject it to. He swirled his tongue around her areole before moving to the exquisitely reactive underside of her breast. He kissed and stroked and suckled in turn, until she was almost breathless with want.

Molly pushed his shirt back off his shoulders, smoothing her hands over the muscled planes of his chest, delighting in the feel of him, so hard and warm and male. He groaned as she slid her hands down over his taut abdomen, his kiss becoming more and more urgent against her mouth. She wriggled out of her wrap and then set to work on the waistband of his trousers. She finally uncovered him, stroking and cupping him until he was breathing as hard as she was. He was gloriously aroused, thick and swollen, hot to her touch, already moist at the tip. She rubbed the pad of her thumb over him, her insides quivering when he gave a low, deep groan of pleasure.

After a moment or two he pulled her hand away and pressed her harder back against the sofa cushions. He kissed his way down her body, lingering over her breasts, down to her belly button, dipping in there with his tongue before moving to the feminine heart of her.

Molly drew in a sharp breath as his warm breath skated over her sensitive folds. She clutched at his head, her fingers digging in for purchase when his tongue gently separated her. 'I don't usually do this…' she said. 'Can we just…? Oh…*oh*…' She closed her eyes as the delicious sensations barrelled through her like a set of turbulent waves. Once it had subsided she opened her eyes and looked at Lucas, suddenly feeling shy. 'That was…amazing… I've never let anyone do that before.'

He leaned his weight on his elbows as he looked down at her. 'You haven't?'

She shook her head. 'I've always felt a bit uncomfortable about it. I know this sounds ridiculous but it always seemed a bit too intimate.'

He brushed back her hair from her forehead. 'You probably weren't with the right partner,' he said. 'Trust is just as important as lust.'

'Speaking of lust…' She stroked her fingers over his erection. 'Don't you want to…?'

'I haven't got a condom on me right now,' he said.

'Do you have any upstairs?' she asked.

'A couple maybe.'

Molly caressed his lean jaw with her fingers. She was used to men who were *always* prepared. 'Let's go upstairs,' she whispered softly.

Lucas carried her in his arms, stopping now and again to kiss her deeply and passionately. Finally he laid her on his bed and came down over her, his weight balanced on his arms so as not to crush her. Molly lifted her hips towards his, her whole body aching and yearning for his deep possession.

He kissed her lingeringly, moving from her mouth to her breasts and back again until she was whimpering and writhing. She clawed at him with her hands, digging her fingers into his buttocks to hold him close to the pulsing heat of her body.

He paused for a moment to apply a condom, and came back over her, his strong thighs imprisoning hers. His first thrust was gentle, almost tentative, as if he was uncertain of whether or not to proceed. But her body gripped him hungrily and with a deep groan of pleasure he surged forward, again and again and again. Molly clung to him as the delicious friction sent her nerves into a frenzy of excitement. He went deeper, his breathing harsh against her neck as he fought for control, his lean, athletic body taut as a bow with the build-up of tension. She caressed his back and shoulders with her hands, feeling the gravel of goose-bumps break out along his skin as he responded to her touch.

He slipped a hand between their rocking bodies to find her most pleasurable point as he continued his rhythmic thrusts. The touch of his fingers, so gentle, so intuitive, triggered her orgasm within seconds. It was like a tumultuous wave that tossed and turned her over and over and over until she was gasping and sobbing with the aftershocks. She had never felt such powerful, all-consuming sensations before. Her body reverberated with them as he laboured towards his own release. She held him tightly against her as he finally let go. She felt every deep pumping action inside her, heard his desperate groan, a primal sound that made her shiver all over in feminine response.

Molly held him to her, unwilling to break the intimate connection. To lie there with his body still encased in hers, to have his arms hold her close, to feel the rise and fall of his chest against hers as his breathing gradually slowed, was too precious, too special to sever just yet.

'I'm sorry if I rushed you,' he said against her neck where his head was resting.

She toyed with his hair with her fingers. 'You didn't,' she said. 'It was perfect.'

He lifted himself up on one elbow to mesh his gaze with hers. It was hard to know what he was thinking. His expression wasn't shuttered but neither was it totally open. 'I guess I should let you get to bed and get some sleep,' he said.

Molly felt a little frown pucker her forehead. 'You don't want me to stay here with you?'

He eased himself away and dealt with the disposal of

the condom, his eyes not meeting hers. 'I'm a restless sleeper,' he said. 'I'll disturb you too much.'

She watched him as he shrugged on a bathrobe, but the thick terry towelling fabric was not the only barrier he had put up. A mask had slipped over his face as well.

'I guess I'd better get out of your hair, then,' Molly said, and got off the bed, taking the top sheet with her to cover her nakedness. Hurt coursed through her like a poison. How could he dismiss her like that? As if she was a call girl who had served her purpose and now he wanted her gone. She had expected more—*wanted* more—from him. Tears prickled and burned behind her eyes as she shuffled to the door in her makeshift covering, almost tripping over the fringe of the Persian rug.

'Molly.'

She held herself stiffly, with her arms wrapped around her middle as she faced him. 'I can see why your sex life has been experiencing a bit of a downturn,' she said. 'Your bedside manner definitely needs some work.'

He put a hand through his hair, a frown carving deep in his forehead. 'I'm sorry,' he said. 'It wasn't my intention to hurt you.' He dropped his hand back by his side. 'Tonight was…perfect. I mean that, Molly. *You* were perfect.'

She let out a long, exasperated sigh. 'Then why are you pushing me away?'

He held her look for a long moment. 'This is all I can give you,' he said. 'You have to understand and accept that. I know it's not what you want in a relationship but it's all I can give right now.'

'Just…sex?' she asked.

A tiny knot of tension flicked on and off in his jaw. 'Not just sex.'

'But not love and commitment,' she said.

He exhaled a long breath. 'You're only here for three months. It wouldn't be fair to make promises neither of us might be able to keep. Besides, you might feel very differently about things once your parents hear we're involved.'

Molly knew that was going to be a tricky hurdle to cross. For so long she had striven for her father's approval and becoming involved with Lucas was going to destroy any hope of ever achieving that. 'I'm hoping both my parents will put my happiness before any misgivings they might have,' she said. 'Isn't that what most parents want—their kids to be happy?'

'Most, I imagine,' he said.

'How will your parents handle it?'

A shadow passed through his eyes. 'I'm not planning on telling them any time soon.'

Molly couldn't help feeling a little crushed. Did that mean he didn't think they would be involved long enough for his parents to find out? Was he ashamed of his attraction towards her? She bit down on her lip, torn between her pride and her passion for him. Why did it have to be so hard to be happy? Was her life always going to be one of compromise? Of never feeling quite good enough?

Lucas closed the distance between them, tipping up her chin to bring her gaze in line with his. 'I've upset you,' he said.

'Why would you think that?' Molly asked. 'You had sex with me and as soon as it was over you told me to leave. You don't want anyone to know about us being involved. And you can't see us having any sort of future. Why on earth would I be upset?'

He brushed his thumb over her bottom lip, his gaze rueful as it held hers. 'You deserve much better than I could ever give you.'

'But what if I only want you?' she said trying not to cry.

He gathered her close, resting his chin on the top of her head, his warm breath moving through the strands of her hair. 'I have this amazing habit of hurting everyone I care about,' he said.

Molly looked up at him. 'You care about me?'

He held her gaze for an infinitesimal moment. 'Are you going to give my sheet back?' he asked.

'You want it back?'

'Only if you come with it.'

'You'll have to fight me for it,' she said with a coquettish smile.

His eyes smouldered as he reached for the edge of the sheet. 'Game on,' he said, and stripped it from her.

CHAPTER EIGHT

LUCAS WOKE TO find one of Molly's arms flung across his chest, her head snuggled against his side and her slim legs entwined with his. He couldn't remember the last time he had woken up beside someone in his bed. His sexual encounters were normally brief and purely functional. As soon as they were over he forgot about them.

But waking up beside Molly was not going to be something he could so easily dismiss from his memory. The way she had responded to him had been one of the most deeply moving things he had ever experienced. He felt like he was her first lover. In a way she had felt like his. Had he ever felt so fully satiated? So in tune with someone that he forgot where his body ended and hers began? His senses had screamed with delight and they were still humming now hours later. The scent of her perfume was on his skin. Her taste was in his mouth. His hunger for her was stirring his blood all over again.

She moved against him and slowly opened her eyes. 'Hello,' she said with a shy smile.

'Hello to you,' he said as he brushed an imaginary hair off her face.

She traced one of her fingertips over his top lip. 'Last night was wonderful,' She said. '*You* were wonderful.

I've never felt like that before. I've always thought it was my fault, you know, that I wasn't very good at sex. But now I can see what I've been missing out on.'

He caught her hand and kissed the end of her finger. 'It was wonderful for me, too,' he said.

She trailed her fingers over his sternum, her grey-blue eyes lowered from his. 'I guess it's pretty much the same for men, no matter who they have sex with,' she said.

He brought her chin up. 'Not always,' he said. 'I agree that it's often more of a physical thing for men than for women, but caring about someone does make a difference.'

Her eyes shone as she put her arms around his neck. 'Is it time to get up yet?' she asked.

He rolled her beneath him and pinned her with his body. 'Not yet,' he said, and covered her mouth with his.

Molly came downstairs after her shower to find Lucas had already left for the hospital. There was a short note on the kitchen counter to say he would catch up with her later at work. She put the note down and sighed. They hadn't really had time to discuss how they were going to manage their relationship in public.

Was it a relationship? Or had she done the same thing she had done with Simon—drifted into something that didn't have a name?

She knew Lucas was keen to keep his private life separate but she couldn't see how they would be able to stop people finding out they were intimately involved unless he planned to be all formal and distant with her at work. It wasn't that she wanted her private life out on show, but neither did she want to hide her relationship with Lucas away as if she was somehow ashamed of it.

She still couldn't believe how amazing he made her feel. Her body was still tingling from his passionate lovemaking. Every time she moved her body she felt where he had been. Holding him tightly within her as he had come had surpassed anything she had ever experienced before. She had felt so deeply connected to him and had felt every one of his deep shudders of pleasure reverberating through her flesh.

She hoped it had been much more than just a physical release for him. She knew it had been a while since he'd been intimate with anyone but, even so, it had felt like he had truly cared about her. He had made sure she'd been comfortable and at ease with him and had made sure she'd experienced pleasure before he'd taken his own. He'd coached her without coercing her to do bolder things. Had been passionate and yet achingly tender with her. How would she be able to pretend he was just her boss at work? Wouldn't everyone guess as soon as they saw her?

When she got to work Kate Harrison and Megan Brent were in the change room, putting their things in the lockers. 'Looks like the boss has got himself a new girlfriend,' Kate said as she hung up her coat and scarf.

Molly kept her gaze averted as she unlocked a locker. Was it somehow written on her face? Had she given off some clue? Could people actually tell she had spent the night in Lucas's arms? 'What makes you say that?' she asked.

'He actually smiled at us as he walked past,' Kate

said. 'Can you believe that? He never smiles. We reckon he got laid last night. Don't we, Megan?'

'Sure of it,' Megan said. 'I wonder who it is?'

Molly stashed her things inside the locker. She could see her cheeks were rosy red in the reflection in the little mirror hanging on the inside of the door. How soon before they put two and two together? Everyone knew she was sharing his house. It wasn't much of a step to sharing his bed as well, or so most people would assume.

How would Lucas deal with everyone talking about them? How would *she* deal with it? She didn't want anything to spoil her relationship with him. It was all too new and precious to her. She wanted time to feel her way with him, to help him see how wonderful being together could be. If a gossip-fest started he might bring things to an abrupt end. He put work before relationships and if their relationship threatened to jeopardise his career, she knew which he would choose.

'I don't think it'd be anyone from the hospital,' Kate said. 'He has a bit of a thing about staff hooking up with each other. He told off one of the residents for getting it on with a nurse in one of the storage rooms. We all thought he was going to have him fired.'

'Do you know who it is?' Megan asked Molly.

'Um…' Molly felt flustered. Should she say something? Oh, why hadn't they talked about this earlier? What was she supposed to do? Deny it? Broadcast it? Lie about it?

'You're renting a room at his place,' Kate said. 'Surely you'd be the first to know if he brought someone home. Who is it? Did you get a good look at her? What's she like?'

Molly turned to close her locker door before she faced the two women again. 'I don't think Dr Banning would appreciate me discussing his private life,' she said. 'I know I wouldn't appreciate him discussing mine.'

Kate lifted her brows as she exchanged a look with Megan. 'Right,' she said. 'Fair enough.'

Molly slipped her lanyard over her neck. 'I'd better get going,' she said, and hurriedly left.

Lucas headed back to ICU after speaking to the infectious diseases doctor about Tim Merrick's antibiotic cover. He hadn't seen Molly since he had left her in the shower that morning. He had intended to talk to her about how they were going to handle their relationship at work but he'd got a call about Tim's rising temperature and had had to rush to the hospital.

He wondered if she would feel uncomfortable about separating their private lives from their work ones. He was good at switching off his emotions but he had a feeling she might not find it as easy. She was the type to wear her heart on her sleeve. She was open and honest to a fault. He, on the other hand, preferred to play his cards close to his chest. He didn't want to be the subject of gossip and loathed people speculating about his private life. The thought of everyone picking apart his relationship with Molly was anathema to him. He didn't want to be ribbed about his involvement with her. He didn't want to be the butt of jokes or on the receiving end of teasing comments.

He wondered how long it would be before the news was out. It was more or less common knowledge that she was rooming at his place. How soon before people assumed they were sleeping together?

Being involved with Molly was an emotional minefield. She was only here for a short time. He wasn't sure how he was going to navigate the next few weeks. A short-term affair sounded good in theory, but how would it play out in practice? What if he didn't want her to leave when her time was up? What if she didn't want to go? His mind swirled with a torrent of thoughts. How would she face her parents if she chose to be with him? How would he face his? Their relationship would cause even more heartache. How could it not?

He was the last person her parents would want her to be with. He had torn apart their family. He couldn't undo the damage of that one moment in time. There was no way he could atone for the death of Matt. He had given years of his life to serving others, to saving others, but it still didn't make an iota of difference.

He could not bring Matt back.

Even if by some miracle her parents and his were OK about him being with Molly, there were still his own doubts over whether he could make her or anyone happy. He had spent so long on his own he wasn't sure he could handle the emotional intimacy of a long-term relationship. He had never been half of a couple before. His relationships—hook-ups was probably a more accurate term—had never involved the sharing of feelings, hopes, dreams, values and goals. He didn't know how to be emotionally available to a partner. He didn't know how to be emotionally available to *anyone*.

He kept that part of himself tightly locked down. His parents and brothers had all but given up on trying to draw him out. He didn't want anyone to see the bottomless black hole of despair deep inside him. He had concreted it over with work and responsibilities that would have burnt out a weaker man. He knew it wasn't healthy, he knew it wasn't going to make him happy either, but he had long ago resigned himself to a life lived without the contentment and fulfilment other people took for granted.

His hope was that Molly would finally come to see he was not worth the effort.

Molly was at Claire Mitchell's bedside as Lucas came into ICU. She had worked tirelessly with Claire each day and he had been impressed by her dedication and patience. Claire had a long road ahead of her and would have to spend months in a rehab facility, learning to walk and talk again. But at least she was going to make it. Her parents would still have their daughter, even if she wasn't quite as physically able as she had been.

Tim Merrick, on the other hand, was an ongoing nightmare. The CSF leak from his ear had increased overnight. The base-of-skull fracture had entered the middle-ear cavity and opened up a potential entry point of bacteria. Lucas had repeated an EEG but there was still little brain activity. The transplant team had contacted him earlier that morning but he had refused to enter into a discussion about harvesting Tim's organs. He was treating Tim hour by hour, refusing to give up hope, even though a part of him was seriously starting to doubt there would be any chance of him recovering. He kept thinking of Hamish Fisher, how shattered he had looked that morning as he had been discharged from hospital. Lucas remembered it all too well—the day he had walked out of the hospital, with his best mate lying cold and lifeless in the morgue.

At least Tim was still alive—for now.

'Claire, can you hear me?' Molly was saying. 'Open your eyes. Lift your arm. Wriggle your toes.'

'Is she responding?' Lucas asked.

'Yes, she opened her eyes a couple of times,' she said. 'She's fighting the ventilator. Her intracranial pressure and all other obs are stable. I think it's time to start weaning her off the ventilator and sedation. I've asked the nurse to let me know if her stats drop. How is Tim Merrick doing? I heard things got worse overnight.'

He gave her a grim look. 'I've started high-dose imipenem and gentamicin and I've just spoken to the ID doctor about recommendations for antibiotic cover. If we don't get on top of this quickly, his chance of a recovery is going to disappear. The next forty-eight hours are going to be critical.'

'Jacqui told me the transplant team called,' Molly said, giving him a pained look.

Lucas drew in a tight breath. 'Yes, but I'm not going to make any decision until we repeat the EEG a couple of times at least.'

'His parents seem resigned—'

'His parents are shocked and upset,' he said. 'They need more time to come to terms with their son's injuries. It's too early to say how things will pan out. Trust me, Molly. I know what I'm doing.'

She caught her lower lip with her teeth. 'I was wondering if you had a minute to talk…in private, I mean.'

'I'll be in my offIce in about twenty minutes,' he said. 'I have a couple more charts to write up first.'

Molly knocked on Lucas's open office door but he was on the phone and gestured to her to come in and sit down. She closed the door and came over to the chair opposite his desk, not sitting down but waiting for him to finish his call.

'Sorry about that,' he said, and placed his phone on the desk. 'It's been one of those mornings. Everyone wants everything yesterday.'

'Yes…'

He studied her for a moment. 'Are you OK?' he asked.

Molly let out a little breath. 'I was wondering how we're going to handle this…um, situation between us. A couple of the nurses were talking in the change room when I came in this morning. I didn't know what to say.'

'There's nothing *to* say,' he said.

'It's not that simple,' she said. 'I think people are going to put two and two together pretty quickly. I'm not sure how to deal with it. We didn't get a chance to talk about it this morning.'

He blew out an impatient breath. 'Personally I can't see why it's anyone's business. I don't go around asking staff members who they're sleeping with, do you?'

'No, of course not.'

He raked a hand through his hair as he leaned back forcefully in his chair. 'What do they want us to do? Release a press statement or something? *God.* Why don't these people have lives of their own instead of speculating about everyone else's?'

'If you'd rather not have people know about us then I'll deny any rumours.'

He leaned forward again and dropped his hand back down on the desk with a little thump. 'These things have a habit of fizzling out after a week or two,' he said. 'It's best just to ignore the speculation.'

'I'm sorry…'

He gave her a wry look. 'Why are *you* apologising?'

Molly dropped her shoulders. 'I seem to have made your life even more complicated.'

'Yes, well, it's not as if it's going to be that way for ever,' he said, making a business of shuffling the papers on his desk.

'You can come right out and say it, you know,' she said, hurt at how he seemed to have filed her away too, as if she was something temporary he had to deal with. 'You don't have to spare my feelings or anything. I understand this is just a fling between us.'

His expression tightened as his gaze met hers. 'The one thing you can't accuse me of is not being honest with you,' he said. 'This is all I can give you.'

'Fine,' Molly said in a perverse attempt to act all modern and casual about it. 'We'll have our fling and once it's time for me to leave, I'll just kiss you goodbye and get on with my life and you'll get on with yours. Does that sound like a plan?'

His jaw worked for a moment. 'As long as we both know where we stand.'

'But of course,' she said. 'If anyone asks, I'll just say we're housemates with benefits. How does that sound?'

His forehead was deeply grooved with a brooding

frown. 'Couldn't you think of a better way to put it than that?' he asked.

'Get with the times, Lucas,' Molly said as she gave him a cheery fingertip wave from the door.

Lucas came back from helping the registrars with a new patient when Jacqui pulled him to one side. 'What's going on between you and Molly Drummond?' she asked.

Here we go, he thought with a roll of his eyes. This would be the first of no doubt many comments he was going to get. 'Why do you ask?' he said.

'Everyone's saying you're a couple now,' she said, her eyes bright with interest. 'Is it true? Are you officially together?'

Lucas was still trying to get his head around Molly's term for their relationship. Call him old-fashioned, but he didn't like the sound of housemates with benefits. It sounded like he was taking advantage of her. He hadn't invited her to stay in his house so he could sleep with her. That had just…happened. OK, well, sure, he'd *wanted* it to happen. He *still* wanted it to happen, but it couldn't happen for ever.

He wasn't a for ever type of guy.

'You know I never discuss my private life at work,' he said as he continued briskly on his way.

Jacqui kept pace with him like a little Chihuahua snapping at his heels. 'Come on, Lucas,' she said. 'What would it hurt to get it out in the open? She's such a sweetheart and it's so cool that you've known each other for years and years. I bet your parents and hers will be thrilled to bits. It's so romantic.'

He threw her a hard look. 'Don't you have work to do?'

'You make such a lovely couple,' she said. 'I bet you'll make gorgeous babies together. Will you invite me to the wedding? I've always wanted to go to Australia. That's where you'll have it, won't you?'

Lucas dismissed her with a look. 'There's not going to be a wedding,' he said, pushing open his office door. 'Excuse me. Some of us around here have work to do.'

Molly was home first and spent some time playing with Mittens before she started cooking dinner. She wondered if she was doing the right thing in setting candles and flowers on the table, but she just couldn't get her head around being *that* casual about things. Somehow waiting naked in bed for him wasn't quite her. She wanted to read his mood first, see what sort of day he'd had. Help him relax and put work stresses aside. She wanted to show she cared about him as a person, not just as someone she was having a fling with. She put on some romantic music on the sophisticated sound system that was wired through the house and opened a bottle of wine she had bought on the way home.

Glancing at her watch a couple of times, she wondered when Lucas would be home. She hadn't seen him since their conversation in his office. She had been busy with a new admission and he had been called to a meeting with the family of an elderly patient who wasn't expected to make it through the night.

He came in just after nine p.m. Molly got off the sofa in the sitting room where she had been whiling away the time with a glass of wine and met him in the foyer.

'Hard day?' she asked when she saw his heavy frown.

'You could say that,' he said, shrugging off his coat.

'I made dinner for you,' she said.

His frown deepened as he hung up his coat. 'You shouldn't have bothered.'

'It was no bother,' Molly said. 'I love cooking. I set up the dining room. It looks fabulous.'

He turned from the coat stand, his frown even darker on his brow. 'What for?' he asked.

'Because it's a beautiful room that's just crying out to be used,' she said. 'What's your problem? You won't eat out. I thought this would be the next best thing. Kind of like a date at home.'

He moved past her on his way to the stairs. 'I'm not hungry.'

Molly felt her spirits plummet. 'What's wrong?' she asked. 'Have I upset you?'

His hands gripped the balustrade so tightly his knuckles whitened beneath the skin. 'Why would you think that?' he asked.

She folded her lips together, feeling horribly uncertain and unsophisticated. 'I was so looking forward to you coming home,' she said. 'I thought you would be looking forward to it, too. I guess I was wrong. You'd obviously rather be alone.' She swung away to the kitchen, determined not to cry.

'Molly.'

'It's all right, I quite understand,' she said, turning back to face him. 'We obviously have different expectations about how this is going to work. I'm afraid I haven't read the latest edition of the *Having A Fling* handbook. Maybe you could give me a few tips. Clearly soft music and candles are out. Perhaps I should've just draped myself over your bed instead.'

He shoved a hand through his hair and blew out a weary sigh. 'I'm sorry,' he said. 'I'm in a rotten mood. It's wrong to take it out on you. Forgive me?'

Molly gave him a huffy look.

'Come here,' he commanded gently but firmly.

She angled her body slightly away from him, her chin up and her arms across her middle. 'I'm not that much of a pushover, you know.'

He moved to where she was standing and gently unpeeled her arms from around her body and gathered her close against him. 'I'm sorry for being a such a bear,' he said. 'I've got a lot on my mind just now. I'm used to coming home and being alone with my thoughts.'

Molly looked up at him with a little pleat of worry on her brow. 'Do you want me to move out?'

He smoothed her frown away with the pad of his thumb. 'That's the very last thing I want you to do,' he said. 'The house feels different with you here. It's warmer, more like a home.'

'I should've checked with you first about dinner,' she said as she toyed with one of the buttons on his shirt. 'I didn't think…I'm sorry.'

'It's fine, Molly,' he said. 'Really.'

'I know it's been awkward for you today with everyone talking about us…'

'They'll stop in a day or two when they realise it's business as usual,' he said. 'I'm usually pretty good at ignoring that sort of thing.'

Molly looked up at him again. 'Are you really not hungry?' she asked.

His eyes smouldered as they held hers. 'My appetite is being stimulated as we speak.'

'I hope I've prepared enough to satisfy you,' she said with a little smile.

He scooped her up in his arms. 'Let's go and find out, shall we?'

CHAPTER NINE

LUCAS WOKE FROM a deep sleep to answer what he thought was his phone. He reached across Molly, who was still soundly asleep, and picked up the phone from the bedside table. 'Lucas Banning,' he said.

There was a shocked gasp and then silence from the other end.

Molly shifted sleepily against him. 'Who is it?' she asked.

He handed her the phone. 'I think it's for you,' he said. 'I thought it was my phone. Sorry.'

She sat up and pushed the tousled hair out of her eyes. 'Hello?'

Lucas heard Molly's mother on the other end. 'I think I called you at a bad time. Do you want me to call back when you're alone?'

Molly glanced at Lucas. 'No, it's fine, Mum… Um, how are you?'

Lucas got off the bed and went to the bathroom to give her some privacy. When he came out again she had hung up was sitting on the edge of the bed with a strained look on her face. 'That was my mother,' she said.

'So I gathered.'

'She was a bit shocked that you answered my phone.'

'I gathered that, too,' he said.

She nibbled at her bottom lip for a moment. 'It's not that she doesn't approve of me getting involved with you…'

'You don't have to pull your punches, Molly,' he said. 'I realise I'm not her top pick as a partner for you.'

'She'll be fine about it once she gets her head around it,' she said. 'It was a shock to find out like that, that's all. I should've called her and told her.'

'I guess it'll be your father calling you next to tear strips off you,' Lucas said, snatching up his trousers and shaking out the creases before he put them on.

She got off the bed and came over and put her arms around his waist. 'I can handle my father,' she said. '*We* are the only people in this relationship. It's got nothing to do with anyone else. Not at work or back at home in Australia. This is about us, here and now.'

Lucas let out a long exhalation and gathered her close. The here and the now wasn't his greatest worry. It was what happened next that had him lying awake at night. Within a few weeks she would be heading home. He couldn't ask her to stay with him, to give up her life back home, all her friends and family, all that was familiar and dear to her. How could he ask it of her? He could more or less cope with the parental opposition but he couldn't cope with hurting her by not being good enough for her. How could he ever be good enough when he had caused her more hurt than anyone?

He kissed the top of her head and put her from him. 'I have to get moving,' he said. 'I have a couple of meetings this morning and another one after work. I'm not sure what time I'll be home.'

'I thought I'd touch base with Emma Wingfield about the fundraising dinner,' she said. 'Would you be agreeable to having it here? It would cut down the costs of hiring a venue. I understand if you don't want to. I know it's a lot to ask.'

Lucas saw the little spark of enthusiasm in her eyes. What would it hurt to let her go to town with the dinner? It would be something to look back on once she had gone. 'Sure,' he said. 'Why not? Let me know what you need. I'll get Gina to give you a hand.'

She stood up on tiptoe and kissed him on the lips. 'Thank you,' she said. 'I'll make sure it's a night to remember.'

Molly hadn't long got home from work that evening when her father called.

'What the hell do you think you're doing?' he said without preamble.

'Hi, Dad,' she said. 'I'm fine, and you?'

'Of all the people in London you could hook up with,' he went on, 'why him? I had to drag it out of your mother. She wasn't going to tell me but I knew something was up as soon as I spoke to her. When were you going to tell me you're sleeping with the enemy?'

Molly rolled her eyes. 'I'm not going to discuss my love life with you, Dad. Lucas and I are seeing each other and that's all I'm prepared to say.'

'He'll break your heart,' he said. 'You just see. It's what he does best. He'll use you and then walk away. He just wants his conscience eased. I reckon he thinks a little fling with you will fool everyone into thinking we've all moved on. But I'll never forgive him. Do you hear me? I will not allow that man to come within a bull's roar of me or any of my family.'

'How is your new family?' Molly asked.

'Don't use that tone with me, young lady,' her father said. 'I'm telling you right now, if you continue to see him I will never speak to you again. Do you hear me? It's him or me. Make your choice.'

'Dad, you're being ridiculous,' she said. 'Isn't it time to move on? Matt would be appalled by your attitude. You know he would.'

'I mean it, Molly. I'll disown you. You see if I won't.'

Molly fought to contain her temper. There was so much she wanted to throw at her father. All the times he had let her and her mother down. All the times he had criticised her for not being as good as Matt at things. All the times she had felt unloved and undervalued by him. It bubbled up inside her like a cauldron of caustic soda. 'You know, that's exactly the sort of thing I've come to expect from you,' she said. 'When things don't go your way, you have a tantrum or throw in the towel, just like you did with Mum. I'm not giving up Lucas just to appease you. If you want to disown me then go right ahead. It's your choice.'

'You're the one making the choice,' her father said. 'Once I hang up this phone, that's it. I won't be calling again, not unless I hear you've ended things with Lucas Banning.'

The line went dead.

Molly pressed the off button on her phone just as the front door opened and Lucas stepped in.

His brows moved together. 'Your father?'

'Yes,' she said with a little slump of her shoulders.

He came over and put a gentle hand on the nape of her neck. 'Hey.'

Molly looked up at him through moist eyes. 'I've never been able to please him,' she said. 'It wouldn't matter who I was seeing, he wouldn't approve. He doesn't love me, not like a father should love his daughter. If he loved me he'd be happy for me.'

He drew her close against his chest, his hand rhythmically stroking her head where it rested against him. 'He does love you, Molly,' he said. 'He's just afraid to lose you. It colours everything he does. I would be the same in his place.'

She gave a heavy sigh and began to fiddle with his loosened tie with her fingers. 'I thought you weren't coming home early,' she said.

'We got through the agenda of the meeting in record time,' he said. 'I thought we could go out to dinner.'

She blinked at him in surprise. 'Dinner? As in out somewhere? In a restaurant? In public?'

He gave her a rueful half-smile. 'I really am dreadfully out of practice, aren't I?' he said. 'Yes, out in public in a fancy restaurant.'

Molly smiled as she flung her arms around his neck. 'I would love to.'

Lucas was putting on his jacket at the foot of the staircase when Molly came down half an hour later. Her perfume preceded her—a fresh, flowery fragrance with a hint of something exotic underneath. He turned to look at her, his mouth almost dropping open when he took in her appearance. She was classy and sexy, modern and yet conservative, sweet and sultry. Her mid-thigh-length black velvet dress clung to her figure like a glove. Her high heels showcased her racehorse-slim ankles and calves, and she had styled her hair in a teased messy ponytail at the back of her head, giving her a wild-child look. Her lips were shiny with lip gloss, her eyes smoky with eye shadow and eyeliner.

It was a knockout combination and he wondered how she had managed to get to the age of twenty-seven without some guy snapping her up and carting her off to be his wife and the mother of his children.

He tried to ignore the pang he felt at the thought of her ripe with someone else's child. He didn't want to think about another man taking her in his arms and making love to her. He didn't want to imagine another man's mouth pressed against those soft, sweet lips.

He wanted her to himself, but how could he have her with the past like a stain lying between them? It would always be there. It would seep into and discolour every aspect of their lives. If they married and had children, he would one day have to explain to them what had happened to their uncle. How would any child look at its father knowing he was responsible for the death of another human being? There had been a time when he had envisaged himself with a family similar to the one he had grown up in. He'd had great role models in his parents. They were strict but fair, loving and supportive, committed to their children and to each other. He had seen them weather some of life's toughest dramas and yet they had never faltered in their devotion to each other and their boys. He had assumed he would have a similar relationship but, of course, that's not how things had panned out.

It was different now.

It had to be.

'You look beautiful,' Lucas said.

Her eyes shone as they met his. 'You look pretty hot yourself.'

He tucked her arm underneath his. 'Shall we go?'

The restaurant Lucas had booked was a fifteen-minute drive from his house. He barely spoke on the journey, other than to point out places of interest like a jaded tour guide.

Molly glanced at him surreptitiously from time to time, but each time she looked at him his brow was lined with a frown as if he was chewing over something mentally taxing. Was he regretting issuing his invitation to have dinner? All her insecurities came out to play. Maybe he was having second thoughts about their involvement.

After all, she had been the one who had made the first move when she had found him sleeping in the library the other night. If it hadn't been for her bending down to kiss him they might not have become involved at all. They might still be just housemates, two ships passing in the night as they went about their busy working lives. Did he regret their involvement? Did he want to put a time limit on it?

What was going to happen when it was time for her to leave? Would he sever the connection or expect her to? They had by tacit agreement avoided mentioning the future. But it was still something that lurked in the background. Molly could even sense the ticking clock on their relationship. She had been here almost three weeks. That left only nine to go. Each day was another day closer to the time she would be leaving. Would he ask her to stay? Or would he be relieved when she got on that plane back to Australia?

'Are you OK?' Molly asked after a long stretch of silence.

He glanced at her distractedly. 'Pardon?'

'You seem a bit preoccupied. You've hardly said a word since you pointed out the Houses of Parliament.'

He reached out and took her hand and brought it up to his mouth and kissed it. 'Sorry,' he said. 'I have a lot on my mind just now. Work stuff. Brian Yates had got a bit behind with some paperwork. It's a nightmare sorting it all out.'

'When was the last time you took a holiday?' she asked.

'I went to a conference in Manchester three months ago.'

She looked at him askance. 'The one where you had the one-night stand?'

His expression tightened. 'Yes.'

'That's hardly what I'd call a holiday,' Molly said. 'I meant a proper holiday. Lying on the beach somewhere, drinking cocktails. That sort of thing.'

He lifted one shoulder. 'I'm not big on cocktails. And I've seen enough people dying with melanomas to put me off lying in the sun for life.'

'All the same, you can't expect to work all the time without a break,' she said. 'It's not good for your health.

People in their early thirties can still get heart attacks, you know.'

'I know,' he said. 'That's why I go to the gym. I go to a twenty-four-hour one a couple of blocks from home. I have a couple of guest passes if you want to try it out some time.'

'I'm not much of a gym bunny,' Molly confessed. 'I prefer long walks in the fresh air.'

'Fair enough,' he said.

Lucas parked the car and came around to open her door. Molly loved it that he had those old-fashioned good manners. He had been brought up to treat women with respect and consideration. She felt feminine and protected as he helped her out of the car with a light hand at her elbow.

Once inside the restaurant they were shown to a cosy table in a candlelit corner. Soft ambient music was playing, making the atmosphere romantic and intimate. 'Have you been here before?' she asked once the waiter had left them to study the menu.

'Not for a long time,' Lucas said. 'I think it's changed hands a couple of times since then but it got a good write-up recently.'

The waiter took their order and left them with their drinks. Molly was conscious of the silence stretching between them. 'I had the meeting with Emma today,' she said. 'She was really excited about the dinner dance at your house. We've marked a tentative date for the first Saturday in May. We're thinking about fifty or sixty couples. The more exclusive it is the better. People don't mind paying top dollar for something that's really special.'

'Sounds like a good plan.'

'And we also thought we might have a theme,' she said.

He gave her a forbidding look. 'Don't ask me to dress up in a ridiculous costume.'

Molly gave him a teasing smile. 'Where's your sense of fun?' she asked. 'I think you'd look fabulous in a Superman costume.'

'No way,' he said, glowering at her. 'Don't even think about it. It's not going to happen.'

'It's all right,' she said, still smiling at him. 'We thought we'd have a black and white theme. Everyone has to wear either black or white or both. We'll decorate the ballroom the same. It'll be very glam.'

'I think I can manage to rustle up a tuxedo,' he said. 'But I should warn you I'm not much of a dancer. I have two left feet.'

'I can help you with that,' she said. 'Mum sent me to debutante school. It won't take me long to teach you to burn up the dance floor.'

He gave a noncommittal grunt as the waiter came over with their meals.

It was raining when they came out of the restaurant. Lucas took off his jacket and used it like an umbrella over Molly. 'Aren't you freezing?' she asked as they made a dash for the car.

'I'm used to it,' he said. 'Mind your step. The pavement's uneven in places.'

It was a quiet drive home but Molly thought Lucas had lost some of his earlier tension. He had started to relax a little after the entrée and had even smiled at one of her work anecdotes. For a while she had felt like they were any other couple having a meal out together. But every now and again she would look across at him and find him with a frown between his eyes.

'I enjoyed tonight,' she said as they walked into the house a short time later.

'I did too,' he said.

'Our first date.'

'Pardon?'

Molly looked at him. 'That was our first proper date.'

'So how did it measure up?' he asked.

'I don't know,' she said. 'It's not over yet.'

A half-smile lurked around the edges of his mouth. 'You seem pretty sure about that.'

She stepped up to him and placed her arms around his neck. 'I want to dance with you.'

'Right now?'

She pushed his thigh back with one of hers. 'Right now.'

A gleam came into his eyes as he started to move with her along the floor. 'I think I could get used to this dancing thing,' he said. 'How am I doing?'

She smiled as he brought her up close to his aroused body. 'You're a natural. You have all the right moves.'

He stopped dancing, his eyes burning as they held hers. 'I want to make love with you. Now.'

Molly shivered as he gripped her hips and held her harder against him. 'Right now?' she asked.

'Right now.'

He swooped down and captured her mouth beneath his in a sizzling hot kiss, his tongue driving through to find hers in a sexy lust-driven tango. Molly felt her senses career out of control as his aroused body probed the softness of hers. Desire was hot and wet between her thighs as he moved her backwards along the foyer in a blind dance of passion until her back was against the wall.

Her hands went to his shirt, tugging and pulling until it was out of his trousers and unbuttoned. She slid her hands all over his chest, caressing, stroking until she came to the fastener on his waistband. She worked on it blindly as his mouth masterfully commandeered hers. Electricity pulsed like a powerful current through her body as his hands shaped her breasts through her clothes. Her nipples felt achingly tight, her breasts full and sensitive.

Her insides quivered as he deepened his kiss, his tongue stabbing and stroking, thrusting and gliding until she was mindless with need. She could feel it building in her body. All the sensitive nerves stretching and straining to reach the pinnacle of pleasure she craved. It was centred low and deep in her body, the feminine core of her alive and aching for the intimate invasion of his body.

Finally she freed him from his trousers. He was thick and full and like satin wrapped steel in her fingers. She caressed him with increasing pressure and speed, delighting in the low deep grunts of approval he was giving. Spurred on by his reaction, she dropped to her knees in front of him and brought him to her mouth.

He gripped the sides of her head. 'No, you don't have to do that,' he said.

'I want to do it,' Molly said. 'I want to taste you like you tasted me.'

He gave a muttered curse as she closed her lips over him. She felt him shudder against the walls of her mouth as he fought to control his response. It thrilled her to have such feminine power over him. He was so thick and so strong and yet he was at the mercy of her touch.

After a few moments he pulled out with a gasping groan. 'No more.' He hauled her to her feet and roughly pulled up her dress until it was bunched around her waist.

She clung to him with one hand as the other peeled away her tights and knickers. Excitement raced along the network of her veins like rocket fuel. She was breathless with it, impatient with it, hungry for every deliciously erotic thing he had in store.

He positioned her against the wall and thrust into her with a deep primal groan that lifted every hair on her head. Her sensitised flesh gripped him tightly, drawing him in, holding him, squeezing him, tormenting him. He rocked against her almost savagely. She held onto his hips, with him all the way, wanting more speed, more pressure, more of that tantalising friction. She was getting closer and closer to the point of no return. She could feel every nerve preparing itself for the free-fall into paradise.

And then she was there, falling, spinning, falling, spinning, delicious contraction after delicious contraction moving like an earthquake through her flesh. She gasped and cried as her body shook and shuddered against his, her hands digging into his taut buttocks as he finally emptied himself.

Molly held him tightly against her as her breathing calmed. She could feel the stickiness of his essence between her legs. It was so incredibly intimate to be that close to him. She had never felt so close to someone.

It was not just the physical experience. There was something much deeper and elemental in how she responded to him and he to her. It was like they were meant to be together—two halves that made a complete whole. She felt a connection with him that went beyond their similar upbringings. It was as if he was the only person who could love her the way she wanted and needed to be loved—with his whole being, his body, his mind and his soul. What woman didn't want a love like that?

Molly knew he was capable of that sort of love. What she didn't know was if he would allow himself to be free of the past in order to act on it.

Lucas brushed her hair away from her face, his eyes dark and serious now the passion had abated. 'I wasn't too rough with you, was I?' he asked.

Molly was touched that he was concerned. 'You were amazing,' she said, looking up at him. '*We* are amazing together. I never thought it could be this good. It keeps getting better and better.'

He tucked some of her hair behind one of her ears, his gaze becoming shadowed, his expression twisted with ruefulness. 'We are amazing together…'

'But,' she said. 'That's what you were going to say, wasn't it? There's always a but with you, isn't there?'

A mask slipped over his features. He drew in a breath and slowly released it. 'Molly…'

'There doesn't have to be a but,' Molly said. 'We can be amazing together for always. You know we can.'

He put his hands on her wrists and unlocked her

hold from around his neck. 'We've already talked about this,' he said. 'I told you what I can give you. There's no point going over it all the time in the hope that I'll somehow change my mind. This is the way it is. You have to accept it.'

Molly blinked back burning tears, her chest feeling as if hard fists were pummelling against her heart. 'Are you really going to just end our relationship when it's time for me to leave?' she asked. 'Have you already circled the calendar or marked it your diary? Have you've written, "*Finish things with Molly*"?'

His features were pulled tight. 'Think about it, Molly,' he said. 'You'd gain me but you'd lose your family. Your father will cut you off. He's probably already threatened to do so. Yes, I thought so. Your mother will make an effort but every time she sees me she'll think of the son she lost. And then, if we were ever to have children...' His throat rose and fell and his voice came out hoarse as he continued, 'What will you tell them when they ask about their uncle? Will you tell them their father *killed* him?'

Molly swallowed the knot of anguish clogging her throat. How could she get him to change his mind? Could they have a chance in spite of everything that had happened? Surely other people overcame tragic circumstances. Why couldn't they? Was it because he didn't love her? He hadn't said anything, but, then, neither had she. He didn't seem the type to be saying 'I love you' at the drop of a hat. But, then, she had never told anyone other than her parents that she loved them. But she sensed that Lucas cared very deeply for her. He showed it in so many little ways.

Was that why he refused to promise her a future? He wanted her to be free to move on from the tragedy of the past and he believed she couldn't do that if she was with him. He was determined their relationship had a strict time limit.

Molly suddenly realised what it must be like for couples during times of war and separation. Of having to live in the moment, of not being sure of what the future would hold, clinging to one another, grateful for every tiny chance to be together. Not making plans but living and loving while they could. It was the same for long-term married couples or even younger couples where one partner was facing the imminent death of the other due to a terminal illness. She had seen them time and time again in ICU. The clock ticking down, each moment more and more precious as it could very well be the last.

How did people do it? How would *she* do it? She wanted fifty, sixty, seventy years—a lifetime to love Lucas, not just a matter of weeks.

Molly couldn't think of a time when she hadn't loved him. When she had been a little kid she had loved him, but that had been more of a hero-worship thing. He had been her older brother's best friend, someone she'd admired from afar. He had always treated her well. He had been far kinder to her than her own brother. Growing up without sisters had made him particularly mindful of the feelings and sensibilities of little girls. He had always treated her with respect and, to some degree, affectionate indulgence. How could she not fall in love with him as an adult? He was the same kind, gentle man—a man who gave up so much of his life for others. Matt's death hadn't caused that other focused part of his personality, rather it had just enhanced it.

But loving Lucas came with a hefty price tag. Her father had already made it clear that he wanted nothing more to do with her if she continued to be involved with Lucas. After the initial shock her mother seemed more accepting, but how long before she too worried that Molly was being short-changed emotionally? No mother wanted to see her daughter with a man who wasn't capable of loving her.

And then there was the issue of children. She wanted a family. She had wanted to be a mother since she had been a little kid. She had nursed every baby animal she had been able to get her hands on, adopting every stray she could in her effort to nurture them.

Lucas was the only man she could imagine as the father of her children. She wanted to feel his baby moving inside her womb. She wanted to feel the march of the contractions through her abdomen that would bring their baby into the world and she wanted to see his face as she gave birth. She wanted to see him hold their baby in his strong arms, to cradle it against his broad chest, to protect and love it as tenderly as he had been loved and nurtured.

But now all those hopes and dreams she had stored in her heart for all this time would never be realised. It was so bitter-sweet to know he loved her but was prepared to give her up because he felt that was best for her.

He was wrong.

He *had* to be wrong.

She would be miserable without him. She would be heartbroken without him in her life. She would be totally devastated to have loved and lost him. She wanted him to live life with her, to share the highs and lows and all the little bits in between: the happy bits; the sad bits; the angry bits; and the funny bits—all the things that enriched a couple's life together.

Surely he would see that eventually? It might take more than the nine weeks left, but surely he would come to realise that it was better to be together than apart? How could she *make* him see it? Would she have to take a gamble on it? To spend the next few weeks in the hope that he would not be able let her go at the end?

Molly looked up at him through misty eyes. 'Can we not talk about this any more?' she said. 'I just want to pretend we are just like any other couple in a new relationship. Can we do that, please?'

He brushed her quivering bottom lip with the pad of his thumb. 'Of course,' he said, and bending his head he softly covered her mouth with his.

CHAPTER TEN

MOLLY WAS AT work a few days later, supervising Claire Mitchell's transfer to the rehabilitation unit. Claire was not fully mobile but she was completely conscious and responding to commands. Her tracheotomy tube had been removed and the hole taped closed, but it would take up to two weeks for the wound to heal over completely. Claire could speak in a whisper but her words were still slurred and a little jumbled and she still had some short-term memory problems. Her parents were relieved but clearly a little daunted at the long road ahead for their only child.

Claire would probably spend months in the rehab centre and was unlikely to regain the full use of her legs. It was a heartbreaking thought that a young woman who had been so fit and athletic, who before the accident had been at the top of her game in equestrian events, was now no longer able to take even a few paces, let alone vault up into a saddle and ride her beloved horse.

Jacqui walked back with Molly to the ICU office once the orderly had left with Claire and her parents. 'For a while there I thought that poor girl wasn't going to make it at all,' she said. 'You should have seen her when she first came in. A bit like our Tim, poor chap.

You just never know how they're going to end up, do you?'

'No, you don't.' Molly glanced to where Tim's parents were by his bedside in ICU, keeping their lonely vigil. They came in each day, spending hours in his cubicle, talking to him, playing his favourite music on an MP3 player, stroking him and praying over him with the hospital chaplain.

Lucas was still treating him hour by hour, stubbornly refusing to give up hope of a recovery. The CSF leak had stopped once they'd got control of the infection, and while a subsequent scan had shown a little brain activity, it was still not as positive as everyone had hoped.

Hamish Fisher had been in just about every day. Molly had watched on one of his first visits as Lucas had taken him aside and talked to him in his quiet, supportive way. It had been particularly moving to see Tim's parents hug Hamish by their son's bedside. There were lots of tears but no harsh words or accusations—so different from her father, who after all this time was still so antagonistic towards Lucas.

'Lucas still thinks there's a chance with Tim Merrick,' Jacqui said, following the line of Molly's gaze. 'He's getting a bit of flak from some of his colleagues, though.'

'Yes, I know,' Molly said, thinking of some of the angry exchanges she'd either witnessed or heard when Lucas had been on the phone. Lucas had given Tim mannitol a couple of times to reduce brain swelling and he had stopped the steroids. This was considered controversial by some as high-dose steroids were commonly used to reduce brain swelling, with mannitol generally only used in the acute situation, straight after the occurrence of an injury. But Lucas was concerned the steroids might suppress Tim's resistance to infection so he had stopped them and closely monitored intracranial pressure.

'So how are things going between you two?' Jacqui asked with a twinkling look. 'Lucas won't tell me a thing, damn him.'

'Things are fine,' Molly answered evasively. She didn't want to talk about her relationship with Lucas. It was precious and private. Their workplace relationship was friendly but professional. She was careful not to overstep the mark in any way. But there were times when she caught his eye and a secret message would pass between them. She would hum with longing all day until she got home. Sometimes she would barely get in the door before he reached for her. Other times he took his time, torturing her with long drawn-out foreplay that had her begging for mercy.

But not a day went past when she didn't long that they were indeed like any other young couple starting out together, without the past casting its dark shadow over them. Over the last few days she had found herself thinking wistfully of an engagement ring and a wedding gown. She had even wandered past a high street wedding designer on one of her walks. She had stood for long minutes in the freezing cold, wishing she was like the young bride in there with her mother, excitedly trying on gowns. She had turned away with a sinkhole of sadness inside her stomach. How would she ever be a bride if she couldn't be with Lucas? She didn't want anyone else. She couldn't think of being with anyone else. She was wired to love him and only him.

'Have you thought of staying on?' Jacqui asked. 'Your time with us is racing away. It'll be over before you know it.'

Tell me about it, Molly thought with a spasm of pain near her heart. 'I have a job lined up at home,' she said. 'It's at a big city teaching hospital close to where my mother lives. They held the post open for me while I came here. I'd feel bad if I didn't show up. Anyway, isn't the person I'm filling in for over here coming back from maternity leave?'

'Yes, but I thought Lucas, being director, might be able to wangle a position for you,' Jacqui said. 'It reeks of nepotism but who cares about that?'

'I don't think Lucas would do anything that wasn't fair and above board,' Molly said. 'Anyway, I wouldn't want him to.'

'You're good for him,' Jacqui said. 'He still works too damn hard but he seems a lot happier in himself since you've been here. I've been quite worried about him, to tell you the truth. I've never met a more driven doctor. I keep telling him he'll drive himself into an early grave if he doesn't let up a bit. He hasn't taken a holiday in I don't know how long.'

'I've been saying much the same thing,' Molly said.

'Maybe he'll take some time off and visit you back in the home country,' Jacqui said. 'Nothing like absence to make the heart grow fonder.'

Molly stretched her mouth in a brief pretence of a smile. 'Let's hope so.'

'You love him, don't you?' Jacqui's expression was full of mother-hen concern.

Molly sighed as she straightened some notes on the desk. 'I'll get over it.'

'Will you?'

Molly looked at the ward clerk's concerned expression. 'I'll have to, won't I?' she said. 'This is just for here and now.'

'But you want the whole package.' It was a statement, not a question. And it was the truth.

'Don't most women?' Molly asked.

'But he's not talking marriage and babies, is he?' Jacqui said. 'He told me point-blank there wasn't going to be a wedding when I asked him about it the other day. It doesn't make sense. Why wouldn't he want to marry you? He's old school right to his backbone. He's not one of these playboys who want their cake and eat it too. He doesn't say much, but anyone can see he's a family man at heart.'

Molly looked at the stack of papers on the desk again, absently flicking through the top right-hand corners of the pages with a fingertip. 'It's complicated…'

'It's because of your brother, isn't it?' Jacqui said. 'I've been watching him with Tim and that young friend of his Hamish, the one who was driving. That's why Lucas is so hell bent on keeping Tim alive. He was driving when your brother was killed, wasn't he?'

'It was an accident,' Molly said, looking at her again. 'It wasn't his fault. A kangaroo jumped out just as he came around the bend. There was nothing he could do. He didn't see it in time.'

'How sad,' Jacqui said. 'I've always wondered why

he's so hard on himself. He works harder than any other doctor I know. Poor Lucas. And poor you.'

'It was a long time ago,' Molly said. 'I'd prefer it if you kept this to yourself. We're all trying to move on from it.'

'But you haven't moved on from it, or at least Lucas hasn't,' Jacqui said. 'But, then, one doesn't move on from something like that. I guess you just have to learn to live with it.'

'I don't think Lucas sees it quite that way,' Molly said. 'He's punishing himself. He's been punishing himself for the last seventeen years. I hate seeing him do that to himself. Matt wouldn't have wanted him to do that to himself. It's all such a mess and there's nothing I can do to fix it.'

Jacqui gave Molly's arm a gentle squeeze. 'Your job is to love him, not to fix him,' she said. 'The rest is up to fate or destiny.'

If only fate and destiny weren't so damned capricious, Molly thought in despair as she walked back to ICU.

Lucas looked at the most recent scans of Tim Merrick's brain with Harry Clark, one of the more senior neurologists on staff.

'There's some activity but not much,' Harry said. 'I've seen a couple of cases where the patient has recovered after scans like this but it's not the norm.' He turned and looked at Lucas with a grim expression. 'He might not thank you for keeping him alive if he has to spend the rest of his days sitting slumped and drooling in a chair. Nor might his parents if it comes to that.'

Lucas tried to ignore the prickle of apprehension that had been curdling his stomach for days. Claire Mitchell had been moved to the rehab unit, which was a positive outcome considering how bleak things had looked when she had first been admitted. But she was going to have a very different life from the one she had known before. He had seen many patients and their families just like her struggle with what life had dished up.

But he didn't want to see Hamish Fisher go through the living hell he had gone through—*was still* going through. He wanted a miracle. He wanted it so badly, not just for Tim and his devoted parents. He wanted it for Hamish and he wanted it for himself. Tim might not have the life he'd had before, but he would still be alive. That was all that mattered.

'Wouldn't most parents want their kid to stay alive, no matter what?' Lucas asked.

Harry let out a long breath. 'Some do, some don't,' he said. 'I've had parents divided over a child's treatment. We had a case a few years back, a kid with severe epilepsy. He'd had one too many seizures and suffered oxygen deprivation. He was virtually vegetative. The father wanted to withdraw treatment. He was adamant about it. He didn't want to see his kid suffer any more. He'd spent fifteen years watching his boy suffer. The mother... Well, I guess that's what us men will never truly understand—the mother bond. She wanted her boy alive, no matter what state he was in.'

'What happened?'

'The parents divorced,' Harry said. 'The mother looked after that kid on her own for a couple of years and then one night he died in his sleep. I've often wondered if the father regretted not being there, helping her.'

'The kid could have lived for another twenty years,' Lucas pointed out.

'Yes,' Harry said with gravely. 'But would he have wanted to?'

Molly was late getting home after sending off the last of the invitations to the dinner dance. Everyone was getting excited about the event. It was the topic of every conversation at the hospital. The exclusivity element had created a furore, which she and Emma had milked for all it was worth. They had kept twenty-five double tickets back and had put them up for bidding on the hospital website.

The money they were raising was beyond anything they had imagined and it was thrilling to think people were so keen to be involved. Even the caterers had offered their services free of charge, and the string quartet—one of whom was a neurosurgical registrar at the hospital—had also offered to perform without charging a fee.

Molly couldn't wait to tell Lucas. She knew he would be pleased that so much money would be raised for the unit. Hospitals had to work so hard to meet their budgets and there was rarely money left over for any extras. With the money she and Emma were raising, new monitoring equipment could be purchased so patients like Emma would benefit in the future.

Mittens came over to Molly with a plaintive meow as soon as she walked through the front door. She bent down to stroke him and noticed he was wearing a new collar with a tinkling bell attached. 'My, oh, my, don't you look smart?' she said. 'Has Daddy been spoiling you?'

Lucas appeared in the doorway of the sitting room. 'He brought in a bird,' he said with a brooding glower.

'Oh... What type?'

'What does it matter what type?' he asked.

'Well,' she said as she hung up her coat, 'if it was a nightingale or a cuckoo I would probably be a little upset. But if it was a sparrow or a starling I wouldn't be as concerned.'

'We need to talk about what you plan to do with him when you leave,' he said. 'Are you planning to take him with you?'

Molly rolled her lips together for a moment. She could sense Lucas was in a tense mood. She wondered if he too was thinking of how quickly her time with him was passing. He hadn't said anything, but she had sensed the increased urgency in his lovemaking over the last few days. Was he thinking of how much he would miss her when she left? 'I hadn't really thought that far ahead...'

'Then you need to,' he said with a jarring brusqueness. 'I didn't sign up for cat ownership. I said I'd babysit him. I've done that. That's all I'm prepared to do.'

'So you'll kick him out when you kick me out, will you?'

His brows snapped together. 'I'm not kicking you out. You're here for a set time. We've both known that from the outset.'

Molly moved past him with a rolled-eye look. 'Whatever.'

'We've talked about this, Molly,' he said. 'You know the terms. I've never hidden them from you.'

She turned to face him. 'Why are you being so prickly this evening?' she asked. 'I came home all excited to tell you stuff about the dinner and you've done nothing but bite my head off since I walked through the door. Sometimes I think you don't really like having me here. I bet you're secretly counting the days until I leave.'

A long tense moment passed as his gaze tussled with hers. But then he expelled a breath and lifted a hand to rub the back of his neck. 'I'm sorry,' he said. 'I didn't mean to rain on your parade.' He dropped his hand back by his side. 'Tell me about your exciting news.'

Molly wasn't going to be won over that easily. 'You probably won't even find it exciting,' she said with a little pout. 'It's not like you really want a bunch of people—most of whom you won't know—wining and dining and dancing in your precious house. You probably only agreed to it to get me off your back.'

'I'm fine about it,' he said.

She gave him a cynical look.

'OK,' he conceded. 'It's not my idea of a fun night at home. But it's obviously important to you so I'm happy to go along with it.'

Molly gave him a haughty look and went to move up the stairs, but he stopped her with a hand on her wrist. 'Do you mind?' she said. 'I'm going upstairs to have a shower.'

His fingers tightened like a handcuff, and his eyes went dark, *very* dark as they locked on hers. 'Have one with me,' he said.

Molly felt a little shiver roll down her spine like a red-hot firecracker. Sparks of awareness prickled over her skin. Her breasts tightened beneath her clothes. Her legs trembled in anticipation of being thrust apart by his commanding possession. But some little demon of defiance pushed up her chin and ignited her eyes. 'What if I don't want to have one with you?' she said. 'What if I want to be on my own right now and sulk and brood and be in a rotten mood?'

He tugged her against him, thigh to thigh, hard male arousal to soft but insistent female need. 'Then I'll have to think of ways to convince you,' he said, and lowered his mouth to the sensitive skin of her neck.

Molly shivered again as she felt his teeth on her skin. It was a playful bite—the primal tug of an alpha male showing his selected mate that he meant business. She tilted her head as he moved down her neck to her left clavicle, his tongue moving over the tightly stretched skin, licking, laving and teasing. Her breasts tingled behind her bra as she felt his warm breath skate over her décolletage.

Sensual excitement sent her heart rate soaring as he pushed his hands up under her top to cup her breasts. His mouth sucked on the upper curve of her right breast pushed up by his hands. She snatched in a breath as she felt his teeth graze her flesh. He went lower, taking her lace-covered nipple in his mouth and sucking on it. It made her all the more desperate to feel his lips and tongue on her bare flesh.

She moved sinuously against him, rolling her hips against the proud jut of his erection, tantalising him with her body, wanting him to be as desperate for her as she was for him.

And he was.

He growled against her mouth as he finally covered it with his, thrusting his tongue through her parted lips to mate with hers in a heart-stopping tango. His hands worked at her clothes methodically but no less hastily. Molly did the same with his, but perhaps with a little less consideration for buttons and seams.

She had only just got him free of his trousers and underwear when he lowered her to the floor. The Persian rug tickled the skin of her back as she felt his weight come down over her. She gasped as he speared her with his body, a deep, bone-melting thrust that made her insides turn to molten lava. It was a frenzied coupling—rough, urgent, desperate and deliciously exciting. Her nerves shrieked in delight, twitching and tensing, contracting and convulsing as each deep thrust drove into her.

She started to climb to the summit. Up and up she went, her body stretching and stretching to reach that blissful goal. He increased his pace as if he had sensed her need for more friction. And then he brought his fingers into play against the swollen heart of her, tipping her over the edge into a tumultuous sea of mind-blowing sensations.

It went on and on, rolling waves coursing through her, each one sending another cataclysmic reaction through her body. She dug her fingers into his back, her teeth sinking into the skin of his shoulder as the riot of sensations shook and shuddered through her until she was finally spent. Still she hung onto him as he reached his own pinnacle of pleasure. She felt it power through her, an explosive release that had him slump against her once it was over.

Lucas eased himself away and offered her a hand to help her to her feet. 'About that shower,' he said. 'Have I convinced you to share it with me yet?'

Molly gave him a playful smile, her body still tingling from his passionate lovemaking. 'I don't know. What's in it for me?'

His eyes ran over her tousled form, leaving a trail of hot longing in their wake. 'You can't guess?'

Her insides fluttered with excitement. 'You're in a dangerous mood tonight, Dr Banning,' she said.

His mouth tilted upwards in a sexy half-smile, his eyes smouldering like hot coals. 'You'd better believe it, Dr Drummond,' he said, and scooped her up in his arms and carried her upstairs.

Molly was in a dangerous mood herself by the time Lucas had turned on the shower. She stepped into the cubicle with him, pushing against his chest with the flat of her hand until his back was up against the marbled wall of the shower. 'Stay,' she said, giving him a sultry look before she slithered down his body.

He gave a groan as she took him in her mouth. She felt his legs buckle and he thrust out a hand to brace himself as she worked on him. It was the most erotic thing she had ever done. She tasted the essence of him on her tongue as she swirled it over and around the head of his erection. He groaned again and she heard his breathing rate escalate. She felt the tension building in him; she could feel the blood surging through his veins, filling him, extending him to capacity and she drove him on relentlessly.

He tried to pull her away but she refused to budge. She drew on him, again and again, using the moistness of her mouth to lubricate him. She used her tongue again to tantalise him, to tease him, to take that final plunge. She felt the intimate explosion, felt the warm spill of his release, heard the raggedness of his breathing, felt the sag of his limbs as the pleasure flowed through him.

Molly got to her feet and rinsed her mouth under the flowing water before trailing her hands over his chest. 'Good?' she asked.

'Where the hell did you learn to do that?' he asked in a husky rasp.

'Instinct,' she said. 'You bring out the wild woman in me.'

He put his hands on her hips and brought her against him. 'You're incredible,' he said.

She turned in his arms and wiggled her behind against him. 'Scrub my back for me?'

He pumped a handful of shower gel from the dispenser on the wall and smoothed it over her back and shoulders. He used slow, stroking movements, caressing all the way down to the dip in her spine. She shuddered in pleasure as he trailed a finger down the crease of her bottom. She shifted her legs apart to give him better access and shuddered again when he found the swollen, pulsing heart of her. She gasped as he played with her, teasing her, taking her to the brink before backing off.

'Please...' Molly leant her weight against the shower wall in front of her. '*Oh, please...*'

'You like that?' he said as he brushed against her from behind.

She shivered as she felt his erection between her legs, every pore of her skin intensely aware of him. 'Yes, oh, yes,' she said.

He guided himself between her parted thighs, rubbing against her, letting her know he was about to mount her but letting her have full control. The sensation of him entering her from behind was wildly, wickedly erotic. There was a primitive aspect to it as he finally possessed her, his groin flush against her buttocks, his thighs braced around hers as he started thrusting, gently at first but slowly building momentum.

Molly was lost within seconds. She tumbled head-first into a whirlpool of such intense pleasure she was gasping and sobbing with it as it rumbled through her. The tight convulsions of her body triggered his release. She felt him pump himself empty, his hands holding her hips with a tight, almost fiercely possessive hold.

His whole body gave a shiver, and then he slowly turned her round and pushed her wet hair back off her face, his eyes dark and intense as they met hers. 'Still want to be on your own to sulk and brood?' he asked.

Molly put her hands on his chest and raised her mouth for his kiss. 'What do you think?'

CHAPTER ELEVEN

MOLLY DIDN'T KNOW if it was because she was so busy with work and organising the dinner dance that time felt like it was set on fast forward, but suddenly it was the day of the dance and she had only three weeks left of her post at St Patrick's.

She had taken the day before the event off to be at Lucas's house to help Gina with the final clean and polish before the flowers and decorations were delivered. The ballroom looked amazing by the time Saturday evening came around.

When Emma dropped by with the after-dinner chocolates a London chocolatier had donated, she gasped in wonderment when Molly led her in to see her handiwork. 'It's like something out of a fairy-tale,' she said turning around to look at the black and white helium-filled balloons festooned in giant bunches with satin ribbons dangling in curling tails.

'Uh-oh,' Molly said as Mittens made a grab for one of the ribbon tails. She scooped him up out of harm's way and hugged him close to her chest.

'Isn't he adorable?' Emma said, reaching to give him a pat.

'He's a little mischief maker, that's what he is,' Molly said. 'He's been unstoppable since he got his cast off.'

'Are you going to take him back with you to Sydney when you go?' Emma asked.

Molly felt the all too familiar pang seize her at the thought of leaving. She took Mittens to the entrance of the ballroom and closed the door to keep him out before she answered. 'I was hoping Lucas might keep him. But nothing's been decided as yet.'

Emma began to chew at her lower lip with her teeth. 'I was kind of hoping you and Lucas were going to stay together...' She looked at Molly and blushed. 'To be honest, I didn't feel like that at the beginning. I feel embarrassed about it now, but I think I was a bit in love with him myself. I suppose it was more of a crush really. But, then, I think a lot a patients fall in love with their doctors. My mum said she fell in love with her obstetrician, her GP *and* her dentist. I think falling in love with the dentist was taking it a bit far but anyway...'

Molly smiled wryly. 'I've had a few crushes over the years myself.'

'The thing is...' Emma continued. 'Dr Banning needs someone like you. You understand the stress and strain he's under because you experience it yourself. You probably think it's none of my business and I shouldn't be so impertinent to comment on your and his private life, but these last few weeks I feel I've got to know you. You love him, don't you?'

Molly gave her a bitter-sweet smile. 'Of course I do,' she said. 'But sometimes loving someone is not enough.'

'How can it not be enough?' Emma asked. 'Love is supposed to conquer all.'

'Lucas isn't ready to commit to a relationship,' Molly said. 'I can't force him to be ready. He has to do that in his own time.' *If he ever does*, she thought with a crippling pain around her heart.

'But he loves you,' Emma said. 'I know he does. It's so obvious. His eyes light up when you walk into the room. And he actually smiles now. He never used to do that before. It must be love.'

Molly wanted to believe her, but Emma was like a lot of young girls caught up in the romantic fantasy of seeing what she wanted to see.

Did Lucas love her?

She had thought so, but if he truly did why wouldn't he promise her the future with him she wanted so much?

Lucas had planned to help Molly with the preparations for the dinner dance but a new patient had come in with severe pancreatitis. He had been caught up with putting in a central line to the forty-eight-year-old man and managing his treatment. Time had slipped away, which it had a rather frightening habit of doing just lately.

As each day came to a close he felt a sickening feeling assail him. He would lie awake for hours with Molly asleep beside him, wondering how he was going to find the strength to let her go. He had thought about it from every angle but he always came to the same conclusion—she was better off without him.

He was concerned that she hadn't spoken to her father since that phone call when Jack Drummond had issued an ultimatum. He knew how much it distressed her to have to choose between him and her family. He had seen relatives torn apart with guilt when an estranged loved one was suddenly taken ill or, even worse, died without being reunited with their family. He couldn't bear to think of Molly having to live the rest of her life estranged from either one of her parents because of her involvement with him.

Her loyalty to him astounded him. And yet he couldn't quite shake the feeling that he didn't deserve it. He kept telling himself she would be better off with someone who didn't have a road train of baggage dragging behind, but every time he thought of her with someone else he felt like a lead boot was stomping on his chest.

Only that day one of the senior surgeons had playfully elbowed him in the ribs and told him to put a ring on Molly's finger before someone else did. Lucas had shrugged it off with an indifferent smile, but inside he'd been so knotted up he had scarcely been able to breathe.

How would he bear it? He'd already started to torture himself with how it might play out. He imagined how he would hear from one of his brothers that Molly had met some other guy—maybe another doctor—and was setting up a home and family with him. Maybe they would even send him photos of her wedding.

Dear God, how was he supposed to cope with that? His life had been pretty bleak before, but that would be taking it to a whole new level of misery.

He imagined the years passing... Molly would have a couple of kids, a little scrubby-kneed boy just like Matt and a gorgeous little sunny-faced princess like herself.

The children *he* wanted to have with her.

He swallowed against the prickly tide of despair that filled his throat. Why did life have to be so hard, *so cruel*? Hadn't he suffered enough, without life dumping more misery on his shoulders? He wanted to be normal again. How long ago that seemed! He had once been a normal kid with the same dreams and aspirations others had. Then fate had cut him from the herd and set him aside, marking him as different.

There was no chance of a normal life now. It would *never* be normal. He had to make the most of what he had and be grateful he had it, because so many—just like Matt—didn't even get the chance.

By the time Lucas came home from the hospital Molly was about to head upstairs to shower and dress for the dinner. He wished he could have spent the evening on his own with her rather than share her with a hundred or so people, but she was terribly excited about the money she and Emma were raising. He was proud of her. She had such a heart for people and the way she had mentored and supported Emma was a credit to her generous and giving nature.

'Sorry I'm so late,' Lucas said as he bent down to brush her lips with a kiss. 'I would've been back ages ago but I had trouble putting in a central line on my last patient. Anything I can do to help?'

She gave him a smile but he noticed it was a little shaky around the edges. 'No, it's all under control.' She crossed her fingers. 'I think.'

He suddenly realised she was nervous about this evening. 'Hey,' he said, tipping up her face. 'You've done a wonderful job. The house looks amazing. Tonight will be fabulous. Everyone is going to be super-impressed with your ability to put on a party to remember.'

Her grey-blue eyes looked misty all of a sudden. 'Lucas…' She blinked a couple of times and bit her lip and began to turn away. 'Never mind…'

He stalled her with a hand on her arm. 'No, tell me, what's worrying you?' he asked.

She looked up at him with a little frown pleating her forehead. 'I want this to be a wonderful night for you too,' she said. 'I want you to enjoy it, not just to endure it for my sake.'

Lucas cupped her face and looked deep into her gaze. 'If I can have the first and last dance and all the other ones in between with you then I will enjoy every single minute,' he said. 'Is it a deal?'

She smiled a smile that was like a blast of sunshine with just a few clouds floating around the edges. 'It's a deal.'

'Great party, Lucas,' Jacqui Hunter said as she scooped up a glass of fizzing champagne from a passing waiter. 'Your house is amazing. You really are a dark horse, aren't you? I didn't know you were such a DIY expert.'

Lucas gave a loose shrug as he took a sip of his soda water. 'It fills in the time.'

She waggled her brows at him. 'Seems to me you might need to find yourself another big old run-down mansion to spruce up in a few weeks,' she said. 'You could end up with a lot of time on your hands.'

He tried to ignore the jab of pain around his heart. 'Yeah, well, I've been looking around,' he said.

'Find anything?'

'Not much.'

'Didn't think so,' Jacqui said, glancing to where

Molly was smiling up at one of the single anaesthetists. 'A house like this is a once-in-a-lifetime sort of find, don't you think?'

Lucas put his glass down on a side table. 'Excuse me,' he said. 'I think someone's cutting in on my next dance.'

Molly smiled at him he approached. 'I thought you were going to stand me up,' she said. 'Tristan was going to fill in for you.'

Lucas gathered her up close and spun her away from the clot of other dancers. 'Yes, well, he can get to the back of the queue,' he said.

She gave him a teasing look. 'Are you jealous?'

He pretended to glower at her. 'When is this party going to be over?' he asked.

She gave him a crestfallen look. 'You're not enjoying it, are you?'

He tapped her on the end of the nose with his finger. 'I'm enjoying seeing you enjoy yourself,' he said. 'It's a great party, not that I'm any judge. I can't remember the last time I went to one.'

She touched his face with the velvet soft caress of her palm. 'Maybe when it's over we can have a party of our own,' she said.

Lucas turned her out of the way of a rather enthusiastic couple who hadn't quite figured out the timing on the waltz they were doing. 'Sounds like a good plan,' he said. 'Do I need to bring anything?'

She stepped up on tiptoe and brushed his ear with the soft vibration of her lips. 'Just you.'

Molly got the phone call just before coffee was served. She wouldn't have heard her phone at all if it hadn't been for Emma needing a sticky plaster for a blister she'd got while dancing with one of the handsome young residents from the hospital. She took Emma upstairs to the main bathroom and she heard her phone ringing in Lucas's room on her way back.

She told Emma to go on without her, and quickly picked up the phone, with the intention of ignoring the call if it wasn't the hospital or anyone important, but then she saw it was her mother. 'Mum? You're calling at an odd hour,' she said. 'Is everything all right?'

'Oh, darling,' her mother said. 'I have some terrible news.'

Molly felt an icy hand grasp at her heart. 'What's happened?'

'It's your father,' Margaret Drummond said. 'He and Crystal have been in an accident. He's OK apart from a broken ankle but Crystal has a ruptured placenta and—'

'Oh, God,' Molly gasped. 'What about the baby?'

Her mother was trying to talk through sobs. 'They had to do an emergency Caesarean. The baby's in the neonatal unit. They're not sure if he's going to make it. The priest has been in to christen him. Poor Crystal… it's just so awful. I don't know what to do.'

'Is she all right?' Molly asked. 'I mean physically?'

'They had to do a transfusion but, yes, she's out of danger now,' Margaret said. 'Your father is beside himself. Can you come home? I know I shouldn't ask you but I can't bear for you to be away at a time like this. Your father needs you right now. We all need you.'

'Of course I'll come,' Molly said, already rushing to her previous room where her suitcase was stored in one of the built-in wardrobes. 'I'll book a flight tonight. Try not to panic. I'll be there as soon as I can.'

Lucas appeared in the doorway a few minutes later just as Molly had turned on her laptop. 'What are you doing, checking emails now?' he said. 'I thought you promised me the last dance and then a private party?'

She clutched at her face with both hands. 'Oh, Lucas, I have to go home. I have to go right now.'

His brows came together. 'Whatever for?'

'My father and his wife were in an accident,' she said. 'Their baby had to be born via Caesarean, but he's so premature he might not make it. I have to go to help them. I can't be away from them at a time like this.'

'Of course you must go,' he said. 'Here, let me make the flight booking for you. You start packing. Just take the minimum. I'll send the rest of your stuff on later.'

Molly moved away from the computer and quickly changed into a travelling outfit. She started to pack, but she had barely tossed a change of clothes in the bag when she turned and looked at him. 'Please come with me,' she said. 'Take some leave from the hospital and come with me.'

Another frown—deeper this time—appeared between his brows. 'I can't leave.'

'Yes, you can,' Molly said. 'What if you were ill or something? They'd find someone else. I want you to come with me. I *need* you to come with me.'

He got up from the computer. 'I can't come with you, Molly,' he said.

Tears blurred her vision. 'That's because you don't *want* to come with me,' she said. 'You don't want to be with me—period. That's why you jumped at the chance to book my flight. You can't wait until I walk out that door for the very last time, can you?'

He went white with tension. 'That's not true,' he said. 'I'm merely trying to keep calm here. You're upset and not thinking straight.'

'Of course I'm upset!' Molly said. 'My father could've died tonight or tomorrow or whatever time it is there. Oh, God. I'll never forgive myself. I should've called him back. I shouldn't have been so stubborn. Now I might never get to meet my little brother.'

'Darling,' he said, and reached for her but she backed away.

'How can you call me that?' she asked. 'I'm not your darling. I'm just a fill-in, just like I was with Simon.'

'Now you really are talking rubbish,' he said in a steely tone.

'Am I?' she asked, challenging him with her gaze. 'Then come with me. Drop everything and come with me.'

A muscle beat like a maniacal hammer in his jaw. 'I will not be issued with ultimatums,' he said. 'That is no way to conduct a relationship.'

'Is that what we have—a relationship?' she asked. 'What we have is an arrangement. A housemates-with-benefits arrangement.'

'You know it's much more than that,' he said with a brooding look.

Molly gave a scornful snort as she flung another couple of things in her bag. 'Sure it is,' she said. 'That's why my stuff is still in this room instead of in your room with yours. And that's why you're not packing a bag right this minute and coming with me.'

'For God's sake, Molly, we have a hundred people downstairs,' he said through tight lips. 'Do you really expect me to drop everything and fly halfway around the world with less than five minutes' notice?'

Molly tried to see it from his perspective. It was a lot to ask at short notice. It was wrong to expect him to drop everything. She wouldn't like him to ask it of her if the tables were changed.

'You're right,' she said, releasing a breath. 'I'm sorry. I'm just all over the place with this.' She pinched the bridge of her nose, trying to keep her emotions under some semblance of control. 'What about in a few days' time?' She dropped her hand from her face to look at him again. 'Will you come then?'

His frown was heavy and forbidding. 'Molly...'

'What about early next week or the week after?' she asked. 'It will give you time to clear your diary, find a locum or someone to step in for you.' *Please, just say you'll try*, she silently begged.

His eyes moved away from hers. 'It's not that simple, Molly. I have patients, responsibilities. I have people depending on me.'

'But what about me?' Molly asked, trying to hold back tears. 'Aren't I important enough for you to put those responsibilities aside for just a few days to be with me when I need you most?'

He looked back at her again, but his expression was masked. 'Your flight leaves in a couple of hours,' he said. 'I've put you in business class so you can sleep.'

'But I can't afford to fly business class.'

'I've paid it for you.'

'I'll send you the money when I get home,' she said.

'Consider it a gift.'

Molly gave him a cynical look. 'A parting gift, Lucas?'

He thrust his hands in his trouser pockets, his expression still as blank as a brick wall. 'Are you coming back for the rest of your term?' he asked.

Molly closed her bag with a click that sounded like a punctuation mark being typed at the end of a sentence. 'You'll have to find someone else,' she said. 'I'll send you a formal resignation as soon as I get home.'

He gave a businesslike nod. 'Would you like me to drive you to the airport?'

I'd like you to tell me you love me, Molly thought as her heart gave a tight spasm. *I'd like you to tell me you can't bear the thought of me leaving. Tell me you love me. Tell me you can't live without me.* 'No, thank you,' she said. 'It'll be quicker if I just leave. I'm sorry to leave you with Mittens. I'll try and sort something out. I'm not sure what the quarantine arrangements are if I were to ship him home. It might be too stressful for him. Cats are funny like that. Maybe one of the nurses at the hospital will take him.'

'It's fine,' he said. 'He might get confused if he was taken somewhere else. This is his home now.'

'Right…well, I'd best get going, then,' Molly said. 'Will you give my apologies to everyone? I'm sure they'll understand it's an emergency.'

'Of course.' He looked at her then, his eyes dark and unreadable. 'Goodbye, Molly.'

Molly came up to him and going on tiptoe gently placed a soft kiss on his lean cologne-scented jaw. 'Goodbye, Lucas,' she said, and then she turned and walked out the door.

* * *

Lucas closed the front door as the last of the guests left. He looked at the emptiness of his house now that the party was over. It was like a big ship after a luxury cruise had ended or a kid's birthday party room after all the children had gone.

Empty.

Even the decorations looked exhausted. Some of the balloons looked as if they had let out a sigh of disappointment now that everyone had stopped playfully punching them about the dance floor. A black balloon bounced listlessly across the floor towards his foot. He gave it a half-hearted kick and let out a string of curses his mother would have washed his mouth out for when he was a kid.

Mittens came mewing through the house. He had stayed away while the party was in full swing. He gave Lucas a quizzical look and peered around as if looking for Molly.

'She's gone,' Lucas said, bending down to pick him up. He held him against his chest and stroked his velvety head.

'Prrrput?' Mittens said, and head-bumped his hand.

Lucas blinked to clear his vision but still the tears kept coming as if a tap had been turned on somewhere deep inside him. 'You're right,' he said. 'This place sucks without her.'

CHAPTER TWELVE

'YOU'RE *ACTUALLY GOING* on leave?' Jacqui asked, swinging round to face Lucas in the office a week later.

Lucas took off his stethoscope and dropped it on the desk. 'Why are you so surprised?' he asked. 'I'm entitled to some time off, aren't I?'

'Well, yes, of course, but you haven't even taken sick leave in I don't know how long,' she said. 'Where are you going?'

'Nowhere special.'

Jacqui folded her arms as she leaned her hips back against the desk. 'So it's finally happened.'

He shot her a quick sideways look as he straightened the papers on the desk. 'What's finally happened?'

'You're finally ready to go home.'

Was he ready?

No, not really. It was a hurdle he had to face—a bridge to cross. He wasn't sure of his reception on the other side but he couldn't waste another moment worrying about it. He wanted to be where Molly was, tell her how much he loved her, how he couldn't bear the thought of the rest of his life without her in it, making him smile, making him feel loved, making him *live* again.

How had he thought he could survive without her? This past week had been one of the loneliest weeks of his life. Even Mittens had joined him in his misery by moping about as if the sun was never going to come out again.

Molly was his sunshine, his only light in the darkness of what his life had become.

She was his second chance, his *only* chance.

'I have a little favour to ask you,' Lucas said.

'Sure,' Jacqui said, eyes twinkling. 'What is it?'

'Do you know anything about cats?'

'He's beautiful,' Molly said as she looked at little baby Oliver Matthew Drummond lying in the neonatal crib.

Jack Drummond brushed at his eyes with his hand, carefully juggling his crutches to do so. 'Yeah, he is,' he said. 'You were too. You were the prettiest baby in the nursery. I felt so proud. Scared out of my wits, though.'

Molly gave him a quizzical look. 'Scared? Why?'

'There weren't a lot of females about the place while I was growing up,' he said. 'Your gran died when I was twelve. Dad had to do things pretty rough and ready, bringing up four boys on his own. Having a daughter terrified me. I guess that's why I left a lot of it up to your mother. I knew how to handle a son because I'd been one myself and I'd had little brothers to help rear. But a little girl dressed in pink? Well, I guess I didn't always get it right with you, did I?'

Molly was still not ready to forgive him. 'No, you didn't.'

He cleared his throat, looking exactly what he was—a rough-and-tumble country man, out of his depth with showing emotion or even witnessing it in others. 'Thanks for coming, love. I reckon the little tyke held on just so he could meet his big sister. The doctors reckon he's out of danger now.'

'I'm happy for you and Crystal,' she said. 'I really am.'

He cleared his throat again. 'Yeah, well, I wanted to talk to you about things.' He let out a long breath. 'I'm a stubborn old goat. Your mother will tell you that— Crystal too, if it comes to that. I wish I'd handled things differently. Not just with the divorce but just…things…'

'You were wrong about Lucas,' she said, looking at the sleeping baby again. 'You were *so* wrong.'

'I know,' he said. 'I've been wanting to talk to you about that all week.'

Molly turned and looked at him again with tears springing into her eyes. 'I love him, Dad. I'm not going to apologise for it. He's the most wonderful man I've ever met. He's suffered so much for what happened with Matt. It wasn't his fault. You know it wasn't. I can't bear to think of him over there all alone. He just works, that's all he does. He works and works and works. He has no life. I *want* him to have a life. I want a life with him. I know it will be hard for you, but I can't live without him. I don't want to live without him.'

'I never really thought of how it was for him until I saw that car suddenly veer in front of me,' Jack said. 'It must have been like that for him when he rounded that bend and that roo jumped out in front of him. In that split second you don't have time to think. You just react. He was a young, inexperienced driver. He did what any young driver would do. It wasn't his fault.'

'Do you really mean that?' she asked.

He looked at Molly with red-rimmed eyes, his throat moving up and down like a tractor piston. 'It wasn't his fault. I want to tell him that. I know it's seventeen years too late, but I want to call him and tell him that. Do you have his number?'

Molly couldn't control the wobble of her chin. Her eyes were streaming and her throat felt raw with emotion but she thought she had never loved her father more than at that point. 'Of course I have his number,' she said. 'Let's go to the relatives' room so it'll be more private.'

Jack handed back her phone a few minutes later. 'He's not answering,' he said. 'I would've left a message but I'd rather speak to him person to person.'

Molly checked her watch. 'He's probably still at the hospital. He works the most ridiculous hours. I told you he was a workaholic.' She looked up at her father and frowned when she saw his expression. 'What?'

Jack gave a crooked smile. 'I wouldn't want him to come anywhere near my little girl if he wasn't dedicated and responsible. He saves lives, Molly. What could be more important than that?'

Molly blew out a breath. 'I'll try the hospital,' she said, and scrolled down for the number. 'If he's not there then I haven't got a clue where else he would be.'

She hung up the phone half a minute later. 'He's on leave.'

'Where?'

'No one knows,' she said. 'He didn't say but, then, he wouldn't. He never tells anyone anything.'

'I'd better get back to Crystal,' Jack said. 'You'll let me know if you hear from him?'

Molly's shoulders dropped on a sigh. 'Yes, but don't hold your breath.'

Lucas breathed in a lungful of hot air as he walked out of Mascot airport. He couldn't get over the Australian accents surrounding him. Even the airport announcements had sounded exaggerated, as if the person on the loudspeaker was pretending to be an Aussie. He hadn't realised his accent had changed until he'd jumped in a taxi and the guy had asked him if it was his first time visiting the country. His brothers had been ribbing him about it for years but now he realised he was one of those ex-pats who didn't really know where they belonged any more.

He checked through his messages as he headed to the taxi rank. There were dozens from the hospital but that wasn't unusual. It was probably hard for the staff to get it into their heads that he was actually on leave.

There was one message he was particularly thrilled about, however. Tim's latest scan had shown some definite activity and his mother had felt his fingers curl around hers when she spoke to him. It was just the sort of response he had been hoping for. The recovery might be slow but he was hopeful it would be like Emma's.

There was a missed call from Molly's phone but no message. He wasn't sure what to make of that. Maybe she had just wanted to let him know she had got home safely.

He headed straight to the private hospital in the eastern suburbs. He had done a quick phone around to track

down Molly and her family. It really helped, being part
of the medical profession. One of the guys he'd worked
with at St Patrick's was now a neonatal specialist at
Sydney Metropolitan. He had given Lucas an update
on Molly's little half-brother. The little guy was out of
danger now. That was great news but Lucas still wasn't
sure how he would be received, turning up in the middle
of a family crisis. But he couldn't stay away. He wanted
to be with Molly, not just now but always. How could
he have thought otherwise? His life without her was
like his house without a party or a cruise ship without
passengers.

Empty.

It was weird, walking into a hospital from the other
side of the counter, so to speak. He was just a visitor here, not one of the top specialists. An officious
nurse gave him directions to the neonatal ward. Lucas
assumed Molly would be somewhere near her little
brother.

And he was right.

He saw her from a way off. She was standing outside
the unit, looking in through the glass window.

But she wasn't alone.

Lucas stopped in his tracks. He didn't want to cause
a scene in the middle of the neonatal unit. But neither
did he want to slink away as if he was scared to stand
up to Jack Drummond. But before he could take a step
forwards or backwards Jack turned and saw him.

'Lucas?'

Molly swung around and her mouth dropped open.
'Lucas?'

'Did you call me?' Lucas said. It was the first thing

that came into his head. There were a thousand things that he should have said instead but it was all he could think of at the time. It was so good to see her. She looked gorgeous. Tired, but gorgeous. She was dressed in tight-fitting jeans and a loose jersey top that had slipped off one of her shoulders. He wanted to crush her to him, feel that soft little body against his hard one and never let her go.

'What are you doing here?' Molly asked.

'I came to see you,' he said. 'To tell you I love you.'

Her eyes widened to the size of dinner plates. 'You came all that way to tell me that?' she said. 'Why didn't you tell me the night of the party?'

'I was an idiot that night,' Lucas said. 'I was caught off guard. I'd worked myself up to you leaving in another three weeks. I wasn't prepared for you to just up and go like that.'

'Can I say something here?' Jack stepped forward. '*Dad.*'

'No, let me speak,' Jack said. He turned to Lucas. 'I was wrong to blame you for Matt's death. I don't expect you to forgive me. I'll never forgive myself. You were like another son to Margie and me. I can't believe I treated you the way I did. For all these years I've blamed you for something that was never your fault.

'I just want you to know that I'm sorry. It's too late to undo the damage I did to Margie. How she still speaks to me is testament to the sort of person she is. But I don't want Molly to suffer any more. She's just like her mother—loving and generous to a fault. I want her to be happy. I think you're the only person who can make her so.'

'Can I have a word with you in private?' Lucas said to Jack. 'There's something I want to ask you.'

Molly put her hands on her hips. 'Excuse me?' she said. 'Hello? Don't I have some say in this?'

Jack grinned from ear to ear as he slapped Lucas on the shoulder. 'She's all yours, mate,' he said. 'She'll drive you nuts and make you tear your hair out at times, but she'll stick with you through thick and thin. She's a good girl. I'm proud of her. I'm proud of you, too. You're a good man. I'll be proud as punch to call you my son-in-law.'

Molly glowered at her father. 'Dad, you're jumping the gun here. He hasn't even asked me.'

'I'm getting to it,' Lucas said with a melting look. 'But you know me, darling, I don't like being rushed.'

Molly felt her heart give a little flip like a pancake, but she still wasn't going to capitulate without a show of spirit. 'You're assuming, of course, that I will say yes?' she said with a pouting, you-hurt-me-and-I'm-not-quite-ready-to-forgive-you look. 'I've been crying myself to sleep for the past week. You didn't even send me a text.'

'I know,' Lucas said. 'I just couldn't say what I wanted to say in a text. I wanted to see you.' He brought her up close, his arms wrapping around her securely. 'Will you marry me, Molly? I want you to be my wife. I want you to be the mother of my babies. I want to spend the rest of my life with you. I want to love you, laugh with you, fight with you, celebrate and commiserate with you. I even want to party with you. I want to live life with you no matter what it dishes up. I just want to be with you.'

'For God's sake, Molly, put the poor man out of his misery,' Jack said.

Molly smiled as she flung her arms around Lucas's neck. 'Yes,' she said. 'Yes, yes, yes, a thousand million squillion times yes.'

Lucas laughed as he swung her around in his arms. It was the first time he had laughed since he'd been a teenager. It felt good. It felt really good.

It felt right.

* * * * *

A FORBIDDEN
TEMPTATION

ANNE MATHER

I'd like to dedicate this book to my loyal readers, whose letters have given me so much pleasure.

CHAPTER ONE

THE PHONE WAS ringing as Jack walked into the house.

He was tempted not to answer it. He knew who it would be. It was at least three days since his sister-in-law had contacted him. Debra seldom ignored him for very long.

But she was—had been—Lisa's sister, and he supposed she was only looking out for him. The truth was, he didn't need looking out for, he thought resignedly. He was doing just fine on his own.

Dropping the bag containing the still-warm baguette he'd bought at the village bakery onto the granite counter, Jack hooked the kitchen phone from the wall.

'Connolly,' he said, hoping against hope that it might be a cold call. But those hopes were dashed when Debra Carrick came on the line.

'Why do you insist on turning off your mobile phone?' she greeted him irritably. 'I called you once yesterday and twice today, but you're never available.'

'And good morning to you, too,' Jack commented drily. 'And why do I need to carry a mobile phone every place I go? I doubt there's anything you need to tell me that can't wait.'

'How do you know that?' Debra sounded offended now and he stifled a groan. 'In any case, what if you had an accident? Or if you fell off that stupid boat of yours? You'd wish you had some means of communication then.'

'If I fell off the boat, the phone wouldn't work in the water,' replied Jack mildly, and he heard Debra give an impatient snort.

'You've always got an answer, haven't you, Jack?' she demanded, her frustration evident. 'Anyway, when are you coming home? Your mother's worried about you.'

Jack acknowledged that the worrying part might be true.

But both his mother and his father—and his siblings, come to that—knew not to ask those kinds of questions.

They'd accepted that he needed to move away from the family. And this house he'd found on the wild Northumbrian coast was exactly where he wanted to be.

'This is my home,' he said now, glancing round the large farmhouse kitchen with a certain amount of pride.

When he'd bought the house, it had been in a sorry state of repair. But after months of his living out of suitcases and cardboard boxes, the renovation—a lot of which he'd done himself—was now complete.

Lindisfarne House had emerged as a comfortable, but elegant, home. The ideal place to find refuge and decide what he was going to do with the rest of his life.

'You're not serious!' He'd almost forgotten what his answer had been until Debra spoke again. 'Jack, you're an architect! A successful architect at that. Just because you've inherited that money doesn't mean you have to spend all your time bumming around some godforsaken corner of England!'

'Rothburn is not a godforsaken corner of England,' protested Jack civilly. 'And certainly no more remote than Kilpheny itself.' He sighed. 'I needed to get away from Ireland, Debs. I thought you understood that.'

Debra sniffed. 'Well, I do, I suppose,' she conceded. 'I'm sure your grandmother's death was the last straw. But all your family's here. Your friends are here. We miss you, you know.'

'Yeah, I know.' Jack could feel his patience thinning nonetheless. 'Look, I gotta go, Debs.' He grimaced at the lie. 'There's someone at the door.'

With the phone hooked back onto the wall, Jack spread his hands on the cool granite for a moment, breathing deeply. It wasn't her fault, he told himself. Just because every time he heard her voice he found himself thinking about Lisa didn't make her a bad person.

For God's sake, he just wished she would get off his case.

'She's in love with you, you know.'

The light, half-amused tone broke into his bleak mood of introspection. He lifted his head to find Lisa seated on the end of the counter, examining her nails. She was dressed in the same cropped pants and silk blouse she'd been wearing the last time he'd seen her. One high-heeled sandal dangled from her right foot.

Jack closed his eyes for a moment and straightened from his stooped position.

'You don't know that,' he said flatly, and Lisa lifted her head and met his brooding gaze.

'Oh, I do,' she insisted. 'Debs has been in love with you for years. Ever since I first brought you home to meet Daddy.'

Jack turned away and picked up the baguette he'd brought home from the bakery. Despite his conversation with Debra, it was still warm, and he switched on the coffee pot and took a dish of butter from the fridge.

Slicing himself a generous wedge of the baguette, he spread it thickly with butter. Then forced himself to eat it, even though he disliked having her watch him do so.

'Are you going back to Ireland?'

Lisa was persistent, and, although Jack despised himself for humouring her, he turned his head. She was still sitting on his counter, a pale ethereal figure that he knew from previous experience could disappear in an instant. But today, she seemed determined to torment him and he lifted his shoulders in a careless shrug.

'What's it to you?' he asked, lifting a mug from the drainer and pouring himself some coffee. Strong and black, the way he liked it. 'You don't like Northumberland, either?'

'I just want you to be happy,' Lisa said, spreading her fingers as he'd seen her do a hundred times after she'd applied a coat of varnish on her nails. 'That's why I'm here.'

'Really?'

Jack was sceptical. In his opinion, she was doing her best

to make people think he was crazy. He was talking to a dead person, for God's sake. How insane was that?

A draught of air blew across his face and when next he looked, she was gone.

She left nothing behind. Not even the faint trace of the perfume she'd always worn. Nothing to prove he wasn't going out of his mind as he sometimes suspected he was.

In the beginning, Jack had dismissed Lisa's appearances as a mental aberration. Even so, he'd gone to see a doctor in Wicklow who, in turn, had sent him to a psychiatrist in Dublin.

The psychiatrist had been of the opinion that it was Jack's way of grieving. And as no one else saw Lisa, Jack had half believed he might be right.

But the visitations had continued, sometimes with days, at other times weeks, in between. Jack had become so inured to them that they didn't worry him any longer.

Besides, he'd never felt that Lisa wanted to hurt him. On the contrary, she always appeared as quirky and capricious as she'd been in life.

Jack scowled and carried his coffee out of the kitchen and across a wide panelled hall into a sunlit living room.

The room was large, high-ceilinged and furnished with dark oak and leather. Pale textured walls contrasted with the beams that arched above his head, long windows overlooking the coastline and the blue-grey waters of the North Sea.

There was a leather rocking chair set in the window embrasure and Jack seated himself in it and propped his booted feet on the sill. It was early yet, barely nine o'clock, and the day stretched ahead of him, silent and unstructured.

Which was also the way he liked it.

As he drank his coffee he pondered the prospect of taking the *Osprey* out for a sail. He knew from previous experience that manning the forty-two-foot ketch demanded all his energies. The North Sea, even at the end of May, didn't take any prisoners.

He frowned. He wasn't sure he wanted that kind of action. He might spend some time on the boat. There were one or two jobs requiring his attention. And he enjoyed exchanging the time of day with the fishermen who also used the small harbour.

Not that he really needed the company. Although he'd suffered in the aftermath of the accident that had killed his wife, he wasn't suicidal. Besides, it was nearly two years since Lisa had died, for heaven's sake. He should be over his grief by now.

And he was. Mostly. Except when Lisa herself turned up to torment him.

When had she first appeared? It must have been about a month after her funeral. Jack had been visiting her grave in the churchyard at Kilpheny when he'd realised that Lisa was standing beside him.

God, she'd certainly shaken him out of his apathy that day, he remembered ruefully. He'd half believed they must have buried some other young woman by mistake.

But no. Lisa had quickly disabused him of that notion. In any case, despite the fact that her little sports car had burst into flames on impact with the petrol tanker, dental records and DNA evidence found at the scene had proved conclusively that the remains they'd found were those of his wife.

The only thing that had survived the crash unscathed had been one of her designer sandals. Which, he assumed, was why Lisa only ever appeared wearing one sandal these days.

He used to ponder that anomaly. Why, if Lisa herself could appear apparently unscathed by the experience, couldn't she have been supplied with another sandal?

It wasn't important. After that first shocking encounter, Jack had learned not to question such prosaic irregularities with her. Lisa had her own agenda and she never deviated from it.

She enjoyed provoking him. Much as she'd done during

the three short years of their marriage. Anything else was apparently beyond her remit.

He scowled, finishing his coffee in a single gulp and getting to his feet. He couldn't spend the rest of his life analysing what might have been. Or, as Debra had said, 'bumming around'.

Or talking to a ghost, he appended drily. Perhaps he ought to be wondering if he was losing his mind.

Eight hours later, he was feeling considerably less gloomy. He'd spent the morning doing some minor repairs to the ketch. And then, because it had been a beautiful afternoon, with only a mild wind flowing from the south-west, he'd taken the *Osprey* out on the water.

By the time he drove back to Lindisfarne House, he'd forgotten how introspective he'd been that morning. He had a bucket of fresh shellfish he'd bought from one of the fishermen and some fresh greens in the back of the Lexus. He was looking forward to making a lobster salad for his supper.

He was propped against the fridge, drinking an ice-cool can of beer, when he heard tyres crunching on his drive. Dammit, he thought, slamming the can down and heading for the front door. The last thing he needed tonight was company...

He scowled. He didn't get visitors. Not visitors who parked in his driveway, anyway. No one, except his immediate family, knew where he was living. And they had strict orders not to give his address to anyone.

When the doorbell chimed, he knew he had to answer it.

'Why don't you open the door?'

Jack swung round abruptly to find Lisa perched on a half-moon console table.

'Say what?'

'Open the door,' she said again, and for the first time she looked almost animated.

'I'm going to,' he said, speaking in a low voice, hoping that whoever was outside wouldn't hear him. 'What's it to you? I'm the one who's going to have to entertain an un-invited guest.'

'Two uninvited guests,' amended Lisa, evidently imply-ing that he had more than one visitor, and Jack's brows drew together.

'So who are they?'

'You'll find out,' she said lightly, her image fading even as her words were dying away.

Jack shook his head, not sure what he ought to make of that. Lisa rarely if ever appeared twice in one day. Did some-thing about the visitor—*visitors*—disturb her? Perhaps he ought to be on his guard. He was alone in the house, after all.

Well, as good as.

Pushing such negative thoughts aside, he released the latch and opened the door.

A man was standing outside. A man he hadn't seen in God knew how long. He and Sean Nesbitt had grown up to-gether. They'd even attended university together, sharing a flat in their final year.

They'd graduated from Trinity College, Dublin, and had been eager to gain advanced degrees, Jack in architecture and Sean in computer science. After leaving Trinity, however, they'd both gone their separate ways, only meeting occa-sionally when they'd been visiting their parents in Kilpheny.

Since Jack's marriage to Lisa, he'd virtually lost touch with the other man. And he had to say, Sean was the last person he'd expected to see here.

'You open for visitors?'

Sean was grinning at him and for the life of him Jack couldn't have turned him away.

'Hell, yes,' he said, taking the hand Sean held out and then stepping back automatically. 'But, my God, what are you doing here? And how the devil did you find me?'

Sean's grin widened. 'I'm a computer expert, remem-ber?' he said smugly, glancing back at the silver Mercedes he'd parked on Jack's drive. 'But I'm not on my own. I've brought my girlfriend with me.' He pulled a wry face. 'Is it okay if we both come in?'

So... Jack lifted a thoughtful shoulder. Lisa had been right. He did have more than one visitor. But...

'Sure,' he said, not without some reluctance, casting a swift glance over his shoulder as he did so. But the table was unoccupied. Lisa had definitely gone.

'Great!'

It was only as Sean turned to go back to the car that Jack realised he hadn't changed since he got back from the marina. His cargo pants were smudged with paint and his black sweatshirt had seen better days.

Ah, well, they would have to take him as they found him, he thought resignedly. He hadn't been expecting visitors. And wasn't that the truth?

Sean had circled the car to open the passenger-side door to allow a young woman to get out. But she forestalled his efforts, sliding out of the car before he reached her door. From his position in the doorway, Jack could only see that she was tall and slim, and dressed in jeans and a white tee shirt.

Sean was only of average height and build and in her high-heeled boots she was almost as tall as he was. She also had a mass of curly red-gold hair, presently caught up in a ponytail.

She didn't immediately look his way and Jack wondered if she was as unenthusiastic about this visit as he was. But Sean was a friend and he couldn't disappoint him. Not as he appeared to have come quite some distance to see him.

Sean attempted to put an arm about the girl's waist to draw her forward, and Jack felt a momentary pang of envy. How long was it since he'd had a woman in his arms?

But to his surprise, the girl shrugged Sean off, striding towards the house with a determination that wasn't matched by the expression on her face.

Uh-oh, trouble in paradise, mused Jack wryly. He must be right. She hadn't wanted to come here.

Then he caught his breath. He felt suddenly as if he'd been stabbed in his solar plexus. His involuntary reaction stunned him, the surge of heat invading his lower body feeling like a fire in his gut.

His response was totally unexpected. Not to say inappropriate, as well. He didn't do lust, but that was what he was feeling at that moment. Dammit, she was Sean's girlfriend; he'd said so. And just because they'd apparently had a lovers' tiff didn't mean he had the right to pick up the slack.

But she was striking. High, rounded breasts, pointed nipples clearly outlined by the thin cotton of her tee. Her thighs were slim and shapely, and she had the kind of legs that seemed to go on for ever.

Thank God for his baggy cargo pants. He had the feeling he had more than his reaction to hide. He almost broke out in a sweat at the possibility that Sean might notice.

He couldn't believe this was why Lisa had been so keen for him to open the door. Yet, wasn't it just the kind of quirky thing she would do? She'd enjoyed baiting him in life and she still enjoyed baiting him now.

Of course, Sean's girlfriend was nothing like Lisa. Lisa had been petite, blonde, bubbly. And okay, yes, she'd been flirtatious. But judging by the look he was getting from this girl, she was anything but flirtatious. She was regarding him with cool—what? Indifference? *Contempt?* As if she'd guessed exactly what was going through his mind.

Right.

Stepping back, he made room for them to come into the house, and Sean quickly made the introductions.

'Grace Spencer, meet Jack Connolly,' he said cheerfully, and, despite the look from her amazingly green eyes, Jack was obliged to take the hand the girl reluctantly offered him.

'Hi,' he said, aware that her slim fingers were cool against his suddenly sweating palm.

'Hello.' Her voice was as cool as her expression. 'I hope

you don't mind, but Sean asked me to come with him, to show him how to get here.'

'I— No. Of course not.'

Jack frowned. He detected a slight local accent. Did she come from this area? If so, how on earth had she met Sean?

Realising he'd been silent for too long, he said awkwardly, 'Do you know the area, Grace?'

'I was born here,' she began, but Sean didn't let her finish.

'Her parents own the village pub,' he said quickly. 'Grace left here when she went to university, and she's been living in London since then.'

Jack nodded. At least that explained the connection. The last he'd heard, Sean had been working in London, too.

'But I've left London now,' Grace inserted flatly, giving Sean what Jack thought was a warning look. 'My mother's ill and I've decided to move back to Rothburn to be near her. Sean is still living in London. This is just a flying visit, isn't it, Sean?'

There was no mistaking the accusation in that question. Jack felt his eyes go wide, and his inhibitions about this visit increased. Whatever was going on here, he didn't want to be part of it. But they were evidently not the happy couple Sean was trying to convey.

'We'll see,' Sean said now. Then, squaring his shoulders, he forced a grin for Jack's benefit. 'I bet you were wondering how I found you out.'

'You could say that.'

'Well, when Grace's pa said an Irishman had bought this old place, I never dreamt it might be you,' Sean continued. 'It wasn't until they mentioned your name that I put two and two together. Small world, eh?'

'Isn't it?'

Jack inclined his head. He hadn't tried to hide his identity from the locals. But no one really knew him here; no one knew about Lisa.

He just hadn't expected Sean Nesbitt to turn up.

'So…' Jack tried to inject a note of interest into his voice now. 'Do you come up here every weekend to see Grace and her family?'

'Yes—'

'No!'

They both spoke at once, and Jack could see the sudden rush of colour that stained Grace's cheeks.

'I come as often as I can,' amended Sean, his pale blue eyes darkening with sudden anger. 'Come on, Grace, you know your parents are pleased to see me. Just because you're feeling neglected, that's no reason to embarrass Jack like this.'

CHAPTER TWO

GRACE WAS ANGRY.

She knew she shouldn't have let herself be persuaded to come here with Sean, but what could she do? Apart from the obvious misconceptions it created, she didn't like arguing with him in public. With Jack Connolly looking on, she felt hopelessly embarrassed. He was not the kind of man to be fooled by Sean's lies.

The trouble was her parents expected her to marry Sean, and they would certainly have suspected something was wrong if she'd refused to come with him. For now she had to accept the situation. But she refused to let Sean make a fool of her.

It had been so different in the beginning. When she'd first met Sean, she'd been fascinated by his easy charm. Okay, she'd been young, and naïve, but that was in the days when she'd taken everything he said as gospel; when just being around such a popular older student had given her a feeling of pride.

How wrong she had been.

Her first mistake had been bringing him to meet her parents. With Sean's promises of easy money, her father had been persuaded to mortgage the pub to help finance Sean's fledgling website.

Grace had tried to stop him. Even though she'd believed she was going to marry Sean, she'd known the website was a huge gamble and her father knew little about websites or their uses.

But Tom Spencer hadn't listened to her. He'd thought he was investing in her future and she'd loved him for it. But even then she'd had some sleepless nights worrying about what would happen if the website failed.

And it had. Like so much else where Sean was concerned, the dream hadn't equalled the reality. Even now, her parents had no idea that Sean had lost their money. Which was why Grace had to do everything in her power to get it back.

Even if it meant lying about her relationship with Sean.

Her parents were still labouring under the illusion that Sean was only staying in London to advance his business. She knew they thought she should have stayed with him, but Grace had had enough. She'd stopped short of telling them about the scene that had finally ended their relationship. Until her mother had recovered her health, she couldn't lay that on them, as well.

She'd let them think that she had been homesick. When the sickness she had felt had been of a different order altogether.

But Sean knew their affair was over. And if she had her way, soon she'd never have to see him again.

But now, here they were, standing in Jack Connolly's doorway, and she for one would have liked to turn around and go home. It was obvious Connolly didn't want them here. And she couldn't exactly blame him. So why didn't Sean get the message and put an end to this embarrassing stand-off?

Unfortunately, their host seemed to realise his manners just as Grace was searching for the words to get them out of this.

'Please,' he said. 'Come in.' And he moved behind them to close the heavy door.

Grace was still wondering why Sean had wanted to come here, anyway. What was it he'd said: that Connolly had lost his wife in a car accident a couple of years ago and that this was his first opportunity to offer his condolences to the man? Grace had had to accept it when he'd strung that line to her father, but she'd have said Sean was the last person to offer sympathy to anyone. Unless there was something in it for him, she appended with the bitter knowledge of hindsight.

Or was she judging him too harshly?

And then she remembered another titbit he'd offered. Apparently Jack Connolly had inherited some money from his grandmother and that was how he'd been able to buy this place. Sean's take on it—or rather the one he'd offered her father—was that Jack had wanted to get away from the pain of familiar places. He'd moved to Northumberland to find a place to lick his wounds in peace.

Having met Jack now, Grace took that with a pinch of salt. Whatever he was doing in Northumberland, he didn't look like a man who had any wounds to lick. He seemed perfectly self-sufficient, and far too shrewd to need anyone's sympathy.

She hadn't forgotten the way he'd looked at her when he'd first seen her. It hadn't been the look of a man who was drowning in grief. On the contrary, if she and Sean had still been together, she would have considered it offensive.

Were all men untrustworthy? she wondered. She didn't think so, but she had no doubt that Jack Connolly wasn't to be trusted, either.

It annoyed her that he was also drop-dead gorgeous. Even the thick stubble of a couple of days' growth of beard on his chin couldn't detract from the stark male beauty of his face.

His skin was darkly tanned, as if he'd been spending time in a sunnier climate. But, according to her father, he'd been living here throughout all the renovations he'd made to the house.

Unruly dark hair tumbled over his forehead and brushed the neckline of his sweatshirt. Thin lips below hollowed cheekbones only added to his sensual appeal.

They crossed the hall and entered a well-lit living room. Whatever she thought of Connolly himself, there was no denying the man had taste. Pale walls, dark wood, much of it antique from the look of it. And a Persian carpet on the floor that fairly melted beneath her feet.

Grace headed for the windows. Despite the attractive appointments of the room, she was fascinated by the view. It was stunning. And familiar. It was still light outside, and she could see the rocky headland curving away, grassy cliffs beyond a low stone wall falling away to dunes.

The sea was calm at present, reflecting the reddening clouds that marked the sun's descent. Lights glinted in the cottages that spilled down the hillside to the harbour and the small marina, the distant cry of gulls a lonely mournful lament.

The outer door slammed and Jack Connolly strode into the room to join them.

'You'll have to forgive the way I look,' he said ruefully, flicking a hand at his paint-stained pants. 'I've been on the boat all day and I haven't had time to change.'

'A boat? You've got a boat?' Sean was enthusiastic. 'Hey, what's it like to be a millionaire?'

Grace, hearing Sean's words, felt her stomach sink within her. Oh, God, why hadn't she asked him how much Jack had inherited? Why had she simply assumed it would be a moderate sum?

What price now his condolences for Jack's wife and his grandmother? Jack's supposed grief had been forgotten. Sean had simply used it as an excuse to get her here.

Jack, to his credit, didn't call Sean on it. 'Let me offer you both a drink,' he said. His eyes shifted to Grace as she reluctantly turned from the window. 'What would you like?'

Well, not you, she thought childishly, disturbed in spite of herself by those heavy-lidded dark eyes. What was he really thinking? She wasn't sure she wanted to know.

'Got a beer?'

Sean didn't wait for her response, but Jack apparently had more respect.

'Um—just a soft drink for me, please,' she said, remembering she was starting a new job the following day. The last thing she needed was to have to face her boss with a fuzzy head.

'A soft drink?' Sean rolled his eyes at Jack. 'Can you believe this woman was brought up in a pub and she doesn't like beer?'

The twitch of Jack's lips could have meant anything. 'I won't be long,' he said and disappeared out of the door.

It was only as Grace heard the faint squeaking sound as Jack crossed the hall that she realised his feet had been bare.

She looked at Sean then, but he only raised his eyebrows in a defensive gesture.

'What? What?' He glanced away to survey the huge comfortable sofas and armchairs, the heavy bookshelves and inlaid cabinets with an envious eye. 'Some place, eh? I bet this furniture is worth a fortune. Aren't you glad you came?'

'Uh—no.'

Grace could hardly bear to look at him. She should have refused to come here. Sean was a pathological liar. She'd known that, but she'd also not wanted to cause an argument and endanger her mother's health.

'A millionaire's pad,' went on Sean, when she didn't elaborate. He turned his attention to a picture hanging on the wall behind him. 'Hey, this is a Turner! Can you believe that?'

Grace didn't want to talk about it. Whatever way you looked at it, she was here under false pretences, and she didn't like it. God knew, she didn't care about Jack Connolly or his money. He couldn't solve her problems.

Jack came back at that moment carrying two bottles of beer and a glass of cola.

'Please—sit,' he said, setting Grace's glass on a low polished coffee table where several expensive yachting magazines were strewn in elegant disarray.

Deliberately? Grace didn't think so. Despite the little she knew of the man, she didn't think Jack Connolly would care what other people thought of his home.

Jack put Grace's glass on the table and, to his relief, Grace seated herself on a plush velvet sofa beside the coffee table. And Sean, after accepting his beer from Jack, did the same.

'Hey, great place you've got here,' he said, waving his bottle around with a distinct lack of regard for the safety of its contents. 'Where'd you get all this stuff? It looks expensive.'

Jack propped his hips against a small bureau he'd picked up in an auction room and said, 'A lot of it was my gran's. The rest I bought and restored myself.'

'No way!'

Sean stared at him, and Jack could see the disbelief in the other man's gaze.

'Yes way,' he said and took a mouthful of his beer. 'It seemed a shame to get rid of it.'

Sean shook his head. 'Since when have you been a furniture restorer, man? You're an architect. You design houses, shopping centres, schools, that sort of thing.'

'Yeah, well—'

Jack didn't want to get into his reasons for doing what he'd done, but Sean wouldn't let it go.

'Oh, I get it,' he said. 'Now you've got private means, you don't need a job.'

Jack bit back the retort that sprang to his lips and said instead, 'Something like that.' He took another gulp from his bottle. 'Beer okay?'

'Oh, yeah. It's cold.' Sean nodded. 'Just the way I like it.'

Then he glanced suggestively at Grace. 'Well, beer, anyway.'

Grace cringed. Why couldn't Sean just drink his beer and stop being so crass? It was so embarrassing.

And, as if he'd sensed her discomfort, it was Jack who came to her rescue.

'So what are you doing these days?' he asked, addressing himself to the other man. 'Still inventing computer games for that Japanese company?'

'Well, no. As a matter of fact, I don't work for Sunyata any more. I've been doing some consulting until I can get my own website off the ground. We can't all have your advantages, can we, Jack?'

Jack blew out a breath. How the hell was he supposed to answer that? He just wished this uncomfortable interview were over.

Forcing a smile to his lips, he met Grace's unwilling gaze with a feeling of resignation. But he pressed on, anyway. 'How about you, Grace?' he asked.

'Grace has a law degree,' broke in Sean before she could say anything. There was pride in his voice, despite the lingering touch of animosity he'd revealed before. 'She used to work for the Crown Prosecution Service.'

'Really?' Jack was impressed.

'Not that there are jobs like that up here,' Sean went on bitterly. 'Grace has had to put her career on hold.'

Grace sighed. 'I'm very happy with the job I've got,' she averred shortly. 'Can we talk about something else?'

'But you, working for an estate agent!' Sean was scathing. 'You know you can do better than that.'

'Sean!'

Grace stared at him with warning eyes, and, as if realising he wasn't doing himself any favours, Sean grimaced.

'It's a living, I suppose,' he conceded. 'I may even try to find myself a job in Alnwick, too.'

Grace shook her head disbelievingly, but Sean's expression didn't change.

'Well, I could,' he insisted annoyingly. 'I might enjoy a change of scene.'

'I don't think so.'

Grace knew he was being deliberately provocative. Was it all for Jack Connolly's benefit? The last thing she wanted was for Sean to move up here.

But as if sensing what she was feeling, Sean reached out and took her hand.

'You know how I feel about you, don't you, baby?' he crooned, bestowing a lingering kiss on her knuckles. 'I know we're having a few problems right now, but once you're back in London…'

Grace gritted her teeth. 'I'm not going back to London, Sean.' She'd told him she wanted to stay near her parents, but he refused to believe it. She'd also made it clear that they could remain in touch—in the hope of recovering her parents' money, although he didn't need to know that—but any relationship between them was over. Did he think that by talking like this in front of Connolly he'd convince her to change her mind?

Meanwhile, Jack stifled a groan. If Sean and his girl-friend were having problems, he didn't want to hear about it.

And despite Sean's mournful expression, he didn't think Grace was too thrilled about it, either.

Or was that only wishful thinking?

And, if so, where had that come from?

Grace had succeeded in pulling her hand away now. For want of something else to do, she wrapped both hands round her glass and concentrated on the cola fizzing away inside.

She'd known Sean was selfish, but his behaviour was un-forgivable. He was supposed to be sympathising with Jack, but he hadn't even mentioned his wife's death.

Taking a sip of her drink, she put her glass down and got to her feet.

'We should be going, Sean,' she said firmly.

Sean swallowed another mouthful of his beer and stood up also, leaving the bottle teetering on the edge of one of the sailing magazines.

Aware of the obvious dangers, Grace had to steel herself not to lean down and rescue it before it fell over and sprayed sticky liquid over the table and the rug below.

Instead, she moved towards the door, avoiding Connolly's narrow-eyed appraisal, desperate to get out of there before Sean could embarrass her again.

But unfortunately he wasn't quite finished.

Looking at Jack, he said, 'We're going to have a proper catch-up, old buddy.' He tried to catch Grace's arm, but she'd already moved out of his reach. 'How about next weekend?' he added. 'I've got to go back to London to-morrow, but I'll try to get up again on Friday evening. What do you say?'

'Well…'

Jack was non-committal. The last thing he wanted was another awkward interlude like this.

'I'd like to tell you my ideas about developing the website,' Sean continued. 'It might be something you'd be interested in. I'd be glad to give you all the details.'

Grace wanted to groan.

She'd been half afraid Sean had been about to bring that up earlier on. As soon as he'd heard that Jack was living in the village, Sean's intentions had been clear.

Jack straightened away from the bureau. He was watching them both through those narrowed eyes, his absurdly thick lashes veiling their expression.

She thought she could guess what he was thinking. He knew exactly what was going on here. She just hoped he didn't think she had any part in it.

'Yeah,' he said at last, without enthusiasm, and, in spite of being innocent of any wrongdoing, Grace could feel the colour pouring into her face. 'I'll think about it.'

Grace crossed the hall, wondering how she could have been foolish enough to believe Sean thought of anyone but himself. All she'd succeeded in doing was making herself look equally avaricious, to a man who probably regarded both of them with contempt.

Jack's eyes were drawn to the unconsciously sensuous sway of Grace's hips as she headed towards the exit. The low-rise waistband of her jeans exposed a tempting glimpse of very fair skin. And, although he couldn't be absolutely certain, he thought she had a small tattoo etched in the hollow of her spine.

She glanced back once and their eyes met, and Jack felt a momentary twinge of guilt. He had no right to be staring at the girl, no right to be thinking thoughts about her he'd believed he'd never have again.

But, no matter what restrictions he might put upon his conscience, he couldn't deny she was a very sexy lady…

* * *

Grace left the Bay Horse with a feeling of relief.

It was good to be home; good to be staying with her parents again. But it had been an extremely frustrating day.

In her room at the pub, the noise from the bar had been penetrating. She wasn't used to the social atmosphere of the Bay Horse these days. And even with the television playing, she could still hear the rumble of men's voices, the shouts of laughter, the sound of car doors slamming in the parking area outside.

And because of this, she intended to find herself other lodgings. Her parents would be disappointed, no doubt, but she was used to living on her own.

Besides, getting herself a small apartment would prove to her parents that she was serious about leaving London. It might also help to get Sean Nesbitt off her back.

It was a pleasant evening, and she'd decided to take a walk. Her mother was resting. Since her bout with breast cancer and the subsequent course of chemotherapy, Mrs Spencer was easily tired and rested often. Evidently the sounds of the pub didn't trouble her.

Grace chose to walk down to the harbour. She hadn't visited the quayside since her return and it used to be a favourite haunt of hers. She was hoping it might help to put the problems of the day into perspective.

She'd wasted the morning at an old vicarage not far from Rothburn, waiting for a client who hadn't shown.

Then, in the afternoon, she'd had to fend off the advances of a property developer.

William Grafton, who was in his late forties, had expressed an interest in some dilapidated cottages that were for sale on the coast. It was an isolated spot, but he'd said he thought they might be suitable for conversion to holiday lets. The area was a Mecca for birdwatchers and other naturalists, and accommodation was limited.

Now, however, Grace wondered if that had only been a

ploy. He'd come into the agency to see her boss, but as soon as he'd recognised Grace he'd switched his attention to her.

She shook her head. Had he really thought she might be interested in him? A married man, moreover, who was old enough to be her father?

Grace had found herself wondering if she was cut out to be an estate agent, after all. Maybe she should try to find a job in a library or doing research. Something that tested her academic rather than her people skills.

Pulling the hairband out of her hair, she tipped back her head to allow the mass of red-gold curls to tumble about her shoulders.

Gosh, that felt good. Even the headache that had been probing at her temples for the past hour was eased by the removal of the confining band.

She hadn't realised it before, but she was still tense from having to deal with William Grafton. The man was a menace, she thought, irritably. Mr Hughes could speak to him next time he came into the agency.

The trouble was he was also a friend of her father's. And a patron of the Bay Horse. And as he was a client of the agency, she had to avoid offending him on three counts.

Leaving the forecourt of the pub, she started down the hill towards the seafront. Rothburn now had a thriving marina, catering to all kinds of leisure craft.

Was this where Jack Connolly kept his boat?

The thought came out of nowhere and she hurriedly flicked it away. She'd reached the quayside now, and she refused to let thoughts of Jack Connolly spoil the evening for her.

The area wasn't busy. The fishing quay was littered with lobster pots and wooden boxes, evidence of the sale that had been held there earlier in the day. But there were few people about.

The marina itself was separated from the working side of the operation by a stone pier. It ran out to a small lighthouse that marked the entrance to the harbour. Rows of slips provided mooring for a surprising number of vessels; small yachts and sailing dinghies rubbing shoulders with larger, ocean-going, craft.

Grace had always liked the idea of sailing. When she was younger, she used to tell her father she was going to be a fisherman herself when she grew up.

Until he'd taken her out on one of the small trawlers and the swell had made her sick.

She half smiled at the memory and exchanged a greeting with an old man sitting on one of the capstans, smoking his pipe. She'd known the man since she was a toddler, she realised. That was the thing about Rothburn: everybody knew who you were.

Resting her arms on the railings that ran along one side of the pier, she scanned the boats moored in the slips with more than a casual eye.

She refused to acknowledge she was curious about the kind of boat a man like Jack Connolly might own. Probably the most expensive, she thought ruefully. Like that gleaming cruiser, with at least three decks.

'Looking for something?'

CHAPTER THREE

GRACE STARTED ALMOST GUILTILY.

Despite the quietness of her surroundings, she hadn't
heard anyone's approach and, glancing down, she could see
why. He was wearing canvas boots, their rubber soles almost
silent on the stone jetty.

Taking a deep breath, she turned.

'Mr Connolly,' she said politely. 'How nice to see you
again.'

'Is it?'

Jack regarded her from between narrowed lids, wondering why he'd chosen to speak to her at all. Not ten days ago,
he'd been hoping he'd never have to see her or her boyfriend
again.

Grace lifted slim shoulders. She was still wearing the
cream shell and navy suit she'd worn for work and, compared to his short-sleeved tee and black jeans, she felt ri-
diculously overdressed.

'I...was just on my way home,' she lied and saw the way
his mobile mouth turned down.

Clearly, he didn't believe her, but she couldn't help that.
She had no reason to care what he thought of her. But she
couldn't deny that she was powerfully aware of him as a
man.

Still, for the present, she had to pretend that she and Sean
were still together. She'd been in danger of denying that fact
when she was at Jack's house.

'A pity,' he remarked now, taking up a position similar to
the one she had adopted. Lean muscled arms rested on the
rail only inches from the hand she'd been using to support
herself. 'I thought maybe you were looking for the *Osprey*.'

'The *Osprey*?'

Trying to ignore the fact that his soft Irish accent stroked like velvet over her skin, Grace managed to sound amazingly bewildered. So much so that Jack turned his head sideways to look at her.

'Yeah, the *Osprey*,' he said. 'My boat.'

'Oh—' Grace moistened her lips. For some reason she was feeling a little breathless and tried to hide it. 'Of—of course.' Did she sound convincing? 'I'd forgotten you had a boat.'

Jack made a sound that was half groan, half laugh. 'Yeah, right,' he said, and suddenly she resented his mockery.

'Yes,' she declared tightly. 'Or do you imagine I came here looking for your boat? Perhaps you even think I was hoping to see you.'

'Hey...' He sounded almost amused now. 'What did I say? I just thought—'

'Yes, I know what you thought, Mr Connolly,' retorted Grace hotly. 'I've met men like you before.'

'I'll bet.' Jack straightened, his own expression sobering. 'I was being polite, that's all. Forget it.' He straightened. 'See you around.'

He turned to stride away along the pier and instantly Grace felt ashamed.

It was evidently her day for annoying people, she thought resignedly, and Jack had every right to be annoyed with her.

For heaven's sake, what had he said? It wasn't his fault that the man had a talent for getting under her skin.

'Mr Conn—I mean, Jack!'

Cursing her high-heeled pumps, Grace hurried after him. The stonework was uneven in places and she'd ricked her ankle at least twice before he stopped and looked back.

Immediately, Grace slowed to a walk, supremely self-conscious as she approached him. He didn't say anything. His lean dark face was closed; enigmatic. And so incredibly sensual, she half regretted giving him a second chance.

'Um—I just wanted to say I'm sorry,' she said, trying to

sound cool and confident. 'It's been a long day. I'm afraid you took the brunt.'

Jack surveyed her silently. Like her, he was conscious of the fact that there was more going on here than a simple apology. He guessed she felt obliged to be civil to him because of Sean Nesbitt. If only she knew.

For his part, he was far too aware of the full breasts rising and falling rapidly beneath her silk top. The top was less revealing than the tee shirt had been, but no less sexy.

She was wearing a short-skirted suit, too, that exposed more of those long, spectacular legs. Were her legs bare? He thought so. And the notion of running his hands up them and under her skirt was as unwelcome as his reaction.

As she drew nearer the fragrance of her perfume drifted to him. It was light, flowery, with just an underlying trace of musk. No doubt her sudden exertion was responsible for the wave of heat that was rising up her throat and into her cheeks.

'It's okay,' he said, when she stopped beside him, managing to sound relaxed even though he was far from it. 'I've had days like that.' He paused, and then, because something more was required, 'How's the job?'

'All right.' Grace shrugged. 'I guess.'

The pause was significant.

'You only guess?'

His dark brows ascended and Grace pulled a wry face. 'Working in Alnwick is great, but I'm not sure if I'm cut out to be an estate agent,' she admitted. 'I'm not a saleswoman.'

Jack pushed his thumbs into the back waistband of his jeans and regarded her sympathetically. 'You haven't been doing it for very long,' he said. 'How do you know?'

Grace sighed. 'This is my second week.'

'So give it more time.'

'I suppose I'll have to.'

Jack thought he sounded amazingly reasonable in the circumstances. But, since Lisa had died, he'd considered himself immune from the opposite sex. And he had been until this girl came into his orbit. He didn't like feeling unsure of himself, but he was.

The urge to tuck a strand of silky red-gold hair behind her ear was almost irresistible. He wanted to touch her, to feel the satin-smooth skin beneath his fingers.

His muscles tightened automatically in anticipation, but somehow he reined his feelings in.

She was waiting for him to go on, so he said deliberately, 'What does Sean think?'

'Oh, Sean...'

If Jack hadn't been so sure he was attributing her with feelings she didn't have, he'd have said she sounded fed up.

'Sean doesn't know,' she said at last. 'I haven't discussed it with him.' And nor would she. She took a breath. 'Yet.'

Jack nodded, and she wondered what he was thinking. Despite this conversation, she didn't think he had a lot of respect for her or for Sean.

Well, that was okay, she decided. She'd had it with attractive Irishmen. With any man, for that matter. And just because Connolly was being sympathetic didn't mean she should trust him, either.

'So what do you plan to do?' he asked now, rocking back on his heels. 'If you left the estate agency, what sort of job would you like?'

'I haven't thought about it.' Which was true. And despite her determination not to get involved with this man, it would be so easy to confide in him.

Her shoulders stiffening, she continued, 'I suppose I'll think about it.' She paused. 'I intend to stay in Rothburn. My mother likes me being nearer at hand. We've always been a close family.'

'You have brothers and sisters?'

'No. I'm an only child.'

'And that's the real reason you want to stay? Because of your mother?'

'What is this? An interrogation?' She moved towards the railings, her fingers curling over the cold metal. Then she sighed. 'I suppose I want to stay here, too.'

O—kay.

Jack gave in to the impulse to go and join her. Where was the harm? he thought, leaning on the rail beside her. The fact that Grace was evidently conscious of his bare arm only inches from her sleeve was a bonus.

Dear God, he was in lust, and that was so not good.

'How is your mother, anyway?'

Jack's voice was a little strained, but he couldn't help it. He'd chosen the words purposely to get his mind off the delights of the slender body almost brushing his sleeve.

It wasn't working, so he added tersely, 'I'm sorry. I should have asked you before.'

'Why?' Wide green eyes turned to look at him. 'You don't know my mother, do you? I asked Dad, and he said that as far as he knew—'

Her voice trailed off in confusion. Oh, God, why had she admitted she'd been asking her father about him? But she had to finish her sentence. 'He—um—he said you'd never been into the pub.'

'I haven't.'

Jack didn't sound perturbed, but Grace was mortified.

'I suppose my enquiry stems from the fact that she's your mother,' he went on reasonably. 'I hope you didn't think I was prying.'

Prying?

Grace swallowed a little convulsively. 'She's—she's much better,' she said. 'Cancer takes some getting over. But thank you for asking.'

Jack shrugged, turning his gaze towards the marina. But he could still see her eyes, open and candid, those words like a mirror to her soul.

Sean was so lucky, he thought, whereas he was being less

than honest with her. And he had no right to be provocative. It couldn't be easy for her and Sean to spend so much time apart.

All the same, he couldn't deny that Grace's mouth was so soft, so generous. A mouth he would very much like to taste...

Not that he ever would, he assured himself grimly. He was celibate, he reminded himself. And he intended to stay that way.

But there was nothing wrong with a little abstract speculation, was there?

Abstract?

Dragging his mind out of the gutter, he forced a polite smile. 'So do you think Sean will like living in Rothburn?' he asked, even though the idea of them setting up home somewhere in the vicinity filled him with dismay.

'Oh...' Grace was grateful to be distracted from her own thoughts. 'Sean likes living in London.' And that was true. She pushed herself away from the rail. 'We'll see.'

Jack turned his back to the barrier, arms spread along the rail where she'd been leaning, hooking one foot onto a lower rung.

He'd been on the verge of saying, *Let me know what he decides*, but it was really nothing to do with him. Besides, hadn't he wanted to avoid Sean in the future? It would be a hell of a lot safer if they both moved away.

'I'd better go.'

Grace was uneasily aware of how disturbing Jack looked lounging against the rail. He was much broader than Sean and, with his arms spread wide, his chest looked strong and muscular.

His stomach was flat, powerful thighs taut against the fabric of his jeans. Jeans that were worn to a much lighter shade in places, places where Grace determined not to look.

Although she did.

She couldn't stop herself. The impressive bulge between

his legs couldn't help but draw her gaze. She felt an unfamiliar shivery sensation in the pit of her stomach.

Which troubled her a lot.

She blew out a breath.

'Goodbye.'

With a nervous lift of her hand, she started back along the pier towards the quayside. But she was intensely conscious of Jack's eyes watching her, of how much less constrained she'd have felt if she hadn't been wearing a skirt.

'Goodbye, Grace.'

The careless farewell drifted after her and she had to steel herself not to turn around and look back.

Jack spent the following weekend half anticipating that Sean would find an excuse to come and visit him again. But, despite his fears, Saturday and Sunday passed without incident.

And he didn't know whether to be glad or sorry.

He knew he wouldn't have objected to seeing Grace again, but it was probably just as well to cool that thought. In any case, he'd spent a goodly portion of both days on his boat, so it was possible he'd missed any visitors. Although knowing Sean, he doubted his temporary absence would have deterred him.

It poured with rain Monday and Tuesday and even Wednesday morning was overcast.

His housekeeper had phoned to say she wouldn't be in that morning. And, unusually, Jack was feeling housebound. With the redecoration complete, and no other restoration project in prospect, he was restless.

Emptying the remains of his coffee into the sink, he left the kitchen and headed upstairs to his bedroom. He'd take the car for a drive, he decided firmly. He felt like driving and there was nothing to keep him here.

'Are you going out?'

Jack was zipping up a pair of khaki pants when Lisa's voice interrupted his thoughts.

He turned to find her slim form balanced on the edge of the windowsill. And he thought how typical it was that she hadn't appeared for over a week, but now that he was planning on going out, she had to interfere.

'Yeah, why not?' He turned to pick up his leather jacket off the bed. 'I've got nothing better to do.'

Lisa sniffed. 'You could get a job.' She paused, pressing a scarlet-tipped nail to her lips. 'You have too much spare time on your hands.'

'And that's my fault, is it?'

Lisa's lips pursed thoughtfully. 'You're going to see that girl, aren't you?'

Jack's jaw dropped. 'I beg your pardon?'

'Don't pretend you don't know who I'm talking about.'

Lisa slipped down off the windowsill and limped on her one high heel across the earth-toned carpet. 'Even so, I doubt if Father Michael would approve.'

Jack's lips twitched with humour now. Father Michael had been the priest who'd married them. He'd also officiated at Lisa's funeral, but he doubted she was referring to that.

'I think Father Michael gave up on me a good time ago,' he remarked at last. 'And I'm sure he'd be the first to suggest I should move on with my life.'

Lisa looked doubtful. 'She's very attractive, I suppose.'

Jack shook his head. 'Do I have to remind you she already has a boyfriend?'

'You mean Sean Nesbitt?'

'That's right. Sean Nesbitt. He's a mate. I'm not about to forget that, am I?'

Lisa pulled a face. 'Really?'

'Hey, I don't tell lies,' retorted Jack, slotting his wallet and his mobile phone into his jacket pockets. 'Which reminds me, you never did tell me where you were going the night you had the accident.'

He didn't get an answer and he didn't really expect one.

It was a question he'd asked many times before. He knew, without even looking again, that Lisa was gone.

The Lexus was still standing on the drive and, dodging the rain, Jack got behind the wheel and started the powerful engine. Then, shoving a CD into the player, he backed the vehicle out onto the road.

So far he'd only seen a small part of the area. Cumbria and the Lake District were only a couple of hours' drive west but, without much hesitation, Jack headed for the A1.

As he drove Jack wondered if he'd intended to visit Alnwick all along or whether Lisa's taunts had piqued his interest. Either way, he refused to concede that he had any anticipation of seeing Grace again.

He was lucky enough to get parked in the town centre.

Despite the lowering clouds, there were plenty of people about, and Jack bought a map of the area before retiring to the nearest coffee shop to study it.

'Looking for somewhere in particular?'

The pretty waitress who'd served him his coffee was standing at his shoulder and Jack looked up at her ruefully, wishing he had an answer for that.

'Not specially,' he replied non-committally. 'I've never been to Alnwick before.'

'Oh, you're a tourist!' The girl evidently thought she had him taped. 'You're from Ireland, aren't you?' She smiled flirtatiously. 'I love your accent.'

'Thanks.' Jack grinned, amused in spite of himself. 'Do you live in Alnwick?'

'Just outside.' She pulled a face. 'It's too expensive to live in town.'

'It is?'

'Oh, God, yes.' She glanced over her shoulder to make sure the proprietor of the café hadn't noticed she was wasting time. 'It's just as well you're not looking for a house.' She dimpled. 'Unless you're a secret millionaire, of course.'

Jack looked down at the map again, not wanting to give

her any ideas. Besides, he reminded himself, he hadn't come here looking for property.

Or estate agents, if it came to that.

'Are you staying in town?'

The girl was persistent and Jack decided he had to nip this in the bud.

'No,' he said neutrally, swallowing the last of his coffee and pulling out his wallet. 'I'm heading north to—' He cast a quick glance at the map. 'To Bamburgh.' He got to his feet. 'I believe there's a castle there, too.'

'Are you interested in castles?'

When Jack started for the counter to pay his bill, she accompanied him, apparently indifferent to the customers still waiting to be served.

Avoiding a direct answer, he said, 'Thanks for your advice.' He accepted his change with an apologetic smile for the cashier, hoping he could get out of the café without offending the waitress hovering behind him.

But to his dismay, she followed him to the door.

'If you need someone to show you around, I'll be finished in an hour,' she offered eagerly. And Jack was just about to break his own rules and blow her off when the door opened and another young woman came in.

'Jack!'

'Grace.'

Jack managed to keep his reaction under control. But he was fairly sure that Grace had immediately regretted the way his name had sprung so effortlessly to her lips.

However, it was the young waitress who looked the most put out.

'Hi, Grace,' she said grudgingly. Then, glancing at Jack, 'Do you two know one another?'

'Um—a little.'

Grace was offhand, and before Jack could say anything in his own defence the waitress spoke again.

'Hey,' she exclaimed disbelievingly. 'Don't tell me this is your boyfriend. I thought his name was Sean.'

In the circumstances, Grace was loath to say anything. She felt hot colour rising up into her face. Of all people to run into—again—it had to be Jack Connolly. And, judging from the other girl's attitude, she wouldn't be averse to him taking an interest in her.

And why should it bother her? thought Grace crossly.

Meanwhile, Jack was feeling significantly peeved. He was all too aware of how the situation must look to Grace and he didn't like it.

'Look, I'm leaving,' he said, uncaring at that moment what either of them thought of him. He nodded to Grace. 'See you around.'

CHAPTER FOUR

GRACE CAME OUT of the café a few minutes later carrying three cups of cappuccino in a paper sack and a bag containing the sugary pastries Mr Hughes was partial to.

She didn't enjoy this part of her job. But being the youngest in the agency, she was expected to do the coffee run. She supposed it was better than having to make it herself, but there were days, like today, when she had other things to think about.

Like explaining to William Grafton why his offer for the cottages at Culworth had been rejected.

She wasn't looking forward to that, either, but Mr Hughes had been adamant that it was her responsibility.

'You have to learn to handle awkward clients, Grace,' he'd told her firmly. 'In an agency like ours, we can't just pick and choose.'

She could have said that handling awkward clients was the least of it. Handling a man who could lose her her job—however undesirable that job might be—was something else.

She glanced about her a little apprehensively as she crossed the street to the agency. But to her relief there was no sign of Jack Connolly waiting outside.

There was a big Lexus parked across the square that she thought might belong to him. But the vehicle was empty. Which was probably just as well.

Probably?

Impatient with herself for even doubting that scenario, she pushed open the door of the agency and stepped inside.

Only to find Jack Connolly standing in the reception area, showing every appearance of being interested in the properties displayed on the walls.

Not that she'd be expected to deal with him, she saw,

with mixed feelings. Standing just beyond Jack was William Grafton, his broad, smug features lighting up when he saw her.

'Grace,' he exclaimed, and Grace was aware that his use of her name had attracted Jack's attention. 'I've been waiting for you. Grant tells me you have some news for me.'

Grace took a deep breath. Then, setting Elizabeth Fleming's coffee on her desk, she did the same with her own before heading for the private office where Grant Hughes worked.

'I won't be a minute, Mr Grafton,' she said, wondering if her day could get any worse.

By the time she'd given Mr Hughes his coffee and doughnuts, Elizabeth Fleming, Mr Hughes's assistant, had left her desk to attend to Jack personally. The two of them were currently huddled cosily beside a free-standing display.

William Grafton, meanwhile, had seated himself in the clients' chair beside her desk.

'Well?' Grafton said as soon as she was seated, and Grace took the opportunity to take a sip of her coffee before getting down to business.

She needed the boost of caffeine, and if Grafton didn't like it, it was just too bad.

'Grant says you've heard from the vendor,' he prompted, when she didn't immediately answer him. 'I hope it's good news.'

Grace sighed. 'I'm afraid not, Mr Grafton. The offer you made has been rejected.' She paused, consulting the papers on her desk, as if she needed confirmation of what she already knew. 'Mrs Naughton wants considerably more than you offered for the properties.'

Grafton snorted, once again drawing Jack's attention.

Despite his apparent absorption in what Mrs Fleming was saying, he was evidently listening to their conversation, too.

'Those cottages are practically dropping to bits,' Grafton exclaimed, his blunt fist coming down hard on Grace's desk, dispelling any other thoughts. 'The old woman knows that. This is just a ploy to get me to offer more.'

He scowled across the desk. 'I want you to get in touch with her again and tell her it's not going to work. She's not dealing with some amateur, you know. When William Grafton wants something, he gets it. You tell her that.'

'Mr Grafton—'

'You heard what I said.'

Rudely, Grafton thrust back his chair, the legs scraping noisily over the wooden floor. Then, after adjusting the collar of his oilskin jacket, he leant forward again.

'You sort this out, Grace, there's a good girl. I'm relying on you.' He tapped his nose with his forefinger. 'No one ever said William Grafton wasn't a generous man. Know what I mean?' He started towards the door. 'Don't let me down.'

Grace could hardly contain her anger. The patronising man! How dared he call her 'a good girl'? And he actually expected her to be flattered because he was giving her his business.

She caught her breath and, as she did so, she was made aware that Jack Connolly must have heard what was said, as well. And how humiliating was that?

All the same, she had to wonder what he was doing here. She didn't believe in coincidence. He must have come here deliberately.

But why?

To see her?

The idea was provocative. And exciting.

But she couldn't let him see how she was feeling. He had a bad enough opinion of her as it was.

She took a generous gulp of her coffee and got to her feet just as Elizabeth Fleming approached her desk.

'Have you a minute, Grace?'

Grace blew out a breath. 'Um—yes. Sure.' She tamped down a feeling of apprehension. 'How can I help?'

Elizabeth gave her a rueful smile. A middle-aged woman,

in her late fifties, she'd been kind to Grace, easing her introduction to the agency and generally being on hand if she was needed.

'Those cottages,' she said in a low voice. 'The ones at Culworth. Are they still for sale?'

Grace blinked. 'You mean the cottages Mr Grafton offered for?'

'I'm afraid so.' Elizabeth pulled a wry face. 'I assume you've told Mr Grafton his offer was declined.'

'Well, yes.' Grace's brows drew together. 'He wants me to speak to Mrs Naughton again.'

'Has he increased his offer?'

'No.'

'I see.' Elizabeth pulled her lower lip between her teeth. 'Well, I'm pretty sure if that's the case Mrs Naughton won't be interested.'

Grace sighed. 'I did try to tell him that.'

'I'm sure you did.' Elizabeth frowned. 'The thing is I've got another client who'd like to view them.'

'To view the cottages?'

Grace's eyes went automatically to Jack, but his face was expressionless.

Not that she was deceived. He had obviously heard what she and Grafton had been talking about. Heavens, she *knew* he had. What on earth was he playing at?

'Yes.' Elizabeth was going on, completely unaware of Grace's agitation. 'But unfortunately I've got the Lawsons coming at twelve o'clock. I don't have time to go out to Culworth this morning, and Mr Connolly wants to see the cottages today.'

Does he?

Grace bit her lip, trying not to let Elizabeth see how uneasy she was.

'So—what?' she asked tightly. 'Do you want me to go?'

'Would you?' Elizabeth looked relieved. 'I'd be really grateful.' She paused. 'I mean, it may come to nothing, but apparently Mr Connolly's an architect and he's looking for development property in the area.' She grimaced. 'I'd love it if you could tell William Grafton that Mrs Naughton has had another offer.'

Grace would love that, too, she admitted wryly. She had few illusions that Jack was serious, but she couldn't let Elizabeth down, so, with a rueful smile, she said, 'Okay. I'll do it.' She turned to pick up her coffee. 'I hope…Mr Connolly… has his own transport.'

As if she didn't know that Jack's Lexus was parked on the square outside.

'Oh, I'm sure he has.'

Elizabeth turned back to speak to her client, and Grace swallowed the remains of her coffee.

Okay, she thought, he wouldn't be the first client she'd had whose intentions might be less than honourable, but she assured herself she could handle it.

And she was probably wrong, anyway.

Feeling eyes upon her, she looked up to find Jack watching her. And chided herself for the sudden frisson of excitement that zinged along her nerves at his cool-eyed stare.

She turned away, but the image of his dark, good-looking face and lean muscled frame stayed with her as she gathered her handbag from the drawer and slipped on her olive-green jacket.

'Mr Connolly has his own car.'

Elizabeth was back at her side, her anxious expression an indication that she wasn't totally unaware of Grace's reluctance to deal with this client.

She moistened her lips. 'Are you all right, Grace?'

'Good. I'm good.' Grace forced a smile. 'Does—does Mr Connolly know the way to Culworth?'

'He says he'll follow you,' said Elizabeth at once. She sighed. 'You know, I would take him myself if it weren't for the Lawsons—'

'I know.' Grace managed to infuse a little more enthusiasm into her voice. 'I'm grateful for your confidence in me. Is Mr Connolly ready to go now?'

'I'm ready.'

Grace had been unaware of Jack's approach, and his low attractive voice caused another shiver to feather her spine.

Elizabeth turned to him with obvious pleasure. 'Miss Spencer will take care of you,' she said, patting Grace's arm encouragingly. 'I'll see you later, right?'

'Right.'

Jack nodded, and Grace was obliged to pick up her handbag and precede him across the room and out of the door.

She waited until they were out of hearing distance and then turned impatiently towards him.

'Just what do you think you're doing?'

Jack's dark brows rose at the obvious accusation in her voice.

'I understood we were going to view a row of run-down cottages at some place called Culworth. Isn't that right?'

Grace sighed. 'Like you're interested in seeing a row of derelict cottages.'

Jack pushed his thumbs into the front pockets of his khakis. 'I am.'

Grace stared at him frustratedly, wishing she didn't have this almost visceral awareness of his masculinity. She struggled to suppress those totally unwelcome feelings and said, 'Why would you be interested in the Culworth cottages? You're not a property developer. It's kind of you to try to help me deal with Mr Grafton, but he's not likely to go away just because someone else has shown an interest.'

'I know that.'

Jack conceded the point, not altogether comfortable with his reasons for getting involved. But when he'd heard Grafton, mouthing off about what he wanted Grace to do, he'd known an immediate urge to thwart the man, any way he could.

'But I am an architect,' he went on mildly. 'With time on

my hands.' He paused. 'It occurred to me that buying another property and developing it—'

'There are *six* cottages,' broke in Grace helplessly, but Jack only lifted his shoulders in a dismissive gesture.

'So? It will be a challenge.'

Grace shook her head. 'You don't mean that.'

'Don't I?' Jack shrugged. 'Forgive me if I think I know my own mind better than you do.'

His words were cooler now, reminding her that she was still an employee of the agency. Whatever her personal feelings might be, Mr Hughes wouldn't be pleased if she inadvertently offended another possible valuable client.

'All right.' Grace pursed her lips. 'I'll get my car.'

Jack's dark eyes assessed her. 'Or we could both go in mine,' he offered evenly, but she just gave him a speaking look.

'I don't think, so,' she said stiffly, looping the strap of her bag over her shoulder. 'I'm parked at the back of the agency. Just give me a couple of minutes to bring my car round.'

Jack made a gesture of assent, wondering seriously why he was doing this. And she was right. This wasn't why he'd come to Alnwick.

Pushing his hands into his jacket pockets, he watched her walk away with a feeling of irritation. He even played with the idea of just getting into his car and driving away, but he knew he wouldn't do that.

For some reason, the rigid cut of her spine and the provocative sway of her hips assaulted his senses. It was crazy, because she was so obviously not interested in him, either as a client, or a friend. And anything else...

But he arrested his thoughts there before they took him places he really didn't want to go. Well, not in the middle of Alnwick High Street, he mused drily as a small red Civic turned the corner at the end of the block and drove towards him.

It was Grace, and, grateful for the distraction, Jack strode across the square and climbed behind the wheel of the Lexus. His eyes met Grace's briefly, and then, with a courteous wave of his hand, he allowed her to lead the way.

They drove north for a couple of miles before turning towards the sea. It appeared at fleeting intervals as the road wound through a series of hidden bends and blind summits to a small hamlet perched on cliffs above a rocky cove.

Culworth.

Jack read the sign without surprise, following the little Civic past a ruined church to where a gravelled area provided a place to park.

Grace pulled in ahead of him and Jack edged the Lexus in behind. Then, switching off the engine, he glanced around.

Their arrival had caused a flurry of black birds to rise out of the crumbling walls of the church and circle excitedly above them.

'Crows!' said Grace, thrusting open her door and getting out just as Jack did the same.

Long legs, corded with muscle, attracted her unwilling eyes. And, as he came towards her, she was uneasily aware of how big he was compared to Sean. Of the casual way he pushed back his hair, of the faint humour tugging at his mouth.

Jack glanced up at the birds. 'Talk about omens,' he said drily. 'Almost scared the hell out of me.'

Grace thought it would take something a lot more frightening than a few birds to scare Jack Connolly, but she let it go.

Instead, adopting her most businesslike tone, she said, 'If you'll follow me, I'll show you where the cottages are situated.'

'Right.'

Jack fell in beside her as she started along a narrow lane that ran beside the church wall. The wind off the sea was funnelled by the wall and the trees facing it.

Meanwhile, for Grace, having Jack Connolly walking beside her was causing a definite rise in her temperature.

Impatient with herself, Grace walked faster than her heels allowed, and almost ricked her ankle in the process.

'You okay?'

Jack had noticed, and Grace sighed.

'Fine,' she said shortly. And then, because she hadn't spoken since they left the cars, 'It's not much further.'

They passed one or two free-standing cottages that obviously still had tenants, and a boarded-up schoolhouse that just as obviously didn't.

The road forked and Grace turned onto the lane that cut across the cliff. Ahead of them, Jack could see what he assumed were the cottages in question. A row of narrow buildings with peeling paintwork and broken windows forming an uneven terrace.

He guessed that the position of the cottages was their main advantage. They had an uninterrupted view of the coastline and the wild and beautiful sea beyond.

Grace glanced up at him as they reached the first of the cottages and said drily, 'Not what you imagined, I expect.'

Jack pulled his hands out of his pockets and pushed back his tousled hair. 'Can we go inside?' he asked, without answering her, and Grace shrugged.

'It will be very dirty,' she said, fumbling in her bag for the set of keys. 'The roofs leak and the rain drives through the broken windows.'

'Yeah, I had guessed that.' Jack regarded her with raised brows. 'Is this your usual way of encouraging a sale?'

Grace had to smile. 'Not usually,' she admitted, brushing past him to open the first gate. It stuck—of course!— but by leaning her weight against it, she managed to get it open. Then she walked swiftly up the path to the front door.

She found the key she wanted without difficulty, but as she opened the door she noticed the damp dirty stain on the jacket of her olive-green suit.

It must have happened when she leant on the gate. She pressed her lips together as she pushed open the door. She should have asked Jack to open the gate. It served her right for behaving like a shrew.

Holding her bag in such a way that it hid the stain, she stepped inside. Straight into a pool of icy water.

And she'd thought the day couldn't get any worse.

Her involuntary shriek of alarm caused Jack to abandon his surveillance of the outside of the cottages. Striding up the path, he stepped into the cottage after her, narrowly avoiding the broken floorboard where the rainwater had gathered.

Of course!

'It's okay.' Grace was already regretting her instinctive outburst. She moved away from the entrance, aware that her black suede pumps were probably ruined. 'I just got a bit of a shock, that's all.'

'What happened?'

Jack was regarding her intently, the concern in his dark eyes clearly visible in the light from the open doorway.

Grace quivered, sure that his sympathy wasn't genuine. And wished she weren't wondering how she would feel if it were.

'Oh—I just stepped in a puddle, that's all,' she said, turning to survey the inside of the cottage.

More peeling paint, wallpaper torn and stained with dampness, a staircase that looked as if it wouldn't take their weight if they tried to use it.

'Are you sure you're all right?'

When she glanced round, Jack was still regarding her with doubtful eyes. And, dear Lord, she felt as if she were drowning in those deep and shadowy depths.

'I—I'm fine,' she assured him quickly, forcing herself to concentrate on the job in hand. 'Um—as you can see, the cottages need a complete renovation.' She managed a tight smile. 'It might be easier to knock them down and start over.'

'Oh, I wouldn't say that.'

Taking his cue from her, Jack made a preliminary examination of the entrance. The walls seemed sound enough, built years ago when breeze blocks weren't in common use. They needed pointing, of course, but if the foundations were solid, that wouldn't be a problem.

'But you have to admit, it's a lot of work,' said Grace, doubtfully. 'Mr Grafton seemed to think there might be rising damp.'

'And he would know,' said Jack wryly, his humour causing Grace to smile again in spite of herself.

'Well, at least he's a proper builder,' she retorted staunchly. 'Not someone only pretending to be interested for reasons of his own.'

'Is that what you think I'm doing?' Jack sucked in a breath. 'Do you think I'm wasting your time?'

'Well, aren't you?'

Grace didn't back down, even though she wanted to.

In an unexpected move, Jack backed up and closed the door, cutting off the chilling breeze off the sea.

Immediately, the light in the hall was narrowed to the broken fanlight above his head. It made the hall seem dark and claustrophobic, and Grace swallowed apprehensively.

'Do you imagine I'm only doing this because of some personal interest I have in you, Grace?'

CHAPTER FIVE

'I— No!'

Grace realised she was in a corner, both metaphorically and physically, and she searched wildly for something to say.

'Um—Mr Grafton has already made an offer for the cottages,' she said valiantly. 'I'm supposed to be contacting the vendor at this moment to try to negotiate a sale.'

'Yeah, I heard.'

Jack moved away from the door and, turning, Grace fairly bolted for the kitchen at the end of the hall.

The cottages were simple affairs, with only a front room and kitchen downstairs, and two bedrooms upstairs. But there was another door opening from the kitchen into a backyard, which offered an escape route should she feel she needed one.

'And do you think Mrs—North, was it?—will eventually accept Mr Grafton's offer?' asked Jack, pausing in the doorway from the hall.

His shoulder was propped against the splintered frame and, despite his dingy surroundings, he managed to look both darkly attractive and dangerous.

And in control.

But she wasn't. And her voice was shriller than it should have been when she said, 'It's Mrs Naughton. And I think the rest is privileged information.'

Jack shrugged, remembering what he'd heard in the agency. Hardly privileged.

'Okay.' He chose not to argue. 'I can live with that. Do you mind if I take a look around?'

He straightened and was instantly aware of her stiffening. She was so tense; so uptight, dammit. What did he expect him to do to her?

He knew what he wanted to do, of course, but that was more privileged information. Nevertheless, he refused to back down at the first obstacle.

'Well, this is the downstairs area?'

It took a minute, but Jack belatedly remembered what he'd asked before his libido took over.

'Downstairs, upstairs, I'd like to see it all,' he said, aware of his own frustration. He regarded her with grudging eyes. 'You do want to sell these properties, don't you?'

Grace straightened her spine. 'Of course I do.'

'You could have fooled me!'

Jack's accent was suddenly disturbingly acute, but Grace couldn't allow herself to be persuaded by its unconscious charm. Starting reluctantly towards him, she said, 'If you'll let me pass, I'll lead the way.'

Grace had never been upstairs before.

William Grafton had taken one look around and decided the insides of the cottages would have to be gutted. It was one of his reasons for reducing his offer; the fact that, according to him, all the inner walls were rotten with damp.

However, despite her reservations, Grace was obliged to behave as if the stairs were sound. If the steps were rickety, and they certainly seemed that way, she had to be the one to find out. Mr Hughes would definitely have something to say if she returned with the news that their newest client had broken his leg.

There'd been a smell of mould downstairs, but it was much worse upstairs. Grace was glad to concentrate on that rather than on the possible thoughts of the man following her.

What was he thinking? she wondered, intensely conscious of the shortness of her skirt. And of the heat that emanated from him, enveloping her in an uneasy combination of shaving lotion and man.

In the first bedroom she discovered why the air upstairs was so much more oppressive. Although the windows had been broken here, too, someone had stuffed a sheet of card-board into the gap. And there were signs of unauthorised occupation in the empty fast-food cartons and chocolate wrappers strewn across the floor.

'Kids,' said Jack dismissively, when Grace gave an ex-clamation of surprise. 'I doubt it's squatters. I think they'd choose something a little more salubrious.'

'You think?' Grace was doubtful. 'I didn't come upstairs with Mr Grafton, so I didn't know about this until now.'

Jack pulled a wry face. 'Hey, I believe you,' he said hu-morously, moving over to the window. He had to step over an old duvet someone had left on the floor to do so. 'I wouldn't want to go upstairs with him myself.'

Grace's lips compressed. 'You think you're so amusing, don't you, Mr Connolly?'

Jack sighed. 'It's not usually such an effort,' he retorted drily. 'Can we make some progress here?'

Grace's expression didn't change. 'Progress towards what exactly?'

'Well, you're not making friends and influencing people,' remarked Jack, as a piece of the windowsill crumbled in his hand. 'For pity's sake, Grace, what have I done to make you treat me like a leper?'

'I'm not treating you like a leper.' Grace was defensive. 'I'm merely trying to do my job.'

'Yeah, right.' Patently he didn't believe her. 'Well, come here and see how dangerous this is. What's left of this win-dow is in danger of falling on someone's head.'

Grace hesitated. 'No one ever comes here.'

'Well, someone does.' Jack indicated the debris on the floor. 'Perhaps you ought to inform your—what was it you called her?—your vendor? I dare say she'd be held respon-sible if somebody sustained a nasty cut or something worse.'

Grace caught her lower lip between her teeth. Then, be-cause it was her job after all, she made her way across the uneven floorboards to where Jack was waiting.

Jack showed her where the frame was crumbling. 'These kids—if it is kids—may be trespassing, but their parents would soon kick up a stink if one of them was badly injured.'

'Yes, that's true.'

Grace believed him. As someone with a law degree, she knew that where children were concerned judges tended to look elsewhere for someone to blame.

Like negligent owners, for example, with no warning signs or danger notices on display.

'I'll tell Mrs Naughton,' she said. 'It's really her responsibility.'

Jack turned to face her and she was immediately aware of how close he was. The heat emanating from his body enveloped her. She couldn't help but be sensitive to his maleness, to the raw sensual magnetism of the man.

Dear God!

She stepped back without thinking, her heel catching in the folds of the duvet lying on the floor behind her. She stumbled and would have fallen on her bottom if Jack hadn't quickly grabbed her flailing arms.

His hands were hard around her narrow biceps, strong hands that caught her and held her without obvious effort on his part.

His swift reaction brought her unceremoniously against him. With her breasts crushed against his chest, she was sure he must be able to feel the pounding of her heart.

It was so unexpected. The whole incident left her breathless. Her hands were trapped between them, one thigh wedged intimately in the junction of his parted legs.

Jack expelled a sharp breath.

Dammit, this was so not meant to happen. Okay, he couldn't have let her fall on her butt. But he'd never intended her to fall into his arms. Or that he wouldn't want to let her go.

Pressed against him as she was, she seemed endearingly

vulnerable. But that was crazy. It was only the shock she'd had that was stopping her from dragging herself away.

Nevertheless, with her curly hair brushing his chin and the faint flowery fragrance of her perfume assaulting his senses, she was utterly feminine. And he suspected the heated scent he could smell was the sudden warmth that skimmed her skin.

His mouth dried as he acknowledged that his racing pulse wasn't just the result of his exertion.

Grace tried to gather her scattered thoughts. Jack's breath was warm as it fanned her cheek and smelled not unpleasantly of coffee.

His body—now why was she thinking about his body?— felt lean and hard and disturbingly hot. When her hands fanned against his midriff, she could feel the heat of his skin through the fabric of his shirt.

And knew she should put some space between them.

She tilted her head and looked up into his dark compelling face and their eyes met.

And clung.

Jack's exclamation was harsh, but unmistakeably passionate. And when his hands tightened on her arms, she felt all the bones in her legs turn to water.

'We—we have to go,' she said, but her voice was thready and barely audible.

Jack nodded. 'Yeah,' he said hoarsely, but then he bent his head and covered her lips with his and she fairly melted against him.

Which was so wrong. But just at that moment it felt so incredibly right.

Jack thought his body might go up in flames. The yielding softness of her mouth beneath his was that devastating.

Her lips were moist, sensuous; igniting a flame inside him that was damn near irresistible. His hands slid down her arms and linked with hers. And it was the most natural thing in the world to wind her hands behind her back and urge her even closer against him.

Grace, meanwhile, could feel her senses slipping. What little resistance she had left was drifting away. And when Jack's tongue parted her lips and thrust hungrily into her mouth, she couldn't prevent her nails from digging urgently into his palms.

She was wearing a lemon silk shell beneath the jacket of her suit, a low-necked item that was so thin Jack could see the lacy curve of her demi-bra through it. He could also see the rounded swells of her breasts rising above it, the swollen nipples pressing against the lace.

Dammit, he wanted to touch her; to touch *them*. To slip his hand up under her top and caress skin that he guessed would be as dewy soft as her mouth.

But that was only part of it, he acknowledged grimly. What he really wanted to do was shove her up against the peeling plaster of this ugly room. To slide that sexy little skirt up her hips and bury the hard-on her hot little body had incited in that wet haven he knew he'd find between her legs.

He blew out a breath.

That wasn't going to happen.

Not in this lifetime; no way.

And the sooner he put a stop to this, the sooner he'd remember who he was; who *she* was.

Sean's girlfriend!

He had to kill these feelings that were so—unwanted?

Right.

With a determination that was enforced by the belief that Grace would blame him for this, Jack reluctantly released her hands and stepped away from her.

Not far, because the window was at his back. But far enough for her to realise what he was doing.

'Like you said,' he declared, his voice a little rough. He cleared his throat before continuing, 'We should go.'

It took a few moments for Grace to get her head round

what was happening. She still felt dazed; disorientated. Half convinced she'd imagined the whole thing.

But as she looked about her she knew it was no illusion. It was real. Jack was real. And the tingling in her lips and—uncomfortably—between her legs brought the whole disturbing scene into sharp focus.

'I— Yes,' she said, her hand going automatically to her hair.

She could feel the knot she'd made that morning had come loose and fiery strands were tumbling about her shoulders.

She probably looked as loose as she felt, she thought painfully, struggling to restore her hair to some semblance of order. But her hands weren't quite steady and the pins refused to stay in place.

'Yes,' she said again, abandoning her efforts in favour of bending to pick up her handbag from the floor. She didn't know exactly when she'd dropped it, but she obviously had, and she imagined it was probably as worse for wear as she was.

She licked her lips, unconsciously provocative in spite of herself. 'I expect you've seen enough.'

Jack wondered if that was a serious comment.

'I think so,' he replied civilly, glad to feel his erection subsiding. Even as his own personal demon reminded him, rather mockingly, that there was a hell of a lot more he'd wanted to see.

They went down the stairs, Jack leading the way this time.

If it was a belated attempt to salvage his self-respect, he had few doubts that it was appreciated. And as soon as Grace had had the time to reconsider the events of the past half hour, he wouldn't get off so lightly.

Perhaps she'd even come to the conclusion that Mr Grafton wasn't so bad, after all.

'Was he interested?'

Elizabeth Fleming was waiting for her when she got back to the agency and Grace managed a tight smile.

'I don't think so,' she said, although in all honesty she had no idea what Jack had thought of the properties.

They'd walked back to their respective transport without speaking, and Grace had been only too happy to get behind the wheel of her car and drive away.

She'd been aware of him following her to the outskirts of town. But then, thankfully, he'd turned off, and she'd been so relieved to see him go that she hadn't considered the questions she might have to face when she got back to the agency.

In fact, as soon as his car had disappeared, she'd found a place to park and restored her hair to some semblance of order. It had been so much simpler to do that without him watching her, although her hands still trembled a little.

Her face hadn't been so easy to deal with. It wasn't difficult to spread a little hydrating make-up, or to add a trace of lip colour to her bare mouth.

But she couldn't disguise all the marks Jack's beard had left on her skin, or hide the swollen fullness of her lips.

'Are you all right?'

Clearly Elizabeth had noticed that she was avoiding her eyes, but there was no way Grace could confide in her. Dear God, she couldn't confide in anybody. And she was so angry with herself for behaving as she had.

Hadn't the experience she'd had with Sean been enough?

'I'm fine,' she said now, heading purposefully for her desk. 'But I've got to get in touch with Mrs Naughton. The window frames in those cottages are downright dangerous.'

'Are they?'

Elizabeth followed her to her desk, evidently waiting for an explanation.

Grace bent to stow her handbag in a drawer before straightening and saying briskly, 'You know the frames are rotten, don't you?'

'Well, I can imagine—' Elizabeth broke off abruptly, gesturing towards Grace's jacket. 'Heavens, how did you do that?'

'Oh—'

Belatedly Grace remembered the stain she'd all but forgotten in her haste to restore other aspects of her appearance.

She smoothed a hand over her lapels. 'It was an accident.' She paused, and then, realising something more was needed, 'The gate stuck. I leant on it and *voila*! Instant ruin!'

'Dear me!' Elizabeth frowned. 'You must get the agency to pay your cleaning bill. If it will clean, of course.'

'I'm sure I can handle it,' averred Grace, not wanting any written reminder of that morning's fiasco.

In actual fact, she was thinking of dropping it into the next charity bag that came through the door. Anything to put the whole humiliating incident behind her.

'I suppose that's why you looked a bit upset when you came back,' remarked Elizabeth sympathetically, and to Grace's relief she turned away.

But then, almost immediately, she turned back again. 'Anyway, what were you saying about the cottage windows?'

'Oh—' Grace had hoped their conversation was over. But with the agency empty of any other clients at this moment, she was obliged to tell the other woman what Jack had said.

'I see.' Elizabeth nodded. 'Yes, that could be a problem. You'd better ring Mrs Naughton and explain.' She grimaced. 'It's just possible it might persuade her to accept Grafton's offer, after all. She's an old woman. The last thing she needs is a potential lawsuit on her hands.'

Grace tended to agree, but the idea that William Grafton might get the cottages was still a tough pill to swallow.

Unfortunately, she was unable to get hold of Mrs Naughton that day. She'd speak to her the following day, even if it meant driving out to Mrs Naughton's house further along the coast. In fact, she thought she would enjoy that.

And it would get her out of the agency, just in case Jack decided to pay them another visit.

CHAPTER SIX

JACK WAS STILL in bed when his doorbell rang.

Muttering an oath, he buried his head under his pillow, trying to shut out the intrusive sound. He wasn't in the mood for visitors, and the uneasy suspicion that it could be Sean, come to seek retribution, wasn't something he wanted to deal with right now.

The doorbell rang again. More aggressively this time. The chimes echoed around the house like the peals of hell and he groaned before flinging back the covers and sliding his legs out of bed.

Then, uncaring that he was stark naked, he went to the window and peered out.

A car was parked at his gate. An unfamiliar car, whose long bonnet and angular lines spoke of another era. It was vintage, there was no doubt about that.

But who did it belong to?

Scowling, he turned back into the bedroom. The jeans he'd worn the night before were lying on a chair at the foot of his bed. Without bothering with any underwear, he pulled them on, snatching up a black tee as he opened the bedroom door.

By the time he'd negotiated the stairs, he was fairly decently dressed. Though his hair was probably sticking up in all directions and his feet were bare.

However, a burly individual, dressed in a double-breasted serge coat, stood on the path outside. The man, who was in his middle sixties, Jack guessed, was also wearing black breeches pushed into knee-high black boots, and for a moment Jack wondered if he'd stepped into an alternative universe.

The man started to introduce himself, but before he could do so an elderly lady emerged from the back of the vehicle.

'It's all right, James,' she said as he hurried to assist her. 'I can manage.' Beady brown eyes sought Jack's face as she brushed down the skirt of her fur-collared coat. 'Wait in the car, will you?'

'Yes, ma'am.'

James was evidently used to taking orders but he waited until his employer had reached the open doorway before getting back behind the wheel of the elderly limousine.

'Mr Connolly, I presume,' the woman said, looking up at Jack. 'I assume you're going to invite me in.'

Jack blew out a breath. 'Mrs Naughton?'

Who else could it be? From what he'd heard, the old lady lived in some style.

'I am.' She lifted artificially dark brows that had been expertly plucked to form a perfect arch. 'Well—may I come in?'

'Oh—yeah, sure.' Jack stepped back automatically, wincing at the chill of the hall floor beneath his feet. 'Come in.' He closed the door and gestured towards the living room. 'Can I get you some coffee?'

'Coffee!' The woman's voice was scornful as she crossed the hall and entered the living room. 'That's all you young people drink, isn't it? Don't you have any tea?'

'Yes, ma'am.' Jack found himself copying James's formality. 'I'll go and put the kettle on.'

Mrs Naughton glanced back at him. 'Don't you have a housekeeper, Mr Connolly?'

'Not today, ma'am.' Jack grimaced, aware that little in the room would escape her notice. 'Make yourself at home.'

In true 'watched pot' fashion, the kettle took for ever to boil. And by the time Jack had made a pot of tea for her and a mug of coffee for himself, fifteen minutes had passed.

He half expected Mrs Naughton to be examining the contents of his cupboards in his absence. But, in fact, she had seated herself in his favourite position by the window, apparently enjoying the view.

Jack set the tray on the low table beside her.

Then, seating himself on the wide windowsill, he said, 'Will you pour or shall I?'

If she was aware of the faint trace of mockery in his voice, she didn't show it.

'I'm not senile,' she said, pulling a face at his excuse for a milk jug. She viewed the milk residing in the small glass vase with a jaundiced eye. 'I trust this is clean.'

'As a whistle,' said Jack drily. 'You'll have to forgive my lack of tableware. I'm still discovering things I'm short of.'

Mrs Naughton snorted. 'And yet you want to take on more responsibilities,' she commented, lifting the teapot and filling her cup. 'Hmm, well, at least you make a decent pot of tea.'

Jack rubbed a hand over the stubble on his jaw. 'Even at nine o'clock in the morning,' he agreed drily.

Jack picked up his mug of coffee and swallowed a mouthful gratefully. Then, holding the cup between his palms, he said, 'So to what do I owe the honour of this visit?'

Mrs Naughton's brows arched again. 'You want to buy the cottages at Culworth, don't you?'

Jack's eyes widened now. 'Well, yes,' he said. Although he hadn't been into the agency again, he had spoken to the manager on the phone. 'But I understood from Mr Hughes that Mr Grafton had improved his offer.'

'He has. Marginally.' Mrs Naughton took a sip of her tea. 'But Grafton thinks he has me over a barrel because the cottages are in danger of collapsing.' She raised her cup again, regarding him shrewdly over the rim. 'I don't like being threatened, Mr Connolly.'

Jack frowned. 'The cottages are not in danger of collapsing,' he exclaimed impatiently. 'The insides need gutting, sure, but the walls seem solid enough.'

'That's what I said,' declared the old lady staunchly. 'I told Grant Hughes I'd had a surveyor take a look at them, and he was of the opinion that they were of no immediate danger to anyone.'

'Well, the window frames are crumbling,' offered Jack honestly.

He had no wish to bolster Grafton's claim, but it sounded as if Mrs Naughton's surveyor was saying what she wanted to hear.

'It looked as if there'd been kids squatting in one of the bedrooms,' he went on ruefully, despising himself for the sudden quickening of his pulse that that memory rekindled. 'The broken glass in the windows is a danger, too. But it shouldn't affect the value of the cottages themselves.'

'My sentiments exactly,' crowed the old lady, setting down her cup and watching Jack with triumphant eyes. 'That's why I've decided to give you the chance to make an offer. I've seen what you've done to this old place and I like the way you work.'

Jack shook his head, pushing all thoughts of Grace aside as he said, 'How did you know I was interested in the cottages?' There was no way Grace would have told her. 'Aren't you employing the agency to handle the sale for you?'

'I am.' Mrs Naughton was unperturbed. 'But Grant Hughes knows which way his bread's buttered, and I've put a lot of work the agency's way in recent years.'

Jack stared at her. 'So?'

'So—I asked him who it was looking around the cottages last week. He tried to put me off by saying that Ms Spencer didn't always consult him before showing a client round a piece of property, but he soon came round when I put a flea in his ear.'

Jack's lips twitched. The old lady was quite a character. But he'd already heard that from Grant Hughes himself.

'Anyway, I understand you were interested in the cottages, before Hughes stuck his oar in,' Mrs Naughton continued unabashed. 'And when I found out it was you, I thought I'd come and see for myself.'

Jack wasn't deceived. 'You'd like to see the house, wouldn't you?' he said flatly. 'Tell me, if you like what you see, do I get what I want?'

'Ah, I suppose that depends what you do want, Mr Connolly,' she replied cheerfully. 'I've checked up on you, you know, and it seems you're not short of a pound or two.'

Jack was amused. 'Do you vet all your prospective buyers?'

'No.' Mrs Naughton got to her feet to look down at him with critical eyes. 'But I'd hazard a guess that your interest was sparked by that foxy little lady who showed you round my property.' She laughed infectiously. 'Oh, yes, I have my spies, Mr Connolly. The church caretaker—who's retired now, of course—saw you pass his cottage. That's how I knew someone had been there.'

Grace heaved a sigh.

She really didn't want to work in the pub that evening. She had a thumping headache, and she'd been looking forward to having an early night.

She refused to accept that her headache had anything to do with the dressing-down she'd received from Mr Hughes that afternoon.

The agency manager had been at pains to tell her that Mrs Naughton had sold the Culworth cottages to Mr Connolly; the same Mr Connolly she'd escorted round the property over a week ago, without first getting permission from him.

To begin with, Grace had questioned his information.

To her knowledge—not to say her relief—Jack hadn't visited the agency again. She'd actually thought he blamed himself for what had happened and was doing her the courtesy of keeping away.

But no.

Mr Hughes had produced paperwork showing that Mr Connolly's legal representative was handling the sale for him. And what was more, he was furious with Grace for allowing it to happen.

'It won't do, you know,' he'd continued, his plump face flushed with irritation.

They'd been in the comparative privacy of his inner office, but Grace had had no doubt Elizabeth—and anyone else who was in the agency at this moment—could hear every word.

'Mr Grafton is a friend, and a long-time client of the agency. I know nothing about this Mr Connolly. Does he live in the area?'

Grace had been tempted to point out that if he studied the paperwork in front of him he could probably answer that question for himself.

'I believe he lives in Rothburn,' she'd told Mr Hughes and seen the way his face had contorted.

'You believe?' he'd said harshly. 'Do you deny that you're the reason Connolly learned about the Culworth cottages in the first place?'

'Yes!' Grace had been indignant. 'Yes, I do.' She'd licked her dry lips. 'I—I didn't mention the cottages to him. He just happened to be in the agency, talking to Elizabeth, and he overheard my conversation with Mr Grafton.'

She would have left it there, but it had been obvious Mr Hughes wasn't satisfied, so she'd continued. 'He's a friend of a friend, as a matter of fact. He and…someone I know were at university together.'

Mr Hughes had frowned. 'And now he just happens to live in this area?'

'Yes.'

The man's nostrils had flared. Clearly he hadn't liked that explanation any better, but, short of calling her a liar, there had been nothing he could do.

'Very well,' he'd said brusquely. 'But you'll have to tell Mr Grafton what's happened. He's your client. I suggest you have a word with him first thing in the morning.'

Which was not an interview Grace was looking forward to. If she knew William Grafton, he'd not like the fact that he'd been outmanoeuvred over the cottages, and he would enjoy making her feel small.

'Grace! Gracie!'

Her father's voice floated up from the bottom of the stairs and Grace knew she couldn't delay any longer.

Swallowing a couple of aspirin with a mouthful of water from the bathroom tap, she surveyed her appearance without enthusiasm.

One of the reasons she was helping out behind the bar was because Rosie Phillips, her father's regular barmaid, had had to go to Newcastle to visit her ex-husband's mother, who was in the hospital there.

Still, she thought ruefully, as her headache began to recede, she might need this job if Mr Hughes decided to get rid of her.

She'd rifled her wardrobe for something appropriate to wear. But now the flimsy voile shirt worn over a jade-green vest looked rather showy for serving behind a bar.

Oh, well, she thought as her father shouted again, nothing ventured, nothing gained. Slipping her feet into wedges, she left the room and clattered down the stairs.

It was only seven o'clock and the bar was still fairly quiet. But there were glasses to dry and cases of soft drinks to stack behind the counter, and she was soon glad she hadn't worn something warmer. It might be a cool evening outside, but she was sweating.

She wasn't used to manual labour, she thought, recalling her life in London without regret. Maybe she could take up running again, now that she was living in Rothburn. For the past few years she'd had to content herself with an occasional trip to the gym.

The public bar got busier, and food orders started coming in, which meant that Grace had to divide her time between serving alcohol and delivering food, and her arms were soon aching. But at least her headache had virtually disappeared, which was a blessing.

She was carrying two plates of food through to the lounge bar when the swing doors that separated the outer and inner lobbies were pushed open.

A man came into the hall, his identity briefly disguised by the daylight streaming in behind him. A big man, tall and broad shouldered, who Grace had no difficulty in recognising as Jack Connolly.

He said he'd never visited the pub, she reminded herself, remembering Sean's comment about it being a small world with some annoyance.

Why had she remembered that? she wondered uneasily. It wasn't as if their conversation had been particularly memorable.

Unlike—

But she would not go there.

'Hi.'

Jack felt obliged to make the first overture. Though in all honesty, he was wondering if this had been such a bright idea.

Why had he felt the need to come and see Grace? Okay, the last time they'd been together, he hadn't exactly behaved honourably. And maybe he did owe her an apology for jumping on her as he had.

But, dammit, she hadn't exactly repulsed him. Someone should have told her that opening her mouth and tangling her tongue with his was not the way to turn him off.

'Hi,' Grace responded now, her voice slightly husky and unknowingly sensual to his ears. She nodded at the plates she was carrying. 'If you'll excuse me…'

'Wait!' Jack didn't know how else to say it. 'I'd like to talk to you.' He glanced about him. 'And I didn't know how else to get in touch with you out of office hours.'

'I don't think we have anything to talk about, Mr Connolly,' Grace murmured, using her back to push open the lounge bar door. 'Goodbye.'

Jack watched her disappear into the adjoining room with

a feeling of frustration. He hadn't expected her to be pleased to see him, but did she have to be so damn offhand?

He scowled. The trouble was he hadn't been able to put what had happened out of his mind. He hadn't been able to think seriously about anything—or anyone—else since that morning at the cottage.

But that wasn't the only reason he was here, he reminded himself.

Getting that visit from Mrs Naughton a few days ago had definitely put him on the spot.

Of course, if he hadn't expected any comeback from the impulsive enquiry he'd had his solicitor make for him, he was naïve as well as stupid.

But he'd convinced himself that he had every right to make a bid for the cottages. The idea of developing them, of using his skill and expertise to create a handful of desirable dwellings, had struck him as eminently sensible.

He needed something to do. Being a gentleman of leisure didn't really suit him. Okay, so he had no intention of getting his own hands dirty, but there was no reason why he shouldn't re-employ the tradesmen who'd made such a success of his house.

He pushed his thumbs into the front pockets of his jeans and considered his options. He could go into the bar and buy a drink and trust she was working there, too.

Or he could just stay here and trust that there wasn't another exit from the lounge bar.

Apparently there wasn't.

Only a couple of minutes had elapsed before the door opened again and Grace reappeared.

She didn't seem surprised to find him still there, but there was no trace of welcome in her expression, either.

Which was a pity, he reflected, because she looked pretty good otherwise. Apart from that first occasion at his house, he hadn't seen her in casual clothes. But the loose-fitting top over low-rise jeans really accentuated her shape and her femininity.

She would have walked past him, probably without saying anything, if Jack hadn't raised his hand to detain her.

But her response was predictable.

'Oh, please,' she said, making sure she remained well out of his reach. 'Isn't this getting rather old?' She sighed. 'Okay, perhaps I gave you the wrong impression that day at Culworth. But it was only a kiss, for goodness' sake!'

'I'm glad you see it that way.' Jack was unaccountably peeved, but he wasn't going to tell her that. He took a breath. 'If you must know, I came to apologise.'

'To apologise?'

Grace's voice squeaked and she silently berated herself for her inability to hide her feelings.

But, dammit, it was the last thing she'd expected him to say and she was momentarily robbed of speech.

'Yeah.' Jack rocked back on the heels of his boots. 'I know you hoped I'd given up on those cottages—'

Cottages? *Cottages?*

Grace blinked.

'—but I really think I can do some good with them.'

Grace's eyes widened.

How stupid could she be? He wasn't apologising for *kissing* her, for pity's sake. And, God, if she was honest, she'd admit that it had been so much more than a kiss. He was talking about the damn Culworth cottages.

She didn't speak and with a rueful little shrug Jack went on.

'I didn't honestly expect I'd get the opportunity to develop them. Not when Hughes told me Grafton had increased his offer. But Mrs Naughton said—'

That was too much.

'You contacted Mrs Naughton?' Grace exclaimed incredulously.

Oh, this just kept getting better and better. He'd actually

gone behind Mr Hughes's back and spoken to Mrs Naughton personally. No wonder her boss had been so mad.

'No.' Jack blew out an aggravated breath. He knew exactly what she was thinking. 'She came to see me.'

Grace's jaw dropped. 'Mrs Naughton went to your house?' She put an unknowingly protective hand to her throat. 'I don't believe you.'

Yeah, he'd gathered that, and Jack was getting pretty annoyed by her attitude.

For God's sake, what was it with this woman? Why did she persist in behaving as if he'd done something wrong?

Because whatever she says, you took advantage of her, his subconscious reminded him mildly, but he refused to listen.

'Well, whether you believe it or not, it's the truth,' he told her in a dangerously bland tone. 'People do come to my house, you know.' He paused. 'You did.'

Grace's lips tightened. 'How did she know where you lived?'

'I'm notorious.' Jack's tone was flat. 'I thought you knew that.'

Grace's face suffused with colour.

Once again, her feelings had betrayed her. And it didn't help that she knew her overreaction had more to do with her own unwilling awareness of the man than with any legitimate grievance she might have over the cottages.

'I have to go,' she said, aware that she'd said that before, too.

But she had spent considerably longer than she should have done arguing with Jack, when her father was working, single-handed, behind the bar.

'Okay.'

Jack lifted his shoulders in a dismissive gesture, and she wished she weren't so hung up on the lean male strength of his body.

But in tight jeans that moulded every muscle and a plum-coloured tee with buttons that were open at his throat, he was undeniably good to look at.

And she was looking, she realised, hurriedly pulling her eyes away.

But he'd noticed.

'Don't beat yourself up,' he said, his voice low and disturbingly attractive. 'You can tell Sean it was all my fault, and if he wants to beat me up—'

Grace gasped. 'Sean doesn't beat people up,' she said tersely.

Particularly not if he thought he'd get the worst of it.

'Doesn't he?' Jack's reaction was enigmatic. 'No? Well, perhaps he should.'

Would that have made you feel better? Grace wondered, annoyed because she knew what had happened had been as much her fault as Jack's.

'He's not an animal,' she said primly, ignoring her conscience. 'I assume you're saying that if Lisa had been unfaithful, that's what you'd have done.'

'Unfaithful!'

Jack was incensed by her attitude. And by her ability to catch him on the raw. The truth was, he hadn't even thought of Lisa when he'd been kissing Grace.

And that was the most infuriating thing of all.

Whatever he might have said next was baulked, however. The swing doors behind him opened and two men came into the lobby.

They were strangers to Grace, but she could tell from the glances that passed between them that they thought they were interrupting a private conversation.

Or a lovers' meeting, she thought uneasily as the two men shouldered their way into the bar.

'I really have to go,' she said again, aware that in some subtle way the situation had changed.

'Be my guest.'

Jack pushed his hands into the back pockets of his jeans, making no further attempt to detain her.

Perhaps because he was tempted to do just that, he thought irritably as she put her hand on the door the two men had just passed through.

Grace hesitated then. She was prone to do that, he'd noticed.

'You—you're not staying for a drink?'

Jack gave her a speaking look. 'You're surprised?'

'Well—it's a public bar,' she muttered defensively. 'I can't stop you.'

'No.' Jack acknowledged the admission, his eyes dark and impenetrable behind the fringe of his lashes. 'But you don't want me here. And I do have some feelings, you know.'

'And if I said I don't mind what you do?'

'I'd say that was pretty obvious,' retorted Jack drily. 'Thanks for the offer, Grace, but no, thanks.'

'Grace!'

Grace recoiled as the door to the bar was propelled open in spite of her resistance.

'Dad!' she exclaimed, half in dismay, half in protest. 'You nearly knocked me over.'

Mr Spencer didn't immediately say anything.

But his eyes moved instinctively towards her companion.

And Jack, who hadn't had the chance to make his escape, thought that, judging by the older man's expression, he and Grace must look as guilty as he felt.

CHAPTER SEVEN

'IS SOMETHING WRONG, GRACE?'

Mr Spencer's tone was more curious than unfriendly and Jack watched the way Grace's tongue moved over her parted lips.

But for once the provocation that evoked was overwhelmed by his need to explain who he was.

'I'm Jack Connolly, Mr Spencer,' he said. 'I was just telling Grace about an offer I've made on some property the agency was dealing with.'

He grinned, and Grace despised herself for thinking how disarming—and disreputable, she reminded herself—he could be.

'I'm sure she was bored silly,' Jack was going on charmingly. 'And I should have known better than to expect her to discuss business matters out of office hours.'

'Well, Grace is working for me at the moment,' Mr Spencer remarked drily.

He turned to his daughter. 'Will's got at least four meals waiting for you to serve.'

'I'll get to it.'

Grace forced a half-rueful smile in Jack's direction before heading into the bar. She thought her father forgot sometimes that she wasn't the schoolgirl she'd been before she left for university. But he'd always been keen to vet any boyfriend she'd brought to the pub.

Not that Jack Connolly was a boyfriend, she reminded herself impatiently. And her father hadn't shown any more sense than she had where Sean Nesbitt was concerned.

Left alone, the two men eyed one another with enforced politeness.

'I'm afraid my daughter doesn't really care for working

in the bar,' Mr Spencer declared pleasantly, more relaxed now that his customers' needs were being seen to. 'I'm Tom Spencer, Grace's father, of course. Have we met?'

'I'm afraid not. I only moved into the village about eighteen months ago,' explained Jack at once. 'I've been renovating that old property on the coast road.'

'Really?'

Despite his words, Jack had the feeling Tom Spencer had known who he was all along.

'You know my daughter's boyfriend, I believe.'

'That's right.'

'Sean.' Tom Spencer nodded. 'He's a good chap, Sean. My wife and I are very fond of him.'

Just in case you have any doubts about that, thought Jack drily.

'Anyway, how is the renovation going, Mr Connolly?'

'Jack,' said Jack politely. 'I finished a couple of months ago. Lindisfarne House has been quite an undertaking.' He wasn't quite sure where this was going. 'But I enjoyed it.'

'I'm sure.'

Tom Spencer considered for a moment and then he gestured towards the bar.

'You must come in and let me buy you a drink,' he said after a moment. 'We always welcome newcomers into the pub.'

'Oh, I don't think—'

Jack started to protest but Tom Spencer was adamant.

'It's the least I can do after interrupting your conversation with Grace.' He pushed open the door of the bar and stood back invitingly. 'I'm interested to hear about this new property you're hoping to buy.'

Ah! Jack was cynical. He had the feeling Spencer didn't want to encourage his association with his daughter, but he was not above hearing a little gossip himself.

But it would have been rude to refuse. So with a slight

shrug of his shoulders, he preceded the man into the warm alcohol-laden atmosphere of the bar.

There was no sign of Grace. She had obviously gone to collect the meals waiting to be delivered. And sure enough, she emerged through a swing door a few moments later carrying a tray on which resided four plates of food.

The only sign that she was surprised to see Jack was the way her eyes widened before darting curiously towards her father.

She was probably wondering what they'd been talking about, Jack reflected half irritably. Did she honestly think her father would be making nice with him if he'd told him about their visit to Culworth?

At Tom Spencer's suggestion, he took a seat at the bar and ordered a pint of beer. He would have preferred a bottle, but the beer when it came was good; rich and creamy, its head smearing his upper lip with foam.

However, before her father could start asking him about the property he was interested in and what he planned to do with it, Grace was back.

She slipped behind the bar, successfully manoeuvring Tom Spencer into a position where he was obliged to serve a waiting customer. Then she snatched up a cloth to wipe the bar in front of Jack.

'You changed your mind,' she said, and Jack couldn't tell whether she was glad or sorry. She glanced sideways at her father. 'I hope Dad's not been giving you a hard time.'

'I can handle it.' Jack took another mouthful of his beer and wiped his mouth on the back of his hand. 'How about you?'

'What about me?'

Grace looked up at him in alarm, and Jack was struck once again by the clear transparency of those green eyes. He wanted to reach out, to cup her anxious face in his hands and smooth the darkness beneath her eyes with his thumbs.

There was a pulse beating urgently in her temple and he

knew he'd find a matching palpitation beneath her ear. Silky strands of red-gold hair had escaped from the knot on top of her head, and he wanted to sweep them aside and taste the slight dampness of her skin with his tongue.

And knew he couldn't answer her question.

Not without betraying feelings he had no desire to put on display. He shouldn't have come here; he shouldn't have accepted her father's invitation.

But, most of all, he so shouldn't have sampled something that was proving to be so damned addictive.

He took another generous swallow of his drink and put his almost-empty glass down on the bar.

Grace glanced at it and then said impulsively, 'Let me get you another beer.'

"No, one's enough,' he assured her easily. 'It was good. Thank your dad for me, won't you?'

'You're leaving?'

'Isn't that what you want?'

Grace blew out a breath.

It had been. It should still be, she knew. Because whatever attraction Jack Connolly might have for her, it was just a fleeting thing.

He must have loved his wife once, and, although it might be too late to regard his behaviour towards her as a rebound, he wasn't seriously interested in her, either.

Nor she in him.

'I—I was going to ask you what Mrs Naughton had said,' she lied, having just thought of that on the spur of the moment. 'What did you think of her? She's quite a character, isn't she?'

'Quite a character,' agreed Jack drily. 'Do you know her?'

'Only slightly.' Grace took a moment to serve another customer and then came back. 'It was me who handled her initial inquiry about selling the cottages.'

'Yeah, I guessed that. To Grafton.'

Grace grimaced. 'I have to tell him the cottages have been sold to someone else tomorrow. He's not going to be pleased.'

And wasn't that an understatement?

Jack frowned. 'Would you like me to do it for you?'

It was certainly a temptation, but Grace shook her head. 'It's my job. Mr Hughes was very definite about that.'

'Hughes? Oh, he's the guy in the agency.'

'My boss, in other words.'

Grace gave him a mischievous grin. Really, she thought, she enjoyed talking to Jack when there were no sexual undercurrents in his conversation. Although, if she was honest, she would admit she didn't exactly dislike them, either.

He was different from Sean. For one thing, his eyes weren't constantly moving round the bar, checking out the other talent. He actually seemed interested in what she was saying, and she wished desperately that Sean's problems weren't still ruling her life.

She moved to attend another customer and when she came back, Jack slid off his stool. 'Hey, I can see you're busy,' he said, wondering if it was only his imagination that made him think the atmosphere between them had changed. 'Don't forget to thank your father for the beer.' He stepped away, uneasily aware that he had forgotten all about Sean for the past half hour. And that wouldn't do. 'Goodnight, Grace.'

Grace knew that her farewell was less than enthusiastic. Dear God, she hadn't wanted him to go. But she was obliged to serve a man who'd come to refill an order and by the time that was done, Jack was long gone.

Almost at once, her father came to join her. 'Mr Connolly's left?' he remarked inquiringly. 'What was he saying to you?'

'This and that.' Grace wasn't in the mood to be tactful. 'We were talking about the cottages. What else?'

'I'm only curious. You seemed very…friendly.'

'Oh, Dad!'

'Does Sean know him well? I'd have my suspicions about him, if I was your boyfriend.'

'Sean's not my boyfriend any more, Dad!' She sighed. Why had she said that?

'I know he still cares about you,' retorted her father impatiently. 'All young couples have rows. But they get over them.'

'Maybe.' If only there was some way she could get her parents' money back. Then she wouldn't have to pretend any longer. 'In any case, Jack Connolly is not interested in me.'

'You don't think so?'

'He's a client, Dad. I may be helping you out here, but the agency is my job.'

Tom Spencer frowned. 'He's your client? You're the one who's dealing with his offer?'

'Well, no.' Grace was already regretting saying as much as she had. Any minute now, her father was going to remind her that William Grafton was a friend. 'But—I did show him the property last week.'

'Hmm.' Her father didn't sound too happy. 'So, you'll know what he plans to do with the property?'

'Yes.'

'Well, go on.'

'Dad, I hardly know Jack Connolly. I believe he's an architect. He probably plans to develop the cottages in much the same way as Mr Grafton.'

'So how come he got the cottages? Wasn't Will first in line?'

'Will? Oh, you mean Mr Grafton. Well, he was, but Mrs Naughton decided she preferred Mr Connolly's offer. It's not my fault. She can sell them to whoever she likes!'

It was getting dark by the time Jack got back to Lindisfarne House. And, when he opened the door and stepped into the hall, he knew instantly he wasn't alone.

When he switched on the lights, he saw Lisa sitting halfway up the stairs, legs crossed, her single sandal balanced precariously on one swinging foot, her silver cap of hair gleaming ethereally in the glow from the chandelier above her head. 'I thought you never went into public houses.'

'Never is a long time,' retorted Jack shortly, and, without waiting for her response, he strode purposefully into the kitchen.

He'd had no dinner, but he wasn't hungry. Nevertheless, he filled the coffee filter and switched it on. He felt aggressive and not a little edgy. And it wasn't Lisa's appearance that was steering his mood.

'There's a casserole in the fridge.' Lisa had come to stand in the open doorway. 'Mrs Honeyman brought it with her this morning.'

Mrs Honeyman was the housekeeper. And, because she worried that he wasn't eating properly on his own, she often left some tasty dish she'd made herself in his fridge.

Jack grunted, but he merely reached for a mug and slammed it down onto the granite counter.

He felt like warning Lisa that he wasn't in the mood for small talk. But he knew from past experience she'd only go when she'd said what she had to say.

'What's got you in such a foul mood?' she persisted, and Jack regarded her with baleful eyes.

'Not your business,' he said tersely. 'And unless you're looking for a fight, I suggest you stay out of my way.'

'Ooh!' Lisa's thin brows rose in mock alarm. 'I'm scared.'

Jack didn't answer her. He was seriously peeved and talking to a ghost simply wasn't going to cut it.

'I gather you've had another run-in with the delicious Ms Spencer.'

Lisa had never known when to keep her mouth shut and Jack gave her a weary look.

'Get lost, Lisa.'

'I was afraid she might be trouble,' she murmured ruefully. 'And I'm not particularly flattered that you can blow me off without a thought.'

'Yeah, right.'

'I mean it.' She was indignant now. 'I've got used to you being on your own.'

Jack scowled. 'Hey, don't look now, but I am on my own,' he stated flatly. 'She has a boyfriend. Remember?'

'Sean Nesbitt!' Lisa spoke scathingly. 'Yeah, well, I shouldn't let that trouble you.'

'What do you mean?'

Jack stared at her, but she was already fading. 'Oh, nothing,' she said, lifting her shoulders in a dismissive gesture.

And just like that, she was gone.

Jack swore his frustration. Pouring himself a mug of strong black coffee, he took a reckless mouthful, almost scalding his mouth in the process.

He was seriously losing it, he thought bitterly. How much longer was he going to go on talking to a ghost? It was just as well he'd found himself an occupation. At least it would get him out of the house.

Three weeks later, he signed the papers that made the Culworth cottages his.

Despite a warning from his surveyor that there could be structural problems down the line, Jack had had the solicitor who'd handled his purchase of Lindisfarne House deal with the legal jargon.

And, in consequence, the sale had gone through without a hitch. Mrs Naughton had been pleased. She'd actually invited Jack to have dinner with her one evening—an invitation he'd not as yet taken her up on.

The agency had been less enthusiastic.

Although Mrs Naughton had paid the agency their commission, on the one occasion Jack had had to go in and see Grant Hughes, he'd been less than impressed.

In his opinion, Grace's boss was an ignorant oaf, whose resentment stemmed more from the fact that she had actually initiated a sale that he'd earmarked for one of his cronies, than from the fact that Mrs Naughton had chosen to interfere in the process.

Jack had wondered if he'd see Grace when he went into the agency. But he hadn't.

Only Mrs Fleming had occupied one of the two desks in the outer office. And although Jack had been tempted to ask where the other girl was, he'd restrained himself.

In fact, he'd come to the conclusion that he was unlikely to see her again. Which was just as well, he told himself.

Then, on Saturday morning, Jack had an unpleasant surprise.

He'd come home after spending the morning out at Culworth with his builder. And once again, he wasn't dressed to receive visitors.

So when he saw the silver Mercedes parked at his gate, his heart sank.

The car was empty, however, and, thrusting open the door of the Lexus, Jack got out and looked around.

There was no one about, and he breathed a sigh of relief, wondering if the Mercedes could conceivably belong to someone else.

Deciding it wasn't his problem, he hauled his jacket out of the back of the Lexus. Then, stepping up to his door, he juggled his keys until he found the right one and inserted it in the lock.

He was looking forward to the shower he'd been promising himself since a wall in one of the cottage bedrooms had collapsed. He and his companion had been covered with brick dust and he could feel it still in the gritty scrape of his scalp.

He couldn't wait to get his clothes off and he was already pulling his sweatshirt over his head as he stepped over the threshold.

'Hey, Jack! Jack, hold up.'

The voice was unmistakeable and Jack fisted the offending sweatshirt even as Sean—and Grace—appeared from around the back of the building.

He was intensely aware that he was sweating. That rivulets of perspiration were moistening the hair between his nipples, and the hair at the nape of his neck.

'We were just admiring your garden,' Sean exclaimed cheerfully, not at all perturbed at being caught out. 'Weren't we, Grace? We guessed—or rather, we hoped—you'd be back for lunch.'

Grace managed a resigned smile of acknowledgement. But her nerves were jumping at the sight of Jack standing, bare-chested, in the doorway.

If she'd thought he'd looked good in a tee shirt, he looked infinitely more disturbing without it. A broad chest, liberally spiked with dark hair, tapered down to a flat stomach, ribbed with muscle.

Faded jeans hung precariously from lean hips and she guessed if they'd been a few minutes later the jeans would have been discarded, as well.

Did he wear underwear? she wondered, feeling her breathing quicken at the images this thought evoked. Probably not, she decided a little grudgingly.

'Well...' Jack stepped back from the door, aware that he was obliged to invite them in. 'Come in.' He gestured towards the living room. 'You know the way. Just give me a minute, will you? I need to freshen up.'

'That you do, old buddy,' said Sean pointedly, touching his nose with a delicate finger, and Grace wanted to slap him.

The scent of Jack's skin got to her, too, but she didn't find it at all offensive. On the contrary, it caused her own skin to prickle with unwanted awareness. And, feeling the sudden dampness between her legs, she was glad she wasn't wearing jeans.

'Okay.' Jack's eyes connected with Grace's for a moment. But his belated, 'Hi, Grace. Nice to see you again,' was in sharp contrast to the heat that was emanating from his body.

It was as if any personal contact between them had been

erased from his memory. And she sucked in a nervous little breath before preceding Sean into the attractive living room they'd seen before.

CHAPTER EIGHT

TOLD YOU, SEAN MOUTHED as soon as they heard Jack vaulting up the stairs. 'I knew he'd be about here somewhere.'

Grace shrugged. 'He could have been over at Culworth. In fact, I think that's where he has been,' Grace averred, eager to keep their conversation impersonal. 'You must have seen the way his hair was coated with grit. It looked as if he'd been working on the cottages himself.'

Which was so not something she wanted to think about.

'Who cares?' Sean spoke carelessly. He dropped down onto a squashy leather sofa and patted the seat beside him. 'Come here. I want to tell you how grateful I am that you agreed to come here with me. It's been ages since you've talked to me. I'm still hoping you might change your mind about staying up here.'

'I'm not just "staying up here", am I, Sean?' Grace exclaimed irritably, making quotation marks with her fingers to emphasise her point. 'And I'm only here because Dad insisted I couldn't let you come on your own.'

In fact, her father was still suspicious about Jack Connolly's visit to the pub to see her. And the last thing she needed was her dad bringing that up in front of Sean.

Nevertheless, she had been taken aback when Sean had walked into the pub the previous evening. It was seven weeks since he'd returned to London, and she'd half hoped he'd got the message as far as she was concerned. It did cross her mind—hopefully—that he might have some good news as far as finding an investor for his website was concerned. Did he ever intend to pay her father back?

But nothing with Sean was that easy.

However, according to what he'd told her father, he had

been busy 'networking'. Grace had no idea how true that was but she'd clutch at any straw in the present situation.

That there'd been no takers was perfectly obvious. And he hadn't been too pleased, either, when Mr Spencer had had to tell him he couldn't stay at the Bay Horse.

A surfing competition was taking place just along the coast and, because they hadn't known he was coming, the pub's two spare rooms had been taken.

Sean had had the sense not to suggest that he share Grace's room. The answer would have been no, of course, and he'd known that. Instead, he'd accepted their suggestion that he stay at a local bed and breakfast down the road.

The trouble was Grace suspected she knew why Sean was here. He'd had no success raising funds in London and she was fairly sure he intended to hit on Jack for a loan.

And while the idea might make her cringe, she couldn't deny the slender hope that Jack might be the way out of her difficulties. She despised herself for even thinking it, but was it possible that Jack's money might save the pub?

Conversely, Jack didn't strike her as the kind of man to be taken in so easily. It was just another website, for goodness' sake. And there were dozens of comparison sites out there already. Sean's idea was not that original. She could only hope and pray that somehow a miracle might happen.

'Come on.' Sean's tone was wheedling now. 'At least pretend we're still a couple. Don't embarrass me in front of Jack.'

Embarrass *him*?

Grace closed her eyes against the images that suddenly assaulted her senses. Was it really better to pretend she supported Sean than to admit she was afraid of her feelings for Jack?

Grace was still thinking about this when Sean got impatiently to his feet.

'Hey, do you think Jack would mind if I helped myself

to a beer?' He was tense and nervy, probably apprehensive about what he was going to say. 'I'm thirsty.'

'You can't go poking around in someone else's kitchen,' Grace protested. She pointed to the window, drawing his attention in that direction. 'Look at that fantastic view! I wonder if the surfing competition has started yet. It might be interesting to watch.'

'Are you kidding me?' Sean was contemptuous. 'If you think I want to waste my time watching a bunch of muscle-heads in wetsuits, trying to stay upright on an ironing board, you're very much mistaken.'

'It wasn't an invitation,' retorted Grace tightly, and then she caught her breath when Jack spoke behind them.

'I think it's a bit more demanding than that,' he remarked, and they both swung round—Grace almost guiltily—to find their host standing in the doorway.

He'd evidently had a swift shower and Grace could see drops of water glistening on his shaggy dark hair. He looked unbearably masculine and so sexy she felt every nerve in her body go on high alert.

In low-waisted khakis that hugged his narrow hips and a black collarless body shirt, he exuded a raw sensual appeal that she'd never experienced before meeting him. And the fact that his body hadn't been completely dry when he'd got dressed meant that the cotton fabrics clung to him in all the most disturbing places.

Thankfully, Sean had his own agenda.

'Jack, my man,' he exclaimed expansively, leaving Grace and turning to Jack. 'We were just admiring your view.'

'Were you?'

Jack's dry comment made Grace almost sure he'd heard every word Sean had said.

'Yeah.' Sean was undaunted. 'So, how are you, Jack? Still living the life of a beachcomber?'

'Don't you mean a beach bum?' suggested Jack, unde-terred, and Sean had the grace to pull a wry face.

'Whatever,' he muttered. He thrust his hands into the back pockets of his chinos and pushed his chest out. 'Anyway, how about offering me a beer? Trailing around your garden is thirsty work.'

'Okay.'

Jack half turned away. Then he looked back, straight at Grace.

'What would you like?'

How to answer that?

Grace felt the treacherous colour rising up her face at the thoughts she couldn't quite keep at bay.

Jack, naked, in her bed, was in there somewhere. As was the compelling prospect of repeating that kiss that had purely blown her mind.

She shivered. How pathetic was that? He could seduce her brain with only a look.

'Um—anything,' she mumbled, aware that Sean was looking at her now.

'So long as it's not beer, eh, Grace?' he said mockingly, and she struggled to find a smile.

Jack's dark brows arched. 'White wine?'

'Fine,' she said. 'That would be nice.'

'I'll come with you.'

Without waiting for an invitation, Sean followed Jack out of the room and Grace sank down rather weakly onto the nearest chair. Right now, it was hard to care what Sean intended. So long as her unwanted attraction to Jack wasn't exposed.

Jack entered his kitchen with Sean behind him.

He was a bit aggrieved at the other man's presumption, but he tamped it down. Remembering the way he'd betrayed their friendship was a rude wake-up call.

Jack pulled open the fridge door, taking out two beers and a bottle of Chardonnay. He handed one of the beers to Sean and then jerked open a drawer, looking for the corkscrew. 'Do you need a glass?'

'Nuh-uh.' Sean borrowed the corkscrew to hook off the cap of his beer, then perched himself on one of the tall stools that faced a central island, surveying the copper pans hanging from the units, the bowls of climbing plants and pots of herbs suspended from the beamed ceiling.

'This is some place,' he said, taking a long drink of his beer. 'I bet it cost a small fortune.'

'Actually, I got it fairly reasonably,' said Jack, despite his dislike of discussing money. 'As Grace's father has probably told you, it was in pretty dire straits when I took it over.'

'Ah, but you didn't do all this,' said Sean, gesturing with his bottle. 'I mean, come on, Jack. You're no do-it-yourselfer, are you?'

'You'd be surprised.' Jack had no intention of telling Sean exactly what he had done during the course of the renovation. 'How about you? Have you found a post in Northumberland, or have you decided to stay in London?'

Sean shrugged. 'As a matter of fact, I haven't been looking. But don't tell Grace that. I'm still hoping to find a backer for my website.' He swallowed the remainder of his beer. 'Got any ideas?'

Jack frowned. 'Do you need a backer to start a website? I'd have thought it was a fairly simple thing to arrange.'

'Not the kind of website I have in mind,' Sean contradicted him shortly. Then he held up his empty bottle. 'You got another one of these?'

'Sure.'

Jack opened the fridge again and handed him another beer. Then he said pointedly, 'Oughtn't we to be getting back to Grace? She'll be wondering where we are.'

'Oh, Grace is okay.' Sean opened his bottle and took another generous swig. 'Man, that really hits the spot.'

Jack said nothing and after a moment, Sean met his gaze.

'Why don't you tell me what you think of her. Grace, I mean.' There was a sly shrewdness to the question. 'You've seen her, haven't you? Since I went back to London.'

Jack kept his reaction securely under control. 'I assume you mean at the agency,' he said neutrally. 'Yes. She showed me the cottages at Culworth.'

'Mmm.' Sean's eyes narrowed. 'So go on. What do you think of her?' His mouth twisted. 'You can tell me.'

Jack could feel a simmering sense of resentment stirring inside him. Where the hell was Sean going with a question like that?

'What do you want me to say?' he asked, restraining his temper with an effort. 'She seems very nice. Very efficient.' The words almost stuck in his throat. 'You're a very lucky man.'

'Yeah, I am, aren't I?' Sean took a moment to enjoy the compliment. 'But she deserves so much more than I can give her.' He grimaced. 'Ever since I lost that job with Sunyata, it's been a struggle to make ends meet.'

Jack suspected that was an exaggeration. Sean's job and the salary Grace had earned as a paralegal would have surely added up to quite a comfortable income.

'Anyway...' Sean wasn't finished '...we all know it's okay for you, Jack. You don't have to go bowing and scraping for every penny you need.'

'Nor do you,' said Jack mildly, but now Sean's jaw jutted aggressively.

'I do, if I want to make anything of myself,' he exclaimed harshly. 'I don't have a wealthy grandmother to help me out.'

Jack sighed. 'I'm sorry you feel like that, Sean,' he said. 'But I haven't had it all my own way.'

Sean's mouth thinned. 'You mean, because of Lisa.'

'Yeah, because of Lisa,' Jack agreed, feeling another twinge of guilt at the realisation that he hadn't thought about his wife in days.

Grace, yes. God help him, he'd thought about her a lot. Because despite his conscious determination to stay well away from her, he couldn't control his subconscious so easily.

Which, let's face it, he thought, was why he was letting Sean Nesbitt pull his strings.

Sean shrugged. 'Lisa was a beautiful woman,' he conceded, though there was little real sympathy in his voice. 'And I know you loved her.' He paused. 'But you have to admit, she was no saint.'

Jack scowled. 'What's that supposed to mean?'

As far as he was aware, Sean had met Lisa only a couple of times; one of them at their wedding. Certainly not enough to pass judgement on her character.

'I'm only saying, it's a couple of years since the accident,' Sean muttered offhandedly. 'And your life has had its compensations, if you know what I mean.'

'Okay.' Jack had had enough of this. 'If you've got something to say, why don't you spit it out?'

Sean hunched his shoulders. 'You always were an arrogant bastard, weren't you?'

'And you know damn well you're only here because you need my help.'

'All right, all right.' Sean pulled a face 'I'll tell you about my idea for a website.' He paused for a moment and then added confidently, 'It's a comparison site. And I know there are lots of them. But this is like nothing you've seen before.'

It was fully half an hour before the two men returned to the living room.

Grace had pulled a sailing magazine off the coffee table and was flicking through the pages in an effort to ignore what she was sure was going on in the other room.

Sean hadn't gone with Jack because he wanted to check out his kitchen. He'd seen an opportunity to speak to him without her obvious disapproval and jumped at it.

Sean's face as he came back into the room mirrored a smug satisfaction. Grace felt her stomach tighten at the realisation that he must have achieved his objective.

But how had he achieved it? Why had Jack succumbed

so easily? Was it because he saw some merit in his website idea? Or because he felt guilty after that torrid embrace in the cottage at Culworth?

She suspected the latter, particularly as Jack's expression was decidedly cynical. It irritated her beyond measure that Sean had put them in such a position and she wished she could just leave him to it.

'White wine?'

Jack was offering her a glass and she was obliged to take it.

But she deliberately avoided his eyes as she did so. Even if she couldn't prevent the little frisson of electricity that shot up her arm when his fingers touched hers.

'Thanks,' she muttered a little ungraciously and felt even worse when Sean came to perch on the arm of her chair.

'Guess what?' he said, and she wondered if he really believed she didn't know exactly what he was going to say.

'What?' she asked dutifully, aware that once again Jack had chosen to remain on his feet, propped against the small bureau at the other side of the room.

He still wasn't wearing any shoes, she noticed out of the corner of her eye. And despised herself for finding the omission unbearably sexy.

But what was new? she asked herself resignedly. Everything about Jack Connolly was sexy, and for some reason her body refused to ignore the fact.

'Jack's agreed to look at my idea,' Sean declared, with a self-satisfied smile. 'I told you he'd be interested. He's like me. He knows a good investment when he sees one.'

Grace had to bite back the words that Jack was nothing like Sean. But that didn't make them any less true, and she felt a weary sense of depression digging at her temples.

Why couldn't Sean have waited until he'd saved enough money for him to speculate on something as risky as this on his own? He'd already almost bankrupted her parents with his lies. And he must know that for every website that succeeded, at least a dozen others failed.

'Well?' Sean knew she resented him sitting on the arm of her chair but he seemed indifferent to her feelings. 'Don't you have anything to say? Aren't you going to congratulate me on being such an astute salesman?'

Grace's lips felt frozen.

She knew she had to say something. But she made the mistake of looking up instead. And the contempt in Jack's brooding countenance was like a chill finger down her spine.

'Um—that's wonderful news,' she managed at last. What else could she say, in the circumstances? And, although it sounded unconvincing to her own ears, Sean evidently only heard what he wanted to hear.

Jack pushed himself up from the bureau and looked away before he said something he'd regret.

But, dammit, it was bad enough having to watch that oaf with Grace without hearing her endorse her boyfriend's sordid little game.

To his relief, Sean seemed to realise he should quit while he was ahead. Getting up from the chair, he said, 'I guess we should be going. Grace's mother worries and we have been out rather longer than we expected.'

Grace bit her tongue until it bled.

Sean had never given a damn about her mother's feelings before.

But perhaps he could see that Jack had evidently had enough of them. Even Sean's thick skin must have some sensitivity, after all.

CHAPTER NINE

'YOU'RE NOT SERIOUSLY going into business with Sean Nesbitt!'

It was the following morning, and, after a restless night plagued with dreams of Grace and Sean together, Jack had decided to make himself a bacon sandwich.

'What's it to you?' Jack demanded, casting a dour glance in Lisa's direction. 'It's not as if you're going to lose anything by it.'

Lisa made a sound of protest. 'I'm hurt,' she exclaimed, lowering her shoeless foot to the floor. She was standing at the other side of the island, arms crossed and ready for a fight.

'I know the feeling,' Jack said now, forking crisp slices of bacon onto a wedge of wholemeal bread. He shrugged. 'But he's right. I have been lucky. Financially, anyway. And maybe I do owe him something for all the years we were good pals.'

Lisa snorted. 'Sean Nesbitt was never a "good pal" of yours,' she retorted shortly.

Then she stifled a groan. 'Uh-oh! Here comes trouble!'

'What do you mean?'

Jack lifted his head to look at her just as Lisa's image began to fade. Instead, he saw Mrs Honeyman through the kitchen window—at least half an hour early, by his estimation—cycling into the yard at the side of the house.

He swore roundly, understanding perfectly what Lisa had meant.

But then he crossed the stone tiles to unlatch the outer door with a certain resignation. Mrs Honeyman always came into the house through the old boot room, changing from her outdoor shoes into the soft-soled trainers in which she preferred to work.

'Mr Connolly!'

Her first words needed no further explanation and Jack sighed.

'Yeah, I know,' he said, 'Fried food is bad for my digestion. But I was hungry!'

Mrs Honeyman merely shook her head and began clearing up the mess he'd made. The frying pan went into soapy water; the utensils he'd used were rinsed and put into the dishwasher. Then, after eyeing Jack, munching on his sandwich, she said, 'I assume you'd like some coffee with that?'

Jack's mouth was full, but he nodded his approval, deciding not to tell her he'd had at least three mugs of his favourite brew already.

A sturdy woman, in her middle fifties, Mrs Honeyman had been the first person to answer Jack's advertisement for a part-time housekeeper. And she and Jack had hit it off at once, making any other interviews he'd conducted superfluous.

Of course, she occasionally despaired of his eating habits. Usually, it had to be said, because she deplored his practice of buying fast food. But in the past few weeks, her attitude had turned to one of concern.

'As I'll be here all day, would you like me to make you some lunch?' she suggested. 'I've got some nice fresh tomatoes in my bag, and I could mince the remains of the steak I used yesterday and make you a dish of bolognese.'

Jack blew out a breath.

'Well, that's very kind of you, Mrs Honeyman—'

'But?'

'—but I won't be in for lunch,' he said apologetically. 'I'm meeting the builder at Culworth, and I'll probably have a sandwich with him!'

'Another sandwich!'

Mrs Honeyman raised her eyebrows, and Jack gave her a rueful smile. He could have told her that while the renovations were going on he'd eaten anything he could lay his hands on. And that included days-old sandwiches whose sell-by date was long past.

'Anyway,' she went on, 'don't you worry. I'll see that you have some fresh vegetables for your dinner. And maybe a fresh steak pie to go with them.'

Jack shook his head. 'You spoil me, Mrs. Honeyman.'

'Well, somebody has to,' she declared. 'It's time you thought about getting yourself a lady friend. Respecting your late wife is all well and good, but a man needs a woman in his—'

She broke off abruptly, her cheeks flushing again, and Jack decided to put her out of her misery.

'Yeah, I know what you mean,' he said ruefully, aware that Mrs Honeyman didn't know how inspired her words had been.

He'd had a woman in his bed last night. Unfortunately, the woman in question had known nothing about it.

Grace drove the last half mile to the church and pulled in behind a battered pickup.

The small parking area was busy, she saw, with a smart little Audi and a more sedate Honda filling the space. But there was no sign of the expensive Lexus SUV and Grace's heart sank.

She'd been so sure she'd find Jack here.

According to what she'd heard in the agency—though no one had actually discussed the matter with her, of course—planning permission for the cottages had been granted without a hitch. With Mrs Naughton's active participation, the whole deal had been accomplished in a little over three weeks.

Of course, Grace reflected now, there was no real reason why Jack should be here at present. If work had started—and it certainly looked as though it had, judging from the unusual activity—he was hardly likely to play an active role.

He might supervise from time to time, but she doubted

he'd want to get his hands dirty. She sighed. She should have gone to his house, after all. Despite her reluctance to set tongues wagging if she did.

She also knew she should have tried to contact him sooner.

It was nearly a month now since Sean had dragged her out to Jack's house. Nearly a month since she'd been embarrassed and humiliated. Nearly a month, and no word from Sean about paying her father back the money he'd borrowed.

And nearly a month since she'd assured herself she'd never see Jack Connolly again.

The way he'd looked at her! She shuddered at the memory. It was so obvious he'd thought she'd been as much to blame for what had happened as Sean.

Perhaps he'd even thought that that was why she'd practically thrown herself at him that morning at the cottage. It was certainly a possibility, despite her original reluctance to go with him.

So why had she come?

Grace thrust open the car door and got out.

It was a beautiful sunny morning, much different from the last time she was here. Even the church looked more appealing, the trees around it colourful now with blossom. And on the horizon, the sea looked bluer than she'd ever seen it.

She could smell the salt on the air, feel its scent coating her skin. And decided to walk along the cliff and see how the cottages were faring. She had nothing else to do until lunch.

As soon as she started along the cliff path she saw the Lexus.

It was parked a few yards from the cottages, with several other vehicles between it and a loaded skip.

Another pickup and two vans showed that work was already in progress, and Grace's determination faltered at the realisation that she wasn't going to be able to speak to Jack alone.

Her footsteps slowed. She might as well turn back, she

thought. She wasn't supposed to be here, anyway. But her morning's viewing had finished early and she wasn't expected back in the office until half past one.

Then a man emerged from one of the cottages and saw her.

It wasn't Jack, but he came towards her, clearly wondering if she needed help. He was a good-looking man, in his late forties, she estimated, and she had the feeling that she'd seen him before.

'I shouldn't come any nearer,' he said, indicating the hard hat he was wearing. 'Health and Safety will have my guts for garters if I let you look around.'

Grace managed a faint smile, realising who he was at the same time that he recognised her.

'You're Tom Spencer's daughter, aren't you?' he exclaimed. 'I've seen you in the pub.'

Grace's smile got even thinner. 'Yes, that's right,' she mumbled now, wondering what the chances were of her meeting someone from Rothburn this far off the beaten track.

But, of course, it was like Jack to employ a builder he knew and approved of. Bob Grady's company had been partly responsible for the sympathetic renovation of Lindisfarne House.

'I knew it.' Grady looked pleased with his deduction. 'But what are you doing out here? You work for an estate agent these days, don't you? Don't tell me Jack has got the properties on the market already!'

'Oh, no. No!'

Grace couldn't let him think that, couldn't risk him going into the agency and mentioning her visit to Mr Hughes. It would be hard enough as it was, explaining her visit to her father. Because she had no doubt that Grady would mention it, the first chance he got.

'So, is it Jack you want to see?'

The man was persistent, but just then Grace had a brilliant idea.

'No,' she said, adopting a note of rueful innocence. 'But I was the one who showed Mr Connolly the cottages when he first became interested. As I was out this way, I thought I'd have a look and see how the development was progressing.'

'Ah.'

If Grady found her explanation just a tiny bit convenient, he didn't say so. Thankfully, he went on, before she could say something else to embarrass herself. 'As far as the development is concerned, it's hardly got off the ground.'

Grace's eyes widened. 'There's been a problem?'

'That's right.' Grady grimaced. 'We've found serious faults in the foundations and we may have to demolish most of the standing walls.'

Grace swallowed. 'I see.'

'Yeah.' Grady turned to survey the group of buildings behind him. 'Jack's brought another architect out to look at the place and he's consulting with him at present. He's got an idea that we might be able to pour concrete into the existing bedrock. That way we might not have to bulldoze the whole site.'

Grace shook her head. 'Is he very annoyed?' she murmured without thinking, and Grady gave her a curious look.

'Annoyed?' he echoed. 'Well, Jack's not pleased, I can tell you that. But if anyone can solve the problem, he can. He's won awards for developments he's designed in Ireland, you know.'

Grace hadn't known, but it didn't surprise her. She had the feeling that anything Jack did, he'd do well.

Incredibly well, she thought. Like making love to a woman. Something told her he'd be as expert at that as he was at everything else.

She shivered suddenly, in spite of the warmth of the day. She was remembering how it had felt to have his hands upon her, the raw sexuality of his mouth.

Oh, God, she thought, she had definitely not been wise to come here. Not when even the memory of his scent assaulted her senses, aroused an insistent need that hadn't been assuaged.

She was trying to remember what Grady had said so she could answer him, when the man spoke again.

'Here's Jack now,' he said. 'And that's the other architect with him. Let's hope they've got some good news. I don't want to have to lay my men off again.'

Grace's throat tightened at the sight of the two men walking towards them. She found it incredibly hard to breathe suddenly as she saw Jack recognise her. Particularly when there was no sign of welcome on his face.

He was wearing jeans again today, the same faded jeans she'd seen before, that hung low on his hips and emphasised his lean athletic frame.

A black cotton shirt, the sleeves turned back over sinewy forearms, hung half open and exposed the strong brown column of his throat.

Both men were wearing hard hats like Grady, but Jack hauled his off as they reached the parked vehicles. He opened the boot of the Lexus and tossed the hat inside.

His dark hair was untidy, evidence of the many times he'd raked his fingers through it. It had grown in the weeks since she'd seen him, and overlapped his collar by a couple of inches at the back.

'You've got a visitor, Jack,' Grady said, without waiting for Grace to introduce herself. 'She says she was the one who showed you the cottages in the first place.'

'Yeah. That's right.' Jack was too well-mannered to make any other response.

Grace squared her shoulders beneath her neatly buttoned shirt and met his gaze with a guarded stare.

'Mr Grady's been telling me you've found some problems,' she said politely. 'Perhaps you should take it up with

Mrs Naughton. She might be prepared to buy the cottages back.'

'In a pig's eye,' said Jack succinctly and then turned to his builder. 'Ralph thinks we can use concrete to shore up the foundations. It's not as if we're planning on building a multistorey car park on the site.'

Grady's relief was palpable. 'Hell, that's great, Jack,' he said, grinning broadly. 'I'll get on to the yard right away. They should be able to fit us in at the beginning of next week.'

'You do that.'

Jack's eyes flickered over Grace's burning face before moving on to the man beside him.

'Thanks for your input, Ralph. It's much appreciated.'

'My pleasure.' The older man lifted a hand in a deprecatory gesture. 'You'd have done the same for me.' He glanced at his watch. 'I'd better get going. Goodbye, Bob. Goodbye, Ms Spencer.'

'Oh—goodbye.'

Grace was touched that he'd thought to include her in his farewells, particularly as Jack hadn't bothered to introduce them.

But then, she evidently wasn't Jack's favourite person at the moment. She shifted uncomfortably. She shouldn't have come here. She should go, too.

'I'll come with you,' she called after Ralph's departing figure, unable to bring herself to use his name. It would have been too familiar.

However, Jack intervened. 'No, that's okay, Ralph,' he said as the other man turned. 'I want to have a word with Ms Spencer myself.' He nodded at Bob Grady as Ralph waved a hand before continuing on his way. 'Do you want to go and tell your men what's going on?'

'Oh—sure.'

Grady looked a little disappointed at being dismissed

so arbitrarily. But, join the club, thought Grace, not exactly thrilled at Jack's arrogance herself.

Yet she couldn't deny the frisson of excitement she felt when Jack came towards her. Whatever way she might want to play this, she couldn't ignore his magnetism. Couldn't prevent her instinctive reaction to his dark masculine beauty.

CHAPTER TEN

'LET'S WALK,' JACK SAID, indicating the path that led past the row of cottages and out onto the cliff. 'I'd suggest we talk in my car, but I know we'd be observed.'

'And that matters to you?'

Grace spoke tartly, and Jack gave her a smouldering look.

'I'd assumed it would matter to you,' he said harshly, urging her to move forward. 'I'd rather not give Grady's men any more to gossip about in the Bay Horse tonight.'

'Oh, God!' Grace swallowed. 'Do you think they will?'

'It's a fair bet.' Jack was sardonic now.

Grace sighed. 'If I'd known you'd employed someone from Rothburn—'

'You wouldn't have come, I know.' Jack shrugged. 'It wasn't the most sensible idea you've ever had.'

Grace's throat tightened. 'I needed to speak to you.'

'I gathered that.'

He fell into step beside her as they passed the cottages and Grace was sure she could feel at least half a dozen pairs of eyes mapping their path. Jack seemed indifferent to her fears, however, adapting his long stride to the restrictions of her suit skirt. But even so, her high heels made it difficult to keep pace.

Beyond the cottages, the route became more uneven, unused in recent years except by walkers or children heading for the steps that led down to the cove.

The breeze was stronger here, but Grace was grateful for it. Despite opening the collar of her shirt, she could feel perspiration trickling down between her breasts.

'So,' he said, when they were safely out of earshot of their audience. 'Do you want to tell me what this is all about?'

Grace's tongue circled her dry lips and she couldn't resist

glancing back over her shoulder. Jack wasn't touching her, but she was supremely aware of him, anyway. And she was sure that anyone watching them would be able to read her body language like an open book.

His warmth, his heat, enveloped her with an uncontrollable sensuality. The clean male scent of his body invading every susceptible pore of her skin.

They'd reached the rocky steps that zigzagged down the cliff to the cove, and Grace halted.

'Um—do you think we could go down to the beach?' she suggested, realising too late how provocative that must sound.

But at least they'd be out of sight of prying eyes, she consoled herself. She didn't like the feeling of vulnerability she was experiencing at present.

Jack stared at her. Then his eyes dropped insolently down the length of her body. Their darkness deepened as they moved over her neat white shirt and narrow black skirt. And her legs in transparent black tights wobbled uncertainly.

'Can you see yourself going down those steps in those heels?' he asked incredulously.

And she breathed a little more easily when his gaze returned to her face.

'I can take my shoes off,' she said at once, bending to do so with more bravado than sense. 'There. You see!' she added. 'No problem.'

Despite her assertion, Jack suspected he should refuse her request and insist they remain on the cliff top. At least up here he could kid himself he retained a modicum of good sense.

He'd been down to the cove only once before, but he knew it would be deserted at this time of day. It was unlikely that anyone would brave the water. Despite its beauty, the sea was cold.

He'd be crazy to agree.

Nevertheless, he found himself saying, 'Okay. But I'll go ahead. Just in case it's not as easy as you think.'

Grace nodded, feeling a little breathless before she'd even started. Which was ridiculous, really. The hard part would be climbing back up again.

Jack, in rubber-soled trainers, had no problem with the steps. They were uneven, but fairly easy to negotiate, so long as he didn't look back.

On the rare occasions when he did—just to check that she was all right, he assured himself—the view was tantalising. Beneath her skirt, long legs stretched provocatively up to her crotch.

Grace had her own troubles to contend with.

The urge to use Jack's shoulder as a crutch being the most insistent. She knew that beneath his shirt, his skin would feel warm and reassuring. And if she slipped...

But she restrained those thoughts, concentrating instead on keeping her feet. Unfortunately, in her bid to appear unconcerned, she hadn't given any thought to fallen stones or broken edges. By the time she stepped down onto the sand, her tights had been shredded in a dozen different places.

Jack was waiting for her and the wry amusement in his gaze was the last straw.

'Just turn away,' she snapped, and, when he did, she ripped off the offending articles, stuffing them into the toes of one of her shoes before saying, 'All right. You can look now.'

It wasn't the most sensible thing she might have said, but she doubted anything would have stopped Jack from staring at her. And without her tights, she definitely felt more exposed. Unlike his skin, her legs looked pale and uninteresting, a stark contrast to the darkness of her skirt.

'Are you okay?' he asked, his eyes narrowing slightly, and she wondered what he was really thinking when he looked at her.

That for someone who was supposed to be going out with

another man, she was absurdly reckless with her reputation? Whatever puerile excuse had brought her out here?

'I'm good,' she said now, putting her shoes down at the foot of the steps and smoothing nervous fingers over her skirt.

Grace pushed her toes into the sand to avoid looking at him. She'd decided it would be easier to say what she had to say if they weren't standing face-to-face.

Jack surveyed the cove that was little more than half a mile from end to end. 'Let's go this way. I believe there are some caves near the rocks.'

'Caves!'

The word escaped on a squeak that Grace managed to disguise by clearing her throat.

But, heavens, she didn't want to go caving with him. Even if the idea did have its temptations.

She frowned then. She wasn't here to repeat past mistakes, she reminded herself severely. She just wanted Jack to understand that Sean's request for finance had nothing to do with her.

'Yes, caves.' Apparently Jack hadn't noticed her exclamation. 'According to one of the locals, they used to connect with a tunnel from some castle near here.'

'Really?'

Grace tried to sound interested, but her awareness of him had jumped to a new level since they'd reached the beach. Without her heels, he was so much bigger than she was, for one thing. And for another, his apparent ability to ignore what had happened between them previously caught her on the raw.

'The guy says the tunnel's been blocked off now because of the dangers of a roof fall,' Jack continued on, regardless. 'Or that's his story. Who knows? Maybe smuggling still goes on along this coast.'

Grace cleared her throat again. 'I—I doubt it's a big concern in these parts,' she murmured, trying to match his detachment. 'The tides are too unstable. And there are currents under the water.'

She forced a smile. 'Besides, some of the locals love to tell a good tale.'

Jack glanced sideways at her. Then his brows drew together. 'What's the matter, Grace? Wishing you'd stayed where we were?'

'No!'

'Sure?' Jack sounded sceptical. 'You're not worried about what might happen now we're alone together?'

Grace's jaw dropped. 'No!'

'That's good.' Jack nodded. 'Because I can tell you you've got nothing to fear from me.'

Never mind what Grace was thinking, he was regretting giving in to her suggestion to come down here. It was so remote, so isolated. And whatever he'd told her, at least one part of his body wasn't listening to his brain.

He sensed rather than heard Grace coming after him.

'Did I say I didn't trust you?' she demanded, and now he could hear that she was out of breath.

What she wasn't aware of was that with every gulp of air she took, the lapels on her shirt gaped invitingly. But she was too busy trying to convince him that she had a handle on the situation to notice it.

'Okay, no,' he said now, dragging his eyes away from that tempting cleft between her breasts. 'So long as we understand one another.'

Yeah, right.

Grace's cheeks were pink, as much with the way she was feeling as with exertion. 'I—I needed to talk to you, that's all.'

'You keep saying that.' Jack regarded her with an expectant expression. 'So why don't you go ahead and talk? I'm listening.'

Grace pursed her lips. 'It's not that easy.'

'Isn't it?' Jack pulled a wry face. 'I haven't noticed you having a problem before.'

Grace trudged on for a while in silence.

Then she halted and said, 'Do you blame me because the cottages are going to be far more expensive to restore?'

It was such a non sequitur that Jack blinked.

'Uh—no,' he said, halting in his tracks to look at her. Then, his brows drawing together, 'Are you saying that Hughes knew there were structural problems when he took them on?'

'No.' Grace was anxious now. 'Mrs Naughton might have. But she's an old woman. She probably hasn't been inside any of the buildings for years.'

'Okay.' Jack stared at her.

Grace pressed her lips together. Why didn't she just admit that the real reason she'd come to see him was to exonerate herself from any resentment he might be feeling towards Sean?

Because that would be far too disloyal, even for her.

Grace was silent for so long that Jack expelled a weary breath. It was obvious she had something else on her mind, but for some reason she was finding it difficult to voice.

He suspected Sean was involved. He couldn't think of any other reason why she might be so hesitant. Which made him somewhat less than gracious when he said, 'What's the matter, Grace? Wasn't the hundred thousand I loaned Sean enough?'

Grace's mouth dried. 'You—you loaned Sean one hundred thousand pounds?'

Jack didn't answer. He was already regretting making such an admission to her.

Instead, he turned and stared out at the ocean. It was amazingly blue, and so calm the horizon shimmered in a haze of heat.

Much different from the first time he'd come here.

He sighed. He really didn't want to be having this conver-

'I—I know,' she breathed, and when he lifted his head, her eyes were wide with a mixture of uncertainty and anticipation.

'Then we should go,' said Jack, but he didn't move. Couldn't move, he thought incredulously, and when she lifted a hand to cup his face, he shuddered uncontrollably.

His jawline was rough with at least a couple of days' growth of beard, but Grace loved the feel of his stubble against her fingers. Loved, too, the way he turned his head and bestowed a lingering kiss on her palm.

Then, with a groan, he gripped her chin and turned her face up to his. This time, his mouth was hot and hungry, and she had no defence against such deliberate sexuality.

She responded willingly, eagerly, uncaring where they were or who might see them. She lifted her arms and wound them round his neck, sliding her fingers into his hair and fisting the damp curls at the nape of his neck.

She arched away from the rock face, pressing herself against him, and felt the unmistakeable thrust of his erection. And wished his body could imitate the tantalising invasion of his tongue.

Jack felt the wilful response of her body with a feeling of desperation. This wasn't supposed to happen, he told himself, even as his fingers traced the hollow beneath her ear, probed inside the neckline of her shirt.

She was wearing a bra, but it was only a delicate shred of lace that gave easily beneath the determined pressure of his hand. And then her breasts were spilling out of her shirt, the buttons parting with little effort on his part.

'God,' he muttered, bending lower to take one swollen nipple into his mouth. 'You are so…beautiful!'

Grace caught her breath as his tongue curled around the sensitive peak and sucked on it. She felt both weak and powerful, her legs trembling with the effort of remaining upright beneath his sensual assault.

Jack tried to hang on to some semblance of sanity, but it was a losing battle. Her feel, her touch, her taste, made any kind of resistance futile, and when he found her mouth again, he knew there could be no turning back.

His hands gripped her hips, urging her back against the cliff as he rocked his throbbing arousal against her yielding body. And felt her part her legs to bring him even closer.

Now his hands found the hem of that prim little skirt, forcing it upwards. His hands slid against cool feminine thighs, against skin as smooth and inviting as silk.

'I want you,' he bit out unsteadily, and she looked up at him with unguarded eyes.

'I want you, too,' she breathed, the words barely audible, and with a muffled oath he pushed her lacy briefs down her legs.

'Here?' he demanded, and she nodded.

'Yes, here,' she said unsteadily, and Jack closed his eyes for a moment, praying for deliverance.

But it never came.

Instead, he felt her fingers unfastening his belt buckle, unzipping his jeans and then taking him in her hot little hands.

Jack's groan was anguished, but he was already lifting her against him. He encouraged her to wind her legs about his hips, pulling himself out of her hands to push into hot, wet nirvana.

Grace sucked in a breath as his thick shaft penetrated her, invaded her, stretching her and filling her in a way she'd never experienced before.

Feeling his length inside her, pulsing deep against her womb, aroused sensations that both scared and delighted her. Her mind went dizzy with visions of spinning out across an endless ocean, of riding on angels' wings, heading irresistibly towards the sun.

Jack drove into her again, withdrawing just enough to leave her weak and begging for more. Her nails dug into his shoulders, and she wanted to tear the shirt from him. But she had to be content with pushing her fingers inside his collar, feeling smooth brown skin beneath her hands.

Again and again, he drove into her until her body felt as if it were on fire. As if the need he had created could only be assuaged if they both went up in flames.

And then it happened.

Just when she thought she couldn't take any more, her body exploded around him. She floated out on waves of ecstasy, the force of her orgasm driving Jack completely over the edge.

He would have withdrawn from her then and spilled himself on the sand. But Grace wouldn't let him.

With a strength she'd hardly known she possessed, she wound herself even tighter about him. She wanted to prolong this moment, wanted to share his release as he had shared hers.

And then, it was far too late for Jack to do anything but slump heavily against her. He shuddered his seed into her waiting body and prayed to Jude, the patron saint of lost causes, that God might forgive this mortal fool...

CHAPTER ELEVEN

'WHERE ON EARTH have you been?'

It was after midnight when Jack got home. And, having spent the past six hours trying to numb his senses with alcohol, he was in no mood for Lisa's accusations.

'Get lost,' he growled, but he could hear the slur in his voice and he knew Lisa would hear it, too.

'Ew, you're drunk!' she exclaimed disgustedly. 'I don't know what's the matter with you, Jack. You never used to care so little about your health.'

Jack wasn't inclined to debate the issue. Slamming the heavy door behind him, he fumbled to secure the deadbolt. It took a few attempts, but at last the key turned in the lock and he sank back against the door, preparing himself to climb the stairs.

Then, without bothering to put on any lights, he started across the hall.

To his relief, Lisa seemed to have given up on him and he wasn't sorry. He was bone-tired. Exhausted, actually. He couldn't wait to strip off his clothes and crawl into bed.

Not that he truly expected to sleep. His mind was still buzzing with the events of the afternoon at Culworth, his senses still humming with what he told himself was the best sex he'd ever had.

But that was exactly why he'd spent so long in the pub. Not her father's pub, of course, but another, smaller, hostelry in the next village. He'd hoped he might erase those events from his mind, temporarily at least.

It hadn't happened.

The memory of Grace's mouth, Grace's body, Grace's sensual sweetness, filled his thoughts to the exclusion of anything else.

But it was wrong; so wrong. Even now, after so many hours of soul-searching, he couldn't begin to comprehend what he'd been thinking of.

Okay, she hadn't exactly resisted him, but that was no excuse for the way he'd behaved. For pity's sake, he'd hit her with Sean's demand and then taken advantage of her stunned reaction to it.

She'd needed comfort, not seduction. Tender understanding, not the raw passion of someone who apparently cared little for her sensitivities and even less for Sean's.

Sean!

He felt sick at the thought of what he'd done to Sean. All right, there was no doubt that he and Sean had drifted apart in recent years, and their goals were not the same any longer.

But he was still Grace's boyfriend; still the man he assumed she would marry.

And yet, today at least, Grace hadn't behaved as if she'd felt guilty for what had happened. On the contrary, she'd responded to his lovemaking with an eagerness and a sensuality that aroused him still. He doubted he'd ever be able to look down on that stretch of sand again without recalling what had happened there in intimate detail.

It was the shriek of gulls that had brought him to his senses. Drunk with passion, reeling from emotions he'd never expected or wanted to feel, it had been an actual effort to drag himself away from her. He hadn't wanted to do it, and, judging from the way she'd clung to him, she hadn't wanted it, either.

He remembered she'd given a little moan of protest as he'd attempted to restore her clothes to some sort of order. And he hadn't been able to resist kissing her again, tasting once more the lush sweetness he'd found with his tongue.

God, what had she been thinking? What had he been thinking? He must have been mad.

Mad with lust, certainly, and blinded by his own selfish desires.

Whatever, they'd eventually walked back along the beach to where she'd left her shoes. He hadn't expected she would have anything to say to him, but in the aftermath of passion, she'd found her voice.

'I—I want you to know, I didn't intend for this to happen,' she'd told him quietly. 'And I don't blame you. I don't blame you at all.'

She'd sighed then. 'I'd just wanted you to know that it wasn't my idea to approach you for...for money. For the past month, I've been trying to summon up the courage to apologise for Sean's...behaviour.'

Sean!

Yeah, right.

At that moment, Jack had felt like the lowest form of pond life. If he'd taken her earlier admission at face value—if he'd believed her, in other words—this wouldn't have happened.

It had occurred to him—belatedly—that maybe that was why she'd allowed him to—

But no. Grace was not venal; he'd known it would never have occurred to her to use her body as a means to an end.

He couldn't remember what he'd said to her then. He did remember climbing the steps, giving her his hand when she'd let out a cry of pain because a pebble had dug into her foot.

And ultimately asking those fatal questions:

Did she love Sean?

And if not, why did she stay with him?

She hadn't answered him. With eyes that were suspiciously bright, she'd simply balled up her tights and pushed them into her bag before slipping her feet into her shoes.

It was that action, as much as anything, that had made him realise that really nothing had changed. It was as if by putting on her shoes she had drawn a line under the reckless events of the day.

And he'd still had no idea how she was really feeling, deep inside.

He remembered escorting her to her car. After she'd

driven away, he supposed he'd been in a state of shock. Disgusted with himself, definitely. But what was worse had been the realisation that the feelings she'd aroused were not going away.

The urge had been to go and get drunk, to bury his sorrows in the bottom of a bottle of Scotch. But instead he'd decided he needed physical exertion, and he'd spent the next couple of hours using a sledgehammer to break up the flags in the kitchen of one of the cottages they were working on.

He guessed the men were curious about his uncharacteristic behaviour. He only hoped Bob Grady wouldn't go blabbing about it in the Bay Horse. He didn't care for himself but Grace's name was bound to be mentioned.

By late afternoon, he'd been unable to control himself any longer. He'd had to try to speak to Grace again. He'd needed closure. He'd told himself he was doing it to salve his conscience, but the truth was he'd been desperate to hear her voice.

Had he hoped for absolution? If so, he'd been disappointed. When he'd rung the agency, Elizabeth Fleming had told him that Grace had phoned to say she wasn't well and was taking the rest of the day off.

Elizabeth had obviously been curious to know why he wanted to speak to Grace. But although he'd known Grace must have a mobile phone, there was no way Mrs Fleming would have given that number to him.

Not that he'd asked her to.

And as for ringing the Bay Horse...

That was how he'd ended up at a strange pub. But the relief he'd been seeking wasn't there. All he'd found was a curdling stomach and a pounding head. And more self-disgust than he could cope with.

The sudden switching on of a light bewildered him.

He was halfway up the stairs and he groped weakly for the banister, clinging to the wood for dear life.

'Dammit, Lisa,' he swore, even though she'd never accomplished such a thing before. 'Give me a break!'

'Oh, Jack!'

The sympathetic voice was both familiar and unfamiliar. And when he looked up it was to find Debra Carrick standing at the top of the stairs, her hand still on the switch.

'Oh, Jack,' she said again, wrapping the folds of her cotton dressing gown more closely about her plump little body. 'I thought you came here to get over Lisa. But it sounds to me as if it isn't working.'

Jack groaned.

This was all he needed. Lisa's little sister come to help him lick his wounds.

Wounds he no longer had, he realised belatedly. Even without what had happened between him and Grace, the pain he'd felt when Lisa died had—like his late wife—passed away.

'I'm good, Debs,' he assured his sister-in-law firmly, straightening away from the banister.

Or he would be, once he'd closed his bedroom door.

'But you were calling for Lisa,' she protested. 'I heard you.' Her eyes grew misty. 'I told your mother you'd welcome some company despite what you said.'

Jack blew out a breath.

Was there any point in denying he'd used Lisa's name?

'You're imagining things,' he said. And then, in an attempt to divert her, 'Anyway, what are you doing here?' His brows drew together in sudden confusion. 'How the hell did you get in?'

'Oh—some woman was still here when I arrived,' declared Debra easily. 'I think she said her name was Honeyman. Is that right?'

'Mrs Honeyman, yes.' Jack frowned. 'But she usually leaves at midday.'

'She did.' Debra started down the stairs towards him and Jack was obliged to back up himself to avoid her. 'I've been here since about half past eleven. I flew into Newcastle this morning and got a taxi from the airport to the house.'

Jack, who had been backing down the stairs, reached the bottom without warning. The sudden impact caused him to stagger a little and Debra hurried down the last few stairs to wrap her arms about his waist.

'It's okay,' she said, as if he were some child in danger of falling. And then the alcohol on his breath caused her to step back in dismay.

'You've been drinking,' she exclaimed. 'Oh, Jack, I'm so glad I didn't take your mother's advice and stay away.'

You should have done!

The words hovered on Jack's tongue, but he didn't utter them. Extricating himself from lingering fingers, he turned rather desperately towards the kitchen.

His mother should have phoned, he thought. She should have warned him Debra was coming. Instead of leaving him to deal with a female who evidently thought he was in danger of falling apart.

'D'you want coffee?' he asked.

'At this time of night?' Debra had followed him into the kitchen, and Jack quickly put the island between them. 'Oughtn't you to have something to eat?'

'I'm not hungry.'

In actual fact, Jack hadn't had anything to eat since breakfast. And right now, the thought of food nauseated him. But however unwelcome her arrival, Debra was a guest, and he was obliged to make the requisite response.

'Have you eaten?'

'Oh, yes.' Debra nodded. 'Mrs Honeyman made me some soup at lunchtime. And she said to tell you, she's left a steak pie in the fridge.' She shrugged. 'I hope you don't mind, I made myself an omelette at dinner time. I suppose I could have cooked the pie, but I didn't know what time you'd be back.'

Jack nodded. Knowing Mrs Honeyman as he did, he

doubted she'd have been best pleased to find they had an unexpected visitor.

Jack switched the coffee on and then turned to prop his hips rather wearily against the dishwasher.

'So,' he said, when she was unexpectedly silent. 'Come on, Debs. Why are you here?'

Debra's lips, a fuller version of her sister's, pursed defensively. 'I should have thought that was obvious,' she said, her expression showing she'd been hurt by the question. 'We're all worried about you.'

Jack sighed. 'Who's we?'

'Your father, your mother.' She hesitated before adding, 'Francis.'

Jack sighed. 'You're wrong, Debs.' He shook his head. 'Ma and Pa aren't worried about me. They know I'm happy here, doing what I want, making a life for myself somewhere new and different. And as for Francis…' his brother '…he's a priest. He doesn't have time to worry about me.'

'Maeve, then,' retorted Debra tartly. 'Did you know she's pregnant? Again?'

Jack hid a grin.

'I think you've answered your own question there, Debs. My sister has a husband and two little girls to care about. Not to mention a new baby on the way. If her brother is too… bullheaded…or too selfish to keep in touch with her, she probably thinks he doesn't deserve her.'

'You know she doesn't think like that.'

'I know.'

Jack knew that was true. Despite the distance between them, they'd always been a close family. Always there for each other when they were needed.

But Debra wasn't family. Not really. And he suspected Debra's reasons for coming here weren't entirely disinterested.

'Anyway,' he said, turning to pour himself a mug of coffee, 'shouldn't you be in school?'

Debra snorted. 'I'm at college, Jack.' She was indignant. 'And it's summer break, as if you didn't know.'

Jack stifled a groan.

'So—what?' he said, turning back, deciding to take his coffee black to try to clear his head. 'Is this the start of a European tour?'

'No!' Debra stared at him impatiently. 'I've just told you, I've come to look after you, Jack. I'm sure you're not looking after yourself properly.'

Jack blew on his coffee before taking an unwary gulp. It was much too hot and it burned his mouth, but at least the pain achieved what a gallon of alcohol couldn't.

'You can't stay here, Debs,' he said, trying to sound mature and reasonable.

But for pity's sake, he didn't want to be accused of taking advantage of a young girl. He had enough on his conscience as it was.

Debra looked shocked now. 'Why can't I stay here?' she exclaimed indignantly. 'You need someone, Jack. Someone who knows you and cares about you.'

'No.' Jack was adamant. 'No, I don't.' He paused and then added as gently as he could, 'It would be different if we were related. But we're not. And can you imagine what people would say if they found out I was living with an attractive young female like yourself?'

Debra's expression softened. 'Do you think I'm attractive, Jack?'

Jack blew out a weary breath.

'Of course I think you're attractive,' he said. But when she would have moved towards him, he held up a hand to stop her. 'But you're Lisa's little sister, Debs. I'm sorry. You'll never mean more to me than that.'

Debra looked sulky now. 'How do you know?'

'I just do.'

'And since when have you cared what people think?' she

persisted, trying another approach. 'Lisa said you never listened to gossip.'

'I don't—'

'Then—'

'But other people do,' finished Jack flatly. 'Come on, Debs. It's not the end of the world. I can't believe you came all this way just to tell me you cared about me.'

'Why not?'

'Because—well, because you're too young, for one thing. And what about that boy you were seeing in Kilpheny? Wasn't his name Brendan or something?'

'Brendan Foyle,' agreed Debra, plucking at the ends of her belt. 'But like you said, he's just a boy. I'm not interested in *boys*!'

Jack felt horribly old suddenly.

He was tired and the last thing he needed was to have to deal with a lovesick adolescent. Debra was—what? Nineteen? Twenty? Her parents should have had more sense than to let her come here.

'I think I ought to give your mother a call in the morning and tell her you're on your way home,' he said at last.

But Debra looked horrified at this suggestion.

'Mummy doesn't know I'm here,' she exclaimed. 'Nor does Daddy. I told them I was going to stay with your parents. I was going to tell them where I really was in a few days.'

'Well, now you won't have to,' said Jack reasonably. 'If you get a flight back to Dublin in the morning, they need never know you've been here. And I'm sure Ma and Pa will be only too happy to see you.' He crossed his fingers as he said this. 'And Maeve, too. I dare say she'd be glad of a babysitter.'

Debra looked mutinous. 'You don't care about me at all, do you? I'm just a nuisance, turning up like this. Well, I was going to tell you something that might make you feel a bit better, but now I don't think I will.'

Jack shook his head. 'I doubt if anything you told me could make me feel better,' he said bitterly.

After the day he'd had, even being told he'd won the lottery wouldn't cut it.

'It was about Lisa.'

Debra clearly had no intention of keeping the information to herself.

But did Jack really want to hear it?

'So—what about Lisa?' he asked at last, realising Debra wasn't about to go to bed without delivering her message. 'If it's something to do with the accident, I'd really rather not hear another version of how it was all her fault—'

'She wasn't alone,' said Debra impulsively, and Jack could only stare at her with uncomprehending eyes.

'What do you mean, she wasn't alone? Of course she was alone. My God, didn't I have to listen to all that testimony at the inquest? The details of how they'd found only one person's remains in the ashes of the car? Don't you think they'd have told me if there'd been more than one fatality? For God's sake, Debra, your sister's dead. Leave it be.'

'She wasn't alone,' persisted Debra doggedly. 'You can rail at me all you want, but I'm not lying.' She licked her lips. 'The man—the man she was with was thrown clear. Just like that sandal they found that belonged to Lisa.' She took a deep breath. 'She was having an affair, Jack. And I thought you deserved to know the truth.'

CHAPTER TWELVE

A WEEK LATER, Grace got a phone call from Sean.

It was five weeks since she'd seen him; five weeks since he'd returned to London, ostensibly to set up the website Jack Connolly had invested in.

Grace had spent part of the time looking for an apartment in Rothburn. She could have got one in Alnwick easily enough, but she wanted to be near her parents if they needed her.

That part of her reason for moving north hadn't changed. Even if so much else in her life had.

Unfortunately, she hadn't been successful. Apartments in Rothburn were hard to find. And she'd had to contend with both her mother and her father assuring her that she could stay at the pub for the foreseeable future. They'd even talked about adding a small extension if the deal her father had with Sean was a success.

For her part, Grace had been in no hurry to hear from him again, unless it was to say he had managed to recover her parents' investment. Goodness knew the money Jack had given him would have gone a long way to repaying the mortgage on the pub. But she could have hardly said that to him without sounding as if she wanted a share.

And she really didn't want to be in Jack's debt.

She hadn't heard from Jack in the past week, either. But that hadn't surprised her. Despite the thrill the memory of that scene on the beach still caused, common sense told her that entertaining any real feelings for a man who was still mourning the death of his wife was plain stupid.

Besides, she was kidding herself if she thought he cared about her. If he'd had any respect for her feelings, he'd never have seduced her when he believed she was still involved with Sean.

But had she given him a choice?

How tempted she'd been to tell Jack the truth about her and Sean's relationship. To admit that the man was selfish, egotistical, that he'd lied about everything she'd ever believed about him.

She would have liked to tell Jack about the so-called business trips abroad that Sean had said would advance his knowledge of computer gaming. That it was only by chance that she'd discovered his latest trip to Las Vegas had not been made alone.

He'd been stringing her a line, and she'd been too stupid— or too naïve—to realise it. It wasn't until she'd actually found him in bed with one of her girlfriends that she'd realised he'd been using her, just as he'd used everyone else.

That was when she'd told him she was going back to Rothburn. She couldn't go on living with a man who had no respect for her at all. He'd objected, of course, and when his pleas for her forgiveness had come to nothing, he'd threatened to tell her parents that he was broke.

That news had sickened her. Despite her contempt for the way he'd behaved, she'd still believed he was trying to get his business off the ground. He'd insisted that he was still making progress, but learning that he'd spent her parents' money as well as hers was devastating.

Consequently, she couldn't explain why she didn't break up with Sean without admitting how her father had been cheated. And with her mother only now recovering from what might have been a terminal illness, how could she risk Tom Spencer finding out?

Just recently, her father had actually asked when she thought Sean might start making some money from his investment, and Grace had had to bite her tongue and admit she didn't know.

No, although she'd cried herself to sleep some nights,

she'd decided it was safer to stick to her original plan and avoid all complications. Telling Jack her troubles would sound too much like hitting on him herself.

It was early evening when the phone rang.

She'd taken to turning off her mobile phone when she got home in the evenings, so it was the phone just outside the bar that her father answered.

'It's Sean,' he said, and, although her heart sank, she could tell he was pleased. 'He says he can't get you on your mobile, and I explained you'd probably left it upstairs and couldn't hear it.' He gestured towards the hall behind him. 'Go on. Ask him when we're going to see him.'

Not soon, thought Grace bitterly. She could imagine he'd spent the past five weeks spending Jack's money. Was he broke again? Was that why he was calling her? If only she could shut him out of her life.

'What does he want?' she asked, and her father looked scandalised.

'I didn't ask him,' he said shortly. 'It's you he wants to speak to, not me.'

'Well, I don't want to speak to him,' she muttered, but her father heard her.

'You don't mean that,' he said. 'Besides, he may have some good news about the website.'

As always, her father believed everything Sean said.

'Anyway...' Tom Spencer scowled '...I hope your attitude towards Sean isn't because of that man, Connolly.' He snorted. 'He's not interested in you, Grace. Apart from the fact that he's just lost his wife, the kind of money he's got to play around with, he won't be staying around here long. We're far too countrified for him.'

'Gee, thanks!'

Grace was hurt that her father could dismiss her so easily. Hurt, too, that he didn't think she had it in her to attract a man like Jack.

She wondered what he'd say if she told him she'd already

had sex with Jack. It would certainly prove she wasn't the small-town innocent he was trying to imply.

Unfortunately, it might also prove that she'd learned nothing from her relationship with Sean, she reflected dourly. But she wished he and her mother would stop trying to push her into Sean's arms.

'You know what I mean,' her father said now, evidently regretting his candour. 'I just don't want you to get hurt.'

'You don't think Sean might have hurt me, do you? What if I told you Sean already had hurt me? How would you feel about that?'

'I'd say it was just a misunderstanding,' averred Mr Spencer, turning away with some relief when a customer snagged his attention. 'Anyway,' he added, taking a glass from the shelf above his head, 'go and have a word with him. I've told him you're here, so I can't go and lie to him, can I?'

'You could,' muttered Grace as she reluctantly passed through the door into the hall of the pub. 'But you won't,' she added, grudgingly picking up the phone.

'Say what?' Sean had evidently heard her grumbling to herself but hadn't been able to distinguish the words. 'Is that you, baby?'

Grace wasn't in the mood to be amenable. 'What do you want, Sean? I thought we'd said all there was to say the last time you were here.'

'Don't be like that, Grace.' Sean sounded hurt, but she wasn't falling for that. 'Come on, sweetheart. Haven't you missed me just the tiniest little bit?'

'Uh—no.' Grace was candid. 'Why don't you tell me what you want? You didn't ring to ask about my health.'

'Well, no.' Sean went silent for a moment, and then he said carefully, 'I've got Jack's financial advisor on my back. He wants to know why I haven't sent him a copy of the contract yet.'

Grace sighed. 'You must have expected that. Jack Connolly's not going to be as easy to deceive as Dad.'

'Grace, Grace. You know I'm doing this as much for you as me and—'

'No!'

'Well, your parents, then. I need your help, baby.' He paused. 'Don't let me down.'

Was there a threat in those words? Grace felt an uneasy shiver slide down her spine. 'I can't help you, Sean. I don't have any money. And if you think I'm going to ask Dad to take out a second mortgage…'

'No, no. I know your parents don't have any money.'

Sean was scornful. 'I used to think pubs were gold mines, but obviously I was wrong.' He took a breath. 'I want you to go and see Jack. Tell him I'm doing my best to get things moving. I need you to explain to him that these things take time.'

'I can't do that.'

Grace was adamant. Although the idea of having a legitimate reason to see Jack again caused her heart to thump almost audibly against her ribs.

'Yes, you can.' Sean had always been persistent. 'He likes you, babe. I know he does. You're just the person to keep him sweet.'

'To keep him sweet?'

Grace was horrified. What did Sean expect her to do?

'The guy thinks you're hot,' he went on, taking her reaction at its face value. 'You're a clever girl, Grace. And it's not as if I'm asking you to sleep with him or anything.'

Too bad, thought Grace bitterly. Been there, done that, bought the tee shirt.

'I just want you to be nice to him,' he continued wheedlingly. Then, when she didn't say anything, his attitude changed. 'Or would you rather have him haul me to court?'

'To court?' Grace was taken aback.

Sean was losing his cool rapidly. 'I'm not saying he would do it but his financial advisor wants things doing all legal and official-like.' He snorted. 'I don't do business that way. Besides, I thought Jack was a friend.'

Grace blew out a breath. She might want nothing more to do with Sean, but she didn't want him to be hauled into court. How could she hide that from her parents? Even if Sean let her try.

After a moment, she said, 'Why can't you just do as he asks and draw up a contract? You have a friend who's a solicitor, don't you?'

'And how much do you think that would cost?' demanded Sean irritably. 'Okay, if you refuse to help me, I'll have to think of something else. But I doubt your parents will be too pleased when they find out you had a chance to save the damn website and you refused to do it.'

'Sean—'

But he'd already rung off, and Grace replaced the receiver with a slightly trembling hand.

She stood for a moment, trying to calm herself. He wouldn't tell her parents. But he was just spiteful enough to try if he didn't get his own way.

She groaned. If she hadn't invited him up to Rothburn, her father would never have got involved. And Sean would never have known where Jack was living. It was all her fault; both the fact of her father's participation and Sean contacting Jack again.

Though not her fault he'd asked Jack for money, she told herself. Not her fault that he hadn't kept his part of the bargain he'd made with Jack.

And what kind of man asked a girl he was supposed to love to be nice to someone just for a business deal? She could answer her own question. The kind of man who'd slept with another woman in their bed.

He didn't know she'd seen Jack again. He didn't know how intimate their relationship had become.

Which was exactly the reason why she felt guilty. She wasn't the innocent pushover he believed her to be.

Without telling her father where she was going, she ran upstairs to her bedroom. Slamming the door, she seated herself at the vanity and stared at her reflection.

Tear-wet eyes stared back at her, dark lashes shading their fractured depths. But her tears weren't for Sean, she thought, scrubbing her cheeks impatiently. The bewilderment she felt was all about herself.

Abruptly, turning her back on the mirror, she surveyed the room with wild eyes. Where was her mobile phone? There, on the cabinet beside the bed.

Snatching it up, she speed-dialled Sean's number before she could change her mind again. She'd go and see Jack, she decided. However painful it was going to be, she felt she couldn't do anything else.

When a woman answered her call, she was taken aback.

'Yes,' the woman said. 'Sean Nesbitt's phone. Who is this?'

'As if you don't know,' said Grace harshly.

It was Natalie West, she realised. The girl who'd professed to be her friend and then slept with Sean. It seemed that despite his pleas of loyalty, Sean was still involved with the other woman.

There was a moment's muttered conversation and then Sean came on the line, apologising fervently.

'Sorry about that,' he said. 'I've got a couple of friends round and one of them picked up the phone.'

'It was Natalie,' said Grace bluntly. 'I recognised her voice and I'm pretty sure she recognised mine. You know, I wish I'd never made this call. You don't change. You never will.'

'Grace!' He sounded desperate now. 'You can't blame me for dating someone else when you won't even let me near you.'

Grace expelled a breath. No, she conceded silently. He was right. She couldn't do that. Not even to avoid an embarrassing interview with Jack.

'Forget it,' she said. 'I just called to say that if I do see Jack, I'll speak to him. But I'm not promising anything, Sean.'

She rang off then, mainly to avoid his gratitude. She didn't want to hear him giving her any credit, when she so felt she didn't deserve it.

Turning back to her mirror, she saw her hair had tumbled down about her shoulders, its red-gold brilliance only accentuating the pallor of her face.

Why had she done it? she wondered. Why had she agreed to speak to Jack? Was it only because she was afraid of what Sean might do without her involvement? Or was she really desperate to prove she didn't care about Jack, either?

Abruptly getting up from the vanity, she opened a drawer and pulled out a black sports bra and matching sweats.

She'd go for a run, she thought. She needed some air; she needed to escape the confines of the pub. Bundling her hair into a ponytail, she pulled on her canvas trainers and left the room.

Jack was tying the aft rope to the mooring when he looked up and saw a tall slim figure, dressed all in black, pounding along the pier.

It was Grace.

He knew he would have recognised her anywhere. Even without the glorious fall of hair, swinging from side to side with every step she took.

He hadn't realised she liked running. But then, what did he really know about her? Just that she was warm and responsive, that she felt and smelled and tasted delicious. That looking at her, even from a distance, caused him to get an instant hard-on.

And when he was with her...

Dammit!

He didn't want to have this reaction to her.

Just because she had full rounded breasts—with those

perky little nipples that had swelled so delightfully against his palms—and slim but curvy thighs, ending in a tight bottom that fitted perfectly into his hands, didn't mean she was unique.

He'd thought Lisa was unique, but Debra had destroyed that image. Okay, he suspected there'd been more malice than compassion in her revelations, but he'd had to accept that her words had aroused some suspicions.

His mother's reaction, when he'd phoned her to ask about Debra's—as he'd thought—jealous claims had clinched it. And, while Siobhan Connolly had done her best to assure him that he shouldn't take anything Debra said seriously, that she was a loose cannon, there'd been something in her voice that had persuaded him she knew more than she'd said.

The call had left him bitter but resigned. He'd thanked God he no longer loved Lisa. Was this why his parents hadn't put up much of a fuss when he'd said he was leaving Kilpheny? Living in the village, there'd always been a chance that someone would say something out of line.

Whatever, he'd noticed that his wife had been significant by her absence since Debra had returned to Ireland. Was that why she'd been hanging around? Had she been waiting for him to find out the truth? He'd decided in the past couple of days that he didn't really care.

Now he climbed the iron ladder to the jetty and called, 'Grace!' before common sense prevented him from doing so.

But what the hell! Sean had been conspicuous by his absence, too, since the money had been transferred to his account. And after what Jack had learned in recent days from his securities expert, he owed the other man no favours, either.

Grace had halted, arrested by the sound of his voice. But then, turning, she put on a spurt and ran back along the pier towards the quay.

Jack blinked. But then, ignoring his conscience, he vaulted

over the handrail onto the pier and raced after her. He easily overtook her, despite the length of those gorgeous legs.

'Hey,' he said, catching her arm and feeling an instantaneous connection. He brought her to a standstill and released her. 'Don't I warrant a hello or something?'

Grace swallowed a little convulsively. Here was her chance to speak to him, so why was she drawing back?

In a tight navy tee and baggy black shorts, Jack should have looked nerdy. But he didn't. He looked incredible and she felt all the muscles in her stomach contract.

'I don't know,' she managed now, trying to control her breathing. 'Do you?'

'Why'd you run away?'

Grace shook her head, intensely conscious of the protective limitations of a sports bra. She couldn't prevent her breasts from peaking, could feel the nipples taut against the tight cotton.

'If you hadn't noticed, I'm running,' she said, with what she hoped was a distracting gesture towards her joggers. 'I can't stand around talking. I'm getting cold.'

'So let me show you my boat,' said Jack recklessly, immediately regretting the invitation. Had he lost his mind? If he took her down onto the *Osprey*, he wouldn't be responsible for his actions.

'I don't think so.'

She'd refused him, and Jack knew he should leave it there. This was the first time he'd seen her since that encounter at Culworth, which was far too prominent in his mind to make any kind of social gesture credible.

'Afraid?' he asked, his brain clearly having no control over his mouth.

'Of course not.' Grace held up her head. 'I just wouldn't want you to put yourself out on my account.'

'I'm not putting myself out,' said Jack drily. 'I really thought you might be interested.'

If she was honest, Grace knew she was interested. But

he hadn't been far from the truth when he'd asked if she
was afraid.

Now she said quietly, 'I think it would be best if I continued with my run.'

'Why?' Jack wouldn't let it go. 'Despite what you said
that night, I get the feeling you resent me for taking advantage of you.' He grimaced. 'Well, believe me, you can't regret what happened any more than I do myself.'

Grace licked her lips. 'I'm sorry.'

'Don't be. These things happen. You're a beautiful woman,
Grace. I wanted you. But I guess that goes without saying.'

Grace pursed her lips. 'I expect you've said that to lots
of women before,' she offered, trying to lighten the mood,
but Jack only grimaced.

'Not as many as you'd think,' he replied with a rueful shrug of his shoulders. 'Come on, Grace. Can't we be
friends?' He paused. 'We could always talk about Sean.
How is your boyfriend, anyway? Has he told you how he's
spending my money?'

It was a crass thing to say, but Jack couldn't help it. He
was doing his best to be friendly, even though it was taking every ounce of self-control he had. When was she going
to get the message about Sean? Dared he tell her? But, no,
there were some things even he wouldn't do.

Grace stared at him. 'Not exactly,' she said now. Not at
all, actually. 'But I imagine he's invested it. In—in starting
up the website.'

'Yeah, right.'

Once again, Jack was tempted, but he couldn't tell her
that half the money had already gone to paying off debts
Sean had probably not told her about. Debts for entertaining, that he suspected weren't business-related. Like hotel
rooms that had been occupied by two.

Grace was frowning now. 'Has—has Sean been in touch
with you?'

She meant this evening, thinking that would be a load off

her shoulders. But then, if Jack had been here on his boat, how could he have spoken to Sean? She doubted Sean had Jack's mobile phone number. Any more than Jack had his.

'I haven't heard a word from him,' replied Jack after a moment. 'Look, forget what I said. Just go and enjoy the rest of your run.' He turned back towards the pier. 'I've got a couple of things to finish off before I go home.'

Grace chewed at her lower lip. Talking about Sean had reminded her what she'd agreed to do. To talk to Jack; to make some excuse for the delay in Sean sending the contract.

To keep Jack sweet!

As if she needed any encouragement, she thought painfully.

Bitterness clogged her throat, but she found herself saying, 'Maybe I would like to see your boat, after all.' She shrugged. 'Can I change my mind? It's a woman's prerogative, isn't it?'

Jack's hands balled into fists, but he forced himself to turn back to her. What could he say? He'd offered the invitation, hadn't he?

'Sure,' he said, ignoring his misgivings. But he couldn't help wondering what had caused this sudden change of heart.

'Okay.'

She wrapped her arms about herself, as if she truly was as cold as she'd claimed earlier.

And Jack's jaw hardened at the thought that he could warm her. Where Grace was concerned, it would be no hardship at all.

Yet he had to keep his head. After all, her sudden change of heart had been unexpected, to say the least. He couldn't help the suspicion that the money he'd given Sean had played a part in it. There was something far too ingenuous about her acquiescence.

But what did that matter? He wanted to spend time with her. He'd take any chance to be with her again.

How the hell was he going to keep his hands off her?

Jack gestured back towards the iron ladder now. 'Can you make it down that thing, or would you rather go round to the steps?'

Grace pulled a face. 'I think I can manage,' she murmured drily.

Then wondered if she'd been entirely wise in her estimate when he went ahead of her to provide a barrier if she fell.

But she didn't miss her footing and Jack didn't touch her, so all was well. She stepped down onto the narrow slip that ran between the rows of craft feeling much warmer than before she'd started.

'It's this way,' he said, going ahead of her again, and, although she'd been expecting a luxury cruiser, the *Osprey* turned out to be a sailing yacht. Some forty feet of polished woodwork and silver-painted hull.

'Oh!'

Grace pressed a hand to her mouth, enchanted by the boat's beauty. Twin masts rose from its gleaming deck, chrome rails adding a touch of elegance.

'D'you like her?'

Jack's tone was surprisingly diffident, and Grace didn't hesitate before giving him an honest reply.

'I love it,' she said, shaking her head in admiration. 'I never expected anything like this.'

Jack's lips tilted. 'I won't ask what you did expect,' he murmured wryly. Then, stepping onto the gunwale, he jumped down onto the deck. 'Give me your hand.'

Grace took his hand without thinking and immediately felt a bolt of electricity shoot up her arm. Jack felt it, too. She was almost sure of it. And she snatched her hand away as soon as her foot touched the planking.

There was a moment when she thought Jack was going to say something. His eyes darkened, and her heart, already pounding in her chest, seemed to rise into her throat.

But the advent of another craft into the marina caused the *Osprey* to rise and fall on the draught.

Unbalanced—physically and mentally—Grace tried to save herself. She groped for the handrail. And, not finding it, suddenly found herself squatting on her bottom on the deck.

It was so unexpected, so unladylike, that she couldn't stop herself from giggling. The tension was released, and Jack, who'd been concerned she might have hurt herself, found a relieved grin spreading over his face.

'I guess you haven't found your sea legs yet,' he said humorously. He held out his hand to help her up. 'We'll have to do something about that.'

Grace didn't want to touch him again, but it would have been churlish not to. His strong, cool fingers curled about her hand, and the electricity she'd felt before fairly sizzled up her arm.

'Thank you,' she said, releasing herself. Then, before he could say anything more, 'Are you going to show me around?'

CHAPTER THIRTEEN

JACK TOOK A deep breath. He told himself he had no intentions to kiss her. But who was he kidding?

From the moment she'd taken his hand to board the boat, he'd been fighting a battle with himself. He wanted her, dammit. He'd acknowledged that. And he'd provided himself with the ultimate temptation.

But she'd drawn back, and he assured himself he was grateful. And how difficult could it be, showing her round the boat? He was proud of the *Osprey*. It was one of the positive advantages that inheriting his grandmother's money had given him.

Turning, he spread a hand to encompass the whole craft.

Then he said, 'Well, this is it. My home away from home. What do you think?'

'It's not as big as I expected,' admitted Grace, taking her cue from him.

'It's big enough for me,' Jack returned, relaxing a little. He pushed his hands into the front pockets of his shorts.

'There's a main cabin. A master suite. A guest cabin, and the galley, of course. Although I have to say, I don't do much cooking on board.'

Grace smiled and he thought how incredibly attractive she was. 'Do you cook?' she asked half mischievously, and Jack pulled a face.

'I do a mean omelette,' he told her drily. 'And I have been known to produce an edible Bolognese, on occasion.'

Grace glanced about her. 'I'm impressed.'

'Which is a first,' he murmured, and she gave him a sardonic look.

'I'm not so difficult to please,' she assured him, wrapping

her arms about herself as the breeze off the marina swirled about them. 'Can we go below?'

'Of course.'

Belatedly Jack took her lack of clothes into consideration. She must be cold. Okay, he admitted, taking her below decks was playing with fire, but what was new?

Expelling a breath he'd hardly been aware he was holding, he gestured towards the companionway. 'Along here,' he said, ignoring the rush of blood that invaded his groin. 'Watch your step.'

A flight of stairs led down to a lower hallway. Jack switched on concealed wall lights as he descended the steps.

Following, Grace sucked in a breath of admiration. Like Lindisfarne House, the yacht was exquisitely designed.

A wide doorway was at the foot of the stairs. Jack had already gone into the main cabin, and Grace hesitated when she reached the entrance.

Comfortable banquettes, bright with cushions in a variety of colours, lined the walls. Bleached oak woodwork matched the sofas and a thick beige shag carpet covered the floor.

'Come on in.'

Jack was standing between the seating areas. Amazingly, despite his half-disreputable appearance, Grace thought he didn't look out of place. Even the growth of stubble on his jawline only added to his dangerous appeal.

And, in the close confines of the cabin, she could smell his heat, the stark masculine scent of his body.

Forcing herself to concentrate on her surroundings, she crossed the threshold and saw that the galley opened off the other end of the cabin. A breakfast bar provided a useful separation between the two areas, tall chrome-legged stools offering a casual seating arrangement.

She shook her head. 'It's amazing!'

'It's practical,' Jack replied without conceit. But she could tell he was pleased with her reaction. 'Does your father own a boat?'

'No.'

Grace wondered what he would say if she told him her father was having a struggle to make ends meet. After the running expenses of the pub, having to pay a mortgage every month was no joke.

'How about you?' he asked. 'Do you like sailing?'

'I used to think I would,' she confessed ruefully. 'But my dad took me out on one of the fishing boats when I was quite young.' She grimaced. 'After spending most of the trip throwing up, it sort of squashed my enthusiasm.'

'I guess it would.' Jack chuckled, realising how much he enjoyed talking to her. He glanced towards the galley. 'Would you like something to drink?'

She watched as he stepped around the breakfast bar, the baggy shorts hanging precariously from his lean hips. He bent to open the door of what she now saw was a fully equipped fridge and freezer, his tee shirt separating from his shorts, treating her to an appealing wedge of smooth brown skin.

'I've got orange juice or cola,' he said, straightening. 'Or beer.'

And that's not all, thought Grace, taking a breath, and admitting to herself how little her agreement to help Sean had to do with her being here.

'Um—nothing, thanks,' she managed after a moment.

Despite the fact that her throat was dry, she doubted if she could swallow anything right now. She sighed, and then, realising she shouldn't delay any longer, she added, 'I have to tell you, Sean phoned before I came out.'

'Did he?'

Jack closed the fridge door with a definite thud. He wished she'd mentioned that before he'd invited her onto the boat. He didn't want to talk about Sean Nesbitt here.

Turning, he regarded her consideringly. 'So you were planning on meeting me?'

'No.' But Grace couldn't deny she'd been hoping to see

him, anyway. 'That is—not exactly.' She shifted uncomfortably. 'As a matter of fact, he said he'd heard from some financial advisor of yours.' She offered a nervous smile. 'He's worried because the website's taking longer to set up than he originally thought.'

Ain't that the truth?

Jack swallowed his annoyance. There was no use blaming Grace for the way Sean had behaved. What irritated him most was that she seemed unaware of his duplicity.

Perhaps she was. He wanted to tell her what her boyfriend was really like, to explode that bubble she seemed to be living in. But he couldn't do it. Not knowing his own motives were anything but impartial.

Jack scowled, turning away again so that she couldn't see his face. But what the hell was he supposed to say? That it didn't matter? That Sean needn't worry? But was he tempted to be generous because he had an ulterior motive?

It seemed he'd got himself into another dangerous situation so far as Grace was concerned.

It certainly put what he'd learned about Lisa into perspective. The feelings he felt when he was with Grace left no room for any other woman—dead or alive—in his life.

'I don't think you have to worry about Sean,' he said now. Then, unable to stop himself, 'Did he say when he was coming up again?'

Jack was regarding her inquiringly and Grace wrapped her arms about herself once more. 'Um—no,' she admitted awkwardly. 'Did you want to see him?'

'Not particularly.' Jack couldn't prevent that answer. Then, keeping a healthy space between them, 'Why don't you sit down?'

Grace licked her lips and he wondered if she had any idea how provocative that was. 'I should go,' she murmured uneasily. 'I haven't finished my run.'

'Okay.'

With a determination born of self-preservation, Jack

moved across the cabin towards the door. If she wanted to go, he wasn't going to stop her. In fact, it was probably the most sensible thing he'd done tonight.

She turned as he would have passed her, and he sensed she was as uneasy as he was. Green eyes met his with undisguised emotion in their depths. And when her lips parted to allow her tongue to escape again, he knew he'd had every reason to be apprehensive.

And let's face it, he thought, she was temptation personified and he'd created this situation himself.

'Dammit, Grace,' he muttered, reaching for her, and she stumbled forward into his arms. 'This was so not meant to happen. It is not why I invited you on board.'

'Isn't it?'

Grace was having her own little crisis of conscience. Not least because she knew she had initiated this, not him.

But for Jack, feeling her lips yielding beneath his was the purest kind of torment. The knot in his belly tightened and a groan vibrated in his chest. God, how much more of this could he take? he wondered. He felt as if he were on the verge of losing his mind.

He couldn't prevent his tongue from seeking the moist cavern of her mouth. Was thrilled when he felt her tongue twine with his tongue and the hungry urgency of her body against his.

She might have been cold before, but she was burning up now.

His leg was wedged between her legs, and he could feel the tremor in her thighs. And knew the urge to lower her onto the soft carpet and strip what few clothes she was wearing from her body.

But some small corner of his brain was still functioning, reminding him that getting involved with her again would be a mistake.

He didn't want to let her go, but he had to. Even if a certain part of his body wasn't with the programme. He had to use his brain, not his sex. He only hoped she wouldn't look down and see the bulge that swelled his shorts.

Grace, meanwhile, had wanted Jack to kiss her. Had wanted more than that, if she was honest. But when Jack drew back and his narrow-eyed gaze raked her face, she knew he was having second thoughts.

'I think we'd better cool it,' he said, a shade harshly. 'Much as I want you, I'm not a complete bastard, whatever you think.'

'Jack…'

'You said you were leaving,' he said, turning aside from her. 'If you want to finish your run, it's getting late. I wouldn't like to think of you out there after dark.'

'Do you care?'

'Of course I care,' he muttered. Then, brushing past her, 'Let's go.'

Grace tucked her hands beneath her arms, aware that her heart was racing. 'Thank you for showing me your boat,' she said, earning a sardonic look from him.

'My pleasure,' he said drily, stepping back to allow her to precede him out of the cabin.

But when he emerged into the small hallway beyond, he almost ran into her. He'd expected her to start up the companionway, but Grace was studying a door at the end of the hall.

'Is—er—is that the loo? I mean—the head?'

Jack looked along the hall and made a negative gesture. 'You need the bathroom?'

Grace's colour deepened. 'My hands are sticky. I'd like to wash them.'

'Hey, you don't have to give me a reason,' said Jack drily. Even if this was the last thing he'd wanted to do.

He eased past her and led the way along the hall. Beyond the door, a double cabin, its wide bed covered with a bronze silk spread, looked far too inviting.

'The head's through there,' he said, pointing to a door across the cabin. 'Take your time.'

When the bathroom door closed behind her, Jack backed out of the cabin. He could have waited, but he decided she could find her own way up onto the deck.

Mounting the stairs himself, he went to check the mooring lines. He'd already checked them once, but what the hell? he thought. You could never be too careful.

In more ways than one.

However, when a good five minutes had passed and there was no sign of Grace joining him, Jack went to the top of the companionway and looked down.

Where was she?

Then he thought he heard a faint cry.

Without stopping to identify it, Jack ran quickly down the stairs again. He glanced into the main cabin, but there was no one there. After only a moment's hesitation, he strode towards the forward stateroom.

'Jack!'

He could hear Grace's voice now. Clearly. She was evidently still in the head and he wondered, not without some apprehension, why she would be calling him.

'Yeah?' he said, pausing only briefly before circling the bed to the bathroom door. 'You okay?'

'Would I be shouting for you if I was?' countered Grace from inside, and it was obvious she was seriously miffed. 'I can't get the door open.'

Jack suppressed a laugh. 'Have you tried lifting the lock?'

'What lock?' Grace sounded confused. 'I didn't lock the door when I came in.'

'No, but I guess the lock dropped, anyway,' said Jack patiently. 'It does that sometimes. If you lift that small circular latch and slide the door along—'

The door opened before he'd finished speaking. Grace stood there, her face flushed with embarrassment, and Jack did the unforgivable. He started to laugh.

Grace didn't laugh.

She stared at him with hurt, angry eyes and then attempted to push past him to get out of the cabin.

'Hey…' Jack sobered. 'I'm sorry. But nobody's locked themselves in my head before.'

'And that's hilarious, isn't it?' Grace exclaimed, frustrated by his refusal to get out of her way. 'Did anyone ever tell you how juvenile that kind of humour is?'

Jack sighed. 'Okay, okay. Maybe I was a bit thoughtless—'

'A bit!'

'All right, a lot thoughtless.' Jack gazed down into her humiliated face and knew an emotion that he'd never felt before. 'I'm sorry, sweetheart—'

'I'm not your sweetheart,' she exclaimed, lifting her hands to push at his chest.

But Jack lifted his hands also, capturing hers in his and bringing the knuckle of first one hand, then the other, to his lips.

'I didn't mean to upset you,' he said softly, his breath, warm and slightly scented with coffee, fanning her hot temple. 'Come on, Grace. You know I was only teasing.'

'Do I?'

Her eyes were still mutinous, but Jack knew she was softening towards him.

'Sure you do,' he said huskily. And then, because he was seduced by her indignation of all things, he pulled her closer.

'Jack!'

But her use of his name, whether encouragement or protest, was lost beneath the urgent pressure of his mouth.

Once again, Grace's lips parted, almost without her volition. Jack's mouth was warm and sensuous, his kiss hard and purposeful. In seconds, she was swept with a feeling of heat and need, numbing her to any thought of resistance.

Hot and weak with longing, she felt his tongue press urgently into the moist hollow of her mouth. It was both a driving assault and an intimate exploration, causing a flood of wetness to make itself felt between her legs.

Her whole body felt consumed by their mutual hunger and a delicious tremor of anticipation caused her to slip her hands about his waist.

Between his tee and the low waistband of his shorts, firm, slightly moist skin spread smoothly beneath her palms. She wanted to push her hands inside his shorts and cup his buttocks, but she wasn't quite that sure of his response.

Nevertheless, when Jack gripped the backs of her thighs, lifting her against the powerful thrust of his erection, she parted her legs eagerly.

She wanted him closer, much closer. Male flesh disappearing into female flesh; brown on white; skin on skin.

She wanted *him*, she thought without remorse. She'd only felt this alive on one other occasion in her life: that morning, on the beach at Culworth.

But what did that make her?

Whatever, she couldn't pretend any longer that she was doing this for Sean.

It was what she wanted, heaven help her! And like an addict, she couldn't get enough of the drug of Jack's lovemaking.

With her nails digging into his hips, she arched against him, telling him without words how vulnerable she was. When his stubble grazed her cheek, she gloried in the sensation, enveloped in a cocoon of sensuality that left her weak and totally lost.

He pushed the sports bra up above her breasts and she shivered in anticipation when his mouth closed on one swollen peak. He nipped at her with his teeth and she trembled violently.

She felt more excited than she'd ever been before.

'Jack,' she choked, clutching at the waistband of his shorts as her legs turned to jelly beneath her. 'God, Jack—please!'

And then the boat rocked as someone came on board.

Grace froze, but Jack apparently retained his mobility.

He pulled her sports bra down over her breasts, the nipples still wet and throbbing from his tongue.

'Stay here,' he said in an undertone, leaving her to stride across the cabin.

She heard him walking swiftly along the corridor and then the sound of his feet climbing the stairs.

Envying him his control, Grace took a moment to check her appearance in the mirror in the bathroom. Her hair had come loose from the ponytail she'd secured before leaving the pub and red-gold strands tumbled about her shoulders. Her mouth looked swollen and bare of any gloss.

But she'd been running, she defended herself. No one seeing her now would necessarily suspect what had been going on.

She pulled a face. Who was she kidding? She looked as if she'd just got out of bed.

She wished.

She ran delicate fingers over her mouth as she moved across the cabin. It did feel bruised and tender. She could only hope no one would notice.

She wondered who would come on board without asking permission. It could be anyone. She didn't know any of Jack's friends.

And then she heard her father's voice and froze again.

'Mr Connolly,' he said politely, and she heard Jack make a similar response.

Then Jack added, 'Can I help you?'

There was a moment's silence while the two men seemed to be taking each other's measure.

'Perhaps.' Tom Spencer sounded less confident now. 'I wonder—have you seen my daughter?'

'Grace?'

As if she had a sister, thought Grace ruefully. But then her father didn't know how much Jack knew about her.

'Yes, Grace.' There was a trace of impatience in her father's voice now, and Grace wondered why he would think

Jack might know where she was. 'Jim Wales, the harbour master, said he saw you talking to her earlier.'

'Ah, yes…'

Grace didn't know what Jack might have said then. Whether he would have condemned himself further by telling an outright lie, which she couldn't allow.

With a feeling of resignation, she left the cabin and ran along the corridor, mounting the stairs two at a time until she was facing the two men.

'I'm here, Dad,' she said flatly, before Jack could answer him. 'What do you want?'

Tom Spencer looked at Grace, then at Jack, before returning his attention to his daughter again.

'Your mother was worried about you. Are you aware of the time?' he demanded tersely.

Grace wasn't, but she took a surreptitious glance at her watch and saw it was much later than she'd imagined.

'It's half past nine,' she said shortly. 'I didn't know there was a curfew.'

'Grace!'

Her father clearly didn't appreciate having to have this conversation in front of Jack.

'It's late enough for a young woman out alone. Particularly one who's barely half dressed.'

'I've been running, Dad.'

'Have you?' Tom Spencer's eyes turned to Jack again. 'Well, it looks as if Mr Connolly caught you. Or were you both going to pretend you weren't here?'

'I invited Grace to look over the boat, sure. I assumed she was old enough to make her own decisions.'

Tom Spencer's lips tightened. 'Of course she is old enough,' he said stiffly. 'I just wonder if that was all you had in mind.'

Jack was taken aback by the accusation. As far as he was aware, Grace's parents knew next to nothing about him.

'Dad,' Grace began, between her teeth, but Jack didn't need anyone to fight his battles.

'I'm sorry if by inviting Grace on board I've upset your wife,' he said neutrally. 'Please give her my sincere apologies.'

Tom Spencer straightened his shoulders. Despite being a fairly tall man, he was still several inches shorter than Jack.

'I'll do that, of course,' he said, even though Jack was sure it pained him to say it. He paused. 'I wonder, has your other female visitor left?'

It was Jack's turn to look confused now. 'My other female visitor?' he echoed. 'I'm not sure I—'

'The lady George Lewis picked up from the airport,' Grace's father said with some satisfaction. 'I believe she told him she was staying with you for a few weeks.'

Jack stifled an oath.

Grace was looking completely stunned by this revelation, and Jack wanted to hit the other man for ruining what had been one of the best—no, *the best*—night of his life.

'Yes. She's gone,' he said, not attempting to avoid the question.

He tried to catch Grace's eye, but she wouldn't look at him, so he continued on regardless.

'Debra Carrick—the young lady you mentioned—is my sister-in-law.'

'Your sister-in-law?'

Grace was looking at him now, but once again her father destroyed the moment.

'You knew Mr Connolly had been married, Grace,' he said, turning to her. 'I'm sure Sean mentioned it to you.'

Jack knew the use of her boyfriend's name had been deliberate, but Tom Spencer wasn't finished yet.

'It's good to know you have people who care about you, Mr Connolly. People who can share your grief at the tragic loss of your wife.'

CHAPTER FOURTEEN

JACK WAS IN a foul mood when he got back to his house.

He couldn't believe what had happened; couldn't believe how strong a desire he'd had to shove his fist down Grace's father's throat.

The man was a complete moron, he thought bitterly. He'd behaved as if Grace were Little Red Riding Hood and Jack were the Big Bad Wolf. Dammit, Spencer knew nothing about him, and that crack about Lisa had been below the belt.

Of course, Grace had left with her father. She'd had little choice when he'd said he'd brought his car. Despite what Jack had said, she probably had her own suspicions about Debra. And who could blame her, with her father looking on as if he'd achieved a coup?

Besides, she was still Sean's girlfriend. Another fact her father had felt the need to emphasise.

Which made the way Jack was feeling now somewhat less than princely. He'd never gone after another man's woman in his life. He ought to be ashamed, not finding reasons to blame her father. He could imagine what Tom Spencer would say if he ever found out the truth.

Yet, in spite of all the obstacles, there was something about Grace that made him act in a way he hardly recognised. He felt an inexplicable mixture of tenderness and lust towards her, feelings that defied any explanation he could give.

And tonight, he'd been fairly sure she felt the same connection, a connection that her father had tried his best to destroy.

Well, Jack had to accept that nothing was going to come of it at present. However Grace felt, she couldn't have mistaken Jack's antipathy towards her father.

He'd been a fool, he thought. He should have cooled it. Right now he felt that if he walked into the Bay Horse, Tom Spencer would have him thrown out.

Of course, good old Sean might turn up this weekend, but Jack wasn't holding his breath. He might even produce the contract he'd originally agreed to provide, but, after Grace's comments, he doubted that was on the cards.

It was a reason he could use to talk to Grace again, but was he really that desperate to regain her trust?

He suspected he was. He suspected he was only kidding himself if he thought this might pass.

Going into the kitchen, he switched on the light and found Lisa sitting on the breakfast bar.

It gave him quite a start. And after tonight's fiasco, he was in no mood to speak to her.

'What's wrong? Did someone rain on your parade?' she said, without her usual air of confidence.

'Apart from you, you mean?' asked Jack sharply, and she pulled a face. 'Oh, yeah, I got the low-down from your sister. No wonder you've never talked about the crash.'

Lisa made a dismissive gesture. 'I told you before, Debs is in love with you. She'd say anything if she thought it would make you notice her.'

Jack had been running water into the coffee pot, but now he turned to regard her with narrowed eyes. 'So it's not true?' he said. 'You weren't having an affair?'

Lisa sighed. 'I was in love with you, Jack, remember? We were good together, weren't we? Why would I need anyone else?'

Jack shook his head and turned off the tap. 'You tell me,' he said, switching the coffee pot on.

But the truth was he didn't care any more. And how depressing was that?

'I was a good wife,' Lisa protested. 'Your house was always clean. You got your meals on time.'

'Yeah, thanks to Mrs Reilly,' said Jack drily. 'I don't recall you doing much about the house.'

'I didn't have to.' Lisa was indignant. 'But that doesn't mean I was unfaithful.' Lisa stretched out a hand to consider her nails. 'And if that's what you're all twisted out of shape about—'

'It's not.'

'Really?' Lisa sounded almost disappointed. Then, staring at him, she said, 'It's that girl, isn't it? The one who came here with Sean.' Her laughter tinkled suddenly. 'Oh, how ironic is that!'

Jack scowled. 'What do you mean?'

But he was too late. Lisa had gone, fading into the darkness as if she'd never been there at all.

He must be going out of his head, Jack thought wearily, aware of a disturbing sense of unease.

But, as he carried his coffee out of the room, he thought he could still hear Lisa's laughter echoing in the quiet house.

Grace worked in the pub on Saturday night.

She hadn't wanted to, but Rosie Phillips had apparently taken another trip to Newcastle. And Grace's mother simply wasn't up to serving behind the bar.

She'd assured herself that if Jack came in, she'd treat him like any other customer. After all, she'd managed to do that before. And although she knew her father had only been trying to cause trouble by bringing up Jack's sister-in-law's visit, all he'd really done was remind her that Jack still loved his late wife.

But she needn't have worried. The bar was busy, but Jack wasn't amongst the customers.

Consequently, by the time she went up to bed, she wasn't feeling very happy.

It was a week since she'd seen Jack; a week since she'd reluctantly accompanied her father off his boat. And while common sense told her she'd be wise to forget all about him, she wasn't having a lot of luck.

She couldn't help thinking about what had happened, couldn't help acknowledging that if her father hadn't interrupted them they'd have ended up in Jack's bed. In that beautiful cabin, she reflected ruefully. She ought to be grateful things hadn't got that far.

Only she wasn't.

In addition, there was an uncomfortable truce between her and her father. He hadn't asked her why she'd been on Jack's boat and she hadn't volunteered her reasons for being there.

In truth, she hardly knew what those reasons were any more. Why had she agreed to his invitation? She'd known the dangers, known how reckless she was being. But somehow when she was with Jack, she forgot everything else.

Grace shed her clothes, feeling utterly depressed. As she stepped into the shower she wondered when her life was likely to return to normal. She seemed to spend her days lurching from one disaster to another.

The water was hot, but Grace ran it as cool as she could bear it. Her whole body felt hot, and, when she soaped her breasts, she felt how aroused she was.

Sean had never made her feel like this, she conceded, soaping the rest of her body. She sighed. How pathetic she was, needing another man in her life.

She slept fitfully, only falling into a deep slumber towards morning. In consequence, it was after eleven o'clock when she opened her eyes.

Something had awakened her, she thought, pushing herself up on her elbows. Then she blinked when the door across the room opened, and her mother's face appeared.

It was unusual to see her mother up so early. Susan Spencer had lost so much weight during her illness that she was only a shadow of her former self.

'Ah, you're awake at last,' she said, pleased to see her

daughter was sitting up. She came into the room and closed the door. 'You've got a visitor. Sean's here.'

'Sean?'

For a moment, Grace had hoped it was Jack.

And how pathetic was that?

Besides, Susan Spencer had never met Jack. And she had no doubt picked up on the fact that her husband wasn't enthusiastic about Grace seeing another man.

Now, however, Grace didn't let any of this show in her face. Since her mum had been ill, there was no question of upsetting her.

'Yes,' said her mother now, bending to pick up the underwear her daughter had discarded the night before. She viewed the scraps of cotton and lace with some bemusement. 'I don't know how you wear these things, Grace. They can't be very warm.'

'They're not supposed to be,' said Grace drily, flopping back against her pillows.

The realisation that Sean was downstairs, probably chatting with her father, filled her with misgivings. What was he doing here? Had he expected her to get in touch with him after she'd presumably spoken to Jack? Was that why he'd decided to make the journey himself? Or was he hoping to persuade her that his relationship with Natalie West wasn't serious?

'Anyway, it's time you were up,' her mother went on, tucking the dirty clothes into the basket in the bathroom. 'It's not like you to spend so long in bed.'

'I didn't sleep well.' Grace raised an arm to cover her eyes. 'When did Sean get here?'

'About fifteen minutes ago,' replied her mother. She still looked a little frail and Grace felt guilty at her making the effort to tidy her room. 'I'll tell him you're coming, shall I? I know he's impatient to see you.'

'But I'm not impatient to see him,' muttered Grace barely audibly, but this time her mother heard her.

She paused. 'Why not?'

Grace groaned. 'It's a long story, Mum.' She was loath to upset her. 'He's not the man you and Dad think he is.'

Mrs Spencer frowned. 'Well, I must admit I wasn't very keen when he persuaded your father to invest in his business.' She hesitated. 'But you know what your father's like. And I know he's hoping that the business is a success. We could all do with some extra cash, couldn't we?'

Grace groaned. 'Oh, Mum…'

'You won't be long, will you?' Her mother moved towards the door, evidently not wanting to hear any more. 'I believe Sean's driven up from London this morning and he's planning on driving back this evening. He looks tired, Grace. Perhaps he's come to give us all some good news. We could certainly do with it, couldn't we?'

'Why?' Grace gazed at her mother anxiously. 'You're not—you're not—'

'Ill again? No.' To Grace's relief, her mother shook her head. 'But I know your father's worried about the pub's finances. He could do with not having to pay that mortgage every month.'

'Oh, Mum…'

Grace shook her head. Of course her father was worried. And it was all her fault. Somehow she had to get Sean to spend some of the money Jack had given him to help her father out.

'I'll have a shower,' she said now as her mother opened the door. 'I won't be long.'

Her mum's smile deepened. 'Oh, good. I'll tell him.'

You can tell him I resent him coming here, preying on my parents, thought Grace bitterly.

But this time she spoke beneath her breath.

By the time Grace went downstairs, it was after twelve.

Apart from having a shower, she'd washed her hair as well, and it had taken a little time to blow-dry.

Then she'd dressed in pleated shorts and a candy-pink halter, high-heeled wedged sandals completing her outfit.

Sean was outside, sitting at a table in the beer garden, enjoying a pint of lager. He was on his own but had apparently struck up a conversation with a couple of girls sitting at a table nearby.

From her position in the doorway, Grace could see there was a lot of giggling going on, and she guessed Sean was exercising his doubtful charms.

Then he saw her and got immediately to his feet.

'Hey, beautiful,' he said, and Grace wanted to die of embarrassment when this caused more giggling from the other table.

She went reluctantly towards him, but when he would have touched her, she kept firmly out of his reach.

Undaunted, Sean grinned. 'You look stunning,' he said, as if she cared what he thought about her.

'Why are you here?' Grace countered shortly. 'Have you come to pay your debts?'

Sean grimaced. 'Don't be like that.' He glanced behind him. 'At least sit down with me. Have a drink.'

Because she didn't want to cause a scene in front of the other girls—and her parents—Grace subsided onto the bench beside the table.

'I don't want a drink,' she said flatly and then had to wait with grim impatience while Sean summoned the youth who helped out at weekends and ordered himself another beer.

'What's going on?' she continued, after she'd regained his attention. 'Do I take it you've been in touch with Jack?'

'Hell, no.' Sean scowled. 'And what do you mean by hanging up on me the other night? I don't like it when people hang up on me and then turn their damn phones off.'

'Well, tough.' Grace wasn't worried about offending him. 'What's happening about the website, or am I not supposed to ask?'

Sean hunched his shoulders. 'I'm getting there,' he muttered. 'I'm getting there.'

'Doing what, precisely?'

Sean glared at her. 'Hey, I don't have to answer to you.'

'Don't you?' Grace arched her brows. 'Don't you think my parents deserve an explanation? And you do have to answer to Jack. From what you've said, he sounds pretty peeved.'

Sean's eyes narrowed. 'Did you go to see him?'

Grace hesitated. 'I've seen him,' she admitted reluctantly. 'I met him when I was out running the other evening. He was working on his boat and he saw me when I ran along the pier.'

'Clever.' Sean regarded her expectantly. 'So I guess you saw his boat, too? What's it like? Some big expensive motor yacht, I'll bet.'

'It's not that big.' Grace was equally reluctant to discuss the boat with him. 'It's not a motor yacht, either. It has sails.'

Sean pulled a face. 'Typical. Jack would go for something that needed a bit of skill to handle it. Lisa always used to say he never took the easy way out.'

'You knew Lisa?' Grace was intrigued in spite of herself. 'You never said.'

'Well, of course I knew her.' Sean's second beer arrived and he took a generous swig before continuing, 'Lisa was a good kid. She—well, she and I had some laughs together.'

Grace didn't know why, but Sean's words troubled her. There'd been a note of arrogance in his voice when he'd spoken of Jack's late wife. Almost as if he knew something that Jack didn't.

'Anyway,' he went on, 'what happened when you saw Jack? What did he say?'

'What did you expect him to say?' Grace was impatient.

'You told him what I was worried about?'

'I'm not a child, Sean. But I got the impression he didn't want to talk about it to me.'

Sean groaned. 'So you didn't try a little…womanly persuasion?'

'No!'

But Grace's colour deepened at the duplicity of her reply.

However, Sean put an entirely different interpretation on her embarrassment. 'I should have known better,' he muttered. 'You always were a cold fish. I bet even a guy like Jack, with all his advantages, would have his work cut out trying to get you into bed.'

Grace was stunned. And hurt.

She wanted to say Sean couldn't be more wrong. That she wasn't cold at all. That Jack was twice the man he was, in more ways than one. But she couldn't do it.

She wouldn't give Sean that kind of ammunition to use against the other man, whatever the provocation. Instead, she schooled her expression and pushed herself to her feet.

'Get lost, Sean,' she said succinctly. 'And don't come back until you can pay Dad what you owe him.'

'Hey, I don't owe your old man anything,' retorted Sean staunchly. 'He chose to invest in the website. If it hasn't worked out, that's not my problem.'

'You're not serious!'

'Of course I'm serious. People invest in stocks and shares all the time and get shafted. He can't come crying to me because his investment hasn't worked out.'

'You bastard!'

Grace got up from the table, her face suffused with angry colour. Sean rose, too, obviously furious that she'd insulted him within the hearing of the other girls.

'Jack's said something, hasn't he?' he demanded. His mouth compressed into a thin line. 'He's been blabbing about where the money's gone.'

'Jack's said nothing about the money,' said Grace contemptuously. 'But if he knows you as well as I do, I'm surprised he lent you any money in the first place.'

'I bet he has.' Sean wasn't listening to her. 'I should have known he'd take any opportunity to put me down. Lisa always said—'

He broke off at that point and although Grace wanted to leave, she felt frozen to the spot. What on earth had Sean been about to say?

'He doesn't understand what it's like for me.' As if regretting his last words, Sean seemed eager to change the subject. 'I've never had any money to splash around.'

Grace groaned. She could hardly believe now that she'd felt sorry for him when he'd lost his job. Or that she'd ended up paying his debts for him while he was out of work. The salary she'd earned at the CPS hadn't been huge, but she'd been happy to contribute to their expenses. Which, in all honesty, was why she had so little money now.

But then she'd discovered he didn't own the apartment they were living in. The money she'd given him to help him out with the mortgage had gone into his pocket. He'd even been behind on the rent.

What a fool she'd been.

Then she'd lost her job, due to cutbacks, just after she'd found him with Natalie. In a way, it had come at exactly the right time. She hadn't needed an excuse to leave, but one had been provided for her. If her parents hadn't been involved, she'd never have seen him again.

But they were involved and she'd been stupid enough to think that, whatever he felt about her, he wouldn't let them down.

'Look, if you want to see Jack, I suggest you go and see him,' she said wearily. 'Tell him you're having problems. He might agree to help you out.'

'You think?' Sean's scowl deepened. 'So—you'll come with me, right?'

'You're joking!'

'No, I'm not.' Sean regarded her derisively. 'If you don't

want me to go into the pub and tell your old man he's not getting his money back, you'll do everything you can to keep me sweet.'

CHAPTER FIFTEEN

JACK WAS IN the study he'd furnished for himself on the first floor of Lindisfarne House when he heard the doorbell.

He'd been engrossed in his study of his plans for the cottages, and trying not to think about Grace. He had decided to knock down the walls dividing the kitchen and living rooms to create a through room, which was both lighter and more contemporary in design.

But the interruption meant he had to abandon the work and go and see who was at the door. The only person he really wanted to see was Grace herself, but he didn't think there was much chance of that.

Then he had an unpleasant thought.

It was Sunday. How could he have forgotten? Sean came to visit his girlfriend at weekends. Bearing in mind what Jack had learned Sean had done with at least a part of the money he'd loaned him, it was possible Sean had decided to come clean about his debts.

His pulse quickened in spite of himself.

What if Grace was with him? He had wanted to see her again, but not with Sean.

Nevertheless, the knowledge served to weaken the bitterness he felt towards the other man. However badly Sean had behaved, his own behaviour beat that hands down.

He had a brief hope that it wasn't Sean. He could see no sign of the Mercedes on his drive through the glass panels in the door.

But when he opened the door, he saw the reason for his error. The car was parked at his gate and Sean was already halfway down the path towards it.

But he heard the door opening and turned, his expression a mixture of disappointment and resignation.

'Hey, Jack,' he said, retracing his steps with evident reluctance. 'I was beginning to think you weren't home.' He grinned. 'Long time no see.'

'Yeah.'

Jack was no more enthusiastic for this meeting than his visitor. And despite his reluctance to see Grace in the other man's company, it was obvious Sean was alone.

'Can I come in?'

'Sure. Why not?' Jack stepped back from the door. Then, because he couldn't help himself, 'Isn't Grace with you today?'

'Uh...no.' Sean shrugged his shoulders indifferently as he passed Jack. 'She's back at the pub. Helping her mum and dad.'

'She didn't want to come?'

Jack knew he shouldn't persist, but he couldn't help himself.

'I guess not.' Sean walked into the living room and flopped down on a leather sofa. Then, shouldering off his jacket, 'That's better. And cooler. Do you have air conditioning or what?'

'No. No air conditioning,' said Jack evenly. 'The walls are thick. They keep the inside of the house cool.'

'And warm in the winter, I'll bet.' Sean nodded sagely. 'There's a lot to be said for old buildings. Present company excepted, of course, but some of these new developers don't have any idea.'

Jack made a non-committal movement of his head and regarded the other man expectantly.

'I agree,' he said. 'But I doubt you came to see me to discuss modern architecture.'

He paused, pushing his hands into the back pockets of his jeans and rocking back inquiringly.

'I imagine you've got some news for me about the website.'

Sean's face reddened. 'It's getting there,' he said evasively. 'I've had a few problems to contend with, actually.'

'Like what?'

Sean was bitter. 'I know you've been checking up on me. You always were a close-fisted bastard!'

Jack's eyes widened. 'I don't think it's unreasonable to show some interest in my investment,' he said mildly. 'I wouldn't be much of a businessman if I handed over one hundred thousand pounds without expecting some feedback.'

'I told you at the time you gave me the money that I'd keep you informed of what was going on,' exclaimed Sean resentfully.

'But you haven't, have you?'

'What do you mean?'

'Correct me if I'm wrong, but it has been over six weeks since we spoke last.'

'Yeah, but I've been busy. Ask Grace, if you don't believe me. This is the first time I've been up to Rothburn since that weekend we came here. And I only arrived this morning, so you can't accuse me of avoiding you, can you?'

Jack frowned.

'I thought you came up every weekend.'

'Is that what Grace told you?' Sean sounded pleased. 'She doesn't like it when I neglect her.'

Jack's nails dug into his palms. 'She'd hardly tell me, would she? It's nothing to do with me.'

'No.' Sean conceded the point. 'But it's not easy, trying to juggle two careers at once. If I'd had more time, I'd have got more done.'

Jack's gaze grew guarded. 'You've had six weeks,' he pointed out, and Sean pulled a face.

'With shift work and a dodgy manager,' he muttered gloomily. 'You try finding inspiration in those circumstances.'

Not to mention Sean's trip to Las Vegas, thought Jack scornfully. Had he spent all his free time in bars and casinos? Just where did Grace figure in that scenario?

'Anyway…' Sean looked up at him. 'If it's an apology you want, you've got it. I haven't been the most reliable of partners, I admit it.' He pulled a wry face. 'I'll try to do better in the future.'

'Right.' Jack conceded the point. 'So tell me, have you found other investors?'

'Other investors?' Sean was suspicious. 'Why would you ask a question like that?'

'It's a reasonable question.' Jack spoke evenly. 'I'm wondering how much money we're dealing with here.'

Sean scowled. 'What has Grace told you?'

'Grace?' Jack's expression was guarded. 'Grace hasn't told me a thing.'

Sean's eyes narrowed. 'So—okay,' he said. 'There are no other investors. It's not that easy to find spare money in the present climate.' He glanced about him. 'Well, how about offering me a beer, Jack? I'm driving back to London tonight and I'm thirsty.'

'You're not staying over?'

'Hell, no. I've got to be back at work first thing Monday morning.'

Jack despised himself for his own reaction to this news. Was it possible Grace hadn't slept with Sean since that first weekend?

'Of course, I'd certainly have more time to work on the website if I was like you,' he continued, apparently unaware that Jack's demeanour had changed. 'I've said it before and I'll say it again, it must be nice to be a millionaire.'

Jack held Sean's gaze for a long minute. Was this the overture to another demand for money? The guy couldn't be serious, he thought. He couldn't possibly think Jack would send good money after bad.

'Hey, I meant to ask you…'

Jack had stepped into the hall to get Sean a beer—as that was all he was likely to get—when the guy's voice called him back.

And Jack prepared himself for the inevitable request. But that wasn't it.

'I understand you saw Grace the other evening, when she was out running,' he remarked casually.

Jack stiffened. 'Yeah, I did,' he admitted, wondering where in hell Sean was going with this.

'I gather you showed her over your boat,' Sean went on, his gaze speculative. 'You and she seem to get along together pretty well.'

Jack shrugged. 'She's a nice girl,' he said tightly, inwardly wincing at his lack of honesty.

But Sean's next words drove every other thought out of his head.

'You know, I wouldn't mind if you wanted to take her out sometime,' he said casually. 'She's lost touch with most of her friends here and I guess you could do with some female company yourself.'

Jack's jaw dropped. 'You're not serious!'

Sean's chin jutted. 'Why not? Don't look at me like that, Jack. It was only an idea.'

'A bad idea,' said Jack harshly, turning back into the hall. His teeth ground together for a moment. 'I'll get your beer.'

'Hey, don't be such a puritan, Jack.' Sean got up from the sofa and came after him. He paused in the doorway, supporting himself with a hand on either side of the frame. 'You like her, don't you? And it's not as if we've never done such a thing before.'

Jack stared at him blankly. 'I don't know what the hell you're talking about,' he muttered.

''Course you do,' declared the other man blandly. 'I mean, when we were at college in Dublin, we used to switch girlfriends all the time.'

'Did we? I don't remember that.'

Jack gripped the frame of the door until his knuckles whitened. Despite Sean's facile response, Jack had the feeling that there was more to this than met the eye.

Was this about Grace, or was it about Lisa? Jack knew, with a feeling of resignation, he couldn't be absolutely sure.

He was grateful when Sean didn't follow him into the kitchen but turned back into the living room. He didn't think he could be civil to the man right now.

Whatever way he looked at it, it seemed that Sean was bargaining with his girlfriend. Was Jack supposed to compensate Sean—financially, of course—for the privilege of screwing Grace?

God, what a situation!

He knew he could never treat Grace that way. In truth, in all this awful mess, she was the only shining light.

He flung open the fridge door, scowling at its contents. Could he honestly drink beer with the other man without giving in to the disgust he was feeling and throwing him out?

His own part in the affair might fill him with loathing, but Sean's behaviour almost compensated for it.

Of course, Jack had never cheated on his wife. But then, he'd never known what temptation was until he'd met Grace.

Thinking of Grace in this context made him feel sick. Pulling out a bottle of beer—he was sure if he tried to drink anything, it would choke him—he tried to control his scattered emotions.

And to cap it all, he couldn't help wondering if Grace had known what Sean was planning to say.

He knew if he wanted to retain any self-respect, he'd stay out of both Grace's and Sean's way in future. She might be innocent of any deception, but for his own sanity's sake he couldn't take that risk.

Sean was standing by the window when he returned to the living room.

'Great view,' he said, accepting the beer Jack handed to him. 'You're a lucky man, Jack. But then, you've heard me say that before.'

Jack frowned. 'Yeah,' he said tightly. 'It was at my wedding, wasn't it? You were complimenting me on finding Lisa. Telling me what a lucky man I was.'

Sean shrugged. 'Well, you were—you *are*,' he amended, flinging himself onto the sofa again. 'You can't deny it, can you?'

'As you are?' suggested Jack, hooking a hip over the arm of the chair opposite. 'What about Grace?'

Jack didn't know what was driving him, but he was heartily sick of trying to humour the other man.

'Grace?' Sean stared at him. 'I don't know what you're talking about.'

'Well, she's a beautiful woman. You're supposed to care about her, aren't you? I'd say that makes you a lucky man.'

'Yeah, yeah.' Sean snorted. 'What are you getting at, Jack? I haven't said any different, have I?'

'You've virtually offered me the chance of sleeping with her,' retorted Jack harshly. 'My God, I'd never offer a woman I loved in exchange for cold, hard cash!"

'You didn't have to.'

The words were barely audible, but Jack had excellent hearing.

'What did you say?' he demanded, getting to his feet, and Sean had the grace to lower his head.

'Nothing. I said nothing,' he muttered in an undertone. 'Forget it. You obviously don't fancy Grace. I don't blame you, actually. She can be a cold fish at times.'

'I want to know what you meant,' Jack persisted, crossing the floor and hauling the other man to his feet. 'Come on, Sean. What are you saying? This isn't about Grace, is it? It's about Lisa!'

'I don't know what you mean.'

'I think you do. I spoke to Debra recently and she made some very interesting comments.'

'Debra!' Sean scoffed. 'Surely you don't believe a word she says. She's been in love with you for years. She'd say anything to get your attention.'

'I don't think so.' Jack stared into the other man's eyes. 'Why don't you tell the truth for once? Or is that too much to expect?'

Sean scowled. 'Don't tell me you never suspected.'

'Suspected? Suspected what?' Jack controlled the desire to get physical with an effort. 'Are you saying you were having an affair with Lisa?'

'As if you didn't know.' Jack's restraint was giving Sean more confidence. 'Yes, I had sex with her, Jack. Lots of times, as it happens. She was bored with you, man. All you could talk about was work—'

His voice was strangled by the grip Jack suddenly had on his collar. Dragging Sean up in front of him, he got seriously in his face.

'You know,' he said almost thoughtfully, 'Debra said as much, but I wouldn't believe her. What about the night she died? Were you with her then?'

Sean struggled to get some air, but it was a losing battle. 'I—I might have been,' he got out through a choked windpipe. 'So what? I didn't cause the crash.'

'She was taking you home, though, wasn't she?' Jack realised that that was where Lisa had been going. She'd sworn to him that evening that she wasn't going out, which was why her death had been such a terrible shock.

'Maybe.'

Sean was evidently weighing his options. The odds of telling Jack the truth against the unlikely event of being able to lie his way out of it.

The truth won out, because he suddenly cried, 'She was mad about me, Jack. You can't blame me because I did what any red-blooded man would do.'

Jack could, and he would. But gauging the satisfaction he'd get out of flooring the other guy, against the story Sean would no doubt make up to account for his injuries to Grace and her family, changed his mind.

With a muffled oath, he opened his hands and let Sean stumble away from him.

'She must have been desperate,' he said flatly.

And the amazing thing was he honestly didn't care.

Recovering a little, Sean tugged at his collar. 'She was crazy, too.' He took several shuddering breaths. 'She drove like a maniac, you know. I thought I was done for when that petrol tanker turned the corner!'

Jack was about to say he didn't care whether the other man had suffered because of the accident or not when Sean's expression abruptly changed. His attempts to defend himself were silenced by the look of absolute horror that crossed his face.

He was looking beyond Jack, towards the doorway into the hall, and, judging by the contortion of his flushed features, Jack suspected they were no longer alone.

He was guessing Grace had decided to join them after all, though he hadn't heard her enter the house. But the room behind him was empty and there seemed no reason for Sean's behaviour, for the unmistakeable terror in his gaze.

Sean blinked several times, his mouth opening and shutting as if he wanted to say something, but couldn't quite get the words past his trembling lips.

Then, almost hysterically, he said, 'What the hell is that?' He swallowed convulsively. 'How— No! No, this isn't happening.' He shook his head as if by doing so he could deny what he was seeing. 'I know what you're trying to do to me. You want me to think I'm going out of my mind.'

And then Jack knew.

He didn't need to hear Lisa's voice or see her slender form wavering in the doorway. Sean's reaction was answer enough. His late wife had chosen to show herself to someone else as well as him.

And although he knew he shouldn't, he couldn't prevent himself from saying innocently, 'What are you talking about,

Sean? As far as I'm concerned, our conversation is over. I never want to see your miserable face again.'

'But—Jack—'

Clearly Sean needed some reassurance, but Jack didn't see why he should comfort someone who had abandoned Lisa when she needed him most.

'Just go,' he said, and Jack guessed Lisa hadn't made it easy for him when Sean practically fell over the coffee table in his haste to get out of the room.

Jack was still standing, hands balled at his sides, when Lisa said wistfully, 'You're never going to forgive me now, are you?'

Jack shook his head. 'I forgave you a long time ago, Lisa,' he said ruefully. 'I just hope Grace understands.'

CHAPTER SIXTEEN

GRACE HAD HAD a particularly tiring day at the agency and she was looking forward to getting home and taking a nice long bath. It hadn't helped that William Grafton had turned up again, asking about a property in Rothburn. He said he'd heard she was looking for an apartment and he was planning on turning an old house on Rothbury Road into three separate units.

As if she'd want to live in some apartment he owned, thought Grace with a shiver. She'd never feel safe from his intrusion, no matter how many locks she had on the door.

She only hoped her father wouldn't hear of it. Knowing that he liked the man would make her position very difficult if that was so. And her heart sank when she arrived home that afternoon, and Tom Spencer asked if he could have a word with her.

He and Grace's mother were having a cup of tea in their living room. The family quarters were at the back of the pub, away from the public rooms and kitchen.

Grace's anxiety lessoned a little when she saw that Susan Spencer looked positively radiant. Surely her mother wouldn't be so pleased if she thought Grace was leaving and getting her own place?

'Would you like some tea, Grace?' she asked, when her daughter came into the room. 'Your father's just made it.'

'No, that's okay, Mum.' Grace wasn't really in the mood for chit-chat. Then a wonderful thought struck her. 'Have you had the all-clear from the hospital?'

'Not yet.' Mrs Spencer pulled a wry face. 'But soon, I hope.' She looked up at her husband, who was hovering in the doorway. 'Do come in and sit down, Tom.' Then, to her daughter, 'We've got some good news for you.'

It was the proposed apartment, thought Grace miserably. Oh, God, how was she going to get out of this?

'Do you mind if I go and get changed first?' she asked, trying to sound positive. 'It's been a long day.'

'Well, this won't take long,' said Mrs Spencer. 'Tom, why don't you spit it out? I have the feeling Grace won't be half as disappointed as you think.'

Disappointed?

Grace frowned. 'Is something wrong?'

'Well, from our point of view, something's very right,' said her mother shortly. 'Tom, for heaven's sake, be grateful that you haven't lost all that money. All right, you haven't made any money, either, but, from my point of view, that's a blessing.'

Grace blinked. 'What money are we talking about?' she asked, hardly daring to believe what her brain was telling her.

'The money I lent that no-good boyfriend of yours,' said her father, shocking her anew. 'Apparently he's had a change of heart. He's not going ahead with the website.' He paused, glancing significantly at his wife, and then added ruefully, 'I hear he's leaving the country and trying his luck in the States.'

Grace's jaw dropped. 'Are you saying you've got your investment back?'

'Every penny of it,' agreed her mother proudly. 'I told your father that I didn't think you'd be too broken-hearted, but he thinks you'll blame him for not kicking up more of a fuss.'

'A fuss about what?'

'Well, you're in love with the man, aren't you?' her father demanded. 'Why do you think I got the money for him in the first place?'

'Oh, Tom, don't blame Grace.' Mrs Spencer regarded her husband with some resignation. 'You know you could see yourself as a company director. Not to mention the fortune you thought you were going to make.'

Grace's father looked a little shamefaced. 'Anything I did, I did for all of us,' he protested, and his wife gave him a reassuring smile.

'I know, Tom. You're a star,' she said mischievously.

'But I can't say I'm sorry Grace isn't going to marry Sean.'

Grace was shocked and stunned. And hardly able to believe it.

'You mean, you'll be able to pay off the mortgage?' she asked weakly. And when her mother nodded, 'Oh, thank goodness. I was so afraid you'd never get your money back.'

'I was afraid of that, too,' confessed her mother honestly. 'So you're not heartbroken at Sean's change of heart?'

Jack entered the bar of the Bay Horse, not without a trace of apprehension.

It was a week since Sean had left and Jack was sure now he wouldn't be coming back.

Sean had driven away from Lindisfarne House ten days ago as if the devil himself were at his heels. Or perhaps a she-devil, Jack decided drily, remembering how he'd felt when Lisa had first appeared to him.

Now, however, Jack had decided to take control of his life and speak to Grace. She might not want to speak to him. He could easily have misread the signals she'd been giving him. But learning about the Spencers' involvement had certainly given him hope.

When he'd asked Sean whether there were any other investors, he'd already known that Grace's father was heavily involved.

Despite his conceit, Sean knew little about business, and he'd had no idea his financial dealings would be so easy to expose. When Jack had first given him the one hundred thousand, the firm of advisors who worked for him in London had immediately investigated the viability of Sean's proposal. That was how Jack had learned how Sean was spending the money; including the trip to Las Vegas and the fact that Sean hadn't been alone.

Jack was praying that, while there were no guarantees that the fact that her parents had been involved explained her reasons for staying with Sean, now that he'd returned her father's money, she was not committed any more.

Or was he only clutching at straws?

He'd chosen a time when he thought the pub might not be crowded. Even visitors staying overnight tended to be gone by afternoon. And it was a nice day; ideal for the beach. He should have been at Culworth himself.

Pushing open the door into the bar, Jack paused to get his bearings. As he'd expected, the place wasn't busy, only a couple of regulars shooting balls around the pool table.

And Tom Spencer polishing glasses behind the bar.

Great!

Jack had hoped to avoid Grace's father. He had no desire to have another argument with the man. But he was here and—oh, joy!—he'd seen him. Jack allowed the door to swing closed behind him and moved across the floor.

'Hi,' he said pleasantly, laying a folded jacket on the counter. He paused, and when the other man didn't say anything, he went on, 'Sean left this at my house a couple of weekends ago. Perhaps you'd give it to him the next time he's here.'

Tom Spencer put down the glass he was polishing and folded his arms. 'Nesbitt won't be coming here again,' he said flatly. 'But I can ask Grace to send it on to him, if you like.'

'Okay,' Jack said, with a shrug of his shoulders. 'That'd be good. Thanks.'

He was turning away, deciding he'd try to speak to Grace some other time, when Tom Spencer spoke again. 'May I offer you a drink, Mr Connolly?' he asked civilly. 'I feel I owe you an apology. I was somewhat less than courteous the last time we met.'

To say Jack was taken aback would have been an understatement. The last thing he'd expected from Grace's father was civility. He'd been fairly sure the man didn't like him, and getting cosy with him now seemed slightly hypocritical somehow.

But he was Grace's father, and time and events had certainly blunted his dislike of the man. So he said, with equal courtesy, 'Thanks. I'll have a bottle of beer.'

Tom Spencer nodded and bent to take a German lager from the chilled cabinet. Then he set the beer and a glass on the counter, levering off the cap with professional ease.

'Do you mind if I join you, Mr Connolly?'

Jack managed not to show his surprise. 'Please,' he said, and the other man drew himself a half of bitter from the tap.

There was silence for a few moments while they both swallowed a mouthful of beer. Jack didn't use the glass, but drank his straight from the bottle.

Then Tom Spencer spoke again.

'Grace won't be seeing Nesbitt again,' he remarked evenly, wiping foam from his upper lip with the back of his hand. He paused, eyeing Jack closely. 'Did you know?'

Jack wanted to say, *How could I?* But this wasn't the time for provocative questions.

So he said, 'No,' with what he hoped was just the right amount of interest. 'I haven't seen Sean since he left my house over a week ago.'

Tom Spencer frowned. 'His choice or yours?'

Jack didn't want to answer that. 'Does it matter?'

The other man sniffed. 'But you're not sorry they've split up?'

'No.' Jack decided to tell the truth. 'Are you?'

'Me?' Spencer grimaced. 'Hell, no. I've known for some time that he wasn't to be trusted.' He paused. 'But I thought

Grace loved him. That was why I acted the heavy father that night on the yacht.'

Jack was taken aback. 'Well…' He was surprised at the man's honesty. 'I don't know what to say.'

'You could tell me if I'm wrong in thinking you want Grace for yourself,' Spencer remarked drily. 'If you don't, then I can only thank you for what you've done for Susan and me.'

Jack caught his breath. 'I beg your pardon…'

'I'm not a fool, Mr Connolly. I know I behaved foolishly in lending Sean all that money, but, believe me, I've paid for my mistake. These past few months have been tough, for all of us. The Bay Horse makes us a living, but, you must know, pubs aren't as popular as they were.'

Jack stared at him. 'I still don't…'

'I'm fairly sure you gave Sean the money to pay us back,' said Grace's father quietly. 'I've not told anyone, but I heard him talking to Grace when he was here that weekend. He as good as told her he'd lost my money, that I wouldn't be getting it back.'

'I see.'

'He wanted her to go with him to see you, but she refused. He said he'd tell her mother and me what was going on, but for once she didn't give in to his threats.'

He paused. 'He never came back. I couldn't understand it, but Grace said he had to get back to London.'

Jack nodded. 'I guess he did.'

Tom Spencer frowned. 'What did you say to him, Mr Connolly? Did you tell him you knew where all the money had gone?'

'I don't remember,' said Jack, taking a mouthful of his beer. 'But I'm glad things have worked out well for you. I wouldn't have liked to see you lose this place.'

'Nor would I, Mr Connolly. Nor would I.' He hesitated.

'But I warn you. I'm not going to allow you or anyone else to hurt my daughter again.'

'Dad!'

The shocked exclamation startled both men.

Jack looked beyond her father's determined stance to where Grace was standing in the doorway to the private quarters beyond.

'Dad, what on earth do you think you're doing?' she demanded. 'Accusing Jack of hurting me!' She swallowed, avoiding Jack's eyes and the look of condemnation she was sure she would see in them. 'He didn't. He—he wouldn't. Don't judge all men by Sean's standards.'

Jack tried to catch her eye, but she wouldn't look at him. And before he could say anything, Tom Spencer turned to speak to his daughter.

'What are you doing home, Grace?' he asked in surprise. 'It's barely half past three.'

'I had a viewing near here and Mr Hughes gave me the rest of the afternoon off.'

She made a helpless gesture. 'It's just as well he did. What have you been saying to Jack behind my back?'

Her father gave Jack an appealing look. 'We've been having a civil conversation, Grace. That's all.'

'I brought Sean's jacket,' Jack broke in. 'He left it at the house. And I don't have his address.'

Grace looked at him then, her beautiful green eyes dark and cloudy. She'd apparently worn a pantsuit to work today, and the slim-fitting trousers emphasised the sexy length of her legs.

'Well—I'm sorry,' she said, shifting a little nervously beneath his disturbing gaze. 'My father had no right to speak to you as he did.'

Her father sighed then. 'You weren't supposed to hear this conversation, Grace. And I have no intention of apologising for speaking my mind.'

He paused, casting another glance in Jack's direction. 'Mr Connolly hasn't had to listen to you crying yourself to sleep every night for over a week now—'

'Dad!'

Grace wanted to die of embarrassment, but her father wasn't finished yet.

'You can't deny it, Grace. We've heard you, your mother and me. And I have to say, we've been worried sick.'

Grace closed her eyes for a moment. And then, holding on to the door frame for support, she said tightly, 'My—my crying myself to sleep has nothing to do with…with Jack.'

'I know.' The older man evidently surprised her with his words. 'But I hope to God you haven't been crying yourself to sleep because Nesbitt has apparently dumped you. I thought you had more sense than that.'

Grace didn't know where to look. Jack was staring at her, she knew it. She could feel those intent dark eyes searching her face.

Oh, God, she thought, what must he be thinking? That the humiliation she was suffering was well-deserved.

'He didn't.' Grace's lips trembled. 'If—if you must know, I dumped him weeks ago.'

Jack felt an incredible sense of relief. Dear God, he did have a chance, after all.

'Well, thank heaven for that!'

Jack's statement came out of nowhere, and Grace rubbed her hands along her forearms under the sleeves of her jacket, feeling the nervous chill in spite of the heat of the day.

Her eyes widened. What was he saying? Had he come here to see her? Dared she believe such a thing?

She was struggling for words, when Jack continued, 'Surely you realised I would want to know?'

Grace's tongue circled her upper lip. 'Why—why would I think that? We haven't even spoken to one another since that night you showed me…your boat.'

And that was such an understatement. But she could hardly say, the night you almost seduced me in the cabin. Not in front of her father.

'Well, I wasn't sure you'd want me to get in touch with

you,' exclaimed Jack drily. 'You must have known I'd want to see you again.'

Grace lifted her shoulders. 'You didn't try very hard to stop me from leaving with Dad.'

'Because I thought you were still involved with Sean.' He sighed, giving her father a rueful look. 'I felt bad enough as it was, knowing how I felt.'

'How did you feel?' she asked a little breathlessly, and at last Mr Spencer realised this conversation wasn't for him.

'I'm going to get a couple of crates up from the cellar,' he said, earning Jack's gratitude. 'If you'd like to stay for supper, you're welcome.'

As soon as he'd gone, Jack groaned. 'You know how I feel about you,' he said savagely. 'Dammit, Grace, I haven't exactly kept it a secret, have I?'

Grace looked at him uncertainly. 'Do you think we should continue this conversation up in my room?'

Jack regarded her narrowly. 'I thought you'd never ask.' He moved quickly along the bar and she lifted the hatch to allow him to step through.

A dog-leg staircase led up to the first floor. Grace went ahead, shedding her jacket onto the banister, revealing a simple vest of coral-pink silk.

The colour should have clashed with her hair, but somehow it didn't. And Jack had to resist the urge to slip his hand beneath its hem and find the soft skin of her midriff.

Her bedroom wasn't big, but it was attractive. Pale walls were complemented by floral curtains and a matching bedspread, a taupe carpet underfoot soft beneath their feet.

Grace was nervous. As she kicked off her heels, going ahead of Jack into the room, she was half expecting a continuation of the awkward exchange they'd had downstairs.

But Jack merely leaned back against the door to close it and then reached for her. He pulled her against him with urgent hands, sliding long, possessive fingers into her hair.

'Sweet,' he said, a little hoarsely, and bent his head.

His mouth nudged hers, took possession of hers, her lips parting to allow the hungry access of his tongue. He licked his way along her lips, causing tremors of delight to consume her, so that when his tongue plunged into her mouth, she heard herself moan with pleasure.

His eyes were open, searching her face for confirmation that she wanted him. She lifted her hand and stroked his jawline, loving the incipient stubble of his beard. She could hardly believe that Jack was here, in her bedroom. She'd despaired of ever being with him again.

Jack knew he had to take this easy, but it was incredibly difficult when what he really wanted to do was tumble her onto her bed. But she deserved to know how he felt about her. For him to hear how she felt about him.

Yet the temptation to just go on holding her and kissing her, feeling her slender body yielding—oh, so deliciously—against his, was almost irresistible.

He had missed her so much. God, even in his best moments he hadn't been able to kill the fear that, despite what they'd shared, she'd forgive Sean and marry him.

Losing her, he knew, would have been so much worse than losing Lisa. He'd loved his wife, of course he had, but it had been such a shallow thing compared to his love for Grace.

He caught his breath.

When had he first realised he loved her? he wondered. At the cottages, when she'd practically fallen into his arms? Or that afternoon on the beach, when he'd made love with her, uncaring that anyone might have seen them?

Or had it been on his yacht, when her father had interrupted them so inopportunely? All of the above, he suspected. He couldn't remember a time since he'd met her that he hadn't felt this amazing connection between them.

He released her mouth to bury his face in the curve below her jawline. Her skin was so smooth, so soft, and the heat of her body came to him in waves. That and the unmistakeable scent of her arousal, an arousal he felt his body mimicking when she lifted one leg and wrapped it around his calf.

'Do you want me?' she breathed, and Jack felt his senses reeling.

'Will the sun rise tomorrow?' he demanded thickly as his hands sought the provocative swell of her butt.

'But we need to talk, Grace,' he muttered, his breathing accelerating. 'Besides, I don't know if your father would approve if I made love to his daughter here.'

'Well, he seemed pretty happy about your being here earlier,' she murmured. 'I thought he was angry with you, but he wasn't, was he?'

'No.' Jack smiled. 'I think your dad and I have come to an understanding. He's not such an ogre when you get to know him.'

'Dad's okay,' said Grace, rising up on her toes to press herself even closer. 'I didn't tell you before because I didn't want you to think I wanted you to bail them out, but Dad had mortgaged the pub to help Sean.'

She paused. 'When Sean was here that weekend, he told me Dad wouldn't be getting his money back, that he'd spent his investment. I was horrified. He threatened to tell Mum and Dad if I didn't help him out.'

'Did he?' Jack wished he'd beaten the guy up while he'd had the chance.

'But I wouldn't do it. And believe it or not, Dad got his money back this week.' She sighed. 'You don't know how relieved I was when I heard what had happened. Sean must have had a change of heart.'

'So it would seem,' said Jack neutrally, thinking he had definitely got the best of the bargain, anyway.

Grace wound her arms around his waist. 'You know, I never thought I'd say such a thing, but I'm actually grateful to Sean.'

Jack's brows descended. 'Sean?' he echoed, and her cheeks dimpled at the darkening expression on his face.

'Leaving his jacket at your house,' Grace reminded him, using her free hand to tug his shirt free of his waistband. Her fingers spread against hot, slightly moist flesh, and she rubbed herself against him. 'Hmm, it's hot in here. Wouldn't you like to get out of this shirt?'

There was nothing Jack would have liked more. His pants, too, he thought ruefully. There was no doubt that they were getting much too tight.

'Grace—love, I want to be sure you know what you're doing here,' he groaned as her fingers slipped inside the waistband of his jeans. His pulse rate went into overdrive. 'I guess Sean didn't tell you what happened when he came to see me?'

Grace closed her eyes for a moment. Then she heaved a sigh.

'How could he? I haven't seen Sean since that afternoon when he went to your house.'

Jack knew this already from her father, but he wanted to be certain. 'He didn't come back to the pub?'

'Well, he wouldn't, would he?' Grace conceded the point. She blew out a breath. 'Okay, perhaps I should tell you that I finished with Sean months ago.' She flushed. 'I found out he was seeing someone else behind my back.'

Jack stared at her. 'But I thought—'

'Yes, I know what you thought,' Grace confessed unhappily. 'But if Sean had thought I was seeing someone else, Dad would never have got his money back.' She gave him a sly look. 'Besides, I'd sworn I wasn't going to get involved with anyone else and you were…well, too much of a temptation.'

Jack caught his breath. 'You're kidding me!'

'No, I'm not.'

'So when Sean came to ask for that loan, and you came with him, it wasn't me you were mad at?'

'No.' Grace sucked in a breath. 'I'm sorry. You must have thought I was a real bitch.'

'That isn't the expression I'd have used,' he remarked wryly, and she gave a little laugh.

Jack shook his head. 'But I have to say I had a few sleepless nights fretting about the way I'd treated Sean.'

'Oh, Jack…'

'It's true.' He gazed down into her anxious face, his own expression softer than she'd ever seen it. 'I was falling in love with his woman, see? I was even thinking of selling Lindisfarne House and moving away.'

Grace shook her head. 'And I thought I was just a diversion. Something to make you forget your grief at losing your wife.'

'Oh, no.' Jack was very sure. 'There's nothing diversionary about my feelings for you, sweetheart. I don't think I've ever felt so desperate as when I thought you loved someone else.'

'You're sure about that?'

Jack's thigh wedged between her legs and he felt her heat in the muscles that drew him in. Her eyes sought his, eyes so green he felt he could drown in them.

'What do you think?' he said as she gazed up at him. 'I just know I've never felt like this before.'

Her lips parted, innocently inviting the invasion of his tongue. She touched his lips with tremulous fingers. 'I love you, Jack. I think I knew it from the moment we first met. Even when I told myself you weren't interested in me, I couldn't deny my feelings. Not to myself.'

'So why didn't you tell me?' he demanded huskily, feeling the rapid tattoo of her heart beating against his chest. 'I've been through hell since you left me on the yacht.'

'Me, too.' Grace pursed her lips. Then, rather tentatively, 'Was that girl my father spoke about really your former sister-in-law?'

'Debra? Oh, yeah.'

Jack caught her chin between his fingers and bestowed a

teasing kiss on the corner of her mouth. He grinned. 'She's been my constant defender ever since Lisa died.'

'Does she love you?'

'So I'm told.' Jack didn't specify his informant. 'But as far as I'm concerned, she's Lisa's little sister. A bit of a nuisance sometimes, but she has my best interests at heart.'

Without her input, would he really have connected all the dots about Lisa and Sean?

Grace considered this. 'My father said she must care about you a lot to come here.'

'I guess she does,' said Jack ruefully. 'But you'll like her when you get to know her.'

'You think?' asked Grace doubtfully. 'I'm going to find it very hard to like someone who loves you. Unless it's your family, of course.'

'I know the feeling,' he said, lowering his head again to nibble at the side of her neck. 'But at least your dad has decided I'm really not such a bad guy. I'm looking forward to him meeting my ma and pa.'

Grace sucked in a breath. 'Meeting your…your ma and pa?' she echoed confusedly. 'Are your parents coming to stay with you?'

'Well, they may do, in the future,' agreed Jack. 'But I was thinking about before the wedding. Perhaps your mother and father might like a trip to Ireland instead.'

Grace's lips parted. 'Is—is that a proposal?'

'Oh, no.' Jack regarded her mischievously. 'I wouldn't be as presumptuous as that.'

'Presumptuous?'

'Of course.' Jack grinned again. 'I haven't got your father's permission yet, have I? But I will get it,' he assured her. 'Even if I have to get down on my knees.'

'Oh, Jack, I do love you.'

'I hope so.' Jack's voice was a little hoarse now, and she could feel the throbbing heat of his arousal against her hip.

'So maybe I'd better go down and tell your father how we feel.'

'In a little while.'

Grace was in no hurry. She looped her arms about his neck and threaded her fingers into his thick dark hair. She loved the feel of his body against hers, the sensual scent of male she associated with him. And the intimacy between them that she'd never shared with anyone else.

'I think, you know,' she said huskily, 'we have other business to attend to first.'

EPILOGUE

GRACE HAD NEVER attended an awards ceremony before, let alone one where she'd been asked to be the guest presenter.

And particularly not one where said guest presenter was in the final trimester of her first pregnancy and feeling like an elephant besides.

'I can't do this,' she moaned, gripping Jack's hand so tightly her nails were in danger of puncturing his flesh. 'I've never done anything like this before.'

'There's always a first time,' murmured Jack, his eyes dancing as he looked at her. 'I'm here and I'm your husband. How difficult can it be?'

'But it's the baby,' Grace protested, and Jack grinned at her words.

'Our baby,' he agreed, with some satisfaction. And ignoring the interested stares of their audience, he leant towards his wife and brushed his lips against hers.

Immediately, Grace felt a surge of emotion. Jack only had to touch her and her body melted with his heat. She badly wanted to touch him, too, but they were on stage in front of more than a hundred people. So she contented herself with squeezing his thigh and hearing his indrawn breath.

'Later,' he said in an undertone, and Grace dimpled.

'Is that a threat?' she whispered teasingly, and Jack gave her a smouldering look.

'It's a promise,' he said hoarsely, removing her hand from his leg as the mayor began to speak.

Grace's attention was definitely fractured, however. Even the baby seemed ominously quiet at present. It was probably a silent protest at the way she'd provoked its father, she reflected. Nonetheless, she was so proud of Jack, so proud of the man she had married.

Her hand traced the prominent mound of her belly almost absently. Just a couple of weeks to go, she thought. She couldn't wait for the baby to be here. The sexy jersey crepe was tight across her abdomen, and she'd wanted to wear something less revealing. But Jack had assured her that he'd be the envy of every man there.

At least the dress was warm. Northumberland in March wasn't the warmest time of year. But at least they were in a warm hall and not out on the cliffs at Culworth. They might have been if her father had had his way.

Jack's renovation of the cottages at Culworth was the reason for this presentation. They'd already won an award for originality of design, and Jack had also received a grant from the government to continue renovating other properties in the area.

Consequently, this ceremony had been arranged by the local Chamber of Commerce. They'd decided to honour Jack and in so doing advertise the attractions of the town, as well.

Asking Grace to present the cut-glass set square had, she suspected, been her father's suggestion.

Since Grace and Jack had got married seven months ago, Tom Spencer and Jack's father had become the best of friends. They shared an interest in fishing, and in Irish whiskey. And Patrick Connolly and Jack's mother were in the audience at present. They were frequent visitors to Rothburn these days, much to everyone's delight.

Then it was her turn to speak and Jack squeezed her hand in encouragement as she got up to make the presentation. She had to say a few words first, which was easy. She loved talking about her husband to anyone.

But the formality of the occasion was what had unnerved her. And only when the ornamental instrument was in Jack's hands did she heave a deep sigh of relief.

Then caught her breath as a stabbing pain pierced her abdomen. It almost caused her to double up, but she managed to keep a smile plastered to her face.

However, Jack, always sensitive to her feelings, saw at once that she was hurting. Cutting short his response, he slipped a protective arm about her waist.

'What's wrong?'

Grace looked up at him, her expression a mixture of irony and regret.

'I think it's the baby,' she said. 'They told me at the clinic that it might come early.' She braced a hand against the lower part of her spine. 'I hate to break up the party, darling, but I think you ought to go and get the car.'

Jack's face mirrored his consternation. 'God, I'm sorry, love. I never should have insisted that you did this.'

'Well, at least you got your award,' murmured Grace, laughing a little breathlessly. 'But right now, I'd like for you to take me home.'

The silence that had first greeted Grace's obvious discomfort was suddenly broken.

Half a dozen sets of footsteps thudded across the stage, among them those of Grace's mother and Siobhan Connolly.

'She needs to go to the hospital,' declared Mrs Spencer, trying to take control. But Grace clung to Jack's hands insistently, not letting anyone else come between them.

'Home,' she said imploringly, her eyes on his. 'Darling, you promised I could have this baby at home.' She took another breath as a second pain ripped through her. 'I'm all right, really I am. Just get in touch with Nurse Forrester and I'll be fine.'

Jack gazed round at his mother and his mother-in-law, hearing their worried protests, and then gave a determined nod.

'Home it is,' he said, ignoring the other women's complaints. 'If you two want to do something useful, offer our apologies to the mayor and his cronies, will you?'

'But, Jack—'

They left the hall with not just the women's protests ringing in their ears, but their husbands', too.

And Jack hoped and prayed he was making the right decision. If anything happened to Grace, his life would be over. He'd realised that a long time ago, and it was never more relevant than at present.

The next few hours were chaotic.

They arrived back at Lindisfarne House to find that Mrs Spencer had contacted Mrs Honeyman and that she had already prepared their bedroom in readiness for the new arrival.

But Grace hadn't wanted to spend the next few hours in the bedroom. She'd insisted on staying with Jack while Mrs Honeyman made them both a strong, sweet cup of tea. In the normal way, Jack would have gagged at the unaccustomed sweetness, but right then everything had taken second place to his concern.

Eventually—and seamlessly—their son was born in the bedroom. Jack had insisted on carrying his wife upstairs as soon as the nurse declared the baby's head was beginning to show.

And John Thomas Patrick Connolly delighted his parents by filling his lungs as soon as Nurse Forrester had delivered him. His lusty cries brought his grandparents to the bedroom, but the nurse wouldn't allow them through the door.

'Give the parents a few minutes,' she said, emerging with flushed cheeks and a smile of satisfaction on her face.

And both the Spencers and the Connollys had to be content with her assessment, forced to kick their heels in the living room while Mrs Honeyman provided them with more tea.

Meanwhile, Jack and Grace were admiring their new baby, whose cries had abated somewhat since he'd discovered his mother's breast.

A mirror image of his father, thought Grace ruefully, aware that Jack was watching his son with awe.

'I told you,' Grace said softly, stroking her husband's cheek with loving fingers. 'I'm tougher than I look.'

'Don't I know it?' Jack pulled a wry face. 'You've always been able to wind me round your little finger.'

'I love you,' Grace said now, reaching up to kiss him, and Jack returned the caress with enthusiasm.

'Love you, too,' he said fervently. 'I've never been happier in my life.'

And he wondered if that was why he'd seen Lisa only the once since she'd scared the bejesus out of Sean.

She'd appeared for the last time the evening after Tom Spencer had told them he'd heard from Sean.

Jack had been sitting at his desk, trying to concentrate on his latest design for a science museum, when he'd become conscious of her presence.

'You're happy,' Lisa had said, a certain wistfulness in her expression. 'Oh, and by the way, you won't be troubled by Sean again. I've taken care of that.'

And apparently she had. The last they'd heard, Sean was emigrating to Australia, and Jack couldn't help wondering if Sean realised that wasn't an escape.

Well, wherever Lisa was, he hoped she'd found her own nirvana at last.

Despite everything that had happened, he'd like to think so.

Now he bent to lift his baby son into his arms. The dark eyes, so like his own, gazed back at him in sleepy contentment.

'He's beautiful,' he said proudly. 'You're beautiful. How did I ever find a girl like you?'

'Just lucky, I guess,' said Grace, her eyes twinkling, and Jack thought how wonderful it was to think they could face the future without any of the ghosts of the past.

* * * * *

A NIGHT OF LIVING DANGEROUSLY

JENNIE LUCAS

CHAPTER ONE

"Is someone here?"

The man's voice was harsh, echoing down the dark halls. Clapping a hand over her mouth, Lilley Smith cut herself off mid sob and ducked back farther into the shadows. It was Saturday evening, and except for the security guards in the lobby downstairs, she'd thought she was alone in the twenty-floor building. Until five seconds ago, when she'd heard the elevator ding and she'd dashed into the nearest private office to hide, dragging her file cart willy-nilly behind her.

Stretching out her foot, Lilley silently nudged the door closed. She wiped her puffy, tearstained eyes, trying not to make a sound as she waited for the man in the hall to leave so she could cry in peace.

Her day had been so horrible it was almost funny. Coming home that morning from an unfortunate, one-time-only attempt at jogging, she'd found her boyfriend in bed with her roommate. Then she'd lost her fledgling dream business. Finally, calling home for comfort, she'd been disinherited by her father. An impressive day, even for her.

Normally it would have bothered Lilley that she'd had to catch up with work on the weekend *again*. Today it didn't even register. She'd worked as a file clerk for Caetani Worldwide for two months, but it still took her twice as long as Nadia, the other file-room clerk, to get her files sorted, delivered and returned.

Nadia. Her co-worker, roommate and, as of this morning, former best friend. Exhaling, Lilley leaned back against her cart as she remembered the stricken look in Nadia's face as she'd tumbled out of bed with Jeremy. Covering herself with a robe, Nadia had cried and asked Lilley for forgiveness as Jeremy tried to make their betrayal sound like Lilley's fault.

Lilley had fled the apartment and gone straight for the bus downtown. Lost, desperate for comfort, she'd called her father for the first time in three years. That hadn't gone too well either.

Thank heaven for work. This job was all she had now. But when would the stranger in the hallway leave? When? She couldn't let him—or anyone—see her like this—with red puffy eyes, working at a snail's pace as every single letter and number shimmered and moved back and forth on the files. Who was the man, and why wasn't he dancing and drinking champagne at the charity ball with everyone else?

Lilley shivered. She'd never been in this office before, but it was cavernous and cold, with stark, expensively appointed furnishings of dark wood, a gorgeous Turkish carpet and floor-to-ceiling windows that revealed twilight across downtown San Francisco and the bay beyond. Her head slowly tilted back to view the frescoed ceilings. It was an office fit for a king. Fit for...

Fit for a prince.

Lilley's lips parted. Panic ripped through her as she realized for the first time whose office this had to be. She gave a terrified little squeak.

The office door creaked open. Lilley reacted on pure instinct, throwing herself through the shadows into the nearest closet.

"Who's in here?" The man's voice was harsh and low.

Heart pounding, she peered through the gap in the door. She saw the hulking silhouette of the stranger's broad-shouldered body in the dim light of the hall, blocking her only avenue of escape.

She covered her mouth with her hands, realizing she'd left her file cart behind the black leather sofa. All the man had to do was turn on the light and he'd see it. Being caught sobbing in the hallway would have been humiliating. Being caught skulking in the CEO's office would be a career-destroying disaster!

"Come out." The man's footstep was heavy on the floor. "I know you're in here."

Her heart stopped in her chest as she recognized that husky, accented voice. It wasn't some random janitor or junior assistant who was about to catch her. It was the CEO himself.

Tall, dark and broad-shouldered, Prince Alessandro Caetani was a self-made billionaire, the CEO of a luxury conglomerate that reached to every corner of the globe. He was also a ruthless playboy. All the women who worked in his San Francisco regional headquarters, from the youngest secretary to the fifty-something female vice president, were madly in love with him.

And now he was about to catch Lilley alone in his office.

Trying not to breathe, she backed farther into his closet, pressing her body behind his jackets, against the back wall. His suits smelled of sandalwood and musk and power. She closed her eyes, praying the prince would turn and leave. For once in her life, she prayed her skill at being invisible to men would actually pay off.

The door was ripped open. The jackets were shoved aside

as a large hand ruthlessly grabbed her wrist. She gave a little shriek as he pulled her out of the closet.

"I've got you now," he growled. He switched on a lamp, and a circle of golden light filled the dark, cavernous office. "You little…"

Then he saw her, and his black eyes widened with surprise. Lilley sucked in her breath as, against her will, she looked straight into the face of her boss for the first time.

Prince Alessandro Caetani was the most handsome man she'd ever seen, from his muscular body beneath his black tuxedo to the cold expression in his dark eyes. His aristocratic Roman nose was offset by the slightly thuggish curve of his sharp, dark-shadowed jawline. He looked—and was, if the legends were true—half prince, half conqueror.

"I know you." Prince Alessandro frowned, looking puzzled in the soft glow of the lamplight. "What are you doing here, little mouse?"

Her wrist burned where he touched her, sending sparks up her arm and down the length of her body. "What—what did you call me?"

He abruptly dropped her wrist. "What is your name?"

It took her a minute to remember. "L-Lilley," she managed. "From the file room."

Prince Alessandro's eyes narrowed. He walked around her, slowly looking her up and down. Her cheeks went hot. Compared to his gorgeous perfection in his sleek, sophisticated tuxedo, she knew she was frumpy and frightful in her sweatshirt and gray baggy sweatpants. "And what are you doing here, Lilley from the file room? Alone in my office on a Saturday night?"

She licked her dry lips, trying to calm her shaking knees. "I was…was…" What had she been doing, anyway? Where was she? Who was she? "I was just…um…" Her eyes fell on the file cart. "Working?"

He followed her gaze, then lifted a dark eyebrow. "Why are you not at the Preziosi ball?"

"I…I lost my date," she whispered.

"Funny." His sensual mouth curved in a humorless smile. "That seems to be going around."

The sexy, deep, accented timbre of his voice moved over her like a spell. She couldn't move or look away from his masculine beauty as he towered over her, strong, powerful and wide-shouldered, with thighs like tree trunks.

Thighs? Who said anything about his *thighs*?

Ever since Jeremy had arranged her file-room job, Lilley had done her best to make sure her billionaire boss never noticed her. And now, beneath the prince's black, hypnotic gaze, she found herself suddenly wanting to blurt out why. She wasn't very good at telling lies, not even white ones. The hot, searing depths in Prince Alessandro's dark eyes whispered that she could tell him anything, anything at all, and he would understand. He would forgive and show mercy.

But she'd been around powerful men before. She recognized the intensity of his gaze for what it actually was: an emotional shakedown.

The ruthless playboy prince, show mercy? No way. If he knew about Lilley's father, about her *cousin,* he'd fire her. Or worse.

"Lilley," he mused aloud in the silent office. He tilted his head, and his eyes suddenly gleamed in the small circle of lamplight. "What is your last name?"

"Smith," she said honestly, then hid a smile. No help for him there.

"And what are you doing in my office, Miss Smith?"

The scent of him, sandalwood and musk and soap and something more—something uniquely *him*—washed over her. She gave an involuntary shiver. "Returning, um, files."

"You know my files go to Mrs. Rutherford."

"Yes," she admitted unhappily.

He moved closer. She could practically feel the warmth of his body through his crisp black tuxedo jacket. "Tell me why you're really here."

She swallowed, looking down at the expensive carpet beneath her old, scuffed jogging shoes. "I just wanted to work for a few hours in peace and quiet. Without anyone bothering me."

"On a Saturday night?" he said coldly. "You were searching my office. Going through my files."

She looked up. "No!"

Prince Alessandro folded his arms. His dark eyes were hard, his expression like chiseled stone.

"I was hiding," she said in a voice almost too soft to hear.

"Hiding?" His voice was silky. "Hiding from what?"

Against her will, the truth was ripped out of her. "From you."

His dark eyes sharpened. He leaned forward. "Tell me why."

Lilley could barely even breathe, much less think, with Prince Alessandro Caetani so close to her.

The soft golden glow of the lamp, the darkening twilight outside the windows filled the enormous, high-ceilinged office with deepening shadows. "I was crying," she whispered over the lump in her throat. "I couldn't stay at home, I'm days behind on my work, and I didn't want you to see me because I was crying!"

Struggling not to cry, Lilley looked away. If she wept in front of her powerful boss, her humiliation would be complete. He would fire her—whether for skulking in his office, for crying in such an unprofessional way, or for being so behind on her work, it hardly mattered. She would lose the last thing she valued. The perfect finale to the second-worst day of her life.

"Ah," he said softly, looking down at her. "At last, I understand."

Her shoulders sagged. He was going to tell her to gather her things and get out of his building.

The prince's gaze was full of darkness, an ocean at midnight, deep enough to drown in. "You were in love with him?"

"What?" Lilley blinked. "Who?"

The corners of his sensual mouth curved upward. "The man."

"What makes you think I was crying over a man?"

"Why else would a woman weep?"

She laughed, but the sound was almost like a sob. "Everything has gone wrong today. I thought I might be happier if I lost some weight. I tried to go for a jog. Big mistake." She looked down at her old running shoes, at her baggy sweatshirt and sweatpants. "My roommate thought I'd left for work. When I came back to the apartment I found her with my boyfriend. In bed."

Alessandro cupped her cheek. "I'm sorry."

Lilley looked up at him, shocked by his unexpected sympathy. Then her lips parted. Sparks spread from his touch, zinging from her earlobes to her scalp, down her neck and spine, causing heat to whirl like lightning across her skin. Her breasts felt strangely heavy, her nipples tightening beneath her workout bra.

His eyes narrowed in surprise. "But you're beautiful."

Beautiful? It was like a slap in the face. She ripped away. "Don't."

He frowned. "Don't what?"

His cruelty took her breath away. She blinked fast, glaring up at him. "I know I'm not beautiful. And it's fine. I know I'm not smart either, and I can live with that. But for you to stand there and taunt me like that…" She gripped her hands into fists. "It's not just *patronizing*, it's heartless!"

Alessandro looked down at her gravely, not saying a word. And Lilley sucked in her breath, realizing she'd just told off her boss.

She clasped her hands together. "I'm fired, right?" When he didn't reply, a shudder of grief went through her. Her hands shook as she picked up a file from the floor and reached for the metal cart. "I'll finish my work," she said miserably, "then collect my things."

He grabbed her arm, stopping her. "So a compliment is a taunt?" Staring down at her, he shook his head. "You're a strange girl, Lilley Smith."

The way Prince Alessandro was looking at her, for an instant she'd almost thought—but no. *Strange* was a code word for *helpless failure*. She said over the lump in her throat, "So my father has always told me."

"You're not fired."

She looked up at him with the first glimmer of hope. "I'm not?"

Leaning forward, he took the file from her hand and set it on top of the metal cart. "I have a different sort of penalty in mind."

"The guillotine?" she said weakly. "The electric chair?"

"You'll come with me to the ball tonight."

Her lips fell open. "W-what?"

His dark eyes were as warm as molten chocolate and hot as embers of fire. "I want you to be my date."

Lilley stared at him, her eyes wide, her heart pounding. Had she fallen into some strange dream? Prince Alessandro could have the most beautiful women on earth—and he'd already had quite a few of them, according to the celebrity tabloids. Frowning, she turned around to make sure he wasn't talking to some movie star or lingerie model behind her.

"Well, *cara?*" he said huskily. "What do you say?"

Lilley turned back. She felt dizzy from his attention, half-drunk beneath the intensity of his dark gaze. She said slowly, "I don't understand."

"What's to understand?"

Lilley cleared her throat. "I don't get the joke."

"I never joke."

"You don't? Too bad. I joke all the time," she said. "Usually by accident."

He didn't even smile. He just looked down at her, his face unmovable and oh, so handsome.

"You're serious?"

"Yes."

"But—it's the Preziosi di Caetani ball," she stammered. "The biggest charity event of the summer. The mayor will be there. The governor. The paparazzi."

"So?"

"So you could have any woman you want."

"And I want you."

His four simple words made Lilley's heart twist in her chest. She clasped her trembling hands together. "But you have a girlfriend. I've read—"

His expression hardened. "No."

"But Olivia Bianchi—"

"No," he said tersely.

Biting her lip, Lilley looked up at him. He wasn't telling her the whole truth. And the waves of danger emanating off his body nearly scorched her. If he found out who Lilley really was, she would lose her job—or possibly get dragged into court on charges of corporate espionage. Every instinct of self-preservation told her one thing: *Run.*

"Sorry," she said. "No."

His eyes widened. She'd clearly shocked him. "Why?"

She bit her lip. "My work—"

"Give me a real reason," he bit out.

A real reason? How about the fact that she was the daughter of a man he hated, and the cousin of another man he hated even more? Or the biggest reason of all: his strength, power and masculine beauty terrified her, making her heart pound and her body break out in a hot sweat? No man had ever had this effect on her, ever, and she didn't know what to do. Except run.

"My boyfriend…my ex-boyfriend," she stumbled, "will be at the ball tonight with my friend—Nadia. So you see I couldn't possibly go."

"He'll be at the ball?" Alessandro's eyes sharpened. "Do I know him—this man who made you weep?"

"He works in the Preziosi jewelry-design division."

His eyes gleamed. "All the more reason to go. When he sees you on my arm, he will remember your value and beg you to come back to him. You can accept his groveling or spurn him, as you choose. And the woman will suffer when she sees you as my date."

She stared up at him in amazement. "You don't have self-esteem issues, do you?"

He looked at her with an even gaze. "We both know it is true."

Lilley pressed her lips together, knowing he was right. If she went as his date, she would be the most envied woman in the city—possibly in all of California.

The thought of Nadia and Jeremy groveling at her feet and begging for forgiveness was a delicious one. All the times Lilley had worked late, all the times she'd asked Nadia to please explain to Jeremy and entertain him, and they'd betrayed her. She had no friends in this city now. None.

She lifted her eyes to Alessandro's. "I'm not a very good dancer."

He slowly looked her over. "I find that hard to believe."

"I took ballroom-dancing lessons as a kid, and my teacher asked me to quit. I was like one of those dancing elephants with tutus. All my boyfriends have complained about me stepping on their feet."

His expression changed, became softer. "Even if that were true," he murmured, "the fault would be your partner's, not yours. It is the man's responsibility to lead."

She swallowed. "Um. I…I never thought of that. I just assumed I was to blame."

"You assumed wrong," he said simply, then lifted his eyebrow. "But just out of curiosity, how many is all?"

"What?"

"*All* your boyfriends."

Oh heavens. She couldn't tell him her pathetic number. She lifted her chin and said with false bravado, "A few."

"Ten?" he persisted.

The heat in her cheeks deepened as her shoulders slumped. "Two," she confessed. "A boyfriend in high school, and…" A lump rose in her throat. "…and Jeremy."

"Jeremy. That is his name? The man who broke your heart?"

"He betrayed me." She looked at the floor. "But that's not what broke my heart."

He waited, but she did not explain. "So go out tonight. Your dancing skills are irrelevant, because we will not dance."

She looked up at him with a crooked grin. "Afraid of getting your toes stomped?"

"I do not dance."

Her eyes widened. "What—never?"

"No."

"But you're the sponsor of the Preziosi di Caetani ball!"

"It raises money for my favorite charity and gets good press for Caetani Worldwide," he said coldly. "That's what I care about. Dancing does not interest me."

"Oh," Lilley said uncertainly. She bit her lip. "I see."

But she didn't see at all. How could a man like Prince Alessandro, the heartthrob of women around the world, sponsor a ball and not dance? It didn't make sense.

He started to reach for her hand. "Come. We must hurry."

She backed away. She was afraid to let him touch her again, afraid of his strange power over her body. She gulped. "Why me?"

"Why *not* you?"

Setting her jaw, she folded her arms. "You're famous for many things, Prince Alessandro, but taking file clerks on charity dates isn't one of them."

He threw back his head and laughed. Turning, he went to the large modernist painting above his desk and swung it open to reveal a safe. Turning the combination to open the door, he pulled out two platinum and diamond cufflinks, then faced her with new intrigue. "You interest me, Lilley Smith. Not one woman in a thousand would have asked me why before saying yes."

"I guess I'm weird that way." She watched him put on his expensive cufflinks one at a time, saw the strength of his wrists and the sensual movement of his hands. He paused.

"My date for the ball fell through ten minutes ago."

"Miss Bianchi?"

"Yes."

She'd seen pictures of the Milanese heiress, who was blond, thin and beautiful—everything Lilley was not. She looked down. "I'm nothing like her."

"That makes you perfect," he said harshly. "Olivia will

learn how I respond to ultimatums. I need a date, and I found you in my office. It is fate."

"Fate," she whispered. He came back around his desk, his body a dark, powerful shadow. His eyes locked with hers.

"I need a date. You need revenge. This Jeremy will be on his knees for you before the night is through."

A low current went up her spine. No matter how much they'd hurt her, she knew revenge was wrong. And being close to Alessandro scared her. She wasn't just afraid for her job. He made her feel so...so strange.

"Why do you hesitate?" he demanded. "Are you in love with him?"

She shook her head. "It's just..."

"What?"

Swallowing, she turned away. "Nothing."

"I've watched you for weeks, little mouse, trying to avoid me."

Her lips parted in shock. "You saw me?"

He gave a single nod. "Scurrying the other way when you saw me in the halls. This type of behavior from a woman is very...singular. It puzzled me. But now I understand."

"You do?" she croaked.

He touched her cheek, forcing her to meet his eyes. "Most women I've met would have deserted their lovers in an instant to be with me. Loyalty is a rare quality. This man who betrayed you, he is a fool."

She couldn't argue with that. She stared up at him, mesmerized.

He dropped his hand. "But you have nothing to fear," he said simply. "Our romance will be only an illusion. I will not call you tomorrow. I will not call you ever. After tonight, you will again be just my employee, and I will be your boss, pretending not to notice as you avoid me in the shadows."

Lilley swallowed, still feeling his touch on her cheek. "You mean if I go with you to the ball tonight," she whispered, "you'll ignore me tomorrow? You'll ignore me forever?"

"Yes."

Lilley exhaled. She had to make him forget her existence. It was the only way to guarantee he wouldn't be curious enough to discover the omissions on her résumé. But in her heart of hearts, she knew that wasn't the only reason.

You're always running away, Lilley. Jeremy's stinging indictment rang in her ears. *You said you came to San Francisco to pursue your jewelry business and spend time with me. Instead you've avoided us both since the day you arrived here. Either you never really wanted me or the business, or you're the worst coward I've ever known.*

Lilley closed her eyes. That morning, she'd been too angry to listen to his words. Jeremy and Nadia had betrayed her, pure and simple. She'd done nothing wrong. Right?

Right?

But suddenly all she wanted to do was prove Jeremy wrong. To be one of the glamorous, carefree, fearless girls who wore sparkly clothes and danced, laughed and drank champagne. To be the girl courted by a knight in shining armor.

To be the girl who attended a ball with a prince.

She wasn't a coward. She wasn't. She could be as brave and ruthless as anyone. She could watch Prince Alessandro and learn!

Lilley opened her eyes. "I accept."

He looked down at her. "Do you understand, Lilley?" he said evenly. "It's not a real date. There will be nothing between us tomorrow. Absolutely nothing."

"Yeah, I get it," she said. "Monday I'll go back to the file room. You'll go back to Rome and probably Miss Bianchi, when you're done teaching her your little lesson. I'll continue to work for you and you'll never bother me again. Perfect."

He stared at her, then snorted a laugh, shaking his head. "You continue to surprise me, Lilley," he murmured, wrapping his hand around her waist. "Come. We haven't much time."

As he led her out of the office, she felt a rush of sensation from the heaviness of his arm around her. Trying to ignore the wobble of her knees, she glanced back at the file cart. "But I haven't finished my work—"

"It will be arranged."

"And I don't have a dress!"

His lips curved. "You will."

She looked up at him, annoyed. "Who am I, Cinderella? Are you supposed to be my fairy godmother? I'm not going to let you buy me a dress!"

In the hallway, he pushed the button to summon the elevator then took her hand in his own. "Of course you will." He gently pushed some strands of brown hair out of her eyes. "You will let me do exactly as I please, and I will give you an evening of pleasure. A beautiful gown, the envy of your coworkers and revenge against the people who betrayed you. It will be…an interesting night."

Lilley breathed in his scent of clean skin and sandalwood, of seduction and power. She felt his palm against her own, rough and hot, and her pulse quickened, sending shivers up and down her virgin body. "All right. Yes."

His dark eyes gleamed in the shadows of the hallway. "Yes?"

"Yes to the dress. To your help." She licked her lips and

gave him a trembling smile. "Yes to everything, your high-ness."

"Call me Alessandro." He lifted her hand to his mouth. She felt the press of his smooth, sensual lips and the heat of his breath against her skin, and gasped as fire raced up her arm and down the length of her body, igniting her like a match thrown into gasoline. "And women always do," he murmured.

She licked her lips, dazed. "What?"

He straightened. His dark eyes were hot as a smile curled his sensual lips.

"Say yes," he whispered. "To everything."

CHAPTER TWO

EVENING fog had rolled in, seeping beneath Alessandro's tuxedo as he stepped out of the limo onto the red carpet outside the hundred-year-old mansion on Nob Hill. It was August, but the fog was clammy and damp against his skin, a cold wet slap across the face.

Alessandro was grateful. A cold slap was exactly what he needed at the moment.

Flashbulbs of the waiting paparazzi popped around him as he heard Lilley's high heels clack against the concrete then step softly onto the red carpet behind him. Alessandro's body tightened. Overwhelming desire crackled through his blood, a shocking need that had begun the moment he'd gotten his first real look at her face in his office.

And now it was a hundred times worse. Just the drive in the limo had been almost unbearable, as he sat beside her. *He hadn't known she was so beautiful.*

He felt Lilley's graceful arm wrap around his, felt the light, gentle pressure of her hand against his forearm, felt the warmth of her touch through his tuxedo jacket.

With a shiver of desire, he looked down at her.

He'd noticed the mousy file clerk weeks ago. Rosy-cheeked and brown-haired, always wearing shapeless, unattractive dresses, she'd looked barely more than twenty and fresh from the country. After watching her veer away from him in a panic with her cart whenever their paths crossed, he'd been curious enough to have Mrs. Rutherford pull a copy of the girl's file. But he hadn't discovered anything very interesting there. She'd moved to San Francisco in June, and the file-room position was apparently her first job since working as a hotel housekeeper in Minneapolis a few years ago. Everything about her was forgettable, even her name.

Except that was no longer true.

Alessandro exhaled. He'd intended to teach Olivia she could be replaced with anyone, even an unfashionable, plump, plain file clerk, fresh from the farm. But the joke was on him, it seemed.

How come he'd never really seen Lilley Smith until today?

Unfashionable? A personal stylist at a luxury boutique had poured Lilley into a long, slinky red dress with spaghetti straps. Backless and daringly low-cut, the red knit gown seemed to cling to her breasts, teasing a man's gaze, threatening at any moment to reveal too much.

Plump? The dress showed off the curves her baggy clothes had hidden. Her breasts and hips were generous and wide, her waist small. She had the shockingly feminine figure that used to drive men wild...and still did. The classic 1950s Marilyn Monroe curves that made any man break out in a sweat. A droplet formed on Alessandro's forehead just looking at her.

And plain? That was the biggest laugh of all. Alessandro had seen the rare beauty of her naked face up close in his office—but now, after Sergio's makeup and hair team had done their work, her loveliness was shocking. Kohl and mascara darkened her deep-brown eyes, and red lipstick highlighted the seductive curve of her full, generous mouth.

Lilley's long, light-brown hair tumbled seductively down her bare shoulders and naked back.

Alessandro had watched her for weeks from a distance, but it was only today that he'd finally seen Lilley Smith for what she truly was.

A beauty.

A sex kitten.

A *bombshell*.

As they walked down the red carpet towards the sweeping steps of the hundred-year-old Harts Mansion, the paparazzi went crazy, shouting questions.

"Where's Olivia? Did you two break up?"

"Who's the new girl?"

"Yeah, who's the sexy brunette?"

Alessandro gave them a half smile and a brusque wave. He was accustomed to being followed and photographed wherever he went, from his palace in Rome to his yacht in Sardinia to his North American headquarters in San Francisco. It was the price he paid for being successful and a bachelor. But as he led Lilley down the red carpet, her feet dragged behind him. He glanced down at her, and realized she was shaking.

"What is it?" he said beneath his breath.

"They're staring at me," she said in a low voice.

"Of course they're staring." Alessandro turned to her, brushing hair away from her eyes. "So am I."

"Just get me through this," she whispered, her beautiful brown eyes looking big and scared. His heart twisted strangely. Tucking her hand more securely around his arm, Alessandro led her swiftly down the red carpet, using his body to block the more aggressive photographers leaning over the ropes. Alessandro usually stopped for photographs—an unfortunate necessity to maximize publicity for the children's charity that would benefit tonight—but he knew Lilley would never manage. Ignoring the shouted questions and frustrated groans, he kept walking, leading her up the sweeping stairs to the shadowy columns of the portico.

Once they were inside the mansion's double doors, past security and into the golden, glittering foyer, Lilley exhaled. Her luminous eyes looked up at him with gratitude. "Thanks." She swallowed. "That was…not fun."

"No?" he said lightly. "Most women think otherwise. Most see it as a perk of dating me."

"Well, I don't." Lilley shuddered. She licked her lips, fidgeting with the low neckline of her tight red gown. "I feel like a dork."

Heat flashed through Alessandro. He wanted to touch everywhere her fingers were tugging, to rip the fabric off her body and cover those amazing breasts with his hands, to nibble and stroke and lick every inch of her.

No, he told himself angrily. He had three rules. No employees, no wives, no virgins. There were too many women in the world, all too easily possessed, to break those cardinal rules. Lilley was an employee. She was also brokenhearted and on the rebound. Too many complications. Too many risks. Lilley was off limits.

But then again…

Alessandro looked at the red fabric barely clinging to her breasts. Looked at the graceful curve of her neck, at the roses in her cheeks and her pale skin beneath thick waves of soft brown hair. He felt a rush of forbidden desire.

Maybe it was a stupid rule, he thought. Maybe taking an employee as his mistress was a great idea. Wasn't his HR department always telling him to promote from within?

Lilley's beautiful eyes looked miserable and vulnerable. "I look like an idiot, don't I?"

Didn't she realize her beauty? Why did she hide it? Why

didn't she use it to gain attention in the workplace to get ahead, as other women would have done?

Was it possible that she really didn't know how lovely she was? He narrowed his eyes. "You are beautiful, Lilley."

Looking up at him, she suddenly scowled, her lovely expression peeved. "I told you never to call me that—"

"You are beautiful," he said harshly, cupping his hand against her soft cheek. He searched her gaze. "Listen to me. You know the kind of man I am. The kind, you said, who would never take a girl on a charity date. So why would I lie? You are beautiful."

The anger slid from her face. She suddenly looked bewildered and innocent and painfully shy. He could read her feelings in her face, something else he found shocking. It was an act—right? It had to be. She couldn't be that young.

He'd been open-hearted and reckless too, long ago. He remembered it like some long-forgotten dream. Perhaps that was why he felt strangely, unexpectedly protective.

He didn't like it.

"You really—" Lilley stopped herself, then bit her lip. "You really think I'm pretty?"

"Pretty?" he demanded, amazed. Lifting her chin, he tilted her head up towards the light shining from the foyer's glittering chandelier. "You are a *beauty,* little mouse."

She stared up at him, then her lips suddenly quirked. "You keep calling me that. Can't you just call me Lilley?"

"Sorry." His lips curved. "It's a habit. It was my name for you, when I was blind."

Lilley's brown eyes sparkled as a smile lit up her face. "So in one breath you tell me I'm beautiful, and in the next you tell me you're blind?"

Her smile was so breathtaking that it caught at his heart.

"Your beauty would make any man blind, *cara,*" he said huskily. "I told you that you'd be envied if you came with me to the ball. I was wrong. *I* will be the one envied to-night."

Her eyes grew big, her dark eyelashes sweeping wide against her pale skin. "Huh. You're not so bad at this complimenting stuff." Her smile lifted into a wicked grin. "Has anyone ever told you that?"

Against his will, Alessandro grinned back at her, and as their eyes locked a seismic tremble raced through his body. How was it possible that he'd ever thought of Lilley as an invisible brown sparrow?

From the instant he'd seen her pushing her little filing cart down the hall, why hadn't he immediately seen her beauty? Lilley's combination of sweetness and tartness, her innocent eyes and lush, sexy curves, caused a spasm of need deeper than his body, down to some fundamental part of his soul.

Soul? The word made his lip curl. *Soul.* What a ridiculous idea. Funny the tricks lust could play on a man's mind.

And he wanted her. Oh yes.

But he wouldn't let himself act on it. He was not a slave to lust. He was a grown man, the head of a worldwide company, and it was past time that he stopped chasing one-night stands and settled down. Olivia Bianchi would make a perfect princess, and when she inherited her father's designer-clothing business, Caetani Worldwide's reach would double in Europe. He did not love her, any more than Olivia loved him, but their union made sense. He'd nearly talked himself into proposing until she'd pulled that little stunt.

He should have expected Olivia's ultimatum. He'd been on the phone in his limo, en route to the office for his forgotten cufflinks, and he'd felt her simmering beside him in her black fur coat. The instant he'd ended the business call, Olivia had turned on him in angry, rapid-fire Italian.

"When are you going to propose, Alessandro? When?

I'm sick of waiting for you to decide. Make our engagement official, or find someone else to be your hostess at the charity ball!"

Five minutes later, he'd dropped Olivia off at her ritzy hotel. No woman, not even one as powerful and perfect as Olivia, would ever give him an ultimatum.

Now, as Alessandro led Lilley towards the ballroom of the Harts Mansion, he felt a rush of relief that he was still a free man. This was already proving to be the most enjoyable, surprising night he'd had in a long time.

Keeping Lilley close beside him, he paused at the landing on the top of the stairs, looking down into the ballroom. A hush fell beneath the soaring painted ceilings and enormous crystal chandeliers as hundreds of guests turned to stare up at them. Alessandro felt Lilley stiffen. She wasn't accustomed to being the center of attention, that was certain. She seemed to expect criticism, which he could not remotely understand.

"I can't tell you you're beautiful, because you'll hit me," he murmured. "But I know every man would kill to be in my place."

Her eyes flashed up at him, and he saw her lips quirk into a nervous smile. "Okay," she said in a low voice, bracing herself. "Let's go."

Alessandro led her down the stairs, where his board members, stockholders and friends waited. He spoke to each of them in turn, then moved across the ballroom, greeting the mayor, the governor, movie stars and visiting royalty by name. The men grinned and asked him for stock tips. The women flirted with him and tossed their hair. And they all gaped at Lilley beside him. None of the upper-level directors of Caetani Worldwide recognized her, he was positive, though they'd likely passed her many times in the hallways.

Insane to think he'd once been just as blind.

Speaking with each of his guests in turn, Alessandro thanked them for their donation to his favorite children's charity. He felt Lilley trembling beside him as if she wanted to take flight, and took her hand firmly in his own, pressing her forward with a gentle push against the naked skin of her lower back. Even that innocent, courteous touch was incredibly erotic. All he wanted to do was leave the gala ball and drag Lilley away to some quiet place. Perhaps his villa in Sonoma, which conveniently had ten bedrooms.

"Your highness," the head of the children's charity said breathlessly, looking up at him through her glasses with dazzled eyes, "won't you say a few words to start the bidding for the auction tonight?"

"Certainly," Alessandro said with a practiced smile. "I'll do it at once."

Gripping Lilley's hand, he crossed the ballroom towards the stage, and the crowds parted for them like magic. He felt her panic as he led her up the stairs, felt her small hand pulling desperately to be freed. It was only once they were behind the wings of the stage that he released her hand, looking down at her.

"Thanks for being my date tonight," he said huskily, and leaned forward to kiss her cheek. It was just an innocent, friendly kiss. Practically nothing. But when he pulled away, her eyes were huge.

His own lips burned where they'd touched her skin. For an instant, they just stared at each other. His blood roared in his ears, his heart pounding with the need to pull her into his arms and kiss her, really kiss her. He had to force himself to step back.

"Excuse me." Years of not showing feelings stood him in good stead. His voice was calm and even, betraying nothing of his tumult within. "This will take just a moment."

"Sure," she said faintly.

Leaving her in the wings, he walked to the microphone at the center of the stage. A hush fell across the ballroom, and Alessandro waited for the hearty cheer of the crowd which quickly followed. He was accustomed to being the center of attention, and far from being nervous, he was bored by it—all of it. There was only one thing that did not bore him right now, one thing that made his blood hum and his body come alive. One thing he wanted.

And he could not let himself have her.

Gripping the podium with his hands, he gave a speech, hardly knowing what he was saying. He could feel Lilley watching from the wings. His heartbeat was quick, his body hot with repressed desire.

"…and so I thank you, my friends," he finished. "Drink champagne, dance and bid high. Remember every penny raised tonight goes to help children in need!"

The cheer across the ballroom was even louder. With an absentminded wave, he left the podium and went straight back to Lilley, who looked as if she'd recovered her senses and was now staring at her watch, keeping time.

"Six minutes." She looked up at him with quirked lips. "I'm impressed. Usually speeches given by important men last for at least an hour. You're fast."

He gave her a lazy smile, then leaned forward to whisper, "I'm slow where it counts."

Alessandro had the satisfaction of seeing her shiver. That was some solace, at least—knowing she was as aware of him as he was of her. It amazed him, how Lilley hid nothing of her feelings. So young, he thought in wonder, so reckless and unrestrained. It reminded him of what he'd once been like himself, before he'd been betrayed. Like her, he'd once been young and hopeful, poor and driven to succeed…

Poor? The sparkle of Lilley's watch caught his eye, and he grabbed her wrist. "What's this?"

She tried to pull her wrist from his grasp. "Nothing."

In the background, he could hear the orchestra start a waltz. He was dimly aware of guests going out to the dance floor. "It's platinum. Diamonds. I don't recognize the brand."

"Hainsbury," she said in a small voice.

Hainsbury's. The damned discount jewelry chain that had recently tried—and failed—to execute a hostile take-over of Caetani Worldwide, solely in order to acquire the cachet of his luxury jewelry brand, Preziosi di Caetani. His eyes narrowed. "Who gave it to you?"

She swallowed. "My mother."

He told himself it was entirely reasonable that someone from the Midwest might own a Hainsbury watch. It was a coincidence, nothing more. His endless battles with the Count of Castelnau, his crafty, vicious French rival, were making him paranoid. He looked at Lilley's face. Clearly he was losing his mind to be suspicious of a girl like this.

"Nice," he said casually, dropping her wrist. "I wouldn't have recognized it. It looks nothing like their usual factory-made junk."

Looking away, she wrapped her hand around her wrist. Her voice was awkward. "My mother had it specially made."

He'd embarrassed her, Alessandro thought. Drawing attention to her Hainsbury-brand watch at a ball sponsored by the far more prestigious Preziosi di Caetani. "Whoever made it, your watch is truly exquisite." He smiled down at her and changed the subject. "Had enough of the ball? Ready to leave?"

"Leave?" Her lips parted. "We just got here!"

"So?" he said impatiently.

She glanced uneasily towards the dance floor. "People are waiting to talk to you."

"They already have my money."

"It's not just a question of money. They clearly want you. Your time and attention." She gave him a sudden crooked smile. "Though heaven knows why. I've yet to see your charm myself."

He gave her a sensual smile. "Do you want me to try harder?"

Her eyes widened and he heard her intake of breath. She muttered, "I'm no good at this."

"To the contrary."

She shook her head. "Forget it. Just don't try to charm me, all right? There's no point, and it might...I mean...we're just using each other tonight. Leave it at that."

Alessandro's gaze fell to her trembling lips. "Right. You're here for revenge. You haven't seen him yet, have you?"

"No." Her voice was quiet.

"He will fall on his knees when he sees you," Alessandro said roughly. "Come."

Grabbing her hand, he led her off the stage and across the dance floor, tracing through the crowds of swaying, laughing couples. Once, Alessandro would have been the first man on the dance floor. He would have pulled Lilley into his arms and moved her against his body in the music's seductive rhythm. But he hadn't danced for sixteen years now. Crossing the floor, he didn't even pause.

The charity director waited for him on the other edge of the dance floor. She beamed at him, gushing thanks and praise, and Alessandro accepted her gratitude with as much grace as he could manage. He was glad to help the charity, but the long line of guests that instantly formed, people waiting to thank him and shake his hand, seemed endless. Almost beyond endurance. He wanted to grab Lilley's hand and jump into his car, and not stop until they were completely alone, away from the crowds of reaching hands and yearning eyes.

But there were some duties from which neither royalty nor wealth excused a man. Standing on the edge of the dance floor like a king holding court, he endured the long queue of wealthy donors and powerful people as best as he could. As solace, he pulled Lilley to stand in front of him, wrapping his arms around her as if he were a child with a comforting blanket.

Except he was no longer a child, and Alessandro had a grown man's idea of comfort. Throughout the endless small talk he found himself distracted by the way her full breasts felt, pressed against his arms. He allowed himself one glance down, and saw that her low neckline barely covered the indecent swell of her breasts. He could see the shape of pebbled nipples though the red knit fabric. It was just as he'd suspected—she wasn't wearing a bra. And he wasn't the only man to notice. All the eyes of the male guests waiting to talk to him lingered long upon her, and Alessandro felt an urge to growl at them.

He was long past hard. He had the sudden bright idea of writing the charity a ten-million-dollar check, if it meant he could leave this ball and take her straight to bed.

He shouldn't. He couldn't. Sex with Lilley was a bad idea on every level. She was his employee, possibly in love with another man, and she was right—they were using each other tonight for mutual gain. He'd told her that straight out. A cheap one-night stand would only end in her recriminations, tears and perhaps a sexual-harassment lawsuit.

But with every passing moment, his self-restraint was growing frayed. Feeling her in his arms right now he felt oddly alive in a way he hadn't experienced in years. She made him feel…young again. As if he still had a beating heart.

And *that* was her biggest danger of all. He couldn't seduce her. He had to send her away. Had to—

Lilley glanced back at him, her lips parted. He saw the tip of her pink tongue dart out to the edge of her mouth and he nearly groaned. He wanted to taste those lips. Plunder her mouth with his. He wanted to rip the clingy red dress off her body, to spread her across his bed, to push himself inside her, to fill her hard and deep—

Basta. He broke out into a hot sweat. As the ambassador droned on to him about the fluidity of Asian exchange rates, all Alessandro could think was that it was a good thing Lilley was standing in front of him, blocking others' view of his trousers. Where was his self-control?

In front of him, Lilley stiffened. For a moment, Alessandro wondered if she'd felt his desire for her—how could she not? Then he saw she was looking over the crowd.

"Jeremy," she said in a low voice.

For a moment, Alessandro couldn't remember what she was talking about. Then his insides burned. He felt envious of this employee in his jewelry-design department, this man who'd had her at his command and let her go.

"Excuse us," he said to the people surrounding them. Ignoring their protests, he pulled Lilley to a quiet corner next to a window.

"Where is he?" he said, keeping his expression impassive.

"Over there."

He followed her gaze. His eyes narrowed in the desire to see this paragon but no one stood out to him at all. He felt irritated. *Irritated* wasn't a strong enough word. *Jealous?* No, impossible. Jealousy was for the weak, for sad, vulnerable men who served their hearts on platters to be shredded and devoured.

So he didn't feel jealous. He felt…annoyed. *Sì.* Annoyed.

He'd said he would help Lilley get the man back. Now he regretted his promise. Why should he help another, less-deserving man get what he himself wanted—Lilley in his bed?

But if Lilley truly loved this Jeremy, Alessandro would do the honorable thing. He would step aside with the noble self-sacrifice of a damned saint.

"Va bene," he ground out. "If you still want this idiot, this imbecile without a shred of sense or loyalty, I will help you win him."

Lilley flashed him a grin. "Um. You're too kind?"

"Just tell me one thing," he demanded.

"Only one?"

His fingers moved down her shoulders, stroking down the warm, bare skin of her back. He saw her eyes widen, felt her shiver and he fought back the urge to yank her body hot and hard against his own. "Why would you want him back, after he made you weep?"

Her smile fell. She took a deep breath, then lifted her left wrist. "Look at this."

A change of subject? He looked down at the bracelet on her wrist. He'd noticed it earlier, a pastiche of welded materials—colorful crystals on a brass chain, interspersed with rusty-looking numbers and held together with a tarnished buckle. "What about it?"

"I made it."

He grabbed her wrist, narrowing his eyes and tilting his head as he tried to make sense of the bracelet. He pointed to the metal number dangling off the chain. "What's that?"

"A room number from an eighteenth-century Parisian hotel."

It seemed strange to him, an artistic hodgepodge of junk. "How do you source the materials?"

"At flea markets and vintage shops, mostly. I create jewelry using old things I find." She swallowed. "I met Jeremy at San Francisco's trade show a few months ago, when my employer thought I was visiting my family. Jeremy loved my jewelry. We decided to be partners and open a boutique together. He was going to handle the financials. I would create the inventory." She blinked fast, and looked away. "When he chose my roommate over me, I lost that dream."

He could see her eyes were shiny with tears, and his insides gave a little twist. "The man's a damned fool," he said roughly. He tried to think of how to comfort her. "Perhaps it's for the best," he tried. "Running a business is a huge risk. You might have lost your investment. People don't want old trinkets. They want their jewelry shiny and new."

Her lips trembled, curving as she looked up. Her eyes were bleak. "I guess we'll never know, will we?"

His attempt at comfort was a clear failure. But Alessandro knew words weren't enough to make anyone forget the loss of a dream. He had no idea how to make Lilley forget her pain. He knew only one way, the same way he used to forget his own.

But he couldn't do it. He couldn't allow himself to make love to her.

The orchestra started a new song, and the notes of an exquisite classical waltz swirled around them like cherry blossoms tumbling from the sky. Lilley looked out at the crowded dance floor wistfully.

She'd told him she wasn't a good dancer, but he didn't believe that for an instant. He'd seen the sensual way she moved. Even walking, her body swayed like sunset against ocean waves.

But he couldn't dance with her. His hands tightened at his sides. He was helpless to offer comfort.

Unless he made love to her.

What could it hurt? His lust argued against his brain.

One night of pleasure. A few hours of comfort. One night wouldn't risk making her fall in love with him. It wasn't as if she were a virgin.

Although she was shockingly close. *Two boyfriends.* He still couldn't believe she'd only been with two men. She truly was innocent. And yet she'd seemed embarrassed of her number. He wondered what she would think if he told her how many women he'd slept with. Something he would never do, even if he knew the number.

"I'm sorry I don't dance," he said slowly.

She looked down. "It's all right."

The scent of her hair was like wild roses. He moved closer, fascinated by the swoop of her neck, by the snub edge of her chin. Her cheeks blushed a soft pink against creamy skin as her dark eyelashes fluttered. He asked suddenly, "How old are you, Lilley?"

"Twenty-three." She furrowed her brow. "Why? How old are you?"

"Ancient to you. Thirty-five."

"Thirty-five, and still not married?" She sounded as astonished as his shareholders. "Where I come from, most people are married by thirty."

"Advantageous for farm life, I assume."

Her brow furrowed. "I don't exactly come from a—"

"In my world," he interrupted, "a man marries to ensure his line, to make sure he has a son to inherit his title and estate when he's dead."

She flashed him a grin. "Gee, you make it all sound so romantic."

"It's not about *romance,* Lilley," he said sharply. "Marriage is an alliance. My wife will be a leader in society. An heiress with proper lineage, the future mother to my heir."

Her grin faded. "Like Olivia Bianchi."

Even hearing her name irritated him. "Yes."

Lilley's eyes were huge beneath the glittering light of the chandeliers. "So if she's the perfect bride for you, why am I here?"

"She threatened to leave if I didn't propose, so I told her to go."

Lilley blinked. "I feel sorry for her."

He barked a laugh. "Do not waste your sympathy on Olivia. She can take care of herself."

"She's in love with you!" She swallowed. "It was wrong of me to agree to this—this charade. When you're just trying to control her."

"I have no desire ever to see Olivia again," he bit out.

She frowned, clearly unconvinced. "When did you decide that?"

His eyes met hers. "I knew it from the moment I saw you in that dress."

Her lips parted in shock. It took her several moments to speak. "Um. Would you get me a drink?" she croaked. "And maybe some food? I haven't eaten all day."

"Certamente," he murmured. "What would you like? A martini? A merlot?"

"You choose."

"We'll start with champagne." Reaching out a hand, he cupped her cheek. "Wait here, if you please, *cara.*"

He felt her shiver beneath his touch, saw her lick her lips as she said with a trembling voice, "I'll wait."

He turned away, but after a few steps could not resist looking back at her. Lilley stood frozen on the edge of the dance floor, gloriously alluring in her red dress, watching him. She was surrounded by men who were already darting her greedy sideways glances.

Damned vultures. Alessandro scowled. He would hurry.

As he strode across the ballroom, he couldn't remember the last time he'd felt such need to possess any woman.

And he could have her. She was free and ripe for the taking. Yes, she was his employee, but he was the one who'd made that rule. He was the boss. He could break his own rules at will.

Alessandro thought again of the ten bedrooms at his villa. An image floated through his mind of Lilley spread naked on his bed, her full, generous mouth curved into a sensual smile, her deep-brown eyes looking up at him with a haze of longing and need. He nearly stumbled over his own feet.

And just like that, his decision was made. His body tightened as exhilaration raced through him. Employee or not, Lilley would be his.

Tonight. He would have her in his bed tonight.

CHAPTER THREE

LILLEY felt men in tuxedos jostle her on the edge of the dance floor, felt the annoyed glare of chic, half-starved women in black designer gowns around her. She took a deep breath, trying to steady her shaking hands. Alessandro's dark head towered above the crowds as he strode towards the bar, trailed by wide-eyed, adoring groupies.

And she was rapidly becoming one of them. Lilley exhaled. What in heaven's name was she doing? He'd told her outright that their date would only be an illusion. And yet, all night, Alessandro's eyes, his touch, had told her differently. Her body felt hot, her skin flushed and pink at the memory of his fingertips stroking her bare back. Of his fingers running lightly along her arm, his lips brushing her cheek.

Just being around him made her feel like a different woman. A bolder, braver one.

She didn't know why or how. Maybe it was the way he looked at her. The way his hard, muscular body felt against her own. Maybe it was his scent, like exotic lands and spice and sunshine. He made her feel tense and tingly and hot, and made her soul feel all jumbled and confused.

He made her feel a hunger she'd never known, and every moment she was near him, the hunger grew.

Lilley swallowed, rubbing her tense neck. She just had

to make it through the night. She'd keep her distance, keep her mouth shut, have some dinner and drink champagne for a couple of hours. Surely she could manage that? And tomorrow, it would all be nothing but a dream. On Monday she could go back to the file room, and Prince Alessandro Caetani would forget her existence.

She couldn't possibly believe his interest in her could be real. There was no way on the green earth that Alessandro would choose Lilley over Olivia Bianchi.

I have no desire ever to see Olivia again. She heard the echo of his husky voice. *I knew it from the moment I saw you in that dress.*

An electric current coursed through her body at the memory. She couldn't forget how he'd pulled her close, wrapping his arms around her as he spoke to politicians and football stars. She couldn't forget how his hot gaze had slowly perused the length of her body when they'd left the boutique, or the way he'd protected her past the paparazzi. A strange new tension had consumed her all night, causing her heart to beat too fast and her breasts to rise and fall in quick, shallow breaths against the snug bodice of her gown.

Maybe it was a good thing Alessandro didn't dance after all. If she felt his hard body swaying against hers, she might have hyperventilated and fallen like a stone on the dance floor. Every time their eyes met, every time he touched her, Lilley wanted things she could barely confess, even to herself.

"Lilley?"

Jeremy stood in front of her, his mouth agape at her tight red dress. He pushed up his black-framed glasses. "What are you doing here?"

"Oh. Hi Jeremy," Lilley said weakly. Licking her lips, she glanced at the black-haired woman behind him. "Hi, Nadia."

Her roommate's face was the picture of misery. She looked as if she were about to burst into tears. "I'm so sorry, Lilley," she choked out. "We never meant to hurt you. We never meant…"

"Stop apologizing," Jeremy told her. His Adam's apple bobbed over his bow tie as he glared at Lilley. "We would have told you days ago, if you'd let us. But you've avoided us. Avoided *me*."

Lilley's mouth had fallen open. "That's ridiculous!"

"I wish you'd just had the guts to tell me from the start you didn't want me, rather than pawning me off on Nadia. Is it any wonder we fell for each other? You were never there!"

Lilley shook her head fiercely. "You're just making excuses. You know I had to work! You're entirely to blame!"

His gaze met hers. "Am I?" His eyes traveled down her full, bouncy hair to the knit dress clinging to her breasts. "You sure never dressed like that for me. You're clearly here with someone you actually care about. Who is he, Lilley?"

It was time for her to lower the boom. Time to get revenge for their betrayal. As soon as she told them her date was Alessandro, they'd be shocked and jealous. Lilley opened her lips.

Then she saw Jeremy's hand on the small of Nadia's back.

It was a protective gesture, one Lilley had resisted every time Jeremy had tried to touch her. The truth was that, after one fun weekend at the trade show, their relationship had always been strained. She'd quit her job in France and moved to San Francisco to start this big new life, but she hadn't done anything to pursue her dreams. When Jeremy had tried to kiss her, she'd pulled away. She'd avoided being with him, coming up with excuses to stay at work a little longer. Looking back at their relationship, Lilley couldn't blame him for wanting to be with Nadia, a girl who actually had time for him, and who, as she'd seen to her shock that morning, actually seemed to relish his kisses.

She'd never loved him. The truth was, what hurt the most was losing her dream of the boutique. She couldn't start a business without Jeremy, she didn't have the remotest idea how to create a business plan or legally register her company or build a clientele. All she knew how to do was design jewelry that was funny and weird and definitely not for everyone.

She'd had such big dreams. And when he'd broken up with her, he'd ended them.

No. She'd done that herself, by never lifting a finger to pursue them.

"Who's your date, Lilley?" Nadia said hopefully through her tears. "Have you met someone?"

Maybe Jeremy had cheated on her, but she'd abandoned and rejected him for months. Maybe Nadia had taken her boyfriend behind her back—but hadn't Lilley begged her roommate to please, please make her excuses to Jeremy as she scurried off to work?

They'd been wrong. But Lilley had been a coward from start to finish.

Trembling, Lilley faced them. "I'm here with…with…" She swallowed, then lifted her chin. "A friend. I'm here with a new friend."

She turned to Jeremy.

"And you were right," she said. "I was never there. Not for you. And not for our business. I had all these dreams, but I was afraid even to try. I'm—I'm sorry."

Jeremy blinked, and the angry light in his eyes faded. "I'm sorry too," he said. "You're a nice person, Lilley, sweet and generous. You didn't deserve to find out about Nadia and me that way." He gave her an awkward smile. "I always liked you. But after you moved to San Francisco, you just…disappeared."

"I know." Her throat hurt. Every time Jeremy had made an appointment for them—at a bank, with a potential investor, with a real estate agent—she'd suddenly had somewhere else to be. She'd hidden behind her work. Her fear had won. "I'm sorry."

"Can you ever forgive me, Lilley?" Nadia whispered.

Lilley tried to smile. "Maybe if you do the dishes for the rest of the month."

"I will. Two months. Three!"

"And I'm sorry the boutique didn't work out." Jeremy rubbed the back of his sandy-blond head sheepishly. "I still think your jewelry is fantastic. You're just not ready to take the plunge. But maybe someday…"

"Right," she said over the lump in her throat, knowing it was a lie. "Someday."

Her roommate was openly crying as she leaned forward and hugged Lilley, whispering, "Thank you."

Lilley's throat hurt as she watched Jeremy and Nadia disappear into the crowd. Then she heard a dark, sardonic voice behind her.

"You didn't tell them about me."

She whirled around. "Alessandro."

"I was waiting to see you take your revenge." His tall, muscular body moved with a warrior's grace as he held out a flute of champagne. "Why didn't you tell them?"

"Because Jeremy was right. I never wanted him. Not really." She took the champagne flute from his hand and said softly, "If I don't have the guts to pursue my dreams, I shouldn't be angry if other people do."

"You could have made them suffer." His dark eyes were puzzled, almost bewildered. "I don't understand."

"That makes two of us," she whispered, and took a long

drink of champagne. The bubbles were a cold shock against her lips as she tilted back her head, gulping it all down. She closed her eyes, waiting for the alcohol to reach her brain and make her forget how she'd been so afraid to risk failure that she'd made it a self-fulfilling prophecy.

What was the point in her avoiding risk, if she ended up losing everything anyway?

"You're crying." Alessandro sounded aghast.

She exhaled, wiping her eyes. "No."

"I saw his face when he looked at you. He could still be yours for the taking, if you chose."

Lilley thought of the stricken expression on Nadia's face. Thought of the way Jeremy's hand had lingered protectively on her roommate's back. Thought of the way Lilley had never, not for one instant, felt a single spark of physical attraction for Jeremy—something she'd never even noticed until she'd experienced the lightning sizzle of electricity with Alessandro.

She shook her head. "I wish them all the best."

"God, you are so nice," he whispered, pushing back wavy tendrils of her hair. "How can you be so—merciful?"

An unexpected bolt of pain went through her. Another man calling her *nice*. Another word for *timid. Terrified. Coward.* No wonder Alessandro had called her little mouse.

Blinking fast, she looked down at her scandalous red dress and sexy high heels. "Do you think I'm a coward?" she whispered.

"What are you talking about?" Taking her empty flute, he pressed his own full glass into her hand. "Here. Drink this."

She looked up at him, her eyes full of unshed tears. "I shouldn't have said that aloud. You must think—"

"I think nothing." His dark gaze seared through her soul. "Never apologize for telling me what you're thinking. You can't hurt me. There is nothing between us, so you risk nothing."

She blinked at him, feeling quivery. "Now you're the one who is being nice."

He snorted, then shook his head, a small smile playing on his sensual mouth. "That is one accusation I've never heard before. Now drink."

Obediently, she took a sip. As she drank, she heard him muse aloud, "Delicious, isn't it? I just bought the winery from a Brazilian. Cost me a fortune." His lips curved. "But it gives me a great deal of pleasure, since I know it infuriates my worst enemy."

Lilley's eyes flew open as she pulled the flute from her lips. She said faintly, "Not the St. Raphaël vineyard."

"Ah, you recognize it?" He smiled in satisfaction. "It once belonged to the Count of Castelnau. Now it is mine."

"You don't say," Lilley said faintly, feeling sick. She'd heard Théo, her cousin and former employer, rage about losing that vineyard in a business deal to a Brazilian. It was only after he'd lost it that he'd realized its value. Typical, she thought. People were so much better at pursuing things they didn't need instead of enjoying what they already had.

But the two men had competed over acquisitions with growing ferocity for the last five years, ever since Théo had bought a small Italian luxury firm that Alessandro considered rightfully his by geography. If he ever found out she was Théo's cousin, he'd never believe Lilley wasn't a corporate spy. Especially after catching her in his office, all alone in the dark!

Her knees trembled. He caught her. "Are you all right?" he asked, looking concerned. "Did you drink the champagne too quickly?"

She looked up at him. She'd left her father's and cousin's names off her résumé because she'd known Caetani

Worldwide would have never hired her otherwise, in spite of Jeremy's recommendation, no matter how honest or hard-working she might be. But telling Alessandro the truth would gain her nothing, and would cost her her job—forcing her to go home to her father and perhaps even consider his demand that she marry his employee, a man twice her age.

"Lilley?"

"I just need something to eat," she managed. "I haven't eaten all day." She gave him a weak smile. "And I did jog a half mile."

"Of course." Taking the half-finished flute from her hands, he set both glasses on the silver tray of a passing waiter and gave her a sudden grin. "I've arranged for a private dinner of sorts. My driver has taken a selection from the buffet to the limo. We'll enjoy a little picnic on the way home."

"A picnic? In your limo?" she said faintly. She shook her head, feeling dizzy in a way that had nothing to do with champagne. With a wistful sigh, she looked back at the glamorous ballroom. "All right. I just—didn't expect it all to end so quickly."

"All good things come to an end," he said, holding out his hand.

Reluctantly, she took it. He led her across the ballroom, stopping many times to say farewell to his friends and admirers before they finally escaped up the stairs, through the foyer and out the double doors.

Outside, beneath the hundred-year-old mansion's shadowy portico, the August night was foggy and cold. "It must be midnight," she murmured.

"Almost. How did you know?"

"Because all night I've felt like Cinderella." She looked up at him, and gratitude, real gratitude, rose above her regret that the night was over. "Thank you for the best night of my life."

He blinked, then frowned. Abruptly, he pushed her against a white stone column. She shivered as she felt the cold, hard stone against the hot skin of her back.

"I don't think you understand," he said in a low voice. "I'm not taking you to *your* home." He paused. "I'm taking you to mine."

She stared at him in shock, hearing only her own hoarse breath and the rapid beat of her heart.

"You're my employee. There are rules." Alessandro's eyes were dark with heat, his dark hair dappled with streaks of silvery moonlight as he held her beneath the shadows of the portico. "But I'm going to break them," he whispered. "I'm going to kiss you."

Staring up at him, Lilley felt as though she was lost in a strange dream. Tendrils of hair whipped across her face; the fabric of her dress moved languorously against her thighs.

"All night I've thought of nothing but touching you." His hands moved down her shoulders to her naked back. He lowered his head to her ear, and she felt his lips brush her tender flesh. "If you want me to stop, tell me now."

She closed her eyes as she felt the warmth of his fingers stroke her bare skin, felt his powerful body, barely constrained by his civilized tuxedo, against her own. His fingertips stroked up her neck, and he tilted her head upwards, his face just inches away. She shivered, her lips parted. The two of them were alone in the foggy, moonlit world.

Then she heard paparazzi yapping like small dogs from the curb, barking out questions that were muffled by a sudden howl of cold wind. He twisted away from her sharply. Moonlight caressed the hard edges of his face, making him look like a dark avenging angel as he scowled behind them. He grabbed her wrist.

"Come on."

He pulled her down the stone steps, past the shouts and flashbulbs of the paparazzi and the reporters who screamed questions and lunged for Lilley as they passed. Alessandro knocked them aside with his powerful arm, gently pushing her into the waiting limousine before he slammed the door behind them.

"Drive," he ordered the chauffeur.

The uniformed driver gunned the engine, roaring away from the curb and plummeting down the steep San Francisco hill. Lilley exhaled as she looked through the window behind them. "Are they always like that?"

"Yes. Take the alleys," Alessandro said. "In case they follow."

"Of course, sir. The penthouse?"

"Sonoma." Alessandro replied, rolling up the privacy divider.

"Sonoma?" Lilley echoed.

He turned to her with a sensual, heavy-lidded smile. "I have a villa. It will give us complete privacy."

She swallowed. This was all happening so fast. "I don't know…"

He gave her a wicked half grin. "I swear I'll have you back in the city safe and sound before work on Monday."

Work! As if that was what she was worried about! Exhaling, Lilley noticed two plates of delicious food and white wine chilling in a bucket of ice. As the divider closed with a thunk, blocking off the driver's view of the back seat, she looked nervously at Alessandro. She'd been starving for hours, but suddenly dinner was the last thing on her mind.

Smiling, he put his hand on her cheek. She could see slivers of silvery light reflected in his fathomless black eyes as he whispered, "I thought a woman like you existed only in dreams."

Her shoulders stiffened. "You mean *nice?*" She felt a sudden lump in her throat. *"Sweet?"*

He gave a low laugh. "You have a way of turning my every compliment into an insult. But yes. You are those things." His hand slowly trailed down her neck, his fingertips stroking the sensitive corner of her shoulder, the hollow of her collarbone. "But that's not why I'm taking you home."

"It isn't?" she breathed.

"I want you in my bed." His gaze was hot. His thumb stroked her sensitive bottom lip, and sparks flashed up and down the length of her body. "I've never wanted any woman this much. I want to taste your mouth. Taste your breasts. To feel your body against mine and fill you until you weep with joy. I won't stop until I am satisfied." He stroked her jawline, tilting her face upward as he whispered, "Until *you* are satisfied."

She trembled, hardly able to breathe. His mouth was inches from hers, and her lower lip fell swollen, burning where he'd touched her. She could feel the warmth of his breath against her skin. Unconsciously, she tilted her head back, lifting her mouth a millimeter closer to his.

His hand slid down her neck, past her bare shoulder. "I offer you a night of pleasure. Nothing more." His palm caressed the length of her arm to the vulnerable pulse inside her wrist. "And nothing less."

Her heart pounded in her throat. She had to refuse him. *Had* to. She couldn't possibly toddle off to his villa in Sonoma and give her boss her virginity. There were a million reasons why this was a bad idea.

But her body refused to heed her brain. She felt as if she was spiraling out of control. She craved his darkness. Craved his fire. "A woman would have to be a fool," she breathed, "to get involved with a man like you."

The ghost of a smile haunted Alessandro's cruel, sensual mouth. He cupped her face with both hands.

"We all must choose in this life," he said, searching her gaze. "The safety of a prison, or the terrible joy that comes with freedom."

She stared up at him, stricken. He seemed to know the secret desires and fears of her innermost heart.

As if in slow motion, he lowered his mouth to hers, whispering, "Live dangerously."

She closed her eyes.

His kiss was electric, like sensual fire. She felt the smooth hot satin of his lips, felt the roughness of his chin, the powerful strength of his arms around her. The heat of his tongue was like liquid silk softly stroking inside her mouth. Sparks of pleasure spiraled down her body, making her breasts taut and heavy, tightening a coil of tension low and deep in her belly. Her nerve endings sizzled from her fingertips to her toes.

She felt as if she were exploding into pure light.

When he pulled away, she heard the low, hoarse gasp of his breath—or was it her own?

She stared up at him, knowing she'd remember that first kiss until the day she died.

Streaks of light moved across their skin as the limousine traveled through the city. They stared at each other, and Lilley's cheeks burned like the rest of her. She'd never known a dream could feel so real. So warm. So hot. She felt as if she were floating—flying. She blinked, feeling dizzy. She could almost see a trail of scattered diamonds sparkling against her skin where he'd touched her, like synesthesia.

Prince Alessandro Caetani could have had any woman he wanted. And he wanted *her.* He moved towards her, gently pushing her back against the leather seat, and she felt the hard weight of his body over her own. She felt his hands on her skin, and suddenly, she no longer felt like a timid, cowardly mouse.

She felt beautiful.

Powerful.

Reckless.

In his arms, she wasn't afraid. Of anything.

She closed her eyes, tossing back her head as he kissed down her throat with his hot, sensual mouth. "No one's ever made me feel like this," she breathed. "Touched me like this."

"I…" Suddenly his hands stilled against her skin. His head lifted. "But you've had other lovers," he said. "At least two."

Her eyes opened. She swallowed. "Not…exactly."

"How many have you had?"

"Technically, well…none."

He sat up, looking at her with wide, shocked eyes. "Are you trying to tell me you're a *virgin?*"

She sat up beside him, her mouth suddenly dry. "Is that a problem?"

He glared at her, his jaw hard. Turning, he pressed the button to lower the privacy shield.

"Sir?" the driver said courteously, not turning his head.

"Change of plans," Alessandro said. "We're taking Miss Smith home."

"What?" Lilley gasped. Her cheeks burned. "Why? That…" she glanced uneasily at the driver in the front seat, "that thing I just told you doesn't matter!"

Alessandro turned to Lilley with cold eyes. "Give Abbott your address."

Folding her arms, Lilley muttered out the address of her apartment building. The driver nodded and smoothly turned left at the next streetlight. Lilley waited for Alessandro to roll the limo's dividing window back up so they could have privacy. But he didn't, and she realized he intended to leave it open, keeping the driver as their de facto chaperone.

Setting her jaw, Lilley turned to stare out the window at the passing lights of the city. Her body felt suddenly cold. She felt bereft. Alone.

As they drove into the increasing traffic of the city, Alessandro wouldn't even look at her. Sulkily, Lilley picked up a plate of food. The dinner was delicious, but cold, and epicurean pleasures suddenly seemed small. The plate was empty by the time they reached her working-class neighborhood, when she realized that Alessandro really, truly did not intend to kiss her again.

Kiss her? He wasn't even going to *look* at her. Her night of magic, her time of feeling reckless and beautiful, was definitely over. But she couldn't accept it. After the brief, explosive joy she'd experienced so briefly in his arms, she couldn't just shrug off her loss and go quietly back to her empty apartment!

Her heart hammered in her throat. "You're making a fuss over nothing. It's not a big deal."

Alessandro looked at her. The lights and shadows of the city swept over the hard, angular lines of his cheekbones and jaw. "It is to me."

Glancing uneasily at the driver, she leaned towards Alessandro. "Just because I am slightly less experienced than your other lovers—"

"Do you not understand what I was offering?" he bit out. "A night. Perhaps two. Nothing more!"

"I wasn't asking for more!" she said, affronted.

"I will never go home to meet your parents, Lilley. I will not marry you." His dark eyes were furious. "I will not *love* you."

A pang went through her at his cold words, but she lifted her chin in defiance. "Who said I wanted love?"

"Virgins always do." He looked her up and down. "Do not be stupid, Lilley."

Stupid. Her cheeks felt suddenly cold as echoes of childhood taunts from school went through her. *Fri-lly, Li-lley, stupid and si-lly!*

Alessandro stared out the window, his jaw like stone. His body language informed her that he was done talking, his decision made.

The limo pulled to a stop at her building. The driver got out and opened her door. The night air rushed in, cool and clammy against her burning skin.

"Good night," Alessandro said coldly, not turning his head.

"This is really how you're going to end our date?" she whispered. "Kissing me—then kicking me to the curb?"

He turned, and his black eyes glowed like dying embers as a hard smile lifted his lips. "Now, *cara,* at last you understand what it means to be my lover."

Lilley stared at him. "I understand, all right," she choked out. Tears filled her eyes as she turned away. "You don't want me."

"Not want you?" he demanded.

She looked back, miserable and bewildered. "Yes, you just said—"

"I am saving you from a mistake," he said harshly. "Be grateful."

She swallowed. "Okay," she said. "Good-bye."

She stepped out onto the curb in front of her 1960s-era apartment building. She took a deep breath of the cool night air and looked down her dark, empty street, littered with parked cars. An old newspaper blew down the black asphalt like a tumbleweed. She'd only lived here two months, but she'd been in this same place for far too long. In France. In Minnesota.

Her apartment building towered over her, seeming almost malevolent in the darkness. She knew what waited for her there, too. Nadia would be out dancing with Jeremy all night, and Lilley would be alone. She'd curl up on the couch beneath her mother's old handmade quilt and watch television shows about other people's lives. Maybe she'd take a long bath, then lights out.

Was that doomed to be her whole life's fate?

She would never have left her cushy job as a housekeeper in France if her cousin hadn't been mean to the mother of his child, causing Lilley to quit her job in solidarity in an instinctive, emotional reaction that would have made her mother proud. But that had been the end of Lilley's courage. From the instant she'd set foot in San Francisco, she'd done nothing but hide.

We all must choose in this life, Alessandro had said. *The safety of a prison. Or the terrible joy that comes with freedom.*

"Lilley." His voice was hoarse in the limo behind her. "Damn you. Just go."

With an intake of breath, she turned back to face him. Without a word, without letting herself think, she climbed back into the limo. She felt his shocked stare, heard his intake of breath as she slammed the door behind her.

"Do you know the choice you're making?" he demanded harshly.

Her body trembled as she looked at him. "I used to dream of my first lover," she whispered. "I dreamed of a knight in shining armor who would adore me forever."

"And now?" he bit out.

"I'm just tired of being afraid." She swallowed, blinking back tears. "Tired of hiding from my own life."

He stared at her for a long moment. Then, pressing the

button to close the divider, he spoke a single word to the driver. "Sonoma."

Lilley watched the divider lift higher, higher. It finally closed with a thunk, the noise reverberating like a door slamming behind her.

Then Alessandro moved. She had a single image of the dark heat of his eyes, the curve of his cruel, sensual mouth, as he pushed her back against the leather seat. Then his powerful body covered hers in a rough, ruthless embrace. His lips seared hers in a hot, hard kiss of sweetly poisonous honey.

Opening her mouth to his plunging tongue, she gave him—everything.

CHAPTER FOUR

AN HOUR later, as Alessandro carried her from the limo, Lilley blinked up at him in the moonlight, feeling drunk on his kisses. She felt hot, so hot. As he held her against his chest, she swayed with every step. The night was clear and the moon glowed in the velvet-black sky.

His Spanish-style villa was surrounded by rolling vineyards frosted with silvery light. In the distance, she could hear night birds calling.

The drive from the city had passed in seconds, it seemed, drenched with kisses. When the limo had arrived at the villa, she'd been so light-headed and breathless that she'd opened the door and fallen into a sprawl on the gravel driveway. Alessandro had picked her up in his strong arms, his gaze full of heat for what was to come.

Now, as the limo disappeared down the driveway, Lilley looked up at him in wonder. The stars seemed to move over his dark head, twinkling magically in the night sky.

She felt intoxicated, and she'd had only a glass and a half of champagne at the ball. There could be no doubt what—*who*—was drugging her senses.

At the door, he held her with one arm and punched in a security code. Around the villa, she briefly saw a pool and tennis courts and vast vineyards beyond. Then he opened the door with his shoulder and carried her inside, kicking the heavy door closed behind him.

Inside, the villa was dark and silent as he carried her up the 1920s-era wrought-iron stairs. He didn't have to say a word. She saw the whole sensual world in his dark eyes.

Upstairs, he pushed open a door at the end of the hall. She saw an enormous bed lit by a flood of moonlight from the windows. Reverently, he put her down on it. She shivered beneath the pool of silvery light as, never looking away from her, Alessandro pulled off his tuxedo tie and jacket and dropped them to the floor. He kicked off his shoes then climbed into bed beside her.

His hands were everywhere as he kissed her swollen lips. His embrace deepened, became hungrier and harder as his mouth pressed against hers, so hot and wet. His tongue twined with her own, and his hands cupped her breasts over the thin fabric of her gown, causing a gasp at the back of her throat. He stroked down to her waist, caressing her bare, shaking arms. Finally, he cradled her face and kissed her again with deepening fervor. She kissed him back with all the reckless passion of twenty-three lonely years.

There is nothing but now, she thought, dazed. *Nothing but this.*

She gasped as his hands moved beneath the clinging fabric of her bodice to her naked breasts. Her nipples tightened to hard points, sharpening in exquisite pleasure as he squeezed each of them gently between his fingers. Suddenly, he yanked the dress down, causing the spaghetti straps to snap as the fabric surrendered.

He showed rough brutality to her dress. But he caressed her body as if she were a precious, fragile treasure. His lips were hot against her skin as he moved down, nibbling her chin, licking her throat. She gasped as his large hands covered her full, naked breasts, squeezing each nipple, holding up each as a delicacy for the pleasure of his mouth. When he lowered his head, she felt the moist heat of his breath against her nipple and gripped the white bedspread beneath her. She held her breath as his entire mouth enfolded her nipple, suckling gently, his tongue swirling against her tight, swollen peak. She inhaled in tiny, desperate gasps as his hot, wet mouth moved to suckle the other breast in turn.

His hand stroked up her bare leg, dragging up the hemline of her long dress. The heavy weight of his hard, muscular body pressed her down into the softness of the bed, and she felt his fingertips languidly explore up her bare calf to caress the hollow behind her knee. As he suckled her breast, his hand continued to move upwards.

Stroking her outer thigh.

Her inner thigh.

She gripped the mattress, holding her breath. Alessandro lifted his mouth from her wet, hard nipple. Straddling her, he slowly unbuttoned his shirt. He tossed his platinum and diamond cufflinks carelessly to the floor. Wearing only his black tuxedo trousers, he moved down, between her legs, and she had her first look at the hard ripples and shadows of his bare chest in the moonlight. She bit down hard on her lip to stifle a gasp. His shoulders were broad, his muscles strong and powerful as an athlete's. The edges of his flat nipples were dusted lightly with dark hair that made a trail down his taut, defined belly before disappearing beneath his waistband. There wasn't an inch of fat anywhere on his body. She could hardly comprehend so much masculine beauty; he was like a dark angel.

At the end of the bed, Alessandro slid the dress off her unresisting body. Looking down, she realized she'd lost her high heels. Where? She couldn't remember. In the limo? Outside the villa? On the stairs…? It was all a sensual blur, and she was lost, utterly lost in sensation.

He pulled off his trousers and silk boxers, and Lilley's lips parted as she got a full look at the first wholly naked man she'd ever seen. And what a man. Her eyes traced over his powerful thighs, the strength of his body. And in the middle. She swallowed as her own breath suddenly choked her. Alessandro was huge. He would never fit inside her. Would he? Could he? How? Someone had made a mistake!

His dark eyes glowed in the shadows as he approached. She felt hypnotized, unable to move, unable even to cover her naked breasts or her lacy panties with her hands. He lay down beside her, turning her body to face him, and ran two fingertips down her side, from her shoulder to the swell of her breast to the valley of her waist and curve of her hip. She trembled, overwhelmed, helpless with desire.

Taking her hand, he gently suckled two of her fingers. Pulling her fingers from his mouth, he held her hand against his naked chest, looking at her. He seemed to be waiting. For what? What could he want…what could he expect from her…?

Taking her courage in her hands, shivering with her own daring, she leaned up and kissed him. His lips were hot and hard against hers, and as he let her set the rhythm, her confidence grew. A sigh of pleasure escaped her as he pushed her back against the soft pillows with a low growl, and covered her body with his own.

He was naked on top of her. Only the thin cotton of her panties separated them. She felt his hardness strain between her thighs, and the ache low in her belly increased. Closing her eyes, she gripped his shoulders as he kissed her, pulling him down harder.

Her head fell back with abandon as he kissed down her throat, kissing the valley between her breasts to the soft curve of her belly. She felt the swift flick of his tongue inside her belly button, but before she could be shocked, his teeth were gently pulling down the top edge of her panties.

He pushed her legs apart and she felt his breath against her thighs. She shivered as he kissed up her legs. He gave a teasing lick beneath the bottom edge of her panties, and her fingernails gripped into his shoulders. She held her breath, eyes still squeezed shut, as his hand cupped the mound between her legs. He sucked her most sensitive spot through the lacy fabric, and she cried out.

He ripped off her panties, tossing them on the floor in a mangled heap of lace. Her eyes flew open and she took a single deep gulp of air before she felt his mouth on her. Right on her. Licking her, spreading her wide with his fingers so he could taste every slick fold. She felt wet, so wet. His tongue played with her, teasing her, one moment lapping her with its full width, then moving to flick her sensitive nub with the tip. The feeling of his mouth on her was like nothing she'd imagined, pleasure so intense it was almost agony. She was being sucked into a maelstrom of ecstasy, drowning in the waves. Her hips lifted of their own accord to meet his mouth as the tension in her deepest core built higher and higher.

She couldn't endure this sweet torture, this agony of pleasure, for much longer. She writhed beneath him, her body twisting as she tried to pull away from the insistent, ruthless pleasure of his tongue. But he held her hips firmly, spreading her wider still, as he suckled between her legs. He thrust one thick finger inside her to the first knuckle. Then two fingers. Then three, going deeper, stretching her wide, giving her a small shock of pain to season and salt the sweet, wide, wet slide of his tongue.

Her body arched off the bed as she tried to move away from his fingers inside her, but he would not let her escape the exquisite agony of her pleasure. She gripped the bedspread as the storm inside her exploded. As if from a distance, she heard the cry from her lips lift to a scream of joy.

Sheathing himself in a condom, Alessandro lifted his powerful body over hers, as she still arched in ecstasy on the bed. Positioning himself, he whispered in her ear, "I'm sorry."

He pushed inside her in a single stroke, shoving himself to the hilt. The sudden pain made her gasp. As he filled her so deeply, ripping the invisible barrier inside her, Lilley's scream of joy changed to a choked gasp. He held perfectly still, letting her get used to the stretch of him inside her.

"I'm sorry," he murmured again. Lowering his head, he kissed her face, her cheeks, her lips. "The only way over it is through it." Her answer was a muffled sob as she turned her face into the pillow.

Then slowly, very slowly, he began to move inside her, and a miracle happened. The ocean of pleasure, which had receded beneath her like a wave, sucking sand beneath her feet, began to rush in like the tide. Having him inside her started to feel…good. She'd thought she was satiated, but to her shock a new need built within her. With each slow, deep thrust, he filled a place deep inside her that made her body tighten with new desire.

As her body accepted him fully, Alessandro moved with increasing roughness, riding her harder and deeper, holding her hips with his hands. Her breasts swayed with the increasing force of his thrusts, the headboard slapping against the wall. The pleasure—the pain—made her writhe, her back arching off the bed as she panted for breath, her body desperate with the need for new release. He held her down as he pushed inside her, and he was so huge, so deep, and it felt good, so good. She held her breath, closing her eyes. Her head tilted back and the tension inside her coiled—and coiled—then sprang.

She gave a silent, mindless scream as explosions ripped through her, shaking her whole body as at, the same moment, she heard his growl rise to a shout and he slammed into her with one final, cataclysmic thrust.

When Lilley opened her eyes, she found Alessandro lying on top of her, holding her protectively. She closed her eyes. For no reason she could explain, she suddenly felt like crying. Except he'd taken her to a whole new world.

Why had she ever been so afraid of something so magical?

"I hurt you. I'm sorry."

At the sound of his low voice, she looked up at his face. The shadowed mystery of his dark eyes held regret and barely satiated desire and something more.

"You didn't," she lied.

He gave her a skeptical look.

"A little," she admitted, then, tossing her arms above her head against the soft pillow, she sighed happily. "But would it be cheesy to say it hurt so good?"

He tenderly kissed her forehead. "Horribly cheesy."

Then he kissed her mouth with something more than tenderness. His kiss deepened, his tongue twining with her own as his hands cupped her cheeks. She sighed with pleasure, then gave an involuntary wince as he crushed her bruised lips.

"I'm hurting you." He started to roll over, but she stopped him.

"You're not."

"You're lying."

"So let me," she whispered.

A sensual smile curved his lips. He kissed her again, his mouth hot and hard against hers. She felt him move against her, and sighed with bliss.

He suddenly rolled her over on the bed, pulling her on

top of his naked body. She gave a little squeak of surprise as he looked up at her with dark, wicked eyes. "Your turn."

Lilley stared at him. He expected her to lead in bed? To ride him? Her heart pounded in her throat. She was so clumsy. She'd make a fool of herself. "I…I don't think I can do this. I don't know how."

"You will." Looking straight into her eyes, he put his hand on her cheek. "I can teach you."

Alessandro leaned up to kiss her, and she forgot to be afraid. Holding on to him, letting him guide her to find her own rhythm, she allowed him to teach her to follow her own pleasure, and lead him to his. She rode him, and joy and freedom filled her soul. For the first time in her life, Lilley was the fearless woman she'd always wanted to be.

Alessandro had never known sex could be like this. Lilley was an intoxicating combination of innocence and fire.

He'd never been so insatiable before. He knew that for the rest of his life he'd remember how he'd had the honor of being her first lover. He'd remember teaching her to control the rhythm and pace as she rode him, timidly at first, then with rising reckless confidence.

Afterward, sweaty and sticky from lovemaking, they'd showered in the enormous, gleaming marble bathroom. Alessandro had watched her as she'd tipped her head back beneath the water. The sight of her arching body as water poured over her breasts and streamed off her tight, pink nipples had been too much for him. She'd flicked him a teasing glance, and he'd suddenly realized she was playing with him. With a growl, he'd pushed her against the cool marble of the shower and made love to her against the wall as hot water sprayed all over them both.

Lilley was a very apt student. No wonder each sexual encounter between them was more explosive than the last.

His innocent virgin was transforming into a wanton sex goddess in front of his eyes.

Rosy-skinned and exhausted, they'd fallen into bed a few hours before dawn and woken up starving a few hours later. They'd made love a fourth time, fast and hot, then ventured downstairs for breakfast.

Alessandro found himself wanting to impress her. He'd given his staff the weekend off, so he made her his signature breakfast dish, a sausage frittata. As he cooked, she scooted around the kitchen wearing an oversized robe, gathering ingredients for her French toast, a delicious confection of nutmeg and cinnamon sugar. They sat together at his kitchen table, basking in the morning light, drinking freshly squeezed orange juice and feeding each other bites of food.

For the first time in Alessandro's adult life, he had no desire to check in with work, or catch up on the morning news. All he wanted to do was look at her, touch her, be with her. He couldn't get enough of her exquisite skin and her curvaceous, soft body.

But it was more than just her body.

Being around Lilley made him feel…different. Made him *feel* his own heart beating. After so many years of being empty and bored, playing the game, making money to keep score, sleeping with women he barely knew and dodging the constant onslaught of people begging for his attention, he could let down his guard. Lilley asked for nothing. She would never hurt him or lie to him. Her openness and honesty reminded him of the person he'd been long ago, before everyone he loved had betrayed him.

For some reason, Lilley liked him. Not his money or his title or even just his body. She liked *him*. The man inside. And looking at her in the morning light, Alessandro realized that whatever he'd promised her yesterday, he had no intention of giving her up. He didn't care if it was selfish.

He wanted more than a one-night stand.

"This is delicious," Lilley murmured, leaning forward at the breakfast table. Her oversized robe fell open to reveal her delectable breasts as she took another bite of frittata. She gave him an impish smile. "To be honest, I didn't expect cooking to be one of your talents."

A moment before, he'd been finishing his last piece of French toast, licking the crumbs off his plate. But looking at her state of undress instantly made him want her again, made him want to sweep their dishes to the floor and make love to her on the table. He swallowed. "I usually don't cook. You inspired me."

She smiled at him, her trusting warm eyes the color of deep, dark caramel, her beautiful face suffused in the soft glow of morning light as she whispered, "Not half as much as you inspire me."

Alessandro stared at her, lost in her gaze. He could no more stop himself from wanting her than he could stop breathing.

But keeping her would be wrong. Very wrong.

I have no reason to feel guilty, he told himself fiercely. He'd tried to let her go once already. She'd made her own choice. He'd told her up front he could never marry her or love her. She could protect her own heart.

Reaching his hand out to her cheek, he slowly stroked down her neck to her swelling breasts half revealed by the gape of her robe. Her lips parted in surprise and he could not resist the invitation. Leaning over the table, he kissed her. He felt her soft lips move against his, matching his passion, and nearly groaned. Selfish or not, nothing on earth could make him give her up. Not now. Not yet.

Rising to his feet, Alessandro pulled her from her chair.

Untying her sash, he dropped her robe to the floor, leaving her naked skin glowing in a pool of morning light. He gave a shuddering intake of breath. "Walk ahead of me," he said hoarsely. "So I can see you."

Her eyebrow quirked. In a quick movement, she jerked open his own robe, dropping it to the floor beside hers.

"You first," she suggested sweetly.

Thirty seconds later, Lilley was giggling with little screams of laughter as he chased her, both of them naked, back upstairs. They didn't even make it to his bedroom, but ended up on the priceless heirloom rug in the upstairs hall.

They spent the rest of Sunday making love in every room of his villa. In the garden, in the library, in the study, and finally, long past midnight, back in his bed. They fell asleep wrapped in each other's arms.

But now, just a few hours before Monday's dawn, Alessandro was wide awake as Lilley slept beside him. He'd lost count of the number of times they'd made love in the last thirty hours. More than ten. He paused, then shook his head, amazed. Less than twenty?

Each time he possessed her, instead of being satiated, he only wanted her more. His passion for her consumed him, and his hunger only grew.

But their weekend was over. He looked down at her, kissing her forehead softly as she slept in his arms. He listened to her breath. She clung to him, naked, sighing sweetly in her sleep as she whispered something that sounded like his name.

Guilt, a very unfamiliar emotion, blew through Alessandro like an icy breeze. Virgins fell in love. He knew that too well. They were not experienced enough in the ways of the world to separate their bodies from their hearts. And a girl like Lilley, so warm, vivid, brilliant and kind, deserved a man who could give her a future. A man who could actually love her.

Unlike his usual sort of mistress, Lilley Smith was not a ruthless coquette who used her body as a weapon for power and gain. He wondered if he could ever again be fully satisfied by a cold-hearted woman like Olivia Bianchi. How could that ever compare to Lilley's intoxicating warmth and joy as she gave all of herself, body and soul?

Already Alessandro wanted her again.

Angrily, he clawed back his hair, which was still damp from the sweat of their passionate night. Careful not to wake her, he rose to his feet and walked naked through the balcony doors, out into the warm, clear August night. Moonlight stretched over his vineyards, frosting the hills with silver as he looked out at his land, trying to calm his unquiet heart.

He closed his eyes, feeling every bit of his thirty-five years. His soul felt old and dark compared to hers. Was that his intention—to suck up her youth and optimism like a vampire, feeding on her innocence until his own darkness consumed her?

"Alessandro?" he heard her murmur sleepily.

Gripping his hands, he went back into the bedroom. He found her lying in bed, her gorgeous curves covered only by a sheet. She sat up in surprise when she realized he'd been standing naked on the balcony. "What's wrong?"

"Nothing," he said.

She swallowed, biting her lip. "Do you regret our time together?" she whispered. "Are you thinking about—Olivia?"

"No!" Shaking his head, he said the first thing that came to mind. "I'm thinking about the Mexico City deal. Wondering how our design team in San Francisco will update the Joyería designs once they take over."

Alessandro closed his mouth with a snap, shocked at his

own stupidity. He'd been so concerned about not hurting Lilley, he'd blurted out something he should never have revealed to anyone except his board of directors. If it became public, it would ruin everything. He'd given Joyería's current owner, Miguel Rodriguez, some legally vague reassurances that he would keep the Mexican designers on staff and the studio in Mexico City separate from Caetani Worldwide's offices in San Francisco, Shanghai and Rome. If Rodriguez heard about his plans to economize, the man could well cancel the deal and sell the company to a competitor.

Alessandro looked at Lilley sharply, but she seemed completely unaware of the import of the information he'd unthinkingly shared. She smiled, shaking her head.

"You always work, don't you?" she said softly. "That's why you're so successful." Her gaze grew troubled as she hugged a pillow over her breasts. "Maybe if I were more like you, I wouldn't be such a screw-up."

He frowned. "A screw-up?" he demanded. "Who said that?"

Her smile became sad. "No one has to say it. I came to San Francisco to start my jewelry business, then chickened out." She looked down at the bed. "I'm not brave like you."

He sat down beside her. "There are all kinds of bravery in the world, *cara*." Reaching over, he lifted her chin, forcing her to meet his gaze. "You have an open heart. You trust people in a way I could not. And your jewelry is unique and beautiful. Like you," he said huskily. Setting his jaw, he gave her a decisive nod. "You will start your business when the time is right. I know it."

Her large brown eyes looked up at him with almost painful hope. "You do?"

"Yes." He dropped his hand. "I failed many times, in

many different businesses, before I made my first fortune. Selling children's plastic bracelets, of all things."

She gave an amazed laugh. "You? Selling plastic bracelets? I don't believe it."

He gave her a sudden grin. "It's true. The trend exploded across America and I made my first million. I was determined to succeed. No matter how many times I failed, I wouldn't give up." He stroked her hair. "You are the same. You just don't know it yet."

"You think so?" she breathed, her eyes huge.

He nodded. "If it's important to you, you'll make it happen. Whatever it costs."

"What made you so driven to succeed?"

His lips flattened. "When my father died, he left debts I had to repay. I dropped out of college and worked twenty hours a day." He looked away. "I will never feel powerless again."

"Powerless? But you're a prince!"

"Prince of nothing," he said harshly. "An empty title I inherited from a fifteenth-century warlord. The men of my family have always been corrupt and weak."

"But not you." Her clear eyes met his. "You are the leader of Caetani Worldwide. You built a billion-dollar company from nothing. Everyone loves you," she whispered.

He felt uncomfortable with the adoration he saw in her eyes. "I'm nothing special," he said gruffly. "If I can start a business, so can you. Start a business plan, work through the numbers."

"That might be hard, since I read letters and numbers in the wrong order."

"Dyslexia?"

She nodded.

"What is it like?"

"It's different for different people. In my case the letters and numbers won't stay put."

He barked a laugh. "And you're working in my file room?"

She gave him a sudden cheeky grin. "Now you understand why I was working late." Her voice became wistful. "I've never been really successful at anything except making jewelry. Maybe that's why my father thinks I'm hopeless at taking care of myself. He threatened to disinherit me if I don't come back to Minnesota and marry one of his managers."

"Disinherit you!" Alessandro pictured a hard-working farmer with a small plot of land in the bleak northern plains. "He wanted you to marry a manager on his farm?"

Lilley blinked, frowning at him. "My father's not a farmer. He's a businessman."

"Ah," Alessandro said. "He owns a restaurant? Perhaps a laundromat?"

Her eyes slid away evasively. "Um. Something like that. My parents got divorced a few years ago, when my mother was sick. The day she died was the worst day of my life. I had to get away, so I found…a job…with a distant relative. My cousin."

She stumbled strangely over the words, looking at him with an anxiety he couldn't understand.

"I'm sorry," Alessandro said in a low voice. "My mother died a few years ago, and my own relationship with my father was always complicated." *Complicated* was an understatement. His father, Prince Luca Caetani, had married Alessandro's mother for her money, then spent it on his mistresses. He'd died when Alessandro was nineteen, leaving debts and an unknown number of bastards around the world. Alessandro was his father's only legitimate child, the heir to the Caetani title and name, but every year some stranger came out of the woodwork, claiming blood ties and asking for a handout from the company Alessandro had built with his own two hands.

Just wait till you're older, son, his father had gasped on his deathbed. *You'll be just like me. You'll see.*

Alessandro had vowed he would never be anything like his father. He was selfish, but not a monster.

Right?

"I actually thought about going back." Lilley's trusting eyes shone at him. "But now I know I won't. You make me feel…brave. Like I can do anything. Risk anything."

Alessandro's heart gave a sickening lurch. He gripped his fists so tightly the knuckles turned white.

Lilley was half in love with him already. He could see it in her face, even if she herself wasn't aware of it yet. If he kept her as his mistress, how long would it be before he obliterated her light completely? Until she, too, had a heart as dark and empty as night?

He'd crossed a line. He'd violated her innocence in a way he could never take back.

If that wasn't the work of a monster, what was?

With an intake of breath, he turned away. In just an hour or two, dawn would break across the purple hills. But there could be no sunrise for Alessandro. He felt cold to the bone.

There was only one way to cut her loss. One way to leave her heart bruised, but not shattered. He exhaled, closing his eyes.

He had to let her go.

"It's almost morning," she said, sounding sad. She splayed her small hand against his chest. "In a few hours, I'll go back to the file room. What about you?"

He opened his eyes. "Mexico City."

Lilley took a deep breath. "Alessandro," she whispered, "I want you to know that I—"

Turning to her almost violently, he put his finger against her lips. "Let's not talk." Pulling her down on the mattress beside him, he breathed in the scent of her, the intoxicating smell of sunshine and flowers. He gloried in her warmth and beauty for the last time.

"This has been the happiest day of my life," she whispered. "I'm just sad to see it end." She gave him a crooked smile. "In a few hours, you'll forget I ever existed."

He looked down at her. "I'll never forget you, Lilley," he said, and it was the truth.

"Oh," she breathed. Relief and gratitude filled her eyes. She thought his words meant they might have a future. She didn't know they were the death knell for any relationship they might have had.

She put her hand on his rough, unshaven cheek. "Then give me a kiss I'll never forget."

He looked at her full, rosy lips, and his whole body shuddered with need.

One last time, he told his conscience savagely. He would give her up at dawn. Set her free before he did any further damage to her soul.

Cupping her face, Alessandro kissed her, as if trying to burn the memory of her lips against his for all time. Tasting the sweetness of her mouth, he spread her lips wide, plundering her with his tongue. Pulling the pillow away from her body, he rolled her beneath him on the bed, covering her naked body with his own.

Alessandro looked down at Lilley's beautiful face. He knew the bitter memory of the joy shining now in her sweet, joyful eyes, her strange trust and belief in his goodness would haunt him for all time. An ache like regret pierced his soul.

Then, closing his eyes, he pushed himself inside her.

CHAPTER FIVE

A MONTH later, Lilley felt sick as she sat in a hard office chair in the basement office of the human resources department. The fluorescent lights above the desk flickered and hummed as Lilley licked her dry lips, praying she'd heard wrong.

"What?" she croaked.

"I'm sorry, Miss Smith, but we must let you go." The kindly older man on the other side of the desk shifted uncomfortably in his chair. "I'm afraid Caetani Worldwide isn't the right place for your skills."

Fighting nausea, Lilley took a deep breath as grief and pain washed over her. She'd known this would happen, known she'd lose her job no matter how hard she tried. Effort couldn't compensate for her slowness in filing numbers and letters that danced in front of her eyes.

Maybe she really was incapable of taking care of herself, just as her father said. Case in point: she'd slept with her boss, and then was surprised when Alessandro disappeared before she woke up on Monday morning and never bothered to contact her again. Exactly as he'd told her he'd do. Her throat suddenly hurt. She really wasn't smart.

"I can assure you," the HR director continued, "there's a very generous compensation package."

"I was too slow, right?" she whispered, blinking back tears. "I took too long to finish my work."

The man shook his head, his ponderous jowls wobbling. He didn't look as if he wanted to fire her. He looked as if he wished the earth would swallow him up beneath his desk. "You did a good job, Miss Smith. You were popular with the rest of the staff. Yes, you took longer than the other file clerk, but your work ethic—" He took a deep breath, tapping a file on his desk. "That's neither here nor there." His voice was clipped. "We will give you an excellent recommendation and I can assure you that you'll find a job soon. Very, *very* soon."

He started to explain the details of her severance package, but Lilley barely listened. The sick feeling was starting to win, so she focused on her breathing, staring hard at the little gray trash can on the floor by his desk. Fighting the desire to throw up into it.

"I'm sorry it turned out this way," he said finally. "But someday you'll be glad that…" He saw that she wasn't listening and was clutching her stomach with one hand while covering her mouth with her other. He sighed. "Please sign this." He pushed a paper towards her on the desk. Grabbing the pen he offered, Lilley skimmed the document—her father had drummed that much into her, at any rate—and saw she was basically promising not to sue the company for sexual harassment. Harassment?

She sucked in her breath. That meant it wasn't her work that was at fault, but she was being fired by—

She cut off the thought, unable to bear his name. Scribbling her signature, she rose to her feet. The HR director shook her hand.

"Best of luck, Miss Smith."

"Thanks," she choked out. Grabbing the file he held out,

she fled to the women's bathroom, where she could be sick in privacy.

Afterward, Lilley splashed cold water on her face. She looked at her wan, green expression in the mirror. She tried to force a grin, to put the cheerful mask back in place that she'd worn for the last month while enduring teasing and innuendo about Prince Alessandro. But today, she couldn't even smile.

Fired. She was fired.

Numbly, she walked to the elevator. She exited on the third floor and went to her desk in the corner of the windowless file room. Other employees had pictures of family or friends or pets hanging at their desks. Lilley had a lonely pink geranium and a postcard that her cousin's wife, Carrie, had sent from Provence a few weeks ago. On the tidy surface of her desk, she saw someone had left a gossip magazine for her to find. Again.

Her body felt cold as she looked down at the latest issue of *Celebrity Weekly*. The cover had a picture of Alessandro in Mexico City, where he'd been living for the last month in his attempt to keep the Joyería deal from falling apart. But last week, Lilley's cousin Théo had made a successful counterbid. It should have made her feel glad, but it didn't. Her heart ached to think of how Alessandro would feel after failing—at anything.

At least she was used to it.

Her eyes moved to a smaller picture at the bottom of the magazine's cover that had been taken at the Cannes film festival months before. Alessandro wore a tuxedo, looking darkly handsome, holding the hand of a beautiful blonde dressed in black. Olivia Bianchi.

Playboy Prince to Wed at Last, the cover blared. Someone had underlined the words with a thick black pen.

Ever since she'd been Alessandro's date at the ball, she'd

been paying for it. Some of her coworkers had worried Lilley might think too well of herself for briefly being their boss's mistress. Well, she thought bitterly, no chance of that.

Lilley jumped as she heard a man clear his throat behind her. Turning, she saw Larry, a security guard she knew. Just yesterday, Lilley had given him advice about how to get ink stains out of fabric, something she'd dealt with fairly often as her cousin's housekeeper. But today, his face was regretful and resigned.

"Sorry, Lilley. I'm supposed to escort you out."

She nodded over the lump in her throat. She gathered up her geranium, the magazine, the postcard from Provence, her nubby old cardigan and the large bag of toffees she kept at the bottom of her desk for emergencies. She packed up her life in a cardboard box and followed the security guard from the file room, trying to ignore all the employees staring at her as she was escorted from the building in a walk of shame.

In the lobby, Larry checked her cardboard box for contraband—what did he think she might take? Pens? Copy paper?—and then took her employee pass card. "Sorry," he mumbled again.

"I'll be fine," she whispered, and was proud she managed to leave the building without either crying or throwing up.

Numbly, Lilley took the bus home. As she reached her apartment, her cell phone rang. She glanced at the number. Nadia had missed all the action, so Jeremy must have told her the news. But Lilley couldn't face her roommate's sympathy right now. Or the suspicions Nadia had voiced lately, which Lilley was desperately trying not to think about: the reason for her frequent nausea over the last week.

Turning her phone to Mute, she threw it on the counter. She gulped down some dry crackers and water to help her stomach calm down, then changed into flannel pajamas and a pink fleece robe. Wrapping herself in her mother's quilt, she lay down on the couch and closed her eyes, even though she knew she was far too upset to sleep.

She was woken by the rattle of her cell phone on the kitchen counter. Sitting up, she saw the deepening shadows and realized she'd slept for hours. Pulling a pillow over her head, she tried to ignore the rattle. The phone finally stopped buzzing, then after a brief pause, it rudely started again. Muttering to herself, Lilley got up and grabbed it. She blinked when she saw the out-of-state number. *Alessandro,* she thought, still half confused by her dream, the dream she'd had over and over all month. She could still feel the heat of his lips against her skin. She swallowed.

"Hello?" she said almost timidly.

"Lilley Smith?" a jovial voice boomed at the other end. "You don't know me, but your résumé has come to our attention, and we'd like to offer you a paid internship with our company in New York."

By the time Lilley hung up the phone, her dreams about Alessandro were gone. She finally understood. He wasn't just ridding her from his company. He was completely erasing her from his life.

Her eyes fell on the magazine, visible from the cardboard box on the kitchen counter. Snatching it up, she stared with narrowed eyes at the picture of Alessandro with Olivia Bianchi. The blond Italian socialite looked like a smug, satisfied Persian cat who'd just licked up a whole bowl of cream.

Another huge wave of nausea overwhelmed her. Tossing the magazine to the floor, she covered her mouth and ran down the hall. Afterward, her eyes fell on the brown paper bag that sat ominously on the sink, like a loaded gun. Nadia had bought it for her days ago at the drugstore, and Lilley had scrupulously ignored it.

She couldn't possibly be pregnant. They'd gone through boxes of condoms! They'd used protection *every single time,* all weekend long.

Except…

She froze. Except that one time. In the shower.

Wide-eyed, she stared at herself in the bathroom mirror.

She exhaled. How could their affair have ended so badly? She'd fallen asleep so happily in Alessandro's arms, foolishly believing they might have a future. Then she'd woken up alone. Wrapping herself in a bedsheet, she'd called his name teasingly as she went downstairs. Instead, she'd discovered only his housekeeper. "The prince has been called away," the woman said stiffly. "Abbott will drive you back to the city." She'd handed Lilley the red gown, mended and pressed, and served her eggs, coffee and toast at the same table where Lilley had enjoyed that joyful, sensual breakfast with Alessandro just the day before. The chauffeur had driven her back home without a word. Lilley's cheeks still burned to remember.

But in spite of everything, she couldn't regret their time together. How could she, when she'd finally discovered what it felt like to take risks? To be truly alive? She'd discovered passion that had been like a fire consuming her body, making her soul blaze like a beacon in the night.

All right, so she'd never see him again. She could accept that, since she had no choice. She could even be grateful for the experience. For the memory.

But what if she was pregnant?

Lilley squeezed her eyes shut, her heart pounding. She would take the test and find out for sure. It would prove once and for all that she'd just eaten some bad Chinese takeout or something.

Her hands shook as she took the test, then waited. She told herself she wasn't worried. Hummed a cheerful little lullaby she'd sung to her cousin's baby in France. Looked at her watch. Two minutes. It was probably too soon to check, but it wouldn't hurt just to—

Pregnant.

Pregnantpregnantpregnant.

Her shaking hands dropped the stick in the trash as she staggered down the hall and into the kitchen. She found herself with a kettle in her hand and realized she was making tea, just as her mother had always done in times of crisis.

"Sweetheart, there are very few problems in the world that can't be made better by a hug, a plate of cookies and a cup of tea," her mother had said, smiling. It had worked like a charm when Lilley was nine and had failed a spelling test, and when she was a teenager and the other kids mocked, "Guess your father can't buy you a new brain." It had even worked when her father had asked her sick mother for a divorce, abandoning their family home in Minneapolis to build a huge mansion for his mistress on the shores of Lake Minnetonka.

She swallowed, trembling as tears filled her eyes. The difference was that her mother had been there. Lilley missed her so much. Paula Smith would have hugged her daughter, told her everything was going to be all right. And Lilley would have believed her.

The kettle screamed. Numbly, Lilley poured boiling water over the fragrant peppermint tea. Holding her steaming, oversized mug in her shaking hands, Lilley went to the couch.

A baby.

She was going to have Alessandro's baby.

Raw, jagged emotion washed over her. He'd arranged for her to be fired and had offered a job that was three thousand miles away. There was no other explanation for her to be spontaneously head-hunted for a fantastic internship with a New York jewelry company at double her current salary. He wanted Lilley out of San Francisco, so he wouldn't have to see her *scurrying in the halls* and could settle down, mouse-free, with his beautiful, sleek bride.

Setting her mug on the end table, she picked up the magazine from the floor. Opening it, she skimmed through the article. Alessandro was holding his annual wine-harvest celebration at his villa in Sonoma. Rumor was that it was going to be an engagement party.

Friday. That was tonight.

Lilley's fingertips stroked the image of Alessandro's handsome, cold face. She'd been so sure he would want to see her again. For the last month, she'd jumped every time her cell phone rang. She'd had such naive faith. She'd expected him to call, send flowers, a card, *something*. He hadn't.

But it turned out he had given her something, the greatest gift any woman could receive. A baby. She placed her hand on her soft belly. She'd always disliked her plump figure, wishing she could be thin and athletic. But now she realized her extra pounds didn't matter. Her amazing body was creating a baby. How could she be anything but grateful to it?

How would Alessandro react when she told him?

The memory of his harsh voice came floating back to her. *I will not marry you. I will not love you.*

She'd known from the beginning that Alessandro only considered her a fling. He'd been honest from the start. If Lilley had a broken heart, she was the only one to blame, because she'd allowed herself to hope for more.

Setting down the magazine, Lilley rose to her feet and walked to the tiny window in her pink fleece robe. Opening the gingham curtains, she looked out into the quiet street, remembering the night she'd made the choice that had changed her life so completely, the night she'd decided to give her virginity to Alessandro.

She would regret leaving San Francisco. She'd come to love the city, and had even become friends again with Jeremy and Nadia. Perhaps she would come to appreciate New York. But she would be going alone.

Then she remembered: she'd never be alone again.

She placed her hand on her belly as a wave of joy, sudden and unexpected as a child's laugh, washed over her. How could she be sad about how her time with Alessandro had ended, when he'd given her such a gift?

And the grip around her heart loosened. She would leave, as he wanted. But there was one thing she had to do first. She couldn't exactly make an appointment to see him via Mrs. Rutherford, who was highly skilled at blocking former lovers from contacting him. And this wasn't the sort of news she wished to convey via his business email address. He'd deliberately never given her his private phone number. So as unpalatable as it was, that left only one option.

Picking up the magazine, she looked down at his hard, handsome face, and at the image of the villa in Sonoma where they'd first made love. Where he'd taken her virginity. Where he'd filled her with his child.

Before she left him forever, she had to tell Alessandro he was going to be a father.

"Alessandro, at last." Olivia's sultry voice immediately set Alessandro's nerves on edge. "Did you miss me, darling?"

Forcing his lips into a smile, Alessandro turned to face her, his shoulders tight. He'd seen her arrive through the window of his study. His first party guest to arrive tonight.

It was unlike Olivia to be early to anything, so that meant she'd heard the rumors. And unfortunately the rumors were true.

The five-carat diamond ring in his jacket pocket felt like an anchor, heavy enough to drag him down through the floors of his villa, through his wine cellar and continuing straight to hell.

"I've missed you." Olivia gave him a smile that showed her white teeth. She was impeccably dressed as always, in a black one-shoulder cocktail dress that showed off her tanned body, muscular and slender from hours of running and self-denial. As she came towards him, her diamond bangles jangled noisily on her skinny wrist. She'd be the perfect Caetani bride, he told himself firmly.

And he needed to settle down before he became every bit as reckless and corrupt as his father. His night with Lilley had shown that all too clearly.

Alessandro pushed away the memory of Lilley's big trusting eyes and soft, sensual body that always hovered on the edge of his consciousness. He never should have allowed himself to touch her. Never.

Olivia came forward to kiss his mouth, but at the last moment, his head twisted away, causing her lips to land squarely on his cheek. His body's abrupt reaction surprised them both. Surely his body, at least, should have been pleased to see her? He hadn't had sex for a month. And what a hellish month it had been.

She drew back, her eyes offended. "What is it?"

"Nothing." What could he say? That he'd missed her while he was in Mexico City? That he'd thought of her when he'd lost his bid on Joyería to his most hated rival, that French bastard Théo St. Raphaël?

The truth was that it hadn't been Olivia's face he'd yearned to see the night he'd suffered that bitter disappointment. He'd hungered for a different woman's face. Her soft body. Her kind heart.

Alessandro took a deep breath. Lilley was likely already packing for New York. She almost certainly hated him now. He could only imagine how she'd felt this past month since he'd abandoned her without even the bare courtesy of a farewell. Usually his one-night stands at least got flowers.

But his coldness was deliberate. He was being cruel to be kind.

Olivia's red lips lifted into a determined smile. "I was so glad when you called me," she murmured. "I was almost starting to think you'd broken up with me."

"I did." He stared down at her. "I do not care for ultimatums."

"Lesson learned," she said, still smiling, though it did not meet her eyes. She tucked her hand into his own. Her skin felt cool. She had no softness, either of body or soul. "I'm glad we're back together. We're perfect for each other, aren't we?"

Alessandro looked down at her beautiful face, her big green eyes and sharp, hollow cheekbones. Physically, she didn't have a single flaw. She would fit well into his world. No one would ever be able to hurt her or criticize her performance as his *principessa.* *"Sì,"* he said tightly. *"Perfetto."*

They walked down the hall towards the two-story foyer. From the landing, he saw many new guests had already arrived. This party had been planned in celebration of the early wine harvest, just for a few friends. But six weeks ago, feeling arrogantly certain of impending success with the Joyería deal, he'd invited business associates, thinking it would be the perfect victory lap.

Instead, the grape harvest was turning weak and the Mexico City deal was a failure. And he was going to propose to Olivia. It wasn't a celebration. It was a wake.

With every step, he felt the dead weight of the diamond ring grow heavier in his pocket. He wondered who'd leaked the story about him purchasing it in Mexico City. Some underpaid store clerk, most likely. He'd carried it for over a week now, but he'd called Olivia only two days ago.

He'd been dragging his heels, but now he'd made his decision and wouldn't go back. He was thirty-five and had defiled one virgin too many. He'd selfishly and ruthlessly possessed Lilley, when he'd known it would ultimately bring her pain. He'd sworn he'd never be like his selfish, callous father. And yet, seducing his innocent, brokenhearted file-room girl, he'd come perilously close.

Olivia's cool, bony arm twisted hard around his as they walked down the stairs. The weather forecast was calling for thunderstorms, so the party had been moved indoors from the pool, although many guests had remained outside. He could hear a jazz trio playing in the ballroom, and he saw friends and business acquaintances from Silicon Valley. The men wore suits similar to Alessandro's, and their wives wore shiny cocktail dresses, and everyone was drinking his wine. He should be enjoying this…shouldn't he?

He heard Bronson arguing loudly at the door. His normally staid butler seemed to be struggling with an unwanted guest. "Service entrance is at the back," Bronson insisted, trying to close the door.

"I'm not here for a delivery!" a woman said, pushing at the door. "I'm here to see Alessandro!"

The butler sucked in his breath as if she'd just insulted his mother. *"Alessandro?"* he repeated in disbelief. "You mean His Serene Highness, Prince Alessandro Caetani?"

"Yes!"

"The prince is currently hosting a party," Bronson said coldly, his tone clearly adding *and is unavailable to the likes of you.* "Make an appointment though his secretary. Good evening."

But as he started to slam the door, the woman blocked him with a foot. "I'm sorry to be rude," she begged, "but I'm leaving in the morning and have to see him. Tonight."

Prickles went down Alessandro's neck.

He knew that sweet voice. It was clear as a fresh-water lake to a man dying of thirst. Dropping Olivia's hand, he went down the stairs to where white-haired, dignified Bronson was struggling with the door like an American bouncer at a bar. The butler panted, "Unhand the door this instant—"

Grabbing the door over his head, Alessandro wrenched it open. The butler turned. "Your highness," he gasped. "I'm sorry for this interruption. This *woman* has been trying to force her way into your party. I don't know how she talked her way past security at the gate, but..."

"It's all right," Alessandro said, hardly knowing what he was saying, staring at the woman from his dreams on the doorstep.

Lilley looked even more beautiful than she had a month ago. Her long brown hair was swept back in a ponytail, her face was bare of makeup. Unlike all the other women squeezed into tight girdles and barely able to move in se-quined dresses, Lilley wore a simple tank top and a flow-ery cotton skirt, a casual summery outfit that effortlessly showed off her stunning curves. She shone like an angel standing in front of the distant dark storm clouds over the horizon.

"Alessandro," Lilley whispered, looking at him. The pupils of her large, limpid eyes seemed to dilate, and the honey-brown gaze pulled him into their endless sweet depths. Hearing her speak his name, he felt electrified.

"Security!" his butler cried, motioning to a bodyguard on the other side of the room. Alessandro grabbed Bronson's arm.

"I will handle this," he growled. "Thank you."

Mollified, the butler nodded and backed away. "Of course, sir."

Taking Lilley gently by the arm, Alessandro pulled her inside the foyer. She looked up at him, her lips parted.

His hand involuntarily tightened, his fingers trembling at the point of contact against her soft skin. Waves of sensual memories washed over his unwilling body. The last time they'd been together, they'd made love in every room here, including this foyer. He looked at the wall behind her. There.

Suddenly choking with need, he felt an overwhelming drive to carry her up to his bed—to claim her body as his own. He'd thought being away from Lilley would make him forget. It had only made him want her more.

Blood roared in his ears as he reached around her and closed the heavy oak door. Dropping Lilley's arm, he folded his hands to keep himself from touching her. He said hoarsely, "You shouldn't have come."

She took a deep breath. "I had no choice."

"What is she doing here?" Olivia demanded peevishly in English behind him. "Did you invite her, Alessandro?"

Oh yes, Olivia. He'd forgotten her completely. He glanced back at her, irritated. "No, I did not invite her." He turned back to Lilley. "Why are you here?"

Lilley moved closer to him, a soft smile on her lips. Her brown eyes were luminous, catching at his soul. She seemed like a creature from another world, a kinder one filled with magic and innocence. Her pretty face was suffused with a strange glow. "I came to see you."

He stared at her, bewildered. *I came to see you.* No pretense? No games? No story about *just being in the neighborhood?* He hardly knew how to deal with such straightforward, vulnerable honesty. He'd had so little experience with it.

"You weren't invited," Olivia said coldly. "You need to leave."

It was clear by her scowl that she'd recognized Lilley as the woman Alessandro had taken to the Preziosi di Caetani ball. Olivia glared at her as if she hoped the hot laser beam of her eyes might cause the younger woman to burst into flame.

But looking back at Olivia, Lilley's gaze didn't have a shred of anger or even fear. Instead, she looked at the Italian heiress with something almost like…sympathy.

"I'm not here to cause a scene," Lilley said quietly. "I just need to speak to Alessandro, alone. Please. It will only take a moment."

"Alessandro doesn't want to talk to you." When he remained silent, Olivia tossed her head, giving Lilley a nasty glare. "Get out before I throw you out, you cheap little— file clerk."

But her attempted insult seemed to roll right off Lilley like water off a duck's back. She turned back to Alessandro with a soft smile. "May I please speak to you? Alone?"

Being alone with Lilley, mere minutes before he planned to propose to Olivia, was a bad idea. A *very* bad idea. He opened his mouth to tell Lilley firmly that she must go. Instead, his body twisted and he heard himself saying in Italian, "Will you please excuse us?"

Olivia drew back with a hiss between her teeth, visibly furious. "Certainly," she said coldly. "I'll go greet the mayor and my good friend Bill Hocking," she said, referring to a well-known Silicon Valley billionaire. Her warning couldn't have been clearer. But suddenly he didn't give a damn.

"Grazie," he answered mildly, as if utterly oblivious of her affronted fury.

With a scowl, Olivia turned on her heel and stomped away, her bare back looking almost skeletal in the black one-shouldered gown.

Alessandro looked back down at Lilley, who, with her soft body and simple cotton clothes seemed even more impossibly alluring than he remembered.

Amidst all the noise around them, the jazz music, the soft clink of wineglasses and laughter of guests, he felt as if they were alone. "I never expected to see you again," he murmured. "I can't believe you crashed my party."

She smiled. "Really brave of me, right? Or really stupid."

"Brave and stupid are often the same thing."

Lilley shook her head, and he saw unshed tears in her eyes as she laughed. "I'm glad to see you, Alessandro. I've missed you."

Hearing her leave herself so vulnerable, he felt it again—that odd twisting in the vicinity of his heart. "But you shouldn't have come here tonight."

Her eyes met his. "Because this is an engagement party."

Alessandro tried to keep his face blank. "You read gossip magazines."

"Unfortunately."

Bracing himself, he waited for the inevitable scene, for her tears and recriminations. Instead, she just gave him a wistful smile.

"I want you to be happy." She lifted her chin. "If Olivia is truly the one, I wish you all the happiness in the world."

Alessandro's jaw fell open. It was the last thing he'd expected her to say. He took a deep breath, suddenly uncertain how to proceed.

"You—aren't upset?" he said finally. His cheeks became

hot as he heard how foolish the words sounded to his own ears.

"There's no point to being upset over something I cannot change." She stared down at the marble floor. "And I truly didn't come to cause a scene."

"Then why did you?"

She looked up, her eyes luminous and wide. Beneath the darkening light of the upper windows, her eyes were the color of a mountain stream. Not just brown, he realized. Her eyes were a thousand shades, depths of green and blue and amber like a deep, ancient river.

"I have something to tell you before I can leave San Francisco."

Leave? Why on earth would she leave? Then Alessandro remembered he'd convinced a friend to offer her a job in New York. When he'd been in Mexico City, enduring night after night of hot dreams, he'd thought sending her three thousand miles away from San Francisco was the only sane thing to do. Now, he thought it the stupidest idea he'd ever conceived. His shoulders tightened. "Lilley—"

The doorbell rang, and as Bronson hesitantly came towards the door Alessandro grabbed Lilley's hand. He pulled her out of the foyer, away from the hubbub of the party, leading her down a side hall.

"Where are we going?" she asked, not resisting him.

His hand tightened around hers. "Where we can be alone."

Turning down a second hallway towards a quiet wing, Alessandro tried to ignore how right her hand felt in his own, tried not to feel the enticing warmth of her soft skin. But as he pulled her into the music room where he often hosted concerts and parties, the large room suddenly felt small, the temperature hot and stifling. As he walked around the grand piano and past the Picasso on the wall, his tie felt tight around his neck. He just kept walking through the music room. Opening the sliding glass doors, he pulled her into a small private garden.

Outside, the air was cool. The garden was green and stark, just a lawn, really, surrounded on three sides by a ten-foot privet hedge that separated them from the pool-side terrace. On the other side of the hedge, he could hear muffled conversation and the clink of wineglasses as guests milled around the Olympic-size pool and terrace.

Alessandro realized he was still holding Lilley's hand. He looked down at their intertwined fingers. She followed his gaze and he heard her intake of breath, felt her tremble.

Their eyes met in the rapidly deepening twilight. The sky above the villa was dark with threatening clouds, and he heard a distant rumble of thunder. He heard the wind howl through the trees. Lilley's full cotton skirt swirled around her legs.

Electricity filled the air as the temperature seemed to drop five degrees around them. But Alessandro still felt hot, burning from the storm inside him. Desire arced though him, and with an intake of breath, he dropped her hand.

Lilley deserved better than a series of cheap one-night stands. For her sake, he couldn't risk her loving him. And for his own sake…he couldn't risk caring for her. He'd learned long ago to trust no one. Sex and money were real. Love was a lie.

He knew this, but his body shook with the effort of not touching her, from not putting his arms around her and sinking into her softness and warmth. He tightened his hands into fists.

"Why did you come?" he ground out.

Colorful fairy lights high in the trees swayed violently in the rising wind. A flash of lightning illuminated Lilley's stricken face.

"You're in love with Miss Bianchi, aren't you?"

He set his jaw. "I told you. Marriage is a mutually beneficial alliance. Love has nothing to do with it."

"But surely you wouldn't want to spend the rest of your life without love." Long tendrils of soft brown hair blew across her face as she searched his gaze. Her expression faltered. "Would you?"

Thunder crackled in the sky above. Alessandro heard gasps from the other side of the hedge as the first raindrops fell, and guests ran back inside the villa.

"Just tell me what you have to say, then leave," he said tightly.

Lilley blinked, then looked down at the grass beneath her feet. "This is hard. Harder than I ever thought it would be."

Rain began to fall more heavily. He watched a fat raindrop slide down her rounded cheek to her full, generous mouth. Her pink tongue unconsciously darted out to lick the thick drop of rain against her full, sweetly sensual lips, and he nearly groaned.

He had to get her out of here before he did something they'd both regret forever. Why had he ever allowed himself to take a single forbidden taste of what did not belong to him by right?

"It was a mistake for me to seduce you," he said in a low voice. "I'm sorry I ever touched you."

She looked up, her eyes bright with grief. "Was it so awful?"

Awful? A new ache filled his throat. He hated that for the first time in nineteen years, he'd found a heart he did not want to break, and here he was breaking it. "Your first time should have been special, with a man who loved you, who might someday marry you. Not a one-night stand with a man like me."

"Don't be so hard on yourself." She tried to give him a smile. "It was two nights."

He nearly shuddered with the memory of how good it had been between them. How she'd tasted. How she'd felt beneath him. He forced himself to say, "You will find someone else."

She stared at him. "That's why you're sending me to New York."

Thunder boomed over them. "You knew it was me?"

"Of course I knew." She looked at him with a tremulous smile. She swallowed, then squared her shoulders. Rain was starting to soak her long brown hair, causing her tank top and cotton skirt to cling to her skin. "Thank you for arranging the internship. It was—very kind."

Her generous spirit only made Alessandro feel more like a brute. His head was throbbing with pain. He tightened his hands into fists. "I wasn't being kind, damn you. I was sending you away because I'm getting married. Not for love. Her father's company will be an asset." His hands tightened. "But when I speak vows, I will be faithful to them."

Lilley searched his gaze. "And if I were an heiress like her?" she whispered. "Would you choose me as your bride instead?"

Looking at her, he held his breath. Then slowly, he shook his head. "You would never fit into my world." His hand lifted. "It would destroy everything about you that I admire most. Everything that is cheerful and bright."

He barely caught himself before he touched her cheek. Thunder cracked again above their heads, as loud and metallic as a baseball bat against the earth, and he dropped his hand. "Olivia will be my perfect bride."

"I can't let you marry her. Not without knowing what I, what I…" She licked her lips. "What I have to tell you."

Alessandro's suit was now completely wet. The two of them were alone in the emerald garden, below the black sky. The scent of rain washed over the leaves, over the earth, over the distant vineyards and the pink bougainvillea twisting up the stucco of his villa.

And looking at her beautiful, stricken brown eyes, he suddenly knew what she was going to say.

"Don't," he ground out. "Don't say it."

She hesitated, her lovely round face looking scared. Her hair and clothes were now stuck to her skin. He could see the full outline of her breasts and hard jut of her nipples beneath her thin cotton tank top. He could see the shape of her curvaceous legs beneath her skirt as lightning flashed above them. "Alessandro—"

"No, *cara*." He put his hand to her lips, stroking the rain off her face with the pads of his thumbs. "Please," he whispered. "Do not speak the words. Leave us that, at least. I can see your feelings on your face. I already know what is in your heart."

Lilley looked up at him, her expression breathless. The rain began to fall more heavily and he realized he'd cupped her face in his hands. Her wet, full, pink lips were inches from his own, and he suddenly couldn't breathe. He was hard and aching, his lips pulsing with the drive to kiss her. His body clamored for him to push her roughly against the hedge and claim her as his own.

Using every drop of willpower he possessed, Alessandro dropped his hands, stepping away. He said harshly, "Go to New York, Lilley."

"Wait," she choked out as he turned away. "You can't go. Not until I tell you—"

He whirled to face her, his expression cold. "Do not fight

me. We must never see each other again. There is nothing you can say to make me change my decision."

She took a deep breath.

"I'm pregnant with your baby," she whispered.

CHAPTER SIX

THUNDER pounded the dark sky, shaking the earth beneath her feet. Lilley held her breath, waiting for his reaction.

The violently swinging fairy lights above the hedge caused shadows to move across the sharp planes of Alessandro's handsome face as he said hoarsely, "Pregnant."

"Yes."

A sharp flash of lightning illuminated his grim black eyes as he took a single step towards her. "You can't be."

"I am."

"We used protection."

She spread her arms helplessly. "That one time, in the shower…"

He sucked in his breath. "No."

"But—"

"No." Clawing back his wet black hair, he paced three steps across the lawn. Lilley watched him with a building sense of despair. Her body felt ice-cold, soaked to the bone. But that was nothing compared to her heart. She'd known he didn't want her, and that he wouldn't want their baby. But knowing it in her head and hearing him say it out loud were two different things.

She wrapped her arms around her shivering body, trying to comfort herself and the baby inside her. *It's all right,* she told herself, using the words her mother had often said to her when she was young and sad. *It'll be all right, sweetheart.*

It worked. She felt the anguish give way a fraction inside her. Lifting her head, she looked at Alessandro. She whispered, "It's all right."

He stopped pacing. "What?"

Love was a gift, Lilley realized. Love was always a gift. Even if the person you loved chose not to love you back.

She looked at Alessandro, so handsome and impossibly sexy even with his expensive suit soaked with rain. His dark hair was plastered to his forehead and tousled. Compassion for him, for this man she'd almost loved, filled her heart, crowding out her grief for the husband and father he could never be. She took a deep breath. "Nothing has to change for you."

The expression on his face was suddenly as dark and ominous as the storm. "What?"

"You told me from the start that our affair would only be a fling." She shook her head. "I don't expect you to help me raise our baby. I just thought you should know."

Alessandro's eyes were black. The muscles of his powerful body tightened. "If you don't expect me to raise your child, exactly what do you want from me?"

She blinked. "Want?"

"What are your demands? A house? Money?"

His words were hard, but she saw the tremble of his body beneath the sheeting rain. And Lilley suddenly wondered what sort of people he'd lived with, that his first thought upon hearing she was pregnant was to expect her to demand money.

"I don't need anything," she said quietly. *Except a father for my baby,* came the painful thought. *Except for a man who can love me.* But she would have to be brave, to be both mother and father to her sweet baby, who would need everything she could give. "Thank you for giving me two nights I'll never forget. Thank you for believing in me. And most of all," she whispered over the ache in her throat, "thank you for giving me a baby."

Blinking fast, she looked up at his face for the last time, trying to memorize his features into her memory. The aquiline silhouette of his nose. The hard angle of his jaw. His eyes like dark embers, blazing fire. "I hope your life is full of joy. I'll never forget you." She turned away. "Good-bye."

Lilley started walking back towards the villa, her sandals squishing in the wet grass, her heart breaking.

His hand grabbed her shoulder, whirling her around. He looked down at her as the rain continued to pound them both. His eyes burned with fury. "You think you can tell me you're pregnant—and just *leave?*"

Lilley sucked in her breath, almost frightened at the darkness in his eyes. "There is no reason for me to stay—"

"No reason?" His voice was nearly a shout. He visibly controlled himself. His jaw twitched as he loosened his grip on her upper arms. "If you truly are pregnant with my child," he ground out, "how can you just turn and leave? How can you be so cold?"

"Cold?" she gasped, ripping away. "What do you want from me? You want me to fall to the ground and cling to your knees, begging for you to love me and this baby, begging for you never to let me go?"

"That at least I would understand!"

"I can't change your nature!" she cried, then took a deep gulping breath. "You made your feelings clear. You want a wife you can be proud of. You want Olivia. And you want me three thousand miles away!"

His eyes narrowed as he said in a low voice, "That was before."

"Nothing has changed."

"Everything has changed, if the baby is really mine."

It took several seconds for the meaning of his words to sink in. Then her eyes went wide. "You think I would sleep with another man, then lie to you about it?"

Alessandro's posture was so taut, he seemed like a statue. Like a stone. She could barely hear his voice as he said, "It happens." His expression looked strange. "You might have gone back to the jewelry designer. Accidentally gotten pregnant, than decided to cash in."

"Cash in?" she said incredulously. "Cash in how?"

He searched her gaze. "Do you swear you're telling me the truth? The child is mine?"

"Of course the baby is yours! You're the only man I've ever slept with in my whole life!"

"I want a paternity test."

She stiffened. "What?"

"You heard me."

The insult was almost too much to bear. "Forget it," she whispered. "I'm not doing some stupid paternity test. If you trust me so little, if you believe I'd lie to you about something like this, then just forget it."

Lilley's body shook as she turned and walked away. Tears streamed down her face, blending with the rain. She was halfway across the empty lawn before he stopped her, and this time, the expression on his face had changed.

"I'm sorry, Lilley," he said quietly. "I do know you. And you wouldn't lie."

Their eyes locked. She exhaled as the knots in her shoulders loosened. Then he spoke.

"Marry me."

She heard the roar of her own heartbeat above the splatter of rain. "Is that a joke?"

His sensual lips curved upward. "I never joke, remember?"

Her head was spinning. She'd never expected him to propose, not in a million years, not in her most delusional dreams. "You...want to marry me?"

"Is that so surprising? What did you expect—that I'd kick you and our unborn child to the curb and merrily go and propose to another woman?"

Biting her lip, she looked up at the ruthless lines of his face. "Well...yes."

"Then you don't know me at all."

"No," she whispered. "I guess I don't." She felt dizzy and still a bit sick. She'd barely made it to Sonoma in Nadia's old car without being sick, she'd been so nervous. And now he wanted to marry her? She licked her lips, feeling as though she might cry. "You want to help raise our baby?"

Alessandro's jaw was tight. "I will protect you both. I will give the baby my name. It is my duty."

Her heart, which had been soaring in blind hope, crashed to the ground. His *duty?* She exhaled. "You don't need to marry me to be involved in our baby's life."

"Yes. I do."

"Why?"

"Because it is necessary."

"You're old-fashioned."

"Yes."

"But you don't love me!"

He folded his arms. "Irrelevant."

"Not to me, it isn't!" She exhaled, clenching her hands. "Listen, Alessandro, I'll never try to keep you from seeing your child—"

"I know that you will not, once we are wed."

"I'm not going to marry you!"

"Of course you will," he said coldly.

She shook her head, causing wet tendrils to slap against

her cheeks. "Be in a loveless marriage for the rest of my life? No thanks!"

"I understand. You still want your knight in shining armor." He set his jaw. "But whatever either of us might have once planned for our lives is over. We are expecting a child. We will wed."

"No—we would be miserable!"

"Miserable?" he said incredulously. "Don't you understand? You will be my bride. A princess. Rich beyond your wildest dreams!"

"I don't care—I don't want it! Not when I know you don't love me and never will!"

He grabbed her by the shoulders, his hands sliding against her wet skin. "You would deny our child a name out of some childish yearning for fairytale dreams?"

"It's not childish." She closed her eyes, which suddenly burned with tears that he'd used his knowledge of her heart against her. "You are cruel."

"I am *right,*" he said grimly. "You have no reason to refuse me." He paused. "I will even be faithful to you, Lilley."

He spoke the words as if being faithful to her would require a huge sacrifice, practically more than any billionaire prince could bear. And it was probably true. "Gee, thanks," she said sarcastically, glaring at him. "But I have no interest in being your duty bride."

"Your objection is to the word *duty?*" He narrowed his eyes. "What do you think marriage is?"

"Love. Friendship. Having each other's backs. A poetic union of souls—"

His grip on her tightened. "And passion?" His voice became husky beneath the rain. "What of passion?"

Her heart fell to her sandals and back again. She felt his strength, his warmth, the irresistible pull of his power. Against her will, she craved him.

"It was good between us." He ran his fingers lightly along her jawline, his thumb along her sensitive lower lip. His soft stroke caused a spark down her body that made her suck in her breath. "You know how it was."

Memories shuddered through her of how it had felt when he'd made love to her. Her breasts felt heavy, her nipples aching and tight. She swallowed. "It was a fling," she breathed. "You said so yourself. I'm not the right woman to be your bride."

"My assessment has changed." He cupped her face. His eyes were dark with heat. "For the last month," he whispered, "I've thought of nothing but having you in my bed."

She licked her lips. "You—you have?"

"I told myself you deserved a man who could love you. But everything has changed. Only our child matters now." His gaze fell to her lips. "But that's a lie," he said in a low voice. "That's not the only reason I want you as my bride. I want you to be mine. I want to possess you completely. Every night. For the rest of our lives."

Lilley could barely breathe. "But Olivia—"

"I would have married her out of duty. Not desire." He looked into her eyes. "You are the one I want, Lilley." His mouth lowered to hers with agonizing slowness as he whispered, "Don't you know that by now? I want you. And now I will have you—forever."

As he kissed her, she closed her eyes, her body shaking as his lips took ruthless possession of her own. His lips were hard and hungry as the rain poured over their skin and thunder pounded across the lowering black sky.

She heard his low growl as in a sudden movement he pushed her back against the hedge. She felt the rough, wet branches of the shrubbery against her back as he held her tight against his wet, muscled body. He moved his hands through her hair, tilting her head to deepen the kiss. In the force of their embrace, their wet clothes slid and clung to their skin. His hands roamed everywhere, over her cotton tank top, over her hips. She felt his hand reach beneath the hemline of her skirt, dragging it slowly up her thighs. His hand slid upwards, and she gasped, placing her hand over his. "No."

"Don't refuse me," he said in a low voice. "It's what we both want."

"I do want you," she panted, then choked out a sob. "But I can't marry you. I'd have to give up everything I believe in. I'm afraid it would destroy me to love you."

"So don't love me." He caressed her hair, looking down at her with serious dark eyes. "It's too late for our own dreams, Lilley," he said quietly. "All that matters now are our baby's."

She sucked in her breath. He was right, she realized. All that mattered now was their child. She closed her eyes. "Will you love our baby? Will you be a good father?"

"Yes," he said simply.

Her heart twisted as she took a deep breath, then another. For an instant, she held her breath. Then she let her dreams for love go.

She opened her eyes.

"I can accept...a marriage without love," she whispered, then shook her head. "But not without trust. Not without respect. I won't be humiliated by a paternity test. Either believe that the baby is yours...or let us go."

Staring at her, Alessandro slowly nodded. "All right, *cara*," he said in a low voice. "All right."

Swallowing back the ache in her throat, she whispered, "Then I'll marry you."

Alessandro drew back. "You will?" The rain had lifted, and a beam of twilight sun burst from behind the clouds, illuminating his hard features with gold. "You'll be my wife?"

Wordlessly, she nodded.

His eyes lit up, and the edges of his lips curved up into a bright smile that made him look younger, almost boyish. She'd never seen him look that way before. As Lilley stared up at him, the noise of the storm faded, and thunder became a distant memory.

Maybe it would be all right, she thought, dazed. Maybe passion and a baby would be enough to start a marriage.

She prayed it would be. Because that was all they had.

CHAPTER SEVEN

LILLEY'S hair flew around her, tangling in the cold night wind as Alessandro drove his yellow Ferrari convertible across the vast, lonely Nevada desert. She couldn't stop looking over at him at the wheel. Moonlight frosted his dark hair with silver.

The party had ended in scandal, when Alessandro had privately informed Olivia that she'd been misled by the gossip columns and he intended to take Lilley as his bride. Olivia had stomped out of the villa, but not before she'd grabbed Lilley's arm in the foyer.

"You'll regret this," the beautiful Milanese heiress had hissed, pressing her fingernails into Lilley's flesh. "You might be pregnant with his child, you piece of trash, but you're not worthy to be his wife. You think you've beaten me. But I will find a way to destroy you."

Turning, the gorgeous blonde had departed, her skinny shoulders straight as she'd stormed out of the villa. In the next room Alessandro was already announcing their engagement to all of his friends, introducing them to Lilley at his side. They'd applauded and murmured congratulations, but she'd felt their bewildered eyes on her, as if they were wondering why on earth someone like Alessandro would choose her for his bride. Something she kept wondering herself. Then he'd announced with a wicked smile, "We're eloping to Las Vegas. Tonight."

Lilley had gasped along with everyone else. They would drive to Las Vegas, he insisted, as his private jet was en route to San Francisco after delivering supplies to a desperate community decimated by a hurricane. "We'll be married by morning," Alessandro had told her after he'd gotten rid of the guests. He paused. "Unless you wish to wait until your father can attend the ceremony..."

She'd felt a prickle at the back of her neck, knowing she had to tell Alessandro the truth about her family before they could possibly marry. She shook her head. "No. I don't want my father at the ceremony, and you wouldn't either. We're not exactly friends. I'm not even sure he loves me." She took a deep breath. "Speaking of which," she said in a small voice, "there's something I need to tell you. Before I can marry you."

"No need." His expression had suddenly become cold, closed off. "I already know what you're going to say."

Alessandro knew about her family? Her jaw dropped. "You—you do?"

He nodded, his eyes hard. "There's no point in talking about it, because there's nothing I can do to change it."

She bit her lip. "So you—you forgive me?" she whispered.

"Yes," he said grimly, then shook his head. "But I will never be able to love you."

Lilley wasn't worried about him loving her at that moment. She'd just been praying he wouldn't utterly despise her. Relief washed through her. He knew her secret. Of course he did, she thought, suddenly so giddy she was almost light-headed. He'd probably known it all along! Alessandro Caetani was a brilliant competitor, which is why her cousin found him to be such an infuriating foe. He knew stuff. With a tearful, joyful sob, she threw her arms around him.

Surprised, he'd put his arms around her. "I'll have my people pack up your things and meet us in Las Vegas. No need to pack clothes," he'd said gruffly. "I'll provide you with those."

"I need my jewelry materials and tools, and the quilt my mother made me."

"You have a passport, yes?"

"Yes." With a whole bunch of stamps in and out of French airports she wouldn't have to hide. "Why a passport?"

"I have a little place in Sardinia." He'd smiled, his eyes hot. "A honeymoon cottage."

They drove all night in his convertible, across the dark, vast Nevada desert. Sometime during the night, she'd fallen asleep against his shoulder. When they arrived in Las Vegas, Alessandro woke her with a kiss to her forehead.

"Welcome to your wedding day, *cara,*" he whispered, and she opened her eyes blearily to see the white light of dawn breaking over the distant craggy mountains.

Alessandro took her to the luxury Hermitage Hotel and Resort, where he ordered a lavish private buffet for two brought up to their penthouse suite. Five waiters with overflowing carts brought up fifty different items for Lilley to sample—waffles, omelets, pecan-stuffed French toast, slabs of bacon, watermelon, fruit salad and chicken-fried steak. Afterward, Alessandro escorted her to an overpriced bridal boutique downstairs in the hotel. Selecting a tuxedo for himself, he casually bought the first wedding dress she admired.

"You can't!" Lilley cried when she saw the twenty-thousand-dollar price tag, even as her eyes traced the beaded white fabric longingly.

Lifting his eyebrow, he gave her a grin. "I can."

They collected their marriage license downtown, then returned to their suite at the Hermitage where a bridal bouquet and boutonniere waited for them beside the grand piano. It was intoxicating. Dreamy. They made love on the huge bed overlooking the Las Vegas Strip, then made love again in the shower before changing their clothes. Then, when Alessandro first saw Lilley in her wedding dress, he pulled her straight back into bed.

Lilley sat astride his lap, riding him as he leaned against the headboard, her necklace bouncing softly against her swollen breasts with every thrust. After their third lust-fueled explosion of the afternoon, he kissed the necklace's pink-heart crystal and brass chain. "Any man on earth would pay a fortune to have such a necklace for his wife." His expression changed. "It's just too bad that…"

"What?"

He exhaled. "Nothing." Taking her hand, he pulled her from the bed. "Let's get to the ceremony before we get distracted."

Two hours after their appointed time, they finally married, surrounded by white candles at the hotel's private wedding chapel. An acquaintance of Alessandro's who owned the hotel, Nikos Stavrakis, was the only witness as they breathlessly spoke their vows.

And just like that, Lilley was a princess. Wearing a white suit he'd purchased for her, she boarded her husband's waiting jet, bound for the Mediterranean.

On board, Lilley found the possessions his staff had packed for her. The box of her life was small indeed—just her mother's homemade quilt, her jewelry tools and an excited, gushing note from Nadia wishing her luck and all the joy in the world. "Jeremy will be moving in with me now—I know you won't mind because you're a happily married princess! I can't believe you *married* Prince Alessandro! You'll be famous now!"

As the jet flew the long miles east across the country and towards the Atlantic, Lilley fell asleep on a couch, holding her mother's quilt to her chest. When she woke up, Alessandro was watching her from a nearby white leather chair.

"I will always protect you," he whispered, leaning forward. His eyes were dark. "I want you to know that. And I will protect our child."

She sat up, clutching the quilt. "Protect us. But not too much." She gave him a weak smile. "My father tried to protect me from the world he didn't think I was strong enough to handle. If not for my mother, I would never have been allowed out of the house."

"Which is why he wanted you to marry one of his employees." His lips lifted in a humorless smile. "When will you tell him about our marriage?"

Her eyes slid away. "I don't know. It's—complicated."

"I understand." He looked down at his folded hands. "My father married my mother for her money, then spent it all on his mistresses, whom he flaunted to her face. He thought condoms were for the weak. He scattered bastards carelessly all over the world."

She sucked in her breath. "Oh, Alessandro—"

He looked up, his handsome face stoic. "He died when I was nineteen, and left us only debts in his memory. My mother would have starved in the street, if I hadn't started work to support her. When she died five years ago, she was living in a palace in Rome. As I vowed she someday would." He exhaled. "I'm trying to tell you that you never need to worry now, about anything. I will always take care of you."

She blinked back tears, giving him a smile as she reached

across the aisle to stroke his face. "We will take care of each other."

He turned his rough cheek into her caress, then placed his hand over her own. "You won't regret giving up your dreams to marry me. I'm no shining knight, but I will treat you well. You won't have a business of your own, but I will work hard for you and the baby. I'll give you all the precious jewelry you could possibly desire."

Frowning, she drew back her hand. "What do you mean—giving up my dream of having a business?"

He stared down at her. "You have no time for a career. Not anymore. Your place is to be my wife, and raise our child."

"You don't tell me this until *now*—after we're already married?"

"I thought it would be obvious," he said stiffly, looking uncomfortable.

"No," she whispered. "You knew I would be upset. Which is why you waited till now." She forced her voice to be calm. "I never agreed to give up my business."

He looked at her. "If that dream had ever meant anything to you, you would have done something about it long ago."

Lilley's eyes widened, then she sucked in her breath. He was right. She could have built her business for years, but instead, she'd squandered her time being paralyzed by fear.

"Money will never be an issue for you again," he tried. "I will provide you with everything you desire." He gave her a smile. "And if you want to make jewelry as a little hobby to entertain yourself, I have no objection to it."

"Generous of you," she muttered.

He stared down at her, then set his jaw. "Once you have properly settled in as my bride, as the mother of our child, well then—we will see," he said grudgingly. His eyes softened as he stroked her cheek. "I want you to be happy, Lilley. I will do everything I can to make that happen."

Feeling his hand upon her skin, seeing the tenderness in his eyes, she exhaled. It would be fine. Somehow, it would all work out. "I want to do the same for you."

His eyes were hot and dark as he gave her a wicked grin. "Ah, but you've made me so happy already. You make me happy on an hourly basis," he breathed, leaning forward to kiss her. He stopped, his face inches from hers. "Just promise you'll never lie to me."

"I'll never lie to you," Lilley promised, and she meant it, with all her heart.

"Io bacio."

"Io bacio," Lilley repeated, balancing a book on her head.

Standing by the window overlooking the bright-blue water of the Costa Smeralda, her Italian tutor smiled. *"Tu baci."*

"Tu baci," Lilley repeated rather breathlessly, walking across the marble floor in four-inch high heels.

"Lui bacia."

As Lilley repeated all the conjugations of *baciare,* she found herself smiling. Her tutor had clearly chosen the verb *to kiss* in honor of her standing as a newlywed. And though her feet ached from the expensive shoes and her body ached from standing up straight in the designer skirt suit for hours, she felt strangely happy. Yes, her head ached from a full schedule of etiquette and deportment lessons, mixed with Italian classes in which she not only learned the word for fork, *la forchetta,* but she was taught which one to use for salad and which for dessert. But she was…happy.

This wasn't the same world she'd left behind in Minnesota, that was for sure. Her father had come from nothing. He'd never given a hoot about etiquette. Now, after a week in Sardinia, Lilley felt exhausted, but it was the best kind of tired. She felt sore, too, but there was a very delicious reason for that as well. A hot blush filled her cheeks as she remembered what Alessandro had done to her in bed last night, and what she'd done to him. The braver she got, the more she acted on her own needs and fantasies, the more he liked it.

"Molto bene," the Italian tutor finally said with satisfaction.

"You are a quick learner, *Principessa,"* said the Swiss woman who'd come from a famous boarding school in the Alps to teach her deportment.

"Grazie," Lilley said with a laugh. A quick learner? She'd certainly never heard *that* one before. But it helped that she didn't have to read, just listen, repeat and practice. Her husband had given the instructors precise instructions.

Her husband.

After a week in Alessandro's white wedding-cake villa in Sardinia, seven blissful days of life as his wife, Lilley still adored the word *husband.* She held the word close to her heart, cuddled it like a child. She had a *husband.* And—she glanced discreetly at her watch, almost causing the book to slide off her head—it was almost five o'clock. Her favorite time of day.

The Italian tutor followed her gaze and nodded. "We are done." He turned to gather his briefcase. *"Buona sera, Principessa."*

Madame Renaud pulled the leatherbound book off Lilley's head. *"Bonsoir, Principessa,"* she said, *"et merci."* Madame followed her tutor out of the door.

Principessa. Another word that still seemed exotic and foreign—nothing to do with her at all.

The instant her instructors were gone, Lilley raced upstairs towards the master bedroom as fast as her tight beige pencil skirt would allow her. She rushed down the hall, past priceless works of modern art that to her looked like a pre-schooler's squiggles, past expensive white furniture that was mostly just hard and uncomfortable in her opinion.

But there was one thing about this villa that she loved: their bedroom. Her high heels clicked loudly as she hurried down the hall. Passing a window, her eyes fell on the view of the turquoise Mediterranean and white sand beach. All right—two things she loved about this house.

A week ago she would have had difficulty placing the Italian island of Sardinia on a map, but now she was in love, because the Costa Smeralda, the island's green coast, was the most joyful and beautiful place she'd ever seen. The open windows lured in a warm, sweet wind to blow against her hair, and the bright golden sun warmed her body and heart. As if those needed any warming.

Running her hand along the curving handrail of the villa's white staircase, she snorted as she remembered Alessandro's description of this vacation home. Some *cottage!* It had eight bedrooms and a full staff, though they always disappeared at five o'clock each night, as Alessandro had ordered, so the two of them could be alone.

Lilley smiled to herself. She enjoyed her lessons during the day, but at night…She shivered. At night, she and her husband set the world on fire.

At the end of the hallway, Lilley pushed open their bedroom door, half expecting to find Alessandro on the bed, wearing only a strategically placed jewelry box. Yesterday, he'd worn only a large black velvet box which held a priceless diamond and emerald necklace. He seemed to enjoy giving her such expensive trinkets, so Lilley always tried to accept them graciously, even though the impersonal, sterile new jewelry was the last thing she cared about.

Spending time in bed with him, on the other hand…well. She'd take all of that she could get.

But today, their bedroom was empty. So was the study where Alessandro had had business meetings all day with high-level board members from his headquarters in Rome. Peeking through the window, she saw him pacing by the pool, talking on the phone. Lilley's eyes devoured his strong physique in a snug white T-shirt, old jeans and bare feet as he paced from the white cabana to the poolhouse. Behind him, palm trees waved against the sparkling blue sea.

The pool! Perfect! She'd get him splashing in there yet!

Squelching a mischievous laugh, Lilley raced back to their bedroom and changed into a tiny bikini, one of the six he'd bought for her in Porto Cervo. Tying the strings at her hips and back, she glanced at herself in the mirror. Funny how she'd once felt so embarrassed about her plump body. She'd worn baggy clothes that didn't fit, trying to hide her shape. But Alessandro loved her body so much, what could possibly be wrong with it? How could she not love her overlarge breasts, her curvy belly, her wide hips, with their child growing inside her?

For the first time in her life, she felt comfortable in her own skin. Even the morning sickness had all but disappeared since she'd become Alessandro's wife. A coincidence? Or were her body and unborn baby in agreement with her, all of them deliriously happy about their new lives?

Lilley looked at the brilliant ten-carat canary diamond ring on her finger. He'd bought it for her at the Caetani boutique in Las Vegas, as if the million-dollar price tag were nothing at all. It was pretty, though it weighed down her hand. As she went outside, the facets sparkled. She saw her husband sitting in a chair by the pool with a computer in his lap, and he was more seductive to her than any diamond.

His dark form shone brighter than the white sun, which on Sardinia was really saying something.

Palm trees waved in the warm breeze, giving a hint of moving shade over Alessandro as she walked around the pool, swaying her hips.

He didn't look up, but continued to stare intently at the screen. She went around to the back of his chair, then bent to rub his shoulders. "Hi."

"Buon pomeriggio, cara," he said absently, typing.

"Buon pomeriggio?" Smiling, she shook her head. *"Buona sera."*

His expression still distracted, Alessandro glanced up at her. Then he got a good look at her bikini, and his eyes widened. He snapped his computer shut. *"Buona sera,"* he replied with interest. "Your Italian is coming along."

"I've always been interested in your native tongue," she said with a suggestive smile. When she saw his gaze linger upon her breasts, she glanced innocently at his computer. "I'm sorry to interrupt, were you done?"

"I am now," he growled. Pushing the computer to a side table, he pulled her into his lap and thoroughly kissed her. As she felt his sun-warmed lips against hers, melting her from the inside, she closed her eyes and breathed in his scent. With his body against hers in the sunlight, she felt intoxicated with pleasure.

There was only one thing that bothered her.

For the last week, they'd made love constantly, eaten delicious meals, slept in each other's arms. Last night, he'd taken her into the village for dinner, and afterward he'd held her hand as they walked through the winding streets. She'd thought she might die of happiness. Then they'd strolled past an outdoor nightclub. She'd eagerly tried to pull him towards the music, towards the dancing couples spilling out onto the street. But he'd shaken his head. "I don't dance. You know that."

"Oh, please," she'd cajoled. "Just this once!"

But he'd refused. Except when they were in bed, Alessandro didn't allow himself to do anything that might make him appear vulnerable or foolish. He didn't dance. He didn't *play.* He didn't splash in the pool.

But that was about to change. It was time he learned to let himself go.

Playfully, Lilley pulled away from his embrace. "I need some cooling off."

She walked over to the pool's steps, swaying her hips as she waded slowly into the pool, relishing the shock of cool water against her skin. She went deeper, until the water level bobbed at her breasts. Then she glanced at Alessandro out of the corner of her eye. Oh yeah. He was watching, all right. With a soft, innocent sigh, she sank all the way into the water, swimming with long, sensual strokes. She bobbed up to the edge of the pool, at the foot of Alessandro's chair.

"Join me," she suggested, smiling up at him.

Looking down at her, Alessandro slowly shook his head. "Not my thing."

Languorously, she dipped her hair back in the pool. She felt his burning gaze as she lifted her head from the water. Droplets trickled down her skin, down her neck and breasts. She stretched her arms over her head, moving her body in a lazy sway against the translucent water.

"Join me," she sighed.

He looked as if he were having trouble breathing. Licking his lips, he shook his head.

Lilley sank fully beneath the water and was down there for several seconds. When she finally resurfaced, he'd half risen from his chair as if alarmed. She swam to the edge of the pool, a sensual smile curving her lips. Leaning against the edge, she threw something at his feet. He looked down at it.

It was her bikini.

"Join me," she whispered.

Alessandro looked at her, his lips slightly parted. She heard the hoarse intake of his breath.

Then he moved. She'd never known any man could move that fast. Still dressed in his T-shirt and jeans, he did a cannonball right into the pool beside her. The water swayed wildly, splashing Lilley's head and face as he rose to the surface, throwing back his dark head like a god of the sea. His wet, translucent white T-shirt clung to his shoulders, pecs and tight abs.

Swimming over to her, he grabbed the edge of the pool with one hand, and with the other, he pulled her against him without a word. Lowering his head, he kissed her in a hot, hungry embrace. As his lips seared hers, his tongue teased inside her mouth, and she blindly reached out to the side of the pool to steady herself. Treading water with his powerful legs, he cupped her face with both his hands, deepening the kiss. A sigh of pleasure escaped her. Lost in the moment, Lilley flung both her arms around his shoulders, letting go of the edge.

She had an instant of weightlessness, of swirling pleasure with no beginning or end, as they sank together into the water. Falling, falling, they held tight together in the intensity of their embrace before his legs suddenly kicked beneath them, bringing them back to the surface.

Gripping the edge of the pool, they coughed water out of their lungs. When they could breathe again, they stared at each other, both of them bobbing in the cool water. The white sun beat down on them, reflecting glittering light against the sky and their tanned skin.

Leaning forward, Alessandro pushed her against the

edge of the pool, splaying his large hands over hers. He kissed her deeply, plundering her mouth. Tilting back her head, Lilley closed her eyes, feeling the heat of his mouth and the sun on her skin. Cool ripples of water moved against her naked breasts as he kissed her throat, nipping her shoulder, suckling the tender flesh of her ear.

"Mi piace stare con te," he whispered. *I like being with you.*

"Baciami," she whispered. *Kiss me.*

With a muttered groan, Alessandro turned around in the water. Pulling her arms around his shoulders, he lifted her onto his back and swam towards the steps of the pool. Her naked breasts pressed against his shoulder blades, her body rubbing against his clingy white T-shirt. As he climbed up the steps of the pool, water poured from his shirt and jeans that clung to his powerful body. He pulled her into his arms and looked down at her. There was a strange expression in his dark, handsome face. One she'd never seen before.

"Mia moglie," he whispered. "My sweet wife."

He carried her across the terrace and into the white villa, trailing water with every step. From a distance, she heard seagulls crying and the honking horns of boats. She breathed in the scent of lemon and orange groves mixed with chlorine from the pool and the salt of the sea. She placed her hand on his wet cotton shirt. It revealed every hard muscle of his torso, and she could feel the beat of his heart.

Inside the villa, it was cool, dark and quiet. The housekeeper and other staff had already left for the evening, going back to their homes in nearby villages. She and Alessandro were alone as he carried her up the stairs to their bedroom, to the enormous bed with the sleek white duvet.

The verandah doors were wide open. The wind blew in from the sea, causing the curtains to oscillate slowly in the breeze as Alessandro set her down on their marriage bed, where she'd already had endless revelations of pleasure and joy.

Never looking away from her face, he slowly pulled off his T-shirt, revealing his muscular, tanned chest and broad arms. His jeans and silk boxers were next, as he stripped the wet fabric off his body and left them on the cool marble floor in a crumpled heap. Naked, he moved beside her on the bed.

His kiss was hot and hard, like the rest of him. Then his embrace grew tender, his lips gentling as he whispered words of adoration in Italian that she only half understood, but that caused her to tremble. He pulled away, looking down at her in the shadowy bedroom, and she could hear their breath mingling in the silence. An inexplicable ache of emotion rose to the back of Lilley's throat.

Reaching up, she put her hand on his rough, scratchy cheek.

I love you.

But she couldn't speak the words. She couldn't be that reckless, or that brave.

Alessandro made love to her slowly, taking his time as he caressed and licked and worshipped every inch of her body, until she exploded in the same instant that he groaned and filled her with his seed. Afterward, they held each other. For several minutes, he slept, and she watched him, looking at the contented smile tracing his sensual mouth. She turned towards the open verandah and the translucent curtains swaying peacefully in the breeze. She could see the distant glint of sunlight sparkling like diamonds against the blue water. And she could no longer deny it, not even to herself.

She'd fallen in love with Alessandro. Fallen? The truth was she'd been in love with Alessandro Caetani from the night he'd found her alone and crying in his office that Saturday night.

Lilley's fingertips stroked the dark hair of his chest. He'd brought her pleasure that she never even knew existed. But was she doomed to love a man who would forever give her expensive jewels instead of his heart? Was there anything she could do to win Alessandro's love?

She thought of the etiquette lessons, the Italian lessons, the designer clothes he'd chosen for her. He was changing her completely, and if she were honest with herself, she didn't like all the changes. Her jewelry tools were collecting dust, and except for her wedding gown, he hadn't allowed her to choose a single item of clothing on her own. Other than the jewelry she had made, nothing she wore was truly hers. He dressed her like a doll. He didn't trust her taste, or her ability to fit into his world.

Lilley took a deep breath. She could live with that, she told herself. She'd be the wife he wanted. She'd keep her mouth shut and focus on being elegant and restrained. She'd try harder at her lessons and wear the clothes he wanted her to wear. She would be whomever he wanted her to be, if it would win his love.

Then it would all be worth it—wouldn't it?

Suddenly shivering, she nestled closer into Alessandro's warmth. In a moment, his eyes would open, and he'd lazily suggest dinner, or perhaps he'd want to make love to her again.

Whatever it took. She would convince him to give her the tiniest fraction of his heart, as she'd recklessly given him all of hers. And it would be enough. She would make it be enough. With a deep breath, Lilley squeezed her eyes shut.

Somehow, she would make him love her.

CHAPTER EIGHT

"Stop him. I don't care how, just stop him!"

Sitting at his desk, Alessandro nearly shouted with fury before he hung up on his company's chief financial officer. Clawing back his hair with a silent snarl, he lifted his hand to throw his phone across his study. Then he stopped himself, clutching the cold metal tightly in his hand.

Exhaling, he set the phone carefully on his desk. Rising to his feet, he paced in front of the window, swearing at Théo St. Raphaël in English and Italian and tossing in a few profanities in French, too, for good measure. Damned vulture. Their rivalry had begun years ago when the Frenchman had bought the Italian firm next door to Caetani Worldwide's headquarters in Rome. The insult had deepened when St. Raphaël had stolen the Joyería deal a month ago. But this was the final straw. The man was brazenly making a play for the takeover of a Japanese company that Alessandro needed to deepen his reach in Asia.

Alessandro growled. He'd spent years building up contacts in Tokyo, in hopes of someday gaining control of the firm. And St. Raphaël had no reason to buy the company. It was pure retaliation for Alessandro's purchase of the French vineyard. It was a taunt, pure and simple.

He must be imagining he smelled Alessandro's blood in the water after the humiliation in Mexico City.

And why wouldn't he? *Someone had betrayed him.* Alessandro's chief financial officer had discovered why Miguel Rodriguez had sold Joyería to St. Raphaël instead of Caetani Worldwide. The Frenchman had learned of his plan to close the Mexico City studio and move it to San Francisco. Rodriguez had sold Joyería to the Frenchman to protect his employees' jobs.

But how had St. Raphaël possibly known?

Sitting heavily at his desk, Alessandro stared at his computer. He'd been working with his team remotely as best he could, but the Tokyo deal was spinning out of control, and that was causing problems. He needed to end his honeymoon early and return to Rome.

Alessandro glanced out of the window, instinctively looking for Lilley. It was past five o'clock. She'd come into his study an hour ago, but he'd sent her away—something he'd had to do too often in the last two days. He'd spent a few hours in bed with her last night, then he'd returned to his study to discuss strategy with his Hong Kong office. Last night he'd fallen asleep over his keyboard.

Alessandro exhaled. He should have gone back to Rome two days ago. By remaining in Sardinia, away from his team, he'd put a woman ahead of his business. Something he'd never done before.

But this wasn't just any woman, it was his wife.

There. He spied Lilley on the beach far below. A smile curved his lips and his shoulders unconsciously relaxed as he watched her frolic in the surf, dressed in one of the bikinis he'd bought her in Porto Cervo. Today the color was violet. He saw her pause and look up towards the sprawling white villa, as if she felt him watching her. Visibly squaring her shoulders, she went to talk to some children playing a distance down the beach. He squinted. He vaguely recognized a dark-haired young boy and small girl, the children of live-in servants from the next villa down the coastline. Lilley flopped down on the sand beside them and started enthusiastically to help build their sand castle.

He watched her as she played on the beach. She was so happy, so natural, so free, so good with children. He'd seen the sweet, tender look in her eyes whenever she spoke to him of dreams for their unborn child. Lilley was everything a man would want in a wife. Everything he'd want the mother of his children to be.

She had only one flaw. She loved him.

She'd very nearly confessed her love before their wedding, but he'd seen on her face what she was going to say and stopped her. He exhaled. As long as the words were never said, they had a chance. They could be lovers, even friends. Once the child was born, Lilley would channel her love into their baby. She would raise their child with a mother's tenderness, while Alessandro would protect them and provide for them, ensuring his children would inherit a vast empire.

His wife and children would never be poor. Never be ashamed of their father. His behavior would be above reproach.

He regretted the shabby wedding he'd given Lilley, in the chapel of a Las Vegas casino, with no family and friends. It had been shabby indeed, but expedient and quiet. He had to give Lilley time to complete her lessons, to be fully polished like a hard-edged gemstone before he exposed her to the cutting, subtle mockery of his friends, or the people who passed for his friends. It was the only way to protect her, helping her become strong enough to protect herself.

No man he knew in Rome would have married a pregnant mistress. He would have simply paid her off with a generous check and perhaps a few gifts at the child's birth. But Alessandro had always vowed his children would know who their father was. After his own father's selfish, callous example, and even more after his mother's sickening revelation after his death, Alessandro had known the risk of sex, and so he'd waited until he was truly in love. When he'd fallen hard for a twenty-five-year-old waitress in his freshman year at Stanford, he'd taken his time, wooing her for months like a perfect gentleman. Until Heather had dragged him to her apartment and begged him to make love to her. She'd told him he didn't need a condom, because she was on the Pill.

"You trust me, don't you?" she'd asked with big eyes. After so many years of waiting, sex had been a revelation. He'd been rapturous with joy. When she'd gotten pregnant, it had seemed like a miracle.

Until his father died, leaving a shocking amount of debt and creditors all suddenly clamoring to be paid. Alessandro had dropped out of Stanford, planning to get a job to support his mother, and to propose immediately to Heather, so she'd know he intended to take care of her and the baby. He'd rehearsed his speech the night he planned to propose. They'd be poor at first, he would say, but he would work full-time by day and invest every penny he could. Someday, he would promise, he'd give her the life of a princess.

He bought a cheap ring he could ill afford and made her a picnic, preparing bologna sandwiches and fruit salad to eat in the park. But things didn't go according to plan. As he gave her the speech, Heather was silent, setting down her sandwich barely tasted. Afterward, he took her out dancing, his favorite thing to do. He was trying to show her how romantic their lives could be, even without money.

But in the middle of the first song, Heather had stopped on the dance floor. She'd looked up at him, her eyes full of tears.

"I like you, Alessandro," she'd whispered. "I really do.

You're lots of fun and an amazing, generous lover." She exhaled. "But the baby's not yours. I lied."

"Not…" He staggered back. It felt like a physical blow. "Not mine?"

She flushed. "You kept saying you wanted us to wait for true love and all that. But I'm sorry, I couldn't go for two long months without sex!" At his expression, her cheeks colored and she looked away. "The first night we slept together, I already knew I was pregnant."

The loud dance music roared in his ears. His throat closed. "But why?"

"I thought you would make a good husband. A good father." She bit her lip. "The other guy's married. He'll never marry me or help raise the baby. But he owns a tech firm in Cupertino. If I tell him, I know he'll give me money." She'd looked at Alessandro beneath the flashing lights and pulsing music. "I don't want my baby to be poor," she'd whispered. "I'm sorry."

And just like that, she'd left him on the dance floor.

It was the last time Alessandro had ever gone dancing or made a fool of himself over anyone. The last time he'd fully trusted a woman.

Until Lilley.

He could have chosen not to marry her. She'd gone out of her way to make it easy for him to abandon her. She'd apparently had zero expectations of his moral character. It had astonished and angered him. Of course he wished to marry the mother of his unborn baby.

Although he hadn't insisted on that paternity test.

A cold trickle went down his spine. He didn't have any actual proof the baby was his. His hand felt clammy as he forked his fingers through his hair. Lilley wouldn't lie to him, he told himself. He didn't need a paternity test, and he wouldn't insult her by asking for one. Lilley had been a virgin before he'd seduced her, and if she said he was the father, he was. End of story.

"Alessandro? Are you still in here?"

He turned in his swivel chair to see Lilley leaning against the door frame. Her hip was jutted out, her plump breasts overflowing the violet bikini top. His mouth felt dry as he surveyed her full, bare thighs and the hourglass curves of her body. His gaze traced down her long, curvy legs and back up to her swelling, pregnant breasts. He was hard in a millisecond.

"Still working, after all this time?" she murmured, smiling as if she had no idea what the sway of her hips did to him as she walked towards him. "Haven't you heard the adage—all work and no play?"

His little wife had become remarkably adept at the art of seduction in the nine days they'd been married. Still smiling, she put her hand on his shoulder, rubbing his neck. "You said you'd join me on the beach an hour ago."

He looked back at her. "I said no such thing."

"You could be building sandcastles with me."

"Running around, kicking the waves? Not interested."

She shook her head, tutting her tongue. "How can you own a villa in Sardinia, and never want to play on the beach?"

"I'll play here," he said huskily, pulling her into his lap. "With you."

Her eyes widened, and Alessandro felt her instant surrender, her body's full attention. It was always like this between them. How many times had they made love since they'd wed? And yet he was still not satiated. He could not get enough of her.

Cupping her face, he pulled her mouth against his. Her lips felt so soft, so warm, and the stroke of her tongue felt like liquid fire. Her legs straddled his on the office chair, with her soft backside barely covered by the tiny bikini. The warmth between her legs pressed against the erection now straining beneath his trousers.

Kissing down her neck, he pressed his face between her large breasts, barely contained in the tiny triangles of fabric. She moaned as she moved against him, unconsciously grinding her body against him. He looked at her beautiful face. Her eyes were closed, her lips parted, her expression rapt. Even a lifetime wouldn't be enough to satisfy his endless desire for this incredible woman.

Twining a hand in her hair, he pulled down her head and gave her a hard, deep kiss as his other hand pulled the strings on her hips. Yanking off the bottom of her bikini, he tossed it to the floor and unzipped his fly, letting himself spring free. Lilley's eyes flew open as she realized what he intended, but it was too late.

Lifting her up, he brought her body down hard over him, impaling her in a single thrust. He groaned as he filled her so hard and deep that her body stiffened, even as she choked out a gasp of shock and pleasure.

He was deep inside her. Stretching her to the hilt. And it was good, so good. And wet. Oh God. Waves of sweet ecstasy washed over him and he closed his eyes. Lifting her a second time, he thrust again and a second, louder groan burst from his lips. But he didn't get the chance to do it again. She picked up the pace, her breasts swaying against his face as she controlled the rhythm. He leaned forward, breathing in the scent of sunshine and salt. Pushing aside a triangle of her bikini top, he suckled a swollen, taut nipple as his other hand gripped her thigh. She let out a little cry as she arched her body, tossing back her head as she rode him hard in his office chair, going faster, faster, deeper, deeper.

The pleasure was too intense. He hadn't taken her since

last night, which seemed like forever ago. His stamina wouldn't last. A low moan came from the back of her throat and he felt her soft breasts bounce against his mouth, felt her deep wet core sucking him further and further into ecstasy. He tried to restrain himself—to hold back the wave that threatened to burst. But he couldn't—hold back—for much longer—

Like a miracle, he heard a soft cry from her lips, which became louder as she clutched his shoulders with her hands, her fingernails gripping into his flesh. She gave a final sharp scream and he felt her convulse and tighten all around him. Just in time. In a rush, he surrendered to the pleasure and exploded into her. Lights danced behind his eyelids as he gave a ragged gasp, groaning as he pulsed and poured himself into her.

He held her for long moments in his office chair. When she finally rose unsteadily to her feet, he stood and zipped up his fly, still feeling disoriented. She was just wearing her bikini top and only half of that, really, since she had one breast exposed. He saw her shiver with cold and pulled off his long-sleeved, button-down shirt, wrapping it tenderly around her nearly naked body.

"Thanks," she murmured. She gave him a mischievous smile. "I love visiting you at work."

He laughed, then looked down at her. His tailored shirt hung down to her mid-thigh. "You look...cute."

"So do you." She ran her hand down his bare chest. "Because now you are far more suitably dressed..." She gave a sudden impish grin. "For the beach!"

He blinked at her.

"Woman!" he thundered. "When will you stop?"

"When you do what I want!"

"Not going to happen." He hesitated. "There's been a complication, Lilley. I need to leave for Rome."

"What's happened?"

He scowled. "Théo St. Raphaël happened."

She sucked in her breath. To his surprise, she seemed to understand the gravity of the situation even before he explained. "What—what about him?"

"It wasn't enough he stole the Joyería deal," he ground out. "Now he's after my expansion in Asia as well. Almost as if it's—personal."

"Maybe it is," she said in a small voice. "I don't get how you guys fight over things you don't even need. You have his winery. Call him. Offer an exchange. A truce—"

"Is that a joke?" he said in amazement. "I'd burn down my palazzo before I'd ask Théo St. Raphaël for a truce." He looked at her, and his voice gentled. "I am just sorry our honeymoon must end."

She licked her lips, then shrugged. "It's all right. I love Sardinia, but I'm sure I'll love Rome as well. I'm excited to see the palazzo. Meet your friends."

"Lilley." His good humor fled. "We've talked about this."

"*You've* talked about it," she said sulkily, her fingertips curling against the dark hair on his chest.

"You're my wife. You promised to obey me."

Indignant, she stared up at him. "I did no such—"

"Your place is at home," he interrupted.

"My home is with you." She looked down at her bare feet. "Unless you're ashamed of me."

Taking both her hands in his own, he pressed them to his lips. "My friends aren't the warmest, friendliest sort of people. I doubt you'd like them."

The cuffs of his long-sleeved shirt hung over her hands, making her look very young as she looked away. "You mean they won't like *me*."

"I'll send for you soon," he said softly, pulling her into his arms. "I promise." And to seal that vow, he lowered his mouth to hers in the gentlest, tenderest kiss he'd ever given her.

To his shock, she pulled away, her brown eyes flinty. "No."

His eyebrows lowered. "Don't you understand? I'm trying to protect you."

"I don't want to be protected, I want to be your wife!"

He exhaled, tried to keep his voice light. "If you're weary of Sardinia, I could leave you at our country estate in Tuscany. You could see the famous paintings of Florence, decorate the nursery, learn how to make bread—"

"No!" She stamped her foot against the marble floor, a gesture marred by the fact that she was barefoot and it caused a grimace of pain across her face. Rubbing the sole of her foot, she scowled at him. "I'm going with you to Rome!"

"Lilley," he tried, "please."

"I'm not afraid of your friends." When he didn't answer, she tossed her head. "What do you think they'll do? Fight me with their bare hands? Wrestle me into the mud?"

"No," he said quietly. "They'll be more subtle. They'll attack any weakness they can find. Your manners, your clothes, even your dyslexia—"

"Are you telling me," she said scornfully, "there'll be some kind of *reading test* before they let me in their little club?"

Trying to keep his patience, he set his jaw. "I am just trying to keep you happy and safe."

"By keeping me a prisoner?"

He folded his arms. "You're not exactly suffering here, Lilley. Most people would call this place heaven, not a prison." At her glare, he amended, "And it's just until your lessons are done. Until you're ready."

"So you *are* ashamed of me."

"Don't be ridiculous!"

"I won't embarrass you," she whispered. She looked up at him with pleading eyes, pressing her fingertips against his bare chest. "Please. Don't leave me here without you. I can't...I can't bear us to be apart."

He felt helpless against that gaze. Setting his jaw, he looked down at the floor. "They will hurt you."

"I'm stronger than you think."

"Olivia is there."

For a second, Lilley fell silent. Then she lifted her chin. "We'll have her to tea."

He snorted in disbelief. "That might be overdoing it."

"I'm serious," she insisted in a small voice. "I feel guilty. She was in love with you, she thought you were going to propose to her, and we eloped. We hurt her."

"*You* didn't do anything," he said sharply. "And if I treated her badly, she can handle it, believe me. She'll find someone else to marry, someone twice as rich and better-looking in the bargain."

"No one's better-looking than you," Lilley said, then her smile faded. She looked away, chewing on her bottom lip. "Do you think she was in love with you? Really and truly?"

Mesmerized, Alessandro watched her white teeth sinking into pink flesh that was full and swollen from days of lovemaking. Then he came back to himself. "Absolutely not," he said sharply. "She just knew as I did, that on paper, we were perfect for each other."

Lilley's expression fell, and it occurred to him that such an honest statement might hurt her feelings. "But now I have you," he said reassuringly. She blinked up at him. "The mother of my precious child," he added. Her lower lip wobbled. He wrapped his arm around her waist and said hopefully, "The woman who's given me the best sex of my life?"

A laugh finally escaped her. Then she shook her head, squaring her shoulders. "And I'm coming with you to Rome."

Alessandro's instincts screamed *No.* But he saw the yearning in her eyes and could not deny her what she wanted. What they both wanted. He didn't want to be apart from her, either.

"Very well, *cara,*" he said quietly. "Rome."

She sucked in her breath.

"Thank you!" she cried, flinging her arms around his shoulders. "You won't be sorry. You'll see. I can handle them. I'm not scared!"

As Lilley kissed his cheeks over and over, murmuring her appreciation, Alessandro almost believed he'd done the right thing. He would protect her, he told himself. And Lilley was strong. She'd gained a great deal of confidence in the days of their marriage. What had caused such a rapid change in her? The Italian lessons? The etiquette classes?

Whatever it was, she would be fine. He was worrying over nothing. After all, they were married now, and expecting a child. What on earth in Rome could possibly break them apart?

CHAPTER NINE

ROME. *Roma*. The Eternal City.

What was the Italian word for *disaster*?

Another fabulous, sophisticated dinner at an elegant restaurant with Alessandro's friends, and once again, Lilley was hiding in a bathroom stall. She was becoming a connoisseur of fancy Roman bathrooms.

Since they'd arrived in Rome three weeks ago, Alessandro had worked endless hours at the office. The only time she saw him—aside from the middle of the night when he made love to her—was at dinner, and that almost always included his friends, who were thrilled to see him.

They were not quite as thrilled about her.

For the last two hours, she'd sat at the table with a frozen smile on her face while Alessandro and his friends talked and laughed in rapid-fire Italian. And it was her own fault. But their first night in Rome, Alessandro had taken her to an elegant restaurant with an English menu. A kind gesture, but Lilley was so nervous, trying to make his glamorous friends like her, that the letters on the menus had refused to stay still. In the end, she'd tried to laugh it off, and her husband had taken over and gallantly ordered for her. But ever since, she'd insisted on only Italian menus. At least then she had an excuse for why she couldn't read them.

And she'd insisted to Alessandro that she preferred that

he speak to his friends in their native Italian. "I'll learn the language more quickly that way," she'd said.

What she'd mostly learned was that his friends made her uncomfortable and she wished that she and her husband could stay home. Home in the bedroom of their palazzo, where Alessandro made her so happy, or creating jewelry in her makeshift studio in the mews, or decorating the large sitting room she was turning into a nursery suite. Heck. Even going for another OB visit, with her chauffeur on one side and her bodyguard on the other, would be more fun than this.

Hiding in the bathroom stall, Lilley stared down at her beige Prada shoes. She'd lasted two hours before she fled to the bathroom. A new record, she tried to comfort herself. It was helpful to be pregnant, because no one questioned long disappearances. Lilley's beige designer suit skirt strained at the seams, feeling too tight around her waist, and she wished she hadn't eaten so much bread. None of the other women ate bread.

No. They seemed to survive on gossip and malice.

It's your imagination, she tried to tell herself. Her Italian was still pretty bad. Alessandro's friends could be saying anything, and she'd likely misread the women's sidelong glances. As soon as her language skills improved, she would no doubt discover his friends were actually quite nice....

The bathroom door banged open.

"Can you believe Alessandro is married to that fat pudding-faced creature who can barely read and has nothing to say for herself?"

Lilley froze, recognizing the voice.

"A tragedy," another woman agreed. "I can hardly believe a fine specimen like Alessandro was trapped by a stupid little nobody."

"Well. I wouldn't say she's *little*," the first woman replied slyly.

Trembling, Lilley peeked through the crack in the stall door and saw Giulia and Lucretia standing at the wall of sleek sinks, refreshing their lipstick in the mirrors. Both of them wealthy heiresses married to still richer men. And they were both so thin they looked like clotheshangers in their designer clothes from Milan.

"Such a shame," Giulia sighed, giving her nose a pat of powder as she stared at herself in the mirror. "Olivia should be with us tonight, like always."

"She will be again," Lucretia said comfortingly. Smacking her lips together, she tucked her lipstick back into a tiny crystal clutch. "The fat little gold digger will realize she doesn't belong here. Once the brat is born, Alessandro will tire of her and send her back to America. Then he will be with Olivia again. As they were meant to be." She glanced at the other woman. "Are we done?"

"I think so," Giulia replied. Smiling at each other, they left the bathroom.

The bang of the door reverberated behind them. Lilley clasped her hands together, her heart pounding. Her skin felt clammy, her body flashing hot and cold. It was her own fault for remaining hidden, she told herself. If she'd come immediately out of the stall, Giulia and Lucretia would never have been so rude. They would not have been so cruel if they'd known she was there, listening.

Then Lilley realized—

The women had spoken in *English.*

"Oh," she breathed aloud, a soft gasp, falling back against the wall as if she'd been punched. Slowly, she swung open the stall door. She saw herself in the mirror, saw how little the stark, minimalist dress suited her taste or her figure. She was wearing the same style as Giulia and Lucretia, but instead of making her blend in with the fashionable set, it only emphasized the rounder shape of her body, and made her normally rosy skin seem washed-out and pale.

Or maybe their words had done that. Alessandro had said his friends could be mean, but she hadn't believed him. She'd never imagined anyone could be so deliberately cruel to a virtual stranger, a new bride far from her home country.

Lilley wondered what Giulia and Lucretia would say if they knew her father was Walton Hainsbury, if that would make her more palatable. But somehow she doubted it. They would simply find new reasons to mock her.

Staring at her own pale, miserable, and yes—a little pie-faced—expression, Lilley swallowed. The ache in her throat felt like a razor blade, but she wasn't going to show them they'd hurt her. No way. Straightening her shoulders, she went down the hall.

Her high-heeled shoes clicked against the floor as she walked across the elegant restaurant, past all the wealthy, gorgeous patrons who actually looked as if they fitted in here. She saw Alessandro sitting beside Giulia and Lucretia and their husbands, tossing his head back in laughter as the women regarded him with sharp, sly smiles. And suddenly, Lilley's courage failed her. Turning, she veered towards the bar.

A handsome young bartender in a white jacket, drying glasses with a white towel, turned to her. *"Sì, signorina?"*

Lilley looked at the wall of liquor bottles behind the bar. If ever a moment called for liquid courage, this was it. But she was pregnant, and anyway she'd never had much experience with alcohol. Except for the night of the Preziosi di Caetani ball, when she'd drunk a glass and a half of champagne. Alessandro had made her feel so precious and beautiful... Her eyes filled with tears.

"Signorina?" the bartender said. *"Prende qualcosa?"*

She wiped her eyes. *"Acqua frizzante, per favore."*

A large hand grabbed her shoulder. With an intake of breath, she turned, but it wasn't Alessandro. Instead, she saw a dark man with ice-blue eyes, an acquaintance of her husband's that she'd met at a cocktail party a few nights before. The Russian tycoon who owned gold mines across the Yukon...what was his name? "Prince Vladimir. Hello."

The man looked down at her with interest. "What are you doing here, little one?" He looked around. "Where is your husband? You do not look well."

"I'm fine. Great in fact." Blinking back tears, she turned back to the bartender as he held out her sparkling water. "Oh no—I forgot my purse!"

"Please. Allow me," Prince Vladimir said, pulling out his wallet. He blinked with surprise when the bartender told him the amount. "So little?"

"It's water," Lilley said. "I'm pregnant."

"Ah," Prince Vladimir said. "Congratulations."

"Thank you. Not everyone knows yet." Lilley glanced back at the table across living room. "Believe me, if I could drink something stronger, I would."

Vladimir followed her glance, and understanding filled his eyes. "Ah. But you have nothing to fear, *Principessa,*" he said quietly. "Your husband is smitten. I've seen the way he looks at you."

Holding the cold glass against the hot skin of her cheek, she whispered, "You mean the way he doesn't look at me."

"Then he is a fool." He put his finger on her bulky crystal necklace. "This is beautiful. Where did you buy it?"

Startled by his touch, Lilley nearly jumped. "I made it."

"You did!"

She shook her head. "Alessandro doesn't want me to wear it in Rome. He said it might make his friends laugh at me, but I don't care. They're going to laugh anyway," she said in a low voice. She straightened. "I have to wear one thing that feels like mine."

"It's beautiful." His finger ran along the bottom edge of her necklace, just below her collarbone. "It's art."

His touch made her uncomfortable. Innocent as it was, the situation might be misconstrued. Even now, Alessandro might be watching them, growing wild with jealousy...

She glanced back at their table, and saw he was busy laughing, having the time of his life with his cold-hearted friends, saying things she couldn't remotely understand.

Clearly, Lilley's plan to make Alessandro fall wildly in love with her was going perfectly.

Tears filled her eyes. How she wished they were still in Sardinia, with nothing but warm sunlight, cool blue water and swaying palm trees around them, far from the rest of the world!

Instead, she was here with him in Rome. As she'd insisted. And as he'd warned her, she was miserable.

Vladimir followed her gaze. "Come, *Principessa*," he said quietly. "I will take you back to him."

As he led her across the elegant restaurant, the tension in Lilley's throat ratcheted up with every step. They reached the table, and the laughter of the group abruptly fell silent.

"Cara." Alessandro turned with a smile. "I was starting to wonder..." Then he saw Vladimir behind her, and the tenderness in his eyes evaporated. He said shortly, "Hello."

"Your wife isn't feeling well," Prince Vladimir said. "I suggest you take her home."

"Yes," Alessandro said grimly, rising to his feet. Throwing money on the table, he said to his friends, *"Mi scusi. Buona notte."*

Placing his hand against the small of Lilley's back, Alessandro escorted her out of the restaurant. Collecting his Ferrari from the valet, he helped her into the car. He didn't speak. He didn't even look at her.

He drove swiftly and silently through the streets of Rome, and Lilley glanced at him out of the corner of her eye. His face was dark, his expression hard. Miserably, she looked away.

The harder she tried to please him, she thought in despair, the worse it seemed to get.

"I'm sorry," she whispered. "I didn't mean for you to have to leave your friends early."

Alessandro changed the gears on the Ferrari with more force than necessary. His jaw was tense as he said in a low voice, "I'm sorry you felt it necessary to tell Vladimir Xendzov you wished to leave, rather than coming to me."

She blinked at him. "I was just trying to—"

"Save it," he cut her off. He pulled past the guardhouse outside their palazzo, driving through the gate.

Parking his car haphazardly in the small courtyard, he stomped into the sixteenth-century palace. Hurt and furious, Lilley followed him. He was far ahead of her, already halfway up the dark, sweeping stairs, when she stopped, clenching her hands.

"You're not being fair!" she bit out.

Alessandro stopped on the stairs, pulling off his tie. He looked down at her, his jaw set. "Are you coming to bed?"

Lilley blinked, taken aback. He stood above her, his button-down shirt tight across his muscular chest, his black trousers fitted low on his hips. Yes. She wanted to go to bed with Alessandro, damn him. Angry as she was, her nipples were hard, her breasts heavy and she felt a spiraling need low and deep in her belly. Her body was instantly at his command.

But—make love with a cold heart? When they both were angry?

She straightened, tightening her hands, and vehemently shook her head.

"I *said*," his voice was deceptively cold as he came down the steps towards her, "are you coming to bed?"

"No," she ground out.

His black eyes glittered.

"Then," he said, "I will bring bed to you."

She saw the intent in his eyes the instant before he grabbed her. Cupping the back of her head, he lowered his mouth to hers in a punishing kiss. As she tried to push him away, his hands gripped her hair, and he deepened the kiss, wrenching her lips apart with his own. He used his tongue like a sensual weapon, plundering her mouth, and, against her will, her body responded. As her sensitive nipples brushed against him, her breasts were crushed against his hard chest, and she melted into his arms.

Leaning her back against the stairs, he kissed her with such brutal ferocity that she surrendered, allowing him to push her down onto the carpet. With a low growl, he yanked her skirt up to her hips. Without a word, he started to unzip his fly.

That woke her up.

"No," she said, grabbing his wrist as she looked straight into his eyes. "No."

His eyes widened. He exhaled, then pulled away. Rising to his feet, he zipped up his trousers, not looking at her.

"I never want to see you with Vladimir Xendzov again," he said coldly. Then, without a look, he walked up the stairs.

Lilley sat up, feeling disheveled and dizzy, her skirt at her waist. He'd nearly made love to her—and she'd nearly let him do it! Then, when she'd refused him, he'd just left her! Her fury returned, redoubled. Standing up, she readjusted her ugly, expensive beige skirt. Her eyes narrowed as she followed him up the stairs to their bedroom, where she heard the shower running in the en suite bathroom. She pushed open the door, and saw him in the shower, standing naked beneath the running water.

Yanking open the glass door, she leaned into the shower and slammed on the handle, shutting off his water.

"What the hell?" he exploded.

Hot steam floated between them, water dripping noisily off the travertine wall. She glared at him, folding her arms. "How dare you treat me like that, you big—jerk!"

"What did you expect?" he ground out. "That I'd kiss your toes with adoration after you spent the whole night flirting with another man?"

"I wasn't flirting! He was comforting me! After—"

Alessandro's eyes narrowed. "After what?"

She swallowed, fighting tears. "It doesn't matter."

He stepped out of the shower, his body naked and dripping wet. His voice was dangerous as he said, "Tell me."

In the mirror, she saw the reflection of his magnificent, naked body, and next to him, she saw herself, fat and dowdy in the unflattering beige suit that made her look like a lump. "I can't."

"Tell me!" he thundered.

She flinched, and her lips turned down. "They were mean to me."

He gripped the door of the shower. "Who? Who was mean to you?"

"You were right," Lilley whispered. "I never should have come to Rome." She blinked back tears. "I don't belong here."

Moving forward, Alessandro grabbed her shoulders. His eyes were dark as he said in a low voice, "Just tell me who."

She tried to laugh it off. "Nothing, really. They followed me into the bathroom where I was hiding at the restaurant—"

"You were hiding?"

"—and spoke to each other. In English, to be sure I'd understand. They called me fat and stupid, and said you'd divorce me. They couldn't wait for you to be back with Olivia."

He stared at her, his mouth a grim line. Then he abruptly released her, turning away. Lilley stared at his muscular backside as he headed for the door.

He was walking away from her without a word. Again.

"Don't you care?" she choked out. "Don't you care at all?"

Alessandro whirled around, and his expression was so full of fury that she gasped.

"I care," he said. "They will regret hurting you."

"What are you going to do?" she whispered, afraid of the strange darkness she saw in his eyes.

"They are women. I cannot physically hurt them. But," he stretched his intertwined hands, "I can take what they care about the most. Their money."

"How?"

He looked past her ear. "A few well-placed calls to the banks…to the businesses that employ their husbands in well-paid sinecures." He gave a smile as cold as death. "They'll be penniless."

She stared at him, her mouth agape. "I thought they were rich."

"It's a front. They're deeply in debt."

"I thought they were your friends!"

His lip twisted. "Friends?"

"You seemed to be having such a good time…"

"I grew up with them," he said tersely. "But we're not close. We share a past. We share a history. But no. They are not my friends."

Staring up at him, Lilley thought of the friends she'd had

in Minnesota growing up, playing marbles with the house-keeper's daughter Lisa, going for long bike rides with Katie from school, ice skating on the pond with her friends and drinking hot chocolate.

Alessandro hadn't had that. His friends weren't real. Pity and grief for him welled up inside her. And suddenly she couldn't hide her feelings. Not any more.

"I don't need revenge." Blinking back tears, she took a step towards him. "There's only one thing I want. One thing I need."

His jaw twitched. "What?"

"You," she whispered. "I love you, Alessandro."

She heard the catch of his breath. Then his eyes became wistful.

"I know," he said quietly. "I've known since before our wedding, when you almost blurted it out, and I stopped you."

"What?" She didn't remember anything like that. "What are you talking about?"

"Don't you remember? You said you had something to tell me before we could marry. I stopped you because I already knew. You were in love with me. I could see your feelings on your face."

Lilley's lips parted as she remembered the moment in Las Vegas when she'd tried to tell him the truth about her family. "That was what you thought I was going to say?" she said slowly. "That I was in love with you?"

He shook his head. "I couldn't let you speak the words. I thought it would ruin things between us, that it would make a good marriage impossible."

He didn't know. Lilley's head was spinning. Alessandro didn't know about her family. All these weeks they'd been married, she'd thought he was so kind not to reproach her, so generous to forgive and forget. But he hadn't known. He still didn't know!

"But now," Alessandro said in a low voice, "I don't know what to think. I don't know if I can love anyone, Lilley." Clenching his jaw, he looked away. "When I was nineteen, I was betrayed by everyone who loved me. The woman I thought I loved told me she was pregnant by another man. My father died after ignoring me most of his life. And then my mother," he took a deep breath, "informed me that I was not his son."

"What?" Lilley gasped.

"By their second year of marriage, she'd already grown to hate him. She had a brief affair, and got pregnant with me. My father never knew. He died thinking I was his son, and still left me nothing but debts and an unknown number of half-brothers and half-sisters around the world."

Grief was shining in his black eyes. She'd never seen him so open with his feelings before. "I'm sorry," she choked out, wrapping her arms around him. "Who is your real father?"

He looked away. "Not someone I ever wanted to know."

"I'm sorry," she breathed again, but it seemed woefully inadequate. Reaching up, she kissed his cheeks, his lips, his chin, his shoulders. She offered comfort by kissing every part of him she could reach. "I'm so sorry." Tears streamed unchecked down her face as their eyes met. "But I'm your family now."

He exhaled as he looked down at her. "I don't know if I can love you, Lilley," he said in a low voice. His dark eyes shimmered. "But if I could ever love any woman on earth... it would be you."

Lilley's heart stopped beating, then suddenly raced at a gallop. "It would?"

"You're the first woman I've trusted in a long, long time,"

he said softly, stroking her cheek. "Because I know you'd never lie to me—about anything."

A tremble went through her. How could she ever tell him about her family now? How could she possibly explain what had started as a fib of omission to help her get a job, but had turned into months of lying straight to his face?

Honey, she could say casually over waffles some Sunday, *a funny thing about how you thought my father owned a shop. He does own a store, but a few more than one!* Maybe they'd have a good laugh. Maybe he'd forgive her.

But then she'd have to tell him about Théo.

She had to tell him. Before he found out some other way. And she would, she promised herself. Once their marriage was on stronger footing. Once his friends didn't hate her. Then she would tell him everything. She *would.* Even though it would make him hate her.

She trembled just to think of it....

"I'm sorry I never gave you the wedding you deserved," Alessandro said, stroking her cheek.

She gasped. "I loved our wedding!"

He shook his head ruefully. "You should have had friends at the ceremony. Family." He looked at her. "Have you told your father about me yet?"

Her father. She swallowed. "Um. No. Not yet." Squaring her shoulders, she forced herself to add, "But I will take you to Minnesota to meet him. Anytime you like."

"How about Christmas?" Holding her in his arms, he smiled down at her, the expression on his handsome face tender and bright. "We'll have a wedding reception in Rome first. Then plan one there."

"A reception?"

"Two. One on each continent. I want to properly celebrate." He stroked her hair. "With our family and friends."

"Oh," she breathed.

"It'll give your father a chance to know me." He gave her a sudden wink. "I'll win him over."

His charm and thoughtfulness just made her feel more guilty. "Of course you will," she said over the lump in her throat. "No one could help loving you."

His expression grew serious. "But I don't need anyone to love me." He pulled her against his naked body, stroking her back over her beige jacket. "I only need you."

Lilley suddenly felt like crying. She felt his naked body stir, and her own immediate response flooded her with need. She shivered as his hands gently caressed her breasts over the fabric, squeezing her plump flesh with his fingers, rubbing her swollen nipples until they were hard and aching beneath her jacket.

Her gaze fell on the bathroom mirrors and she saw their image, his naked body and muscular backside, as his lips lowered to her neck. The image caused a wave of immediate pleasure as he unbuttoned her jacket.

"You're mine," he murmured against her skin. She felt him hard between her legs, felt the gentle, insistent stroke of his fingertips as he pulled off her silk camisole and bra, running his palm down the valley between her pregnant breasts to her small waist and softly rounded belly. "Say it."

She opened her eyes. "I'm yours."

"Forever," he demanded.

She swallowed. "Forever."

Alessandro fell to his knees in front of her. Lifting her skirt to her hips, he yanked her panties to the floor. Moving his head between her thighs, he lifted one of her legs over his shoulder.

Her hands gripped his naked, hard-muscled shoulders as she felt his hot breath between her thighs. Then, the last moment before he kissed her, he lifted his head to look at her face.

"Never lie to me, Lilley," he whispered. "And we'll last forever. No one will ever be able to break us apart."

He lowered his mouth between her legs, and as waves of pleasure exploded inside her, Lilley tilted back her head with a gasp, closing her eyes. Her heart pounded as she realized what she'd done. She should have told him the truth from the beginning. From the very first day. She'd thought it would be better to wait until he had a reason to care. But when he discovered she'd lied to him for months, after he'd allowed himself to be so vulnerable and care for her—trust her—it would be the beginning of the end.

No. She felt his wet, slick tongue between her legs and shuddered with need, closing her eyes with anguish. She couldn't lose him. Not now. Not ever.

She would find a way to tell him the truth. And pray it wasn't the end...of everything.

CHAPTER TEN

ALESSANDRO'S jaw dropped when he first saw his wife at the top of the stairs.

After five weeks of planning, he'd known she was choosing her gown with care for their wedding reception at their palazzo tonight. She'd insisted on picking her dress herself, in utmost secrecy. Now he saw why. Lilley was wearing a ball gown of watered silk in blending swirls of purple and fuchsia, with a snug corset tight beneath her breasts and loose over her swelling belly. Pink flowers adorned her long, flowing brown hair which tumbled over her shoulders.

She paused at the top of the landing, waiting for his reaction. "Well?" she asked with a deep breath. "What do you think?"

Alessandro opened his lips to tell her she must change, to tell her she couldn't wear such an outrageous gown, not when they'd be surrounded by the critical eyes of the most stylish citizens of the most stylish city in the world. He opened his mouth to tell her that fitting in was the only way to survive.

Then Alessandro saw the hope in Lilley's vulnerable brown eyes. He realized what a risk she'd taken, choosing a dress like this for the night of the reception she'd spent weeks planning.

She was, quite deliberately, taking a risk.

And the truth was she looked beautiful. Looking at her face, Alessandro suddenly didn't give a damn what anyone else thought. He didn't care about anyone but her.

He held up his hand with a smile. "You look beautiful."

Relief and gratitude rushed across Lilley's beautiful face before she gave him a mischievous grin. *"Grazie,"* she said, swishing her skirt as she came down the stairs. She adjusted his tie with a dimpled smile. "You don't look so bad in that tuxedo yourself."

Then, standing on her tiptoes, she reached up and kissed him so long and hard that if guests for the reception hadn't already started to arrive, he would have taken her straight upstairs and ripped the colorful ball gown right off her.

As they went to the ballroom to greet their guests, Alessandro marveled at the changes Lilley had made in the palazzo. In the two months they'd been in Rome, Lilley had tossed out all his elegant, creaky antiques and replaced them with furniture that was both comfortable and warm. His palazzo had once been a showplace. Now it was a home.

And it had never looked better than it did tonight. It was early December, and there was a fire in every fireplace, white twinkling lights on the trees outside and holly and pine boughs on all the mantels, to celebrate the upcoming season.

Looking across the ballroom, Lilley gave a sudden intake of breath. "Uh-oh. The ambassador is hitting on Monica Valenti." He followed her gaze to see the gray-haired ambassador clearly invading the personal space of the nineteen-year-old starlet. Lilley threw him an apologetic glance. *"Mi scusi."*

As he took a flute of champagne from a passing waiter, Alessandro watched his wife with admiration. Their ballroom was packed. Lilley had invited everyone: aristocracy, government officials and entrepreneurs, from the highest circles of Roman society. She'd even invited Lucretia and Giulia.

His wife had a forgiving soul. He did not.

Alessandro had called both women and disinvited them in no uncertain terms. Now they were missing this reception, which somehow—he wasn't sure quite how—had turned into the social event of the year. The humiliation would teach the two women to show his wife a little more respect. His lips curled. The next time Lilley saw them, he suspected they would be in a far friendlier mood.

Finishing the glass of St. Raphaël champagne, he placed his empty flute on a silver tray and watched as his beautiful wife disengaged Monica Valenti from the ambassador with such friendly, warm charm, that instead of taking offense, the gray-haired man smiled at her, clearly enchanted.

And who wouldn't be enchanted? Surrounded by skinny women who wore drab designer gowns of beige and black, Lilley stood out like a bird of paradise. Guests followed her, waiting to speak with her, and Alessandro suddenly remembered how shy and terrified Lilley had been when he'd taken her to the Preziosi di Caetani ball. That was just a few months ago. So much had changed since then.

Lilley's eyes met his across the crowded ballroom, and he gave her a wicked half smile, thinking of what he intended to do to her later. Her brown eyes widened, and her cheeks turned a charming shade of pink. Ah, she was so adorable, his wife. So innocent and easy to read.

She looked away, their eye contact broken as a man came to speak with her, blocking Alessandro's view of her face.

He scowled as he recognized Vladimir Xendzov talking to Lilley, touching the bulky necklace around her neck. It was her newest strange concoction, created from gold and sapphire gem clusters she'd found in an antique shop in Venice. He wondered what they were talking about. He trusted his wife, but he didn't trust Xendzov. Setting his jaw, he grabbed a glass of bubbly pink champagne, then gaped at the raspberry in the bottom. He'd look like a fool drinking *that.* Setting the flute back on the tray, he barked at the waiter, "Get me a Scotch."

The man bowed and backed away, and Alessandro looked slowly around the crowded ballroom. Lilley had thrown herself into planning this reception as if her life depended on it, finding caterers and musicians and florists. The end result was as unique and offbeat as Lilley's jewelry. No one was dancing yet, but the mood was lively with a brash, lilting Irish rock band Lilley had hired from Dublin, just for fun. Dinner was being served buffet-style, with exotic dishes representing every country where Caetani Worldwide owned a subsidiary. The hodgepodge of cultures should have been a disaster. Instead... He looked around and saw powerful men laughing, saw their beige-clad wives giggling like schoolchildren. It was a hit.

Lilley was a hit.

Emotion rose in Alessandro's heart.

Why had he never realized it before? Lilley was perfect as she was. She didn't need to change. She didn't need to fit in. She was born to stand out.

The feeling in his heart expanded to his throat, choking him, and suddenly he had to tell her. He had to take her in his arms and tell her how proud he was of her, how much he cared about her, how much he...that he...

His feet moved across the marble floor, beneath the twinkling lights of the multicolored, sparkling glass chandeliers she'd bought in Venice. Alessandro moved faster, pushing through the crowds. His view of Lilley's face was still blocked by the people clustered around her, by the Russian who called himself a *prince*. Alessandro needed his wife in his arms. Now.

"Darling." Olivia suddenly stood in front of him, blocking his way. Skinny and pale, dressed in a black sheath that showed her complete lack of décolletage, she looked like an angel of death.

"What are you doing here?" he demanded.

"I was invited." Her lips curled up on the edges, reminding him of a cat, although that seemed disrespectful to cats. "By your *wife*."

She spoke the word as if it left her mouth with a foul taste. He set his jaw, glaring at her. "Lilley is too generous."

"Of course she is generous," Olivia's smile widened. "She can afford to be."

"What are you talking about?"

"She's rich."

Alessandro snorted. "Lilley doesn't come from money. That's one of the things that makes her so trustworthy. So different from you," he said pointedly.

She gave a tinkling little laugh. "Oh, this is delicious. Do you truly not know?" She walked slowly around him, running one red-painted fingertip along the shoulder of his tuxedo jacket. Her thin face was smug as she leaned forward to whisper, "She's Walton Hainsbury's daughter."

Alessandro stared at her. As if from a distance, he heard the lilting rock music, heard the laughter and low conversation of the Italian guests around him, the crème de la crème of Roman society. Then the marble floor seemed to move beneath his feet.

Walton Hainsbury's daughter. The man who owned the huge discount jewelry chain that had tried to seize control of Caetani Worldwide in a hostile takeover last spring. He shook his head fiercely.

"You're insane," Alessandro said. "Lilley comes from a little town in the midwest."

Olivia threw back her head and laughed. "You mean

Minneapolis? Oh, darling." She made a show of wiping her eyes. "It's a large city. The headquarters of many international corporations." She lifted a perfectly groomed eyebrow. "Including…"

Including Hainsbury Corporation, he remembered with a sickening twist of his gut. And Walton Hainsbury lived nearby. An icy chill went down his spine. He lifted his chin. "Lilley is not his daughter."

"Not just a daughter, but his only child. His heir."

My father threatened to disinherit me, her voice whirled through Alessandro's brain, *if I didn't come back to Minnesota and marry one of his managers.*

She'd had that platinum Hainsbury watch, which her mother had had especially made. How? How had she done that?

My father's a businessman.

He owns a restaurant? Perhaps a laundromat?

Um. Something like that.

Alessandro ignored the sudden pounding of his heart. He wouldn't believe it. He couldn't. "When we met, Lilley was working in my file room. My *file room,* Olivia."

She looked down at her finely sharpened red fingernails. "What better place for a corporate spy?"

A strangled noise escaped Alessandro's throat. He remembered finding Lilley alone in his private office that first night. *I just wanted to work for a few hours in peace and quiet. Without anyone bothering me,* she'd said.

His throat closed. And most damning of all. She'd known. She'd known about his plans for the Joyería deal. She could have given that information to Théo St. Raphaël.

Impossible, he told himself harshly. Lilley had no connection to the French count. Perhaps she'd had a motive to hate Alessandro back then, after he'd seduced and abandoned her in Sonoma. But she'd had no opportunity to…

"I'm surprised your company even hired her," Olivia said thoughtfully. "Considering her last employer."

Alessandro tried to remember the job Lilley had mentioned, the most recent one, which for some reason she'd left off her résumé. It all seemed like a million years ago. "She worked as a maid. In Minneapolis. And she worked for a relative…"

She looked at him in disbelief. "I've never seen you so stupid and slow. Until six months ago, she was Théo St. Raphaël's housekeeper in the South of France. He's her cousin, you know. She left his employ just days before she started working for you."

It felt like getting hit in the face. Alessandro staggered back. "Théo St. Raphaël?" he said faintly. "The Count of Castelnau is Lilley's cousin?"

"She's lied to you all along." Olivia regarded him. "But you expected that, didn't you? You always expect women to lie to you. Surely you had her background checked before you married her?"

His heart hammered in his chest, so hard and fast he thought it might break through his ribs. "No."

"Prenup?"

The ballroom, the noise of the guests, seemed to be spinning around him. The crowds parted, and he saw Lilley's face. She smiled at him across the room, her face shining, as honest and bright and beautiful as ever. He turned his head away, feeling sick. "No."

"Clever girl," Olivia murmured. "I wonder what else she's lied to you about." She gave him a sideways glance. "How well do you really know her?"

His jaw was tight. "I know she's pregnant with my child."

"Do you?" Her eyes were steady and cold. "Do you really?"

It felt like an ice pick through Alessandro's brain. He

heard the echo of Heather's voice from long ago. *The baby's not yours. I lied.*

He tightened his hands to fists. "Of course the baby is mine," he ground out. "Lilley wouldn't lie about that."

"You know how conniving and ruthless people can be."

"I know how conniving *you* can be," he said harshly.

"Me? I'm an amateur." Olivia laughed, covering her mouth with her hand. "All this time you believed her to be some small-town innocent, didn't you? And she probably planned this from the start. Perhaps her goal is full control of Caetani Worldwide, split equally between her father and her cousin."

He stared at her. "I don't believe you," he choked out.

But that was a lie. He did believe her. That was the problem.

Olivia's eyes met his. "So ask her."

With a low curse, Alessandro pushed past her. Shoving through the crowd, Alessandro stalked towards his wife. Just moments before, he'd felt such reckless joy, a strange breathless certainty about Lilley. Now, that feeling had evaporated as if it had never existed. All that was left was cold despair.

And fury. As he walked towards her, blood started to pound through his body, boiling hot, thawing him out limb by limb. He welcomed the anger. Stoked it.

He'd given Lilley everything, and she'd made a fool out of him. She'd lied to him from the beginning. Faked her name. Her résumé. And perhaps even—

No. He cut off the thought savagely, his hands clenching at his sides. Guests saw his face and backed away, the crowd parting for him like magic.

Lilley was laughing as she talked to Vladimir Xendzov, and the man's eyes caressed her face with admiration. Was

Lilley flirting with him? Toying with him? Using him, as she'd used Alessandro?

Lilley looked over Xendzov's shoulder and blanched when she saw Alessandro. "What's happened?" she breathed. "What's wrong?"

"Tell me your name," Alessandro said in a low voice.

The other guests clustered around Lilley glanced between them, suddenly uneasy at his tone of voice. Looking bewildered, she answered, "Lilley Caetani."

"No." He set his jaw, hating her soft, deceptive beauty that had lured him into trusting her. And more. "Tell me your *name.*"

More guests fell silent, turning to look. The Irish rock music abruptly stopped. Suddenly, amid hundreds of people, it was quiet.

His wife swallowed, looking to the right and left. Then with a deep breath, she whispered, "Lilley Smith."

"Tell me!" He thundered. "Your *name!*"

She suddenly looked as if she was going to cry. "Alessandro, I was going to tell you."

"When?" he bit out. "After you'd stolen my company for Hainsbury and your cousin to pick through?"

"No!" she gasped. "I tried to tell you before our wedding. You said you already knew. You always know so much. I believed you!"

"You believed I would actually marry you, knowing that? You lied from the start, even about your name!"

She flinched. He saw the tremble of her eyelashes. "I changed my name three years ago, when my father divorced my mother while she was dying. I didn't want to be a Hainsbury anymore. So I took her maiden name—"

"You knew Caetani Worldwide would never hire you with either Hainsbury or Théo St. Raphaël's name on your résumé."

"Yes," she admitted in a small voice.

"You came as a spy."

"No! I was just desperate for a job while I tried to start my business!" She shook her head tearfully. "I went to San Francisco to follow my dream—"

"Bull," he said brutally. "You went to San Francisco to seduce Jeremy Wakefield into giving you information about Preziosi designs, so your father could have them copied in China in advance. Until I took you to the Preziosi ball and you realized a greater prize was possible for you." He gave a hard laugh. "You decided to become my mistress, so you could funnel information to your family."

"I would never betray you!" she said with a sob. "I was going to tell you everything! I swore it to myself, when I finally realized you didn't know about my family. All this time, I thought you did, until the day I first told you I loved you."

Her voice trembled, but her tears weren't going to work on him, not this time. "That was weeks ago." He grabbed her by the shoulders, looking fiercely into her weepy eyes. "All this time, I thought I could trust you. And you were waiting to stab me in the back. What was your goal? How are they going to work against me? Are your father and cousin planning a hostile takeover of my company?"

"You know me better than that!" She hiccupped, and her eyes became huge as she looked up at him. Unchecked tears streaked her rosy cheeks as she whispered, "Don't you?"

"I wish to God I'd never met you." Alessandro's pulse hammered in his ears, and he couldn't breathe. Couldn't even think. "There's just one last thing I need to know."

"What?"

He gently touched her full bottom lip, the lip he'd once thought could only speak the truth. "How deep do your lies go?"

Her lips parted beneath his touch. His hand slowly traced down her neck, skimming over the breasts and corset to the bright pink-and-purple skirts that covered her swollen belly. "Is the baby mine?"

Her eyes widened as she gasped.

"Tell me the truth, Lilley," he said in a low, dangerous voice. "Did you sleep with another man?"

A sob came from the back of her throat. As he stared down at Lilley's beautiful, tortured face, Alessandro suddenly forgot about the crowded ballroom, forgot Caetani Worldwide, forgot Olivia behind him. All he could think was that he'd loved Lilley. That had been the feeling swelling in his heart moments before. That had been what he'd wanted to tell her. *He loved her.*

But now he knew the woman he'd loved was a lie. Lilley had deceived him from the beginning. He'd asked for a paternity test, and she'd talked him out of it. She'd lured him into loving her, so she could rip out his heart. Just like all the rest.

Unwilling memories rushed through him. Lilley's teasing smile as she tried to get him to play. Lilley naked in the pool in Sardinia. Lilley defending everyone, even people who didn't deserve it. Lilley clinging to him for comfort and strength. Lilley's deep, loving eyes that promised eternity. All a lie.

She stood in front of him now, swaying on her feet, looking as if she might faint. "You really think I would do that?" she whispered. "That I'd sleep with another man, then marry you and spend the rest of my life lying to you? How can you think that? I love you!"

"Nice," he murmured. Touching her cheek, he tilted her face towards the light of the chandelier. "The tears in your eyes, the catch in your voice." He dropped his hand and said acidly, "You'd almost have me believe that you cared."

"I do care!" she choked out. "I love you—"

"Stop saying that," he said harshly, then set his jaw, glaring at her with hatred. "Fine. Don't tell me. I wouldn't believe a word you said anyway."

Lilley clasped her hands together, looking pale and small in her vivid ball gown, flowers tumbling from her long brown hair. Then she glanced at Olivia behind him.

"She did this, didn't she? She took my white lie and twisted it into evidence of a black heart." A tremble filled her voice as she looked back at him. Tears were streaking her face. "And you believed her. You never thought I was good enough to be your wife. You never wanted to love me. And this is your easy way out."

"I despise you," he said coldly.

She gave a sob, and Vladimir Xendzov placed a hand on his shoulder. "Enough. You've made your point."

Alessandro twisted out of the man's grasp, barely restraining himself from punching his face. "Stay out of this." He suddenly hated Xendzov, Olivia and every other vulture in his colorful, festive ballroom. Setting his jaw, he looked around the ballroom and shouted, "All of you—get the hell out!"

"No," Lilley said behind him. "Stop it, Alessandro."

Her voice was harder and colder than he'd ever heard from her lips before. Surprised, he turned back to face her.

Lilley's eyes were still grief-stricken but her shoulders were straight, her body rigid. "Our guests haven't done anything to deserve your abuse. And neither have I." She squared her shoulders and said, "Either tell me, *right now,* that you know this baby is yours, or I will leave you. And never come back."

An ultimatum. He stiffened. "I'm just supposed to trust your word, am I?"

Lilley's face turned pale, almost gray. "I'm not going to

stay in a marriage you don't know how to fight for." She glanced back at Olivia bitterly. "She's the one you always wanted. A woman as perfect and heartless as you."

In a swirl of purple-and-pink skirts, Lilley turned away.

Alessandro grabbed her shoulder. "You can't leave," he ground out. "Not without a paternity test."

She looked at him, and he could have drowned in the deep grief of her brown eyes. "I'm done trying to make you love me," she whispered. "Done."

Alessandro couldn't show weakness. Couldn't let her know how close she'd come to breaking him entirely. "You'll stay in Rome," he said harshly. "Until I allow you to leave."

Her eyes glittered.

"No," she said. "I won't."

Her face looked strange, her eyes half-wild as she took a deep breath.

"I slept with a different man, just like you said." Blinking back tears as she looked up at him, she choked out with a sob, "And I loved him."

Her words were like a serrated blade across Alessandro's heart. He staggered back, stricken. "And the baby," he breathed, searching her eyes. "What about the baby?"

Lilley's brown eyes were dark as a winter storm. Tears streamed down her face like rain. For answer, she pulled her canary-yellow diamond ring off her left hand and word-lessly held it out to him.

Numbly, he reached for it. Lilley turned away, pushing through the crowds, not looking back.

And this time, he didn't try to stop her. Gripping the ten-carat diamond ring tightly against his palm, Alessandro closed his eyes, leaning his head against his fist as he felt the first spasms of grief course through his body.

CHAPTER ELEVEN

A week later, Alessandro sat in his study staring at divorce papers, feeling numb.

He hadn't seen Lilley since she'd fled the reception, running out into the streets of Rome with only her passport and wallet, still dressed in the fuchsia ball gown. He had no idea where she was, and didn't care. Let the lawyers find her.

He looked down wearily at the documents spread across his desk. He didn't need Lilley, he told himself. He didn't need their baby.

Except a hard lump rose in his throat every time he passed the room that would have been the nursery. The walls were soft yellow, and Lilley's painting of baby elephants, monkeys and giraffes was propped against the wall. Alessandro's car still held the stuffed elephant he'd bought the day before the reception, and it was in his trunk right now, wrapped in festive paper decorated with baby animals, tied with a bright yellow bow.

The ache in his throat increased. Alessandro clenched his jaw. He'd burn the toy, he thought savagely. Then he'd repaint the nursery's walls with a color that wouldn't remind him of either Lilley or the baby. No blue. No pink. He couldn't use brown, either, the color of her eyes. Nor red, the color of her lips. So what was left?

Black. Just black.

He leaned his forehead into his hands. He was better off without them. Better off without Lilley constantly pestering him to jump in the pool or dance or play. Without hearing her soft voice speak dreamily of their future children, of a happy marriage that would last fifty years. Without seeing the sensual, breathless expression in her face as she looked up at him in bed, the moment before he pushed inside her.

Va bene. He didn't need them. He'd go back to the life he'd had before, working all day to earn money he didn't need, having meaningless affairs that were forgotten by morning. Trusting no one. Forever alone. *Perfetto.*

He covered his face with his hands.

His phone rang. "*Buon giorno,* darling," Olivia said cheerfully. "Now you're rid of your mistake, I want to ask you to lunch. To celebrate."

"I'm not divorced yet," he said in a low voice.

"Come to lunch anyway. I don't mind."

Her low, smug voice jarred him. Swiveling in his chair, he turned towards the window, towards the view of the city and hazy blue sky. Where was Lilley? Was she with another man? He remembered the way Vladimir Xendzov had looked at her. Remembered Jeremy Wakefield's awed face when he saw her in the red dress.

Who was the father of her baby?

I slept with a different man, just like you said. And I loved him.

His lips twisted. That meant she'd lied when she'd told Alessandro she loved *him.* Another lie to add to the pile.

Through the window, he saw a limo park at the gate of his palazzo. A driver got out of the limo, opening the door for a well-dressed, dark-haired man, who went to talk to the security guard. Frowning, Alessandro sat up straight, narrowing his eyes, trying to see the man's face.

Then he did. And he rose to his feet with a half-strangled curse.

"Darling, what's wrong?" Olivia asked. "What is it?"

"Someone's here," he said curtly. "I have to go."

"Who could possibly pull you off the phone with me?"

"Théo St. Raphaël."

"What?" Olivia's voice was suddenly sharp. "You don't need to see him. Wait at your house, I'll pick you up and take you for lunch—"

"Sorry," he said shortly, and he hung up, tossing his phone on his desk. As he ran down the stairs, his blood was pounding for battle. His hands were clenched into fists, ready for a fight, any fight. Brushing past his bewildered housekeeper, he went into the courtyard.

"Let him in," Alessandro ordered his guard in Italian. Théo St. Raphaël came through the gate, looking polished and powerful in a suit and yellow tie, holding a leather briefcase. He looked calm, cool and under control, all things Alessandro hadn't felt for a week. The hot Italian sun shone down on his scrubby T-shirt and jeans as Alessandro stalked through the dusty courtyard to finally meet his rival.

"What the hell do you want?" he demanded. "Come to gloat?"

Théo St. Raphaël stared at him as if he were insane. "Gloat?"

"I bet you and—" he still couldn't say her name out loud "—your cousin had a good laugh after she helped you steal the Mexico City deal. It was clever for her to lure me into giving information in bed!"

In a swift movement, St. Raphaël leapt five steps across the courtyard in a flutter of dust and punched Alessandro solidly across the jaw.

"That's for Lilley," he said, panting as he rubbed his wrist. "Damn you."

It would have knocked a lesser man to the ground. As it was, Alessandro felt the impact of the blow all the way to his knees.

His own fist flew back on instinct. Then he straightened, rubbing his jaw. "At least you have the decency to attack me to my face, St. Raphaël," he said. "Rather than stabbing me in the back."

"Lilley kept one small secret from you. *One.*"

"Small?" Alessandro said incredulously. "She told you my plans for the Mexico City deal! Convinced me to marry her when she was in love with another man! And worst of all…" He cut himself off, and his voice hardened. "Why are you here? What more could she possibly want?"

The Frenchman glared at him. "In your office."

Alessandro stiffened, then realized his security guard was watching with interest, as were the paparazzi who'd been parked across the street ever since the scandalous night of their reception. He set his jaw. "Fine."

Turning on his heel, he led the count silently into the palazzo.

"I'm here to collect Lilley's things," St. Raphaël informed him once they reached his study. "Her tools. Her mother's quilt."

"And the clothes I bought her?"

"She doesn't want them."

Alessandro sank into his office chair, feeling weary. He swiveled towards the window. He'd nearly thrown her most precious belongings away in his rage after she'd disappeared, but he hadn't been able to do it. The tools and quilt were too much a part of what he'd loved about her. "It's boxed up by the front door. Help yourself." He glared at the other man. "I'll be glad to get it all out of here."

St. Raphaël stared at him coldly, then set his briefcase

on the desk. Opening it, he pulled out a file and held it to Alessandro.

"What's this?" he asked, not touching it.

"The Mexico City deal," St. Raphaël said scornfully. "If you still want it."

Alessandro opened the file. Skimming through it, he realized it was a contract to exchange Joyería for the St. Raphaël vineyard. He looked for a catch. He couldn't find one.

"I will step away from the Tokyo deal as well."

Alessandro looked up in bewilderment. "I don't understand."

"Lilley's idea."

"But why would she arrange this, when she's the one who betrayed me?"

"Lilley didn't betray you," St. Raphaël bit out. "Someone else gave me that information. She said she wanted payback for the way you replaced her with some cheap fileroom girl." He paused. "I had no idea she was talking about Lilley."

"Olivia?" Alessandro said in a strangled voice. "Olivia Bianchi?"

St. Raphaël's eyes settled on his. "The two of you deserve each other."

Was it possible he was telling the truth? Had Olivia betrayed him? Alessandro suddenly remembered all the times he'd done business on the phone in the back of the limo, with Olivia sitting bored beside him. She'd certainly known about his rivalry with St. Raphaël.

She'd had motive, means and opportunity.

The Frenchman leaned forward, his knuckles white against the desk. "But you must promise, in writing, that you will keep the design studio in Mexico City. I gave

Rodriguez my word that none of his people would lose their jobs. And, unlike you, I do not wish to be a liar."

Alessandro's eyes narrowed. "I didn't lie. I might have *implied*—"

"You lied. Worse than Lilley ever did. All she was trying to do was get a job. You were trying to enrich your own pockets at the expense of someone else's honor. You lied to Rodriguez. Just as you lied to Lilley when you didn't mention until after you were wed that you wouldn't allow her to work."

Alessandro's cheeks grew hot. Then his chin lifted coldly. "Lilley slept with another man, then tried to pass off her unborn child as mine."

With a snort, St. Raphaël stared at him, then shook his head. "If you believe that, you're even more stupid than I thought." He pulled out one last paper. "Here. Give that to your lawyers."

I slept with a different man, just like you said. Alessandro remembered Lilley's wide, stricken eyes as she stood in her pink ballgown amid the holly and ivy. He remembered the strange way her voice had trembled. *And I loved him.*

Alessandro's heart gave a sickening lurch.

What if Alessandro was the man she'd loved—before he'd turned on her so brutally, in public, with his ex-mistress egging him on, practically chortling with glee?

He'd vowed to honor and protect his wife. Why hadn't he cared for her enough to speak with her privately? To ask, to listen, to give her the chance to explain? Instead, he'd turned on her like a rabid dog. He'd attacked her, his beautiful wife who had never done anything but love him with all of her gentle, loyal heart.

"Where is she?" he whispered.

"She left France a few hours ago." The other man's lips

pressed together in a thin line. "She wanted to visit her father, then scout out locations for her jewelry line."

"She's doing it?" Alessandro said faintly. "Really doing it?"

St. Raphaël glared at him. "My wife says Lilley's jewelry is a sure thing. And she should know." He drummed his fingers on the desk. "You know, I should thank you. For doing the right thing by my cousin."

Alessandro's lips lifted humorlessly. "You mean marrying her?"

"Divorcing her," he replied coldly. "Lilley is the kindest person I know. She doesn't have a mean bone in her body. She and her baby deserve better than you." He closed his briefcase with a snap. "But business is business. I have wanted these vineyards back for some time. Have your lawyers review the documents. There is no need for us to meet again. *Adieu.*"

Without another word, Théo St. Raphaël left. Numbly, Alessandro stared down at the file, and at the divorce papers still spread across his desk beneath. Picking up a page, he tried to read it, but the words seemed to move and jump across the pages. It was as if he were suddenly seeing the world from Lilley's point of view.

Pushing the papers aside, he rose to his feet. From the window, he saw St. Raphaël carry a large box out through the gate. His limousine soon disappeared back into the streets of Rome.

Alessandro looked up. The bright-blue sky seemed smeared violet. As if the world were going dark.

I love you, Alessandro.

I'm yours. Forever.

He closed his eyes, pressing his hot forehead against the cold glass of the window. But even with his eyes closed, even if he covered his ears with his hands, he could still hear Lilley's shaking voice, still see the grief in her eyes. *I'm done trying to make you love me. Done.*

And the truth hit Alessandro like a blow.

Lilley hadn't betrayed him.

He had betrayed her.

His eyes flew open. He'd told her she wasn't good enough to be his wife, or good enough to be liked by his friends. He'd insisted on buying her clothes. He'd told her why her jewelry would never sell, then insisted that she give up her own dreams in order to sit alone in their palazzo, waiting for him to come home.

He'd let her love him without offering her anything in return, except coldly expensive jewels, which he should have realized long ago, she would never, ever want.

No wonder when he'd turned on her so viciously at their reception, Lilley had finally given up. For months, she'd bent over backwards trying to please him. She'd convinced herself he was worthy of her love. That night, even her romantic, loyal heart had been forced to see the truth.

He'd finally proven that he wasn't her knight in shining armor, and never could be.

She was right. He'd been afraid to love her, terrified to let himself be vulnerable again. For sixteen years, he'd kept his heart locked up. When Olivia had given him an escape, his cowardly heart had taken the first chance at the exit door.

Lilley was right. Cold rage filled him. Rage at himself.

Alessandro turned back to the window, staring at the early twilight of December. The blue sky was streaked with pink and orange, like a brilliant fire on the horizon.

We all must choose in this life, he'd told her once. *The safety of a prison. Or the terrible joy that comes with freedom.*

He'd thought of her as a timid little mouse. But all along,

she was the one with the courageous heart. He was the one who'd been hiding.

But not anymore. *Not anymore.*

Whirling around, he grabbed the phone off his desk so fast he nearly it knocked to the floor.

He would bring the laughter and trust back to her eyes, even if it made him look like the biggest fool on the face of the earth. If he couldn't even do that…then that bastard St. Raphaël was right. Lilley and his child really would be better off without him.

Alessandro would find her. Win her.

Squaring his shoulders, he set his jaw.

He would deserve her.

After six hours, Lilley's backside was well and truly sore.

She shifted on the hard cushion of her father's reproduction Louis XIV couch as she sat in his fancy parlor. She looked down at her watch. Six hours he'd made her wait now. *Six.* It was her first visit in three years, and he'd just left her here, alone and unwelcome in the sprawling house he'd built for his mistress, a forty-thousand-square-foot mansion on a sprawling estate near Minneapolis.

Clearly this was her punishment for not coming home in June to marry his employee, as he'd demanded.

Her lower back gave a sudden stab of pain, and she rose to her feet. The parlor had beautiful views of snowy Lake Minnetonka through the black, bare trees, but it still felt like an office, not a home. There were no personal photographs, just posters from various Hainsbury's advertising campaigns. The closest framed poster showed a happy young couple embracing on a park bench with the image of an engagement ring superimposed around them. Beneath it in big letters was the tagline, Hainsbury Jewelers. When Only Perfection Will Do.

Perfection. Engagement rings. Love in general. Lilley hated them all right now. But most of all, she hated her knack for loving men who did not have the capacity or desire to love her back.

Her father's abandonment had left a hole in her heart. But Alessandro had done far worse. He'd cut through that hole with a machete, leaving one side of her heart drenched in acid, the other smashed with a meat mallet.

She'd given her husband everything, and it still hadn't been enough. Alessandro hadn't even tried to hear her side. He'd just taken Olivia's every word as gospel—even believing it was possible Lilley might have slept with another man!

Well, she *had* slept with another man. Without thinking, she reached up and touched the brass-and-pink-rock-crystal necklace hanging around her throat, a gesture she'd repeated many times over the last week. A tragedy that the man she'd loved, the man she'd been so sure Alessandro could be, had been entirely a figment of her imagination.

She swallowed, blinking fast. But work would see her through. After all she'd endured, she was no longer afraid of failure.

She just hadn't been thinking big enough. Instead of opening a boutique, she was starting her own line of handmade, unique jewelry art, as Vladimir Xendzov had called it. After Alessandro had effectively ended their marriage, Lilley had spent days weeping in her old housekeeper's suite in her cousin's castle before she'd resurfaced to play with her cousin's baby. Théo's wife had demanded, "Where did you get that fabulous necklace?"

"I made it myself," Lilley had replied, turning away. Then something inside her made her pause. Made her turn back around. With a deep breath, she'd added, "I've decided to start my own business. I'm going to sell handcrafted jewelry to luxury boutiques and exclusive department stores across the world. I'm going back to the States to try for a business loan."

Carrie had shaken her head vehemently. "No!" she'd cried, and for a moment Lilley was taken aback. Then her friend smiled. "Don't take out a loan with some banker, please. Let me do it! This is just the investment I was looking for."

Closing her eyes, Lilley took a deep breath. Her dream was coming true in a way she'd never imagined. She had her financing now and was dependent on no one, not even Carrie. She'd finally been brave enough to take a risk. Alessandro had helped her do that, she admitted quietly to herself. He'd taught her how to have the confidence to follow her dreams. Her business might succeed or fail, but either way, it was all up to her.

She'd finally become strong enough to stand up for what was right, even if it terrified her. And she would rather be alone than be with a husband who didn't love or trust her.

Lilley was no man's housekeeper. No man's helpless wife. And apparently, no man's daughter.

As the sun started to set, scattering pink light over the snow beneath a black lattice of trees, Lilley finally gave up and turned for the door.

"What do you want?" Her father's voice was low and hard. Lilley saw him in the doorway, and her mouth fell open with shock.

Walton Hainsbury seemed to have aged decades in the three years since her mother's funeral. His beady eyes glared at her through his wire-rimmed glasses, but his face looked pale as he took a long suck of his cigar.

Her nose wrinkled at the smell. Cigars had become her least favorite smell in the world. He'd been smoking the day he'd left Lilley and her mother, when he'd announced he would go and build a mansion on Lake Minnetonka for his far younger mistress. Eighteen-year-old Lilley had cared for her mother at their family home in Minneapolis for two years, until she died.

"What are you doing here?" Walton rasped, looking contemptuously at the powder-blue coat and dark, fitted jeans. "Have you come crawling here to try to worm your way back into my will? It's too late, missy! I've left everything to charity!"

Lilley stiffened. "I didn't come for money."

"Likely story."

The accusation stung. "I've never asked you for money. Not once. You know I haven't." Lifting her chin, she looked at him. "I just came to tell you you're going to be a grandfather."

He stared at her. She noticed that the color of his skin was ashy, his jowls flabby, as if he'd lost weight. He took several puffs of his cigar before he said in a low voice, "You're pregnant?"

She nodded.

His eyes narrowed at her bare left hand. "And no husband." He glared at her. "You couldn't marry the man I chose for you. Had to throw yourself away!"

"The man you chose for me was twice my age."

"If you'd married him, I could have left him my company. I would have known you'd always have someone to take care of you. But you wouldn't see sense, as usual. And now it's too late."

She heard a wistfulness in his voice. A lump rose in her throat. "I'll be all right. I can take care of myself."

"You can't," he barked. "You've just come back with another mouth to feed, expecting me to solve things for you as I always do."

The accusation was so unjust, she sucked in her breath.

"You've never solved anything for me! You just made me feel helpless and stupid as a kid. The instant you knew about my dyslexia, you treated me differently. Same as you did when Mom got sick!"

"I loved your mother," he said harshly. "As I loved you. I tried to take care of you both—"

"By divorcing her when she was dying? By deserting us both so you could build—" She looked around the gilded parlor. "—*this* for your mistress? Where is Tiffany, by the way?"

Walton looked away. "She left me a few months ago."

"Oh." Lilley blinked at him, not knowing what to say. *Good riddance* seemed rude.

"I never wanted to leave your mother," he added gruffly. "Paula's the one who told me to go."

Lilley's brow furrowed. "What?"

He exhaled. "I've never dealt well with illness, I'll give you that. But when I told your mother about Tiffany, I was trying to wipe the slate clean. I vowed to her that if she could forgive me, I'd be a better husband, a better man." His lips trembled in a smile. "But she told me to get the hell out of our house. She refused to see me again. And so I didn't." He clawed back his wispy hair. "Not until the funeral, when she couldn't stop me."

"I never knew. I just assumed—"

"Your mother didn't want to drag you into our quarrel. I respected her wishes."

"And took all the blame," she whispered.

He looked at her. "I reckon I deserved it." He looked away. "So who's your baby's father? Some penniless musician? An artist? Any chance the man has a shred of honor or decency?"

"If you're asking if he's married me, the answer is yes. We were married in September in Las Vegas."

His face grew more ashen. His long eyebrows shook as he said, "You got married! Without telling me!"

"You disinherited me. I didn't think you'd care."

"Tell me you got a prenup."

"No."

His hand trembled as he stabbed the cigar towards her. "I haven't worked hard all my life to let some greedy fortune hunter steal it all now!"

"He doesn't want your money," she whispered. She looked away. "And anyway, he's about to divorce me."

"After such a short marriage? Who will take care of you and the child?"

"I will." She took a shallow breath, trying not to inhale his smoke which was making her feel sick. "Théo offered me a spot at his headquarters in Paris, in his mergers and acquisitions department. He said I have a fresh take on things, an original mind. But his wife Carrie and I had already decided—"

"Original mind?" her father interrupted derisively. "You can't survive on your own, and take care of my grandchild alone. You will come home," he ordered. "You'll move in with me."

Lilley sucked in her breath. "Why can't you believe in me, Dad? Just once?" she whispered. "Why can't you forget my dyslexia and tell me you believe in me, tell me I can do anything I put my mind to?"

Walton scowled. "Lilley—"

"Forget it." She turned away. "Good-bye."

Leaving the parlor, she fled the mansion. Outside, the frigid Minnesota air hit her skin with a vengeance, making her shiver in her warm jacket. Cold December light gleamed off Lake Minnetonka, and she could see a white cloud of fog rising up from the ice as she climbed back into her rental car. Starting the engine, she drove down the gravel driveway, her back tires sliding over the packed snow.

But when she reached the gate, the security guard ignored her. She waved at him furiously, but he turned the other way, a phone to his ear. Finally, she got out of the car and stomped to the guardhouse. "Open it," she demanded. "Right now!"

The guard pushed the button to open the gate, but leaned out of his window. "Mr. Hainsbury wants you to wait."

Lilley muttered under her breath. She was done waiting for anyone, especially men who'd proven over and over in every possible way that they didn't love her. Climbing into her car, she gunned the engine. "Let him wait."

But as she pulled out of the long driveway and out onto the quiet country road, she saw her father run through the gate, waving his arms as he shouted after her. For a moment, she stared towards the inviting open road. Then, cursing herself aloud, she slammed on the brake.

Lilley closed her eyes, heart pounding as she leaned her head against the steering wheel. Then, slowly, she turned off the engine.

She climbed out of the car, turning back towards her father. He was wheezing loudly and his run slowed to a walk. But she didn't take a single step. She let him walk all the way.

"You don't know, do you?" he said in a low voice. "Before I found out about the baby, I thought that was the only reason you turned up here. Because you found out."

"Found out what?"

He looked at her. "I'm dying, Lilley."

She stared at him, not moving. "What?"

He gave her a wan smile. "That's why Tiffany left." He held up the lit cigar between his fingers and stared down at it. "Doctors give me a few months, maybe a year. I wanted you to marry Gerald because...then I'd have known," he whispered. "That you'd always be all right."

Trembling, Lilley looked at her father in the gray December light. She'd had a happy childhood, back when her parents had loved each other. Her father had taught her to ride a bike. Taught her how to weld. He'd taught her how to evaluate uncut gems, and the different names for the stones. He'd shown her, through his example, the value of hard work and big dreams. She exhaled.

"There's no hope?"

He dropped the cigar, crushing it beneath his feet. "Nope." His lips creased. "I've made a lot of mistakes, Lilley. First with your mother—then with you. But even I couldn't be stupid enough to make this last one, and let you leave, knowing I might never see you again." He lifted his head. "I do love you, Lilley," he whispered. "And I've always been proud of you. I know I wasn't always a good father, and I'm sorry. But before I die, I need...I'm asking—" His voice cracked. "—for you to forgive me."

Lilley stared at him, her heart squeezing in her chest. Even her mother had forgiven Walton at the last. He'd treated them both badly. But she suddenly knew she wasn't going to let him die alone.

Narrowing her eyes, she shook her head decisively. "Not going to happen."

Her father's face fell. Then she added with an unsteady smile, "There's no way you're going to die. I know you, Dad. Death itself wouldn't be able to talk you into a deal you didn't like."

He exhaled. He looked up, and his eyes were filled with tears. "I told you that you needed me. That was a lie. The truth is—I'm the one who needs you." He swallowed. "I swear to you, if I live long enough, I'll be a better grandfather than I was a father."

She felt a lump in her throat. "You weren't so bad. Really."

"No?"

"Well." She gave him a crooked smile. "You did teach me how to ride a bike." He smiled back at her. But as she started to reach out to him, the road suddenly rumbled and shook beneath her feet. She heard a loud honking behind her.

Turning in surprise, she saw a delivery van barreling down the country road, followed by a semitruck so huge it hung over the edges of the asphalt. The delivery van drove by, honking.

"What the devil?" her father sputtered, coughing.

"Abbott," she whispered in shock. What was Alessandro's chauffeur doing in Minnesota, driving a delivery van on this small country road?

The semi parked behind her car, blocking her on one side as the delivery van blocked the other. Confused, she started walking towards Abbott, who'd leapt out of the driver's seat and was swiftly walking around to the back of the van.

"Abbott, what are you doing here?"

She stopped as he opened the van's back doors. Looking inside, Lilley sucked in her breath, her hand over her mouth.

There was a knight in the back of the van. A medieval knight in full armor.

The knight pushed up his visor, and she saw Alessandro's dark, handsome face. His warm black eyes were glowing with such adoration that her heart caught in her throat.

She exhaled, tilting her head to look up at him in the back of the van. She'd slipped on the ice and fallen into some kind of coma. She was dreaming. That was the only explanation for Alessandro wearing armor in Minnesota, standing in the back of a van, in front of a snowy white lake.

"What are you doing here?" she breathed.

"I've come for you," Alessandro said, his eyes looking straight into hers. "I was a coward and a fool. Come back to me, Lilley," he whispered. "Let me show you I can be the husband you always dreamed of."

Tears filled her eyes as she went towards the van. With a scrape of metal, he hopped off the van's edge. But the heavy weight of his armor seemed to take him off guard. His visor snapped shut with a loud clang as he fell heavily on the snowy road.

Lilley was beside him in an instant, kneeling as she gathered him in her arms. "Are you all right?" she said anxiously. "Are you hurt?"

Sprawled out across the road, Alessandro didn't move. Dear God, what if a sharp blow in that tin-can suit had knocked him out? Lilley's hands shook as she pulled up his visor.

But she saw he was silently laughing. She fell back on her haunches in wonder.

"Oh my God. You've totally made a fool of yourself," she breathed in awe. She shook her head, suddenly smiling. "Dressing up in armor? What were you thinking?"

"I've never seen any angel half as beautiful as you." He lifted his armored hand to touch her cheek. "I would battle far more than armor to be in the arms of the woman I love. I would slay dragons for you," he whispered.

What had he said? *What had he just said?* That he loved her? She felt her heart expand and bend and swell until it was big enough to swallow the whole world. She looked down, her lashes brushing shyly against her cheek. "Come on," she murmured. "I'll help you up."

But the armor was even heavier than she'd thought. First Abbott, then her father, had to come and help him to stand up.

"Hello, sir," Alessandro said to her father, smiling.

"I don't think we've ever met in person. I'm Alessandro Caetani."

Walton blinked, his eyes wide. He looked at Lilley. "This is your husband?" he asked faintly.

Unable to speak, she nodded, then turned back to Alessandro.

Behind her, she heard her father give a low whistle. "What a merger this will make." But as she turned with a scowl, Walton quickly said to Abbott, "Care for a drink at the gatehouse? Something to warm your blood?"

"You bet."

Lilley and Alessandro stood alone on the snowy, empty road. A wind blew off the lake, whipping through her hair, but she no longer felt the cold. She felt warm all over, filled with light.

"What possessed you to do this?" she whispered, putting her hand on the side of his shiny helmet. "This crazy thing?"

He moved his metal glove over her hand. "I wanted to show you I'm sorry," he said in a low voice. "I never should have asked if the baby was mine."

She swallowed, looking down.

"I shouldn't have let a single white lie keep me from trusting you for thousands of reasons," he said. "One most of all." He lifted her chin with his finger. "I love you, Lilley."

The winter sun burst through the gray winter clouds. A beam of light caught his armor, making him sparkle like diamonds.

"It took losing you in Rome to make me realize you were right. I was afraid. Now, the only thing that scares me is losing you. I'll do anything to win you back, Lilley," he whispered. His dark eyes met hers. "Absolutely anything."

The white, gray and black of winter suddenly filled with

the beautiful pinks and greens of spring in Lilley's eyes. He loved her. And their lives together were only beginning.

"I love you, Alessandro," she whispered, throwing her arms around his hard, cold armor.

For a long moment, they held each other on the quiet road. Then Lilley pulled back, her forehead furrowed as she glanced back at the huge semitruck, still parked behind her car. "But why did you bring that?"

"Oh." Alessandro gave her a sudden grin. "I was afraid I'd kill us both if I actually tried to sit on a horse, so I made other plans." Looking at the truck's driver, he motioned with his hand. The driver hopped out and went to the back of the truck. She heard the distant roar of an engine, and then a vintage Cadillac De Ville—in hot pink—rolled off the ramp to park beside them.

As the driver disappeared for his drink at the gatehouse, Lilley walked slowly around the Cadillac, her mouth open.

It was a classic convertible from the 1960s, the exact same fuchsia as the ball gown she'd worn to their reception in Rome. "What is that?"

He grinned at her. "Our getaway vehicle, *cara*. To ride off into the sunset."

She looked back at him. "And what if you hadn't found me? What if I'd already been gone?"

"Then I would have sold my business and driven all over the country, looking for you," he said gravely behind her. "Everywhere. Until you were in my arms."

She gasped a laugh. "Dressed as a knight? Driving a hot-pink Cadillac? The paparazzi would have had a field day! They'd have said you'd lost your mind!"

"I have," he said softly. "Along with my heart. All I want to do, for the rest of my life, is make a fool of myself. Over you."

Tears fell from Lilley's lashes. Standing on her tiptoes,

she held up his cold visor with her fingertips and kissed him. Her husband kissed her back fervently, reverently, passionately. They had been standing in the snowy road for hours, or perhaps minutes, when she finally pulled away for air. His black eyes glimmered down at her. She had no idea if the tears on his cheeks were hers or his. But what did it matter? They were one.

"Thank you for being a fool," she said, her heart welling with joy. "Thank you for making all my childhood dreams come true."

He looked down at her, his handsome face glowing with love and shining with the strength of steel. "And thank you," he whispered, stroking her cheek, "for making me want to dance."

They danced at their first anniversary party the following September. As Alessandro led Lilley to the dance floor in their Sonoma ballroom, he whirled her in a circle, making her colorful skirts twirl. She heard a soft *"awww"* from their fifty or so guests, just family and friends, including a deep sigh from her father, who was holding his baby grandson, Teo.

Alessandro pulled her close on the dance floor. Lilley looked up at him breathlessly as he swayed against her.

"My, oh my," she murmured, fluttering her eyelashes. "You're quite the dancer. Have you been taking lessons?"

"You know I have. You've been taking them with me." He twirled her, then gave a mischievous grin. "No broken toes in sight."

"Because you're leading me."

"No," he whispered, pulling her close. "We lead each other."

Lilley looked up at him, dazed with happiness. Their lives over the past ten months had been filled with one

joy after the next. They now split their time evenly between Rome and San Francisco, where Lilley had started
her fledgling jewelry company, Lilley Caetani Limited.
Her first collection had already been a great success at the
international jewelry trade show in San Francisco.

So much had changed in the last year. Lilley was still
awed to think how, just fifteen months before, she'd attended the trade show as a guest with a dream. Now she
was an exhibitor. With Carrie's financial backing, her fledgling company had already made a splash in the trade dailies
and orders had started to flood in from around the world.
She would have to hire more employees soon. Lilley often
traveled with her husband and their baby to Singapore or
Norway or Namibia, getting inspiration for her designs.
She happily traveled wherever the continuing expansion
of Caetani Worldwide took them.

There was only one of Alessandro's potential acquisitions that she absolutely wouldn't allow. Alessandro had
made multiple offers to buy her company and merge it with
Caetani-Hainsbury Worldwide, which she'd refused in no
uncertain terms.

"Sorry, my company is not for sale," she'd said breezily.
"I'm not interested in being part of some soulless, heartless
conglomerate—"

"Hey!"

She'd grinned. "Sorry. But my company is small and I
like it that way."

He'd tilted his head thoughtfully. "We could double your
growth projections, especially in Europe. And there might
be other fringe benefits as well," he'd murmured. "Think
about it."

"Not for sale at any price," she said primly.

He'd lifted a wicked eyebrow. "Oh? Are you sure?" And
he'd pulled her into bed. Lilley sighed at the memory. Of

course, she would never sell him her company, but it was sure fun to let him try.

Tonight's anniversary party in Sonoma had been Alessandro's idea. He'd planned the whole thing from start to finish. The wine harvest looked to be excellent this year, and all their friends and family beamed as they held up glasses, toasting Alessandro and Lilley on the occasion of their one-year anniversary.

Olivia Bianchi, alas, was not in attendance. Lilley hadn't even tried to invite her. She'd learned she couldn't please everyone, and she didn't need to impress anyone. The only people she cared about were right here: her friends Nadia and Jeremy, who were now engaged. And her family. Her cousin had come all the way from France, along with Carrie and their baby. Alessandro and Théo might never be friends, but they'd managed to achieve a sort of détente. They'd moved their rivalry to the realms of basketball and extreme sports like skydiving. Great, Lilley thought with an inward groan. Just what she needed. A husband and a cousin who were fighting to jump out of a perfectly good plane.

Even her father was doing better, now that he'd retired and given up day-to-day management of Hainsbury's to Alessandro. The company was on track to merge with Caetani Worldwide, and all of it would be left in trust to Walton's grandchildren. Her father had moved to San Francisco to be closer to them, and to focus on getting healthier. And, like a miracle, he seemed stronger every day. Especially on the days he played with his grandson.

Friends and family were all that mattered, Lilley thought. Not fame. Not the glitter of wealth. The only diamonds that mattered were the ones in the bright smiles of the people she loved. As her dance with Alessandro ended and their friends applauded wildly around them, her father brought the baby to the dance floor.

"I think the kid wants to dance," Walton said gruffly.

A new song began, and Alessandro took baby Teo in his arms. Nuzzling his chubby cheeks and downy head, he looked down at his son tenderly. "I can teach him."

Lilley's heart swelled as Alessandro held their cooing baby against his tuxedo jacket, and wrapped his other arm around her. Smiling, she leaned her head against her husband's strong shoulders as they swayed together in time to the music. Listening to Teo's baby giggle and Alessandro's joyful baritone laugh, Lilley suddenly knew their lives together would always be happy like this. Their days would shine with endless brilliant facets, in a hodgepodge of sparkling gemstones and tarnished brass, rough rock crystals and gleaming platinum, that when welded together…formed a family.

* * * * *

JOIN THE
MILLS & BOON
BOOKCLUB

* **FREE** delivery direct to your door

* **EXCLUSIVE** offers every month

* **EXCITING** rewards programme

50% OFF
YOUR FIRST
PARCEL

Join today at
Millsandboon.co.uk/Bookclub

MILLS & BOON
Desire

Indulge in secrets and scandal, intense drama and plenty of sizzling hot action with powerful and passionate heroes who have it all: wealth, status, good looks…everything but the right woman.

LET'S TALK
Romance

For exclusive extracts, competitions
and special offers, find us online: